Praise for Barbara Samuel

"Not only does she write of the love between and men and women, but of the powerful friendships between . . . women and a man's need to be free and respected."

—*Romantic Times*

"Samuel sprinkles period sounding language with the light hand of a master chef, providing enough to flavor her story without overwhelming it."

—*Old Book Barn Gazette*

"Rarely has any author so captured the incredible power of physical attraction between a man and a woman. Barbara Samuel creates, with narcotic, evocative language and haunting imagery, a world which engages all your sense and emotions. She carries you to the dark side of passion and then spirals you toward a happy and satisfying ending you were convinced was impossible."

—*Romance and Women's Fiction*

"Discover the magic of Barbara Samuel."

—*Painted Rock Reviews*

"Barbara Samuel writes with . . . poignancy and pathos."

—*Under the Covers*

Also by Barbara Samuel

A Bed of Spices

A Winter Ballad

Lucien's Fall

Dancing Moon

Heart of a Knight

Published by HarperPaperbacks

The
Black Angel

Barbara Samuel

HarperPaperbacks
A Division of HarperCollins*Publishers*

HarperPaperbacks
A Division of HarperCollins*Publishers*
10 East 53rd Street, New York, NY 10022-5299

This is a work of fiction. The characters, incidents,
and dialogues are products of the author's imagination and
are not to be construed as real. Any resemblance to actual events
or persons, living or dead, is entirely coincidental.

ISBN 0-06-101389-7

HarperCollins®, 📖®, and HarperPaperbacks™ are trademarks of
HarperCollins Publishers Inc.

Cover illustration © 1999 by Jon Paul

First HarperPaperbacks printing: September 1999

Printed in the United States of America

Visit HarperPaperbacks on the World Wide Web at
http://www.harpercollins.com

❖ 10 9 8 7 6 5 4 3 2 1

For Luerelean and James Samuel,
who not only raised the wonderful man who is
my husband, but are the best in-laws
a woman could ask for.

Lady Adriana St. Ives rode well, the result of a childhood spent more savage than civilized. On this dark, wet morning, she rode astride, and rode hard, her hair uncombed and streaming down her back as she raced to beat the dawn threatening at the edge of the horizon. Wet leaves slapped at her face and arms, and her skirts were soaked. Later, she would pay with a fever.

But all that mattered now was that she halt the folly about to take place here, a duel between her brothers and Everett Malvern, Baron of Wye, the King's nephew, and until last week, Adriana's lover.

"Please," she whispered to whatever celestial beings might still be listening to her.

She broke from the trees into a wide, grassy clearing. Relief washed cold down her spine, for they had not yet begun. Her brother Julian, tall as a cedar, his wheat-colored hair shining even in the gloom, stood sober and straight beside a phaeton. Their half brother, Gabriel, as handsome and swarthy as the pirates of their childhood games, stood next to him, the box of pistols in his hands.

Thank God.

She slowed, her breath coming in ragged gasps from her chest. Not even enough air left for a cry.

And then movement from the trees on the opposite side of the clearing caught the edge of her vision and Adriana jerked her head around to see Everett Malvern. The rake was visibly in his cups, weaving as he tossed off his woolen cloak and gestured for his pistol to be put in his hand. The fine satin waistcoat and breeches that had begun the night before in such splendor were now stained with the night's revels, and the elegant, almost pretty face framed with golden curls was decidedly less attractive by the morning light. His sleeves, trimmed with tumbles of Belgian lace, fell over his hands, and he laughed uproariously to his entourage, who only summoned the most polite of chuckles in response. They knew, even if Malvern did not, that he faced a most deadly—and furious— opponent.

Adriana narrowed her eyes. The fool. Only he was arrogant enough to think he'd go unwounded at Julian's hand. His second, a foppish dandy named Stead whom Adriana disliked heartily, plainly understood the danger. He tugged at Malvern's sleeve, his mouth moving with words Adriana could not hear. Malvern shook the hand away and swaggered out to face Julian, who stood cold and still in the midst of the clearing, his dark gold hair glittering with moisture.

Humiliation and anger and regret welled up in

Adriana, but there was no time to indulge it. "Wait!" she cried, dismounting, and ran forward.

The men glanced at her, but quickly turned back again, all intent upon this foolish duel. She tried to rush, tripped on her skirts and tumbled in the wet grass. The jolt slammed her teeth together and jarred her entire head.

She scrambled to her feet, putting her hand in a muddy puddle, and stumbled forward.

Too late.

In horror, Adriana halted, tasting blood on her tongue where she'd bitten it. Sweat and cold mist dampened her clothes, and her breath still came raggedly. Hands limp at her sides, she watched them take their paces.

Turn.

And fire.

Involuntarily, she slammed her hands over her ears and squeezed her eyes closed. A man cried out in surprise. Her eyes flew open.

Blood bloomed in the shape of a peony over Malvern's chest. Adriana saw the stain leak into the embroidered satin of his waistcoat, spreading like doom, saw the surprise steal away his drunkenness. Abruptly unfrozen, she raced forward and grabbed Julian's arm. "God, Julian, you've killed him! You killed the Duke's bastard."

Julian dropped the pistol, and the icy calm over his face shattered. He raised gray eyes to Adriana's face, and in them she glimpsed misery and resolve. "He'll trouble you no more."

She flung her arms around him, weeping. "I am so

ashamed," she whispered against Julian's neck.

Gabriel touched her back, her hair, and she embraced him fiercely. "Take care of him," she whispered, then pulled away. "Now, go. Go!"

Without a word, they turned together, and disappeared into the mist of the dark morning.

✤ 1 ✤

HARTWOOD HALL, ENGLAND
1786

Just before the bells awakened her on her wedding day, Lady Adriana St. Ives dreamed of her brothers. They rode white horses over a muddy road, and even in the damp, they looked splendidly heroic, one so fair, the other so dark. There was urgency in the air all about them; their hair and cloaks flew, and the horses' hooves kicked up a spray of mud over the men's legs. Firm intent marked their faces.

They were coming. Coming to save her.

Bolting awake, she found herself alone in her cold chamber, blinking at the pale light coming through mullioned windows. Only her own bed. And no sound of horses beyond. She fell back to the pillows, heart pounding, and blinked at the dark-beamed ceiling.

A dream. Only a dream. But after a moment she rose, taking a wrapper from the chair, and padded over to the window to peer out. The grounds of Hartwood Hall spread in wet emerald beauty below a drizzly sky, the leaves of the boxwood glistening along the edge of the road. A road that was empty, as she'd known it would be.

She leaned her forehead against a pane of glass, the improbable hope withering in her breast. It had been almost five years since Julian and Gabriel had fled England after defending her honor, or rather, avenging her shredded pride. She was quite certain they were dead, drowned at sea or captured by Indians or fallen to some exotic fever.

No, there would be no rescue from her brothers, as there had been when they were children, playing pirate in the lush landscape of their father's Martinique estates. But that did not keep her from wishing to be saved.

Shivering a little in the damp, she walked over to her desk and took out her pen, and ink, and a small bound book. She and her sister Cassandra had both acquired the habit of journals, a way to amuse themselves on the long passages between the islands and home. Long, long, long days for children. She began to write:

> *In an hour, I must allow them to know I have awakened, but this last hour is mine, perhaps the last I can call my own for a good many years. It is, at the outside, the last in which I will be free.*
>
> *At noon, I am to be married to a man I have never seen, a distant Irish cousin my father thought would make me a suitable husband.*
>
> *Cassandra has been most insistent I should resist this match, as have all those glittering renegades who grace her salon. They are too scandalous and mixed a lot to approve this move I must make in behalf of my family. They thought me too much like them, I think, seeing in*

me a freedom of character and heart that does not truly live in my soul, thinking those months of passion with Malvern meant I have some wild freedom of attitude, which is not true. In fact, I am only a ruined spinster who so disgraced herself that she is lucky to find even an Irishman for husband.

But it is to Papa that I owe my allegiance. He worried so much about us toward the last! If he chose this Black Angel for me, I suppose he imagined some good would come of it.

But foolishly, I've harbored a fantasy that somehow my brothers would hear of this marriage, and come home in time to set things right. Foolishness, but I know Papa never gave up watching for them to return, either, so at least I am not alone. They were likely slain in the uprising that cost Papa his fortune, but I feel I would know if they were dead, if their spirits no longer walked the earth.

Ah, I promised myself I would not be maudlin, but here it is, a gray cold morning, and I find I cannot help myself. I miss them most terribly.

Now I've splotched the page and my ink will smear. For it is Julian who is most emphatically in my thoughts this morn, golden Julian who tossed all away to avenge his sister in a duel. And disappeared to save his neck. Now, to do my part to save our estates, I must take this rake they call Black Angel as my husband and somehow make the best of it. For all of us.

With a sense of finality, she scattered sand over the page, then bent to add coal to the fire. In the passage-way beyond her door, she heard the first stirrings of her sisters, probably the youngest two, by the excitement and hushed giggling. Fondly, she smiled, and the tight knot of worry eased a little.

Without her knowledge, her father had arranged the marriage before his death a year ago. As his consumption stole the breath from him, he worried obsessively over the fate of his daughters and wrote at length to the Earl of Glencove, Tynan Spenser, whom he'd met in London a few years before, to offer his eldest daughter's hand in marriage.

Spenser had written to Adriana two months ago, almost a year to the day after her father's death. Although she had at first been appalled at both her father's belief that Julian was dead—else there would be no need to arrange the marriage at all—and at his high-handedness in arranging the match, Adriana knew how desperately the family estates needed the influx of capital Spenser would bring.

And he, by trading on her father's good name, hoped to buy a seat in the English House of Commons. It amused her, and she'd written him an acerbic letter, making sure that he knew of his future wife's scarlet past before he committed himself.

The return mail had carried a very short missive. "It does not matter," he wrote. "Will be arriving in London, 10 September. Will correspond further then."

And in many ways, the solution had been the answer to a prayer, so Adriana tried to make the best of it. Knowing nothing of him, save the blatant facts of his title and holdings in the west of Ireland, she had conjured a picture of him from clues she could gather from his letters. The handwriting was bold and sprawling, marred with blotches of ink and hastily crossed-out words. It suggested to her a man of energy, a plain-speaking country Irishman with political ambitions. Someone near her father's age, perhaps, portly or balding. Yes, she could make such a trade.

Such bliss in ignorance!

Wrapping a warm woolen shawl around her shoulders, Adriana heard a squeal, quickly hushed. Her sisters again. They were so young, she thought with a pang. A wedding, no matter how it was arranged, was to them the height of excitement.

She peered once more toward the road, and saw with despair that it remained empty.

It was Adriana's sister Cassandra who'd brought the truth of the Black Angel, gleaned in gossip. Tynan Spenser was no portly, balding squire. Instead, he was the very stuff of Adriana's nightmares, a rake with a silver tongue obscuring a heart as black as a winter night. He was rumored to have slept with every great beauty in London, and a good many wives of the Irish Parliament, and was said to make a fine game of it, passionate one moment, cold the next, so the women sighed in longing for him.

The Black Angel.

Adriana tried not to think what he might look like. She tried to remind herself of the way Malvern had looked that misty morning in Hyde Park, dissipated and sodden and distasteful.

Instead, her rogue imagination insisted upon dishing up other memories: the feel of her lover's mouth upon her throat, the brush of his hands over her breasts and gliding up her thighs—

She put her face in her hands, hating the betrayal of her flesh. Five years, and she still remembered. Not him, not her foolish, vain lover, but the pleasure he gave.

This was her most dangerous, and most private, failing—that she still ached for that pleasure. That she had not yet found a way to keep it from her thoughts, the wish for it. And now she would be forced to lie with a rake who'd made such pleasure his trademark, and she feared desperately that it would be her undoing. As it had been in the past. Somehow, some way, she had to armor herself.

Adriana clapped her hands sharply, and the noise of a half-dozen girls and women abruptly ceased. "Enough chatter! If we do not settle my attire, the bride will be late."

The chastening lasted barely an instant before the voices rose again. All four of her sisters, aged fourteen to twenty-one, plus two of the younger house maids, even Adriana's new girl, Fiona—oddly enough the first Irish maid she'd had—chimed in with opinions.

"Riana, please not the bombazine!" Ophelia begged. Fifteen and prettiest of them all, she clasped her hands under her chin in a prayer. "At least the blue silk."

"Oh, you only think of blue because it suits *you*," Cleo said with a toss of her head. Dusky as her half sister was fair, she rivaled her in beauty. "But, Riana, perhaps at least the gray brocade? It *is* more festive."

Cassandra, a widowed twenty and languid, sprawled over a divan, one hand on her cheek, a tendril of red hair falling down her forehead. "Since she's inclined to throw herself to sacrifice for our benefit," she drawled, "at least let her choose the gown of her doom."

Adriana, exasperated, looked to Phoebe—twenty-one and prim. "Help!"

"If you want to stay, halt your chatter," Phoebe said, her voice stiff as whalebone. Briskly, she pushed the maids out of the way and plucked a brush from one of their hands. "Can't you find some work elsewhere? We'll tend to our sister."

Summarily dismissed, they left. And as Phoebe's reign took hold, the others lit on the bed and the trunk. "There," Phoebe said with a smile. "You have some peace."

Adriana closed her eyes and took in a breath of air to steady the race of her heart. "I'm terrified," she whispered, and put her hands to her bloodless cheeks. "And it shows."

"You've let yourself be swayed by the gossip," Phoebe said, yanking the brush through Adriana's long, thick hair. "No man could live up to that reputation."

"I've heard otherwise," Cassandra drawled. A happy widow with no intention of marrying again, she kept a house in London. Her drawing room was famed for the wit and gossip batted about. "But in that you should find some comfort, sister. If he's the rake they say, he'll not want to molder about at Hartwood. He'll come in, and bed you, and be off again in a day. You'll be free."

"Cassandra!" Adriana hissed, tossing a warning glance in the direction of the two youngest girls.

"Perhaps he'll be so handsome you'll fall in love on

sight," Ophelia offered. Her eyes went misty. "'The Black Angel' is such a dangerous nickname. I think he sounds exciting."

Adriana stared resolutely at her reflection, watching Phoebe purse her lips as she twisted her hair away from her face and pinned it severely in place. "His reputation matters very little to me," Adriana said. "He has the fortune and we have the political connections. Marriages have been made on worse."

"Indeed." Phoebe met Adriana's eyes in the mirror for a sober moment. Of all of them, Phoebe, who had kept a hawk's eye on the accounts the past year, knew how critical that infusion of wealth had become. A good deal of the family fortune had been sunk into their father's island estates—all but lost to them in the current wave of revolutions in the colonies. "It's his fortune that matters—as it will be when you marry, Ophelia."

"I intend to marry for love."

"Intend all you wish, my sweet," Cassandra said dryly. Her foot swung monotonously, up and down, showing the tip of a boot every second. Every third or fourth time, she wiggled it a bit.

"Cassandra," Adriana said, "please be still."

"Ophelia is beauty enough to find love *and* fortune," Cleo declared.

Adriana only nodded mildly. "Perhaps." Suddenly weary of the pretense she had to maintain for the sake of the younger girls, she added, "Why don't you two check to be certain all is ready for our guest's arrival?" With a smile, she added, "Perhaps he'll bring an entourage."

Interest sparked between them, arcing from Ophelia's Dresden blue eyes to Cleo's dark brown as they smiled at each other in secret mischief. The pair were only ten months apart in age, and were close as twins. For a moment, looking at the contrast between fair and dark, Adriana thought again, this time with a pang, of her brothers.

"Let's!" they said together, and giggled.

When they'd departed, the room grew quiet. "They don't really remember the scandal," Cassandra said.

"Which is just as well." Adriana pinched her cheeks in a vain attempt to bring some color to them. "I have a more than vivid enough recollection for all of us."

"Riana, you wrong yourself in this." Phoebe put her hands on her sister's shoulders. "You were foolish, and young—he was powerful and beautiful and turned your head. It has happened thousands of times."

Adriana bit back her sharp reply: *How would you know?* But of course it was mean-spirited, and no one could be so evil to Phoebe.

Cassandra leaned close to take Adriana's hands. "Listen to her. Malvern was relentless in his pursuit. A far more sophisticated girl than you would have been swayed."

A familiar ache, half regret, half humiliation, rose in her throat. "Please . . . I cannot bear to speak of it. Even now."

Cassandra slid from the sofa to kneel before her sister, tightening her hands around Adriana's. "I despise that you feel you must sacrifice yourself this way, that you feel you must atone for your sins by marrying some rake you've never seen."

"You are too dramatic, Cassandra." Adriana pulled her hands free. "There is no sacrifice here. Papa arranged the matter before he died—he must have had some reason to do so." She smoothed a wisp of hair from her face. "I am simply being practical. Besides, as you said, if he's the rake they all say, he'll be little inconvenience."

A sound of shouts reached them, and all three turned toward the window. For a moment they froze together. "I expect that is the groom's party," Adriana said, and stood, smoothing her skirts and lifting one hand to her tightly coiled hair. "Shall we greet him?"

Cassandra gripped her hand. "Are you absolutely certain, Adriana?"

Adriana lifted her chin. "Yes."

Tynan Spenser, Earl of Glencove, Baron of Tynagh, had carefully orchestrated his arrival at Hartwood Hall. He rode a black gelding, fifteen hands of glorious Irish horseflesh, aristocratic and graceful enough to have pleased one of the ancient kings. The saddle was made of Spanish leather, and worked with silver, and in a moment of fancy he'd braided the beast's mane in the old way, with ribbons of scarlet.

He'd considered gathering a small party of young lords for this event, but had discovered he could not bear the company of them on the long ride. As a result he rode in alone, with only his man Seamus for company. They'd spoken little, for Seamus disapproved of the match. Disapproved of anything English, come to that. Some might consider three days of sulky silence an impertinence, but Seamus had been Tynan's father's man before him, and one permitted a servant of forty years some leeway.

And as no family of his own remained, Tynan wished some familiar company on so momentous a day.

Tynan himself was splendidly attired in close-fitting breeches and tailored coat and tall boots, mud-spattered a little now, but none the worse for all that. He'd allowed one clue to his true nature, donning a black cloak embroidered around the edges by the women in his village with a bright Celtic design. At his throat was an ancient brooch, in his family for longer than anyone could remember, woven of red and white gold, set with a ruby the color of the fuchsias that grew along the road to Glencove castle.

Even Seamus had grunted a miserly approval.

A twist of anticipation rose in Tynan as they rode between the neatly clipped boxwoods lining the drive, past acres of wide lawns dotted with tiny white daisies, surrounding the house like a carpet. Here it was— Hartwood Hall. An English earldom if his wild gamble paid off; and the lost earl, Julian St. Ives, did not return. Tynan suspected his chances were better than even. There had been not a word of St. Ives in five years. Likely, he lay at the bottom of the sea, victim of some ill-built packet.

But even if his gamble did not gain him the title, Tynan knew he'd gain political power through his highborn wife. Scandals could be overcome. One way or the other, he planned to win this hand.

Against the gloomy sky, the hall rose in ancient

grandeur. 'Twas more of a castle than the manor he'd expected. He'd known it was old, in the family for centuries, since it had been awarded to the first Earl of Albury in 1342. The main hall, a square four stories, was the only remnant of that time, though Tynan thought he could make out the uneven swell of ground that once marked the curtain wall. He sought—and found—the dry moat, now filled with earth and flowers.

The rest of the rambling structure had been added over the centuries, a little here and there, a wing, a room, a tower, all shaped by native red stone that brought unity and a certain dignity to the hodgepodge of styles.

Gathered on the wide steps leading to the main entrance stood a group he assumed must be the sisters and their servants. Undoubtedly one of them was Lady Adriana. Faced now with the finality of the act he was about to commit, Tynan suddenly hoped she would not be too plain. With curiosity, he studied the faces of the five ladies, flanked by servants in green livery, who awaited him on the wide sweep of steps leading to a pair of carved wooden doors.

The first girl was a beauty, blond and sweet—very young. She linked arms with another girl with long dark eyes, mulatto by the look of her, but as finely dressed as the first. Just behind them stood a woman as plain as a country mouse, her pale brown hair swept up from a strong, kind face. She resembled her father, Tynan thought with some fondness. The Earl had been a good, kindhearted man of no particular attractiveness but that in his clear blue eyes.

Next to the plain girl stood a tall, straight woman

whose ill-fitting black bombazine obscured the shape of her body and leeched all color from her face. Her hair appeared to be blond, but he thought it must be a poor texture, for it had been pulled back tightly and braided in a coronet.

The last one stood on the top steps, her arms crossed, her face hard. Even her legs were slightly askance, as if to give her firmer grip on the world, and he noticed with some amusement that she wore boots, not slippers. Her hair was a particularly glorious shade of red-gold, and though he could see an attempt had been made to tame it, wisps slipped free to drift around her face. He pursed his lips, measuring. This one might own that brisk voice he'd read in her letters, and yes—he could see her falling to passion too young.

His spirits lifted and he dismounted with a spring in his step. "Good morning, ladies," he said, and bowed.

The young girls giggled, and Tynan favored them with a broad grin, as rakish as he could summon. It pleased him when they blushed happily. "You must be Ophelia and Cleopatra."

They curtsied prettily, and nudged each other over the hothouse flowers he bestowed upon them from the armload Seamus carried behind him. He looked to the next sister.

"You do favor your father, lass," he said, offering a handful of some yellow blossom he couldn't name. Up close, he saw that her skin was fine, and her eyes were of a singularly piercing blue. "A good man he was."

Her gaze was clear and direct, and in it he saw that he had found her softness immediately. "He was, sir."

That left the final two, who awaited at the top of the

steps. Yes, the one in black must be the widow—Cassandra. Poor girl was paler than the moon, and she kept her eyes carefully downcast. From the bouquet, he selected a perfect white rose, and one of deepest red.

Only then did he allow himself to raise his eyes to the glorious redhead, and was startled to see active dislike on her face. He cocked a brow ironically and gave her the red rose. "My lady," he said with a slight bow.

"I am Cassandra, sir." She gestured with a slim white hand. "This is my sister, your bride-to-be, Lady Adriana St. Ives."

Tynan had learned to control his expression in a thousand circumstances, and had polished his gift for flirtation to an art, but for a single instant he stumbled. His gaze flew to the pallid blond, and sought some single beauty he could admire, flatter her about.

But he could find nothing. The features were even enough, he supposed, with no glaring flaw he could pinpoint aside from the paleness. Pale lips, pale hair, pale cheeks. Her figure looked plump in the ill-fitting stiff gown.

And in that heartbeat's length of time that passed before he could hide his dismay, she raised her eyes and saw his true feelings. Her nostrils flared and her chin tilted faintly, and he read in the expression the haughtiest disdain.

A bad show, that lapse of his expression. In an instant he gathered himself and smoothly took her cold hand in his own. With all of his charm—and there were many who said it was considerable—he pressed a warm kiss to it. "At last we meet, my lady," he said in a voice meant to roll down her spine.

She raised one sharp, arched brow—darker by far than her pale hair—and he saw he'd moved her not at all.

Taking her hand back, she said only, "My lord," in a voice as distant as her cool nod.

The lady of the manor, soiled by Irish riffraff. The message could not have been more clear. Tynan smiled, coldly, and offered his arm. "Shall we?"

2

Adriana's hands shook as she took the Earl's arm and allowed herself to be led into the house. There was a hot roaring in her ears as they walked down the old stone passageway, a noise that blocked out the rest of the party, which she knew must be gaily tracking in behind them. She could not hear them.

There was only room for the sense of the Black Angel beside her, towering over her, both taller and broader than she'd first thought. Not stout, but hale—wide in the shoulder, deep in the chest—arms and legs hard with the strength of a vigorous sportsman. Adriana had been tall her entire life, and disliked this sudden sense of small powerlessness he gave her.

Against the wool of his coat, her fingers grew damp, and beneath his sleeve she felt the ungiving muscle of a man who did not take his horses lightly. His boots clicked authoritatively against the stones, while hers only whispered. When they arrived at the doors to the chapel, one of her favorite places in the house, Adriana discovered that not even the ancient hush and stained glass could give her peace this day.

Throughout the short ceremony, she held herself rigid, eyes fixed upon the sloped shoulders of the village parson who'd been summoned for this task. Her groom seemed not to notice the trembling of her fingers, only stood next to her, straight and strong, smelling of damp wool and coriander and something evocative and musky she could not name. From the corner of her eye she kept catching on the vivid embroidery on the edge of his cloak, an extravagance that somehow frightened her.

The service went quickly, and abruptly it was time to solemnize their agreement with the kiss of peace. Adriana was forced to turn toward him and raise her eyes and look again in that face.

That face.

Lush, untamed black hair framed it, hair that misbehaved in the damp, and tumbled heathenlike down his back. The face itself was made of lean angles and winged brows and a mouth created from the fantasies of maidens. She remembered an old story, told by her Irish nanny in Martinique, about the beauty of Irish kings. This face, unholy in its beauty, would have ruled all.

But it was his eyes that were most dangerous. Eyes of clearest aquamarine, not quite blue, not quite green, gazed down at her, eyes whose faintly mocking expression revealed both his intelligence and the easy seductive flirtation of a rake. But just as she had in that brutal moment outside on the stairs, Adriana saw again the darkness that lurked in the depths of that impossible color. To her despair, she found it made him all the more attractive.

Oh, God, did he have to be so beautiful?

He lowered his head, and against all her will, Adriana's gaze fell to his mouth. Kisses. From the first, kissing had ever been her downfall. As a young girl, she'd restlessly imagined kissing the beautiful stable boy, had found a way to do it, and it was even more delicious than her fevered imagination had anticipated. Malvern had seduced her with his sweet, sweet kisses.

And neither of them had had a mouth like this one. It made no pretense to sweetness or innocence. It was a wide, mobile mouth, but the worst of it was that the upper lip, crisply cut, arched ever so slightly over the seductive lower in an arrangement she found desperately erotic.

As if he noticed her fixation, one side of that mouth quirked, very slightly, and he bent his head to kiss her. She clenched her teeth hard against it, and the mouth that met his was hard and unyielding. It was mercifully brief, but even the brush of that mouth over her own was promising. He would, she knew in an instant, kiss as if kissing could change the world.

"Such a warm welcome from my bride," he murmured, cocking one brow.

She cocked one of her own and lifted her shoulder the slightest bit in imitation of the ennui she'd seen in the women at Cassandra's salons. "One cannot expect passion from a stranger."

His face shuttered. "Especially for an Irishman." His voice was so low, none but she could hear it.

She frowned. "I do not understand your meaning, sir."

"Then you are far more naïve than your past would lead me to believe."

Stung, she raised her chin. "Do not ever speak of that again," she replied.

A pause, so brief it could barely be discerned. Then he gave her a curt nod. "So be it."

Tynan circled the party warily, taking the measure of this new group. In the wide, windowed ballroom a string quartet played minuets, and when the guests were not eating the feast laid out on tables around the edges of the room, they danced and flirted and laughed. With some amusement, he noted that the two youngest girls, Ophelia and Cleopatra, dazzled the young men who'd come from the surrounding country to celebrate the wedding. Soon, he thought with proprietary ease, the girls would need husbands of their own.

The plain Phoebe circulated, pausing now and again, gesturing for new wine here, a stool for a gouty baron's foot there. A gentle hand on a shoulder, a beatific smile at an old man's joke, snagging a child to retie a ribbon that had come undone. In Phoebe lived the heart of the family.

The redheaded sister had left soon after the ceremony in order to arrive in London before dark. Tynan thought it just as well. Someone told him she held salons in her town house, a center of the artistic and creative communities. He'd do well to avoid that set, and Cassandra herself. The fire was too tempting.

Sitting stiffly to one side was Adriana, her hands

folded tightly in her lap, her face unyielding. She had not eaten that he'd seen, nor taken a sip of wine. When their eyes caught, her gaze sidled away in a rush, as if she were frightened.

Tynan pursed his lips, measuring her from his post across the room. Of all the sisters, she seemed the least likely to have fallen prey to the talents of a rake, but 'twas fact that she had, and that her brothers had killed the man in a duel.

Which had led to him standing here now. Though dueling was strictly outlawed, it was not a crime ordinarily punished by juries—especially a nobleman avenging a sister's honor.

But the murdered man in this case was a bastard born to a mistress of the King's brother, and that mother cried out loud and long for justice for her fallen son. Should Julian St. Ives, twelfth Earl of Albury, and his half brother Gabriel, ever set foot on English soil again, they would be arrested.

Tynan saw Phoebe pause by her sister and put a hand on her shoulder. Lady Adriana nodded at something she said, and accepted a cup of brandy pressed into her hand.

Again, he tried to see some hint of passion or the promise of sensuality—anything—that might have sent a powerful youth into wild pursuit of this woman when all the beauties of London had been available to him. He could see nothing. Nor could he discern any hint of the recklessness that might have led a well-bred young lady to give in to such machinations. He saw only the straightness of her spine, the stiffness of her neck, the unsmiling rigidity of that unyielding mouth.

Still, there had to be something. And whether or not he discovered it, he had promised her father to be a husband to her, and though the old man asked no more than he would have from any businessman, Tynan had been very fond of James St. Ives. In his honor, he would at least try to create more than a mockery of a marriage.

Tugging on his coat, he lifted his glass and carried it over to her table, aggressively straddling a chair beside her. Tossing hair from his eyes, he said, "Good evening, wife."

A pulse beat in her throat. "Good evening."

He lifted his glass and took a swallow of fine port, then gestured with it toward Cleo, dancing with splendid form. "Tell me about your family," he invited, knowing it was a rare woman who could resist talk of her siblings. More than one maid or matron had been wooed to his bed by just such a gambit.

"Do you mean my family, sir, or specifically Cleo?"

He inclined his head in acknowledgment of a point scored. "Touché. Cleo, of course. The rest is clear enough."

"She's beautiful, isn't she?" Lady Adriana said quietly.

Cleo wore a turquoise silk gown, a color that glorified her flawless golden skin and black hair, which had been swept into a tumble of curls that teased at the joining of neck and shoulder, a breathlessly graceful spot. "Indeed," Tynan agreed.

"I worry about her," Adriana confessed, and he found in her voice a quality that was appealing. A richness that would lend itself well to singing. "She has not yet come to understand that—" She broke off, sighed. "She and Ophelia have shared a perfect childhood. Ophelia will go on to marry a duke, or at the least, an earl, while Cleo will have to content herself with a tradesman or even less. A man who will have no sense of the finer things Cleo loves."

"Did your father not consider that?" He sipped his wine again. "I assume she is his daughter."

"Yes, she is." A faint smile touched her lips. "My father adored her, as he loved all his children, and he wanted her to have what he could give. He did the same for Gabriel."

"Gabriel." Tynan frowned. "Your brother?"

"Half. He's the oldest of us all, born also to Cleo's mother."

"Ah." He nodded. "But 'tis an easier world for a man than for a woman," he said. "No matter the race of the man."

She glanced at him, and he spied the sharp intelligence in her eyes. "It is rare enough that a man knows it."

He shrugged, uncomfortable suddenly under that sharp gaze. "Did your mother not object to your father's mistress?"

"He had no mistress while she lived, sir." She swiveled her proud head. "My father served in the wars and was given a plantation for his efforts. As a second son, he had few prospects in England, so he settled in Martinique, to make what he could of his life. There he met Cleo's mother and they had a child, who was Gabriel." She looked at Tynan down her aristocratic nose. "He granted both mother and child their freedom, and gave Gabriel all that he desired. He loved them, sir, because he was not blinded by the world's values."

Tynan grinned at the lecturing tone, and sipped his port. Finding the glass empty, he gestured for another, which was quickly delivered. "But in the end, he betrayed them, did he not?"

She made a noise of outrage, a tsk. "He did not! His brother died, making my father Earl, and he came home to do his duty and find a wife with whom to make an heir. Gabriel and his mother wanted for nothing."

"And your mother did not mind?"

"She forgave him his youthful indiscretions." Now her face softened, and she warmed to the family legend. "He met her at a cotillion. She was quite beautiful." She gestured to the small, tiny blond sister who danced elegantly with a London fop. "Ophelia is her very image, and my father was smitten on sight. Theirs was an honorable love, rare, but true. While he was married to her, he did not stray."

"So how did the lovely Cleo come about, hmmm?"

"My mother traveled with him to Martinique one year," she said quietly, her face turned from him, "and en route conceived a child. The climate did not agree with her, and although she managed to deliver Ophelia into the world, she did not survive the birth."

"So your father took refuge in the arms of his mistress."

Her gaze moved back to him, even and calm. "She saved him, I think. He was quite mad with grief and guilt."

A strange pluck of emotion ached in his chest at the steady honor in her face as she said that. He felt chastened without knowing why. And suddenly he thought of his twin, his black-shrouded body on a litter carried by grim-faced villagers up the long hill to the estate. He bowed his head.

"My father could not bear to return to England and the life he had shared with my mother," Adriana continued, "so he sent for us, and we lived there four years. Gabriel and Cleo were part of our family. When we returned, because of the brewing war in the colonies, they came with us." She gestured to a tall, straight black woman in a brightly colored cotton gown. "So did Monique."

Intrigued in spite of himself, he asked, "Did you like living there?"

Her gaze flickered away. "It changed us."

"Did it, now?" Tynan leaned forward, hearing something in her voice. "How did it change you, Lady Adriana?"

He saw a shift in her eyes, a worry, and then her posture softened, and her neck seemed longer as she inclined her head. He thought of a swan. Her nostrils flared, as if she scented wild blossoms and humid evenings, and her gaze focused on something distant. "It changed everything," she said softly. Then her lips tightened and she shook her head, as if in rejection. "Everything."

For a brief moment Tynan spied the tall leafy plants, vowed he could feel heat and wet against his flesh. The rigidness that had lived on his spine since his brother's murder eight months before eased the smallest bit. A tiny bit of the bitterness he slept with slid away from his mouth, and for the space of five heartbeats he longed to sustain himself on something besides hatred.

Then the music ended abruptly, and the polite clapping and soft murmurs of approval from the dancers interrupted him. He realized he was leaning close to her, thinking not of himself and his goals at all, but some far distant land he would never see—and longing for it.

But it was a colony, as Ireland was, and the love Adriana felt for the land as a colonist was not the same pleasure the slaves forced to work the land would feel. Contained in her body was all that he loathed—and he would do well to remember it.

Tynan straightened. "Well, much as I enjoy your story, my lady, perhaps it is time we . . . retired."

It caused her a moment's discomfort, quickly hidden. Smoothing her black skirts, she raised an imperious chin. "First, sir, tell me why you have married me."

"Your father asked it."

The steeliness in her eyes did not fade. "You waited a year to offer."

Tynan discarded the easy lie—that he'd waited out of respect for the mourning period. For one long moment he met her gaze, wishing briefly once again that she were in some way a little more attractive. From his pocket he took a heavy, engraved ring, set with a ruby, and put it in her hand.

She made a small, choked noise. "Where did you get this?"

"A peddler, believe it or not. He came straight away

to my estate, knowing there'd be no one else in the district able to pay for such a prize. I recognized it immediately, and wrote to you the very same day."

Now there were deep sparks in her hard eyes. "What good is it to you if he's dead? The title will pass forever out of reach."

"Ah, but there's the point of it." He smiled coldly and plucked the ring back again. "If he is dead, we wish to keep that knowledge among ourselves as long as possible."

A shimmer of tears covered the blue eyes, and her cheeks and lips grew rosy with emotion. A braid of desire, regret, and pity rose in him, and he reached for her hand, slim and white, on the table. "Madam, forgive—"

She yanked away. "Don't," she said fiercely. "Don't ask it. You wish my brother dead for your own gain, and I cannot but hate you for that." She stood, the movement furious and graceful at once, and regally, she pushed the chair into place. "I will send for you shortly."

He captured her wrist. "Sit down."

She resisted, peering down her nose at him. "I need not. You may speak as I stand."

Their gazes clashed in a battle of wills. He simply stared hard at her, and though few had ever met his will at such moments, Lady Adriana did. Color increased in her face, and he saw the agitated rise of her breasts below the stiff, unflattering fabric, but she simply stared right back.

He kicked the chair with his foot. "Sit and listen, madam. I have a tale to tell you."

Abruptly, she perched on the edge of the chair and tugged at her wrist, still clasped in his hand. "Let me go."

He released her. "Listen well, for I will not say it again."

She waited, back straight, chin high.

"I've my reasons for what I do here, and they are good ones. I mean you no harm—I'll be as good a husband as I am able. I have money for your land," he gestured, "for your home and your sisters. I'll give you children, if you wish it."

At that, there was a flicker over her eyes, a glimpse of hunger, and Tynan nodded. "Ah, so there's your reason for wedding me, is it?"

She swallowed. Took a breath. Nodded with a bowed head, as if it shamed her. But it made him like her the more, that small admittance.

"I do not wish your brother dead, Lady Adriana," he said, and took a hand to prove he meant it. "I'd rather the House of Lords still thinks him missing, for as long as he is alive, there will be no move to do anything about the title and estates. All I ask of you is the connections your family has cultivated these many years, to smooth my way a little."

A bewildered, faintly bitter expression came on her face. "You might have chosen a bit more wisely if it was political power you wanted, sir. It may have missed your notice that I . . . that my . . ." She pressed her lips together. "That my reputation leaves much to be desired."

"Your father was most insistent it should be you."

She winced visibly. "I do not think I like your brand of honesty."

"Do you not? Isn't it easier to have it all on the table here, where we know what is what and who is who?"

She looked up. "I suppose it is." For a moment she did not move. "You are not what I expected," she said, and stood. "I will send for you shortly."

"Braid it," Adriana said, "tightly."

"But milady!" Fiona protested, spreading the gilded length over Adriana's shoulders. "It's so beautiful! It will please the lord a good deal."

An ache—part terror and part despair–pulsed through her. "Do as I say."

When she was finished, Adriana gave her instructions. "Tell him to come to me in ten minutes."

Fiona bobbed politely and left her mistress alone.

Adriana had not come back to her own chamber. She would keep it to herself. Her retreat. This was an old chamber, part of the ancient keep. An embrasure hung with heavy velvet curtains took up most of one wall, and the enormous, high bed with its draperies engulfed another. On the stone walls hung tapestries woven by the St. Ives women in gentler centuries.

On the wall in front of Adriana was a silver mirror, round and dark, which reflected far more than she wished. In the candlelight, she looked luminous and overheated, her skin aglow with desire. Without the black to leech color from her flesh, the natural peach tones of her skin shone free, and even Adriana could see the invitation in her limpid eyes.

She took off the wrapper to examine herself in the fine lawn nightrail she'd chosen. It was modest enough, with long sleeves and a drawstring neckline that covered her to her collarbone, but in the chill, her nipples pressed outward against the cloth, and candlelight shining through the fabric showed the outline of her legs.

She nearly wept at the overwrought emotions welling up in her, a volatile mix of sorrow over the ring and fury over Tynan Spenser's cavalier attitude toward it, dread over the coming hour, and worst of all—anticipation.

It was that creeping, insidious desire that caused the most distress. She wanted him. Wanted to tear off the gown and lie next to him, wanted to wrap his long black hair around her wrists, wanted to open her mouth to those sensual lips—

"Stop it!" Adriana closed her eyes and willed herself to breathe deeply.

Whatever else her experiences had taught her about men, she had learned that there was a great gulf between the way men and women experienced sensuality. Tynan Spenser, that Black Angel, could stride in here with laughter in his eyes and skill in his hands, and have sex with her, then amble away whistling and never look back.

Women were not made the same way. Her heart would be snared along with her sex. In a month or a week or a year, when he tired of the novelty of a passionate wife and took up his old life, she'd be shredded, humiliated.

And wouldn't they all laugh at her then!

Whatever else transpired in this marriage, she vowed she would resist the temptation of enjoying him. It only led to trouble.

A heavy booted heel sounded in the passageway beyond her door. In terror, Adriana blew out all the candles and rushed to the bed, clambering up to it and lying down before he entered. There, rigid and afraid, she waited for her husband.

Tynan lifted his candle higher in the gloom of the chamber. It was dark, but for the fire in the grate, and even that had burned down to low, red embers. "My lady?"

"I am here." The words were astringent, and came from the bed.

He chuckled. This one wanted a little port, he'd wager, and was glad he'd brought a bottle along with him. Carrying both candle and bottle to the bed, he set them down on a table nearby and unlaced his shirt. "I neglected to bring a cup for the port. D'you have one here?"

"I do not."

She lay flat on her back, staring at the ceiling, her gown carefully arranged about her, except at the shins, where it was in a little pile that suggested haste. Her ankles were white and trim, and impulsively he circled one with his hand. She jumped.

Even worse than he expected. "I won't hurt you," he said quietly, rubbing the fine bones with a gentle hand.

She said nothing, but a fine tremor shook her.

Puzzled, Tynan asked, "Did we misfigure, my lady?"

"What?" She turned her head to at least look at him.

How to ask it? "This is a matter of some delicacy, but are the gossips wrong? Are you still a virgin?"

"Oh. No."

"I see." He lifted the bottle and took a swig from the mouth, then took her hand. "Have a little. We needn't rush."

"I don't take spirits, sir."

"Ah, but now you're lying. I saw you nipping some brandy not an hour ago."

"That was medicinal."

He smiled. "Am I so terrifying?"

"No." With an exasperated sigh, she said, "I would just as soon be done with this."

"Doesn't speak well of your lover."

She stared at the ceiling. "I asked you not to speak of that."

Amused and oddly challenged by her coldness, Tynan set the bottle down. "Very well. Let's be done with it." Quickly, he stripped off his shirt and boots, and paused a moment to see if she would glance at him. Most women found his form pleasing enough.

She did not look at him. Exasperated, he mounted the steps and stood at the top, right next to her. His body cast shadows over the deepness of the bed and over her white-shrouded form, leaving only a single rectangle to illuminate the curve of her cheek and the tip of her nose.

He inclined his head, waiting for her to look toward him. She displayed remarkable stubbornness, however, laying still for a long, long moment, her fists curled beside her, her body utterly motionless, the hair slicked back and hidden away in a braid that snaked out beside her. Tynan tried to make out the shape of her body, but the single, guttering candle was no match for the gloom.

At last she turned her head and cold eyes flickered over his torso. "I do not wish to kiss," she said. "And I would much prefer to extinguish the candle."

A prick of annoyance stabbed him. "Are you determined to make this difficult, madam? It needn't be unpleasant."

"I have wed you, sir. I will lie with you to solemnize our vow and to get us some children, which I would like, but do not expect more than that." As if she could not help herself, she folded her hands across her belly. "For the rest, you may go to your mistress. A man such as yourself must have any number of them to choose from."

He narrowed his eyes. "And if I do not?"

She made a soft, disbelieving noise, and suddenly turned her face toward him. "I shouldn't think you'd have trouble finding a new one."

In the moment of her turning, the gilding of candlelight washed over her face, and Tynan spied quite another woman than the one bound up in black bombazine. In this light, her eyes were sultry, a color of bruised grapes, and her mouth was fuller than he had first believed, and he saw, before she could hide it, the flickering of her gaze over his torso, reluctantly snaring in the region of his hips.

He smiled and rubbed his belly with an open palm.

She jerked her head away. "You forget, sir, that I'm quite familiar with the habits of rakes."

His eyes narrowed. He'd not expected so cold a

woman, but he'd be damned if he'd leave her without consummating the vow. With a shrug he said, "So be it," and turned to pinch out the candle.

In darkness, he climbed to the bed and sank down beside her. She smelled of lavender, unexpectedly pleasant, and he leaned close to her neck to breathe it. His breath crossed her shoulder, and he felt a tiny ripple of reaction in her, but whether revulsion or desire, he could not have said.

He'd never faced the prospect of bedding an unwilling woman, and found it went against the grain to simply mount her. Thinking of nervous horses, he reached out a hand and stroked her arm. When she didn't shy, he took her hand and rubbed the limp fingers, kneaded her wrist, worked his way up to her shoulder. She went rigid again—he supposed it was the thought of his hands on her breasts.

So instead he slid a hand over her waist. He'd expected the giving softness of a plump belly, but instead found hipbones and a smooth, flat plane that was very nice indeed. He roved in a circle, exploring warm flesh beneath crumpled lawn, and touched ribs, thinly veiled with flesh, and the sleek flare of a hip. She simply lay there, unprotesting, silent, but his body responded with anticipation.

"It is not necessary to try to arouse me," she said into the dark. "Just be done."

Uttering an expletive, Tynan lost patience. Roughly he positioned himself between her legs, shoved up her gown, and set himself free. "I'd have spared you this," he said, and plunged—into the quivering moistness of aroused female flesh, flesh that gave a pulse as he moved within her. It so startled him that he halted, buried within her, and looked up. In the faint red from the fire he could see that her chin was upthrust, her jaw rigid as if she strained to keep from crying out. Her fists were tight at her sides.

With a flash of intuition, Tynan slid his hands under the fabric of her nightrail, over that sleek belly, upward to the ribs, then into the plush, unbelievable weight of glorious breasts.

He could not halt the murmur of approval that rose in his throat, and braced himself on his elbows to gather the luxurious flesh into both palms, feeling his body—and hers—leap in pleasure as his thumbs grazed aroused nipples. A faint, helpless noise came out with her breath, and impulsively Tynan bent his head to kiss her breasts. She cried out a little as his mouth closed around her, and distinctly mewed when he began to suckle. Pleased, he moved his hips ever so slightly, teasing from her the response he knew awaited. He felt it building around him, a quivering and pulsing that grew with each flicker of his tongue, each thrust of his hips, until she at last was moving with him, and her hands flew up to his hair, gripping it tightly, pulling him closer, deeper, with the innate, sensual gestures of a woman who knew what pleased her. Her orgasm was violent, shattering. Her shoulders rocked beneath his hands, and her knees closed hard on his hips, and her body spasmed with such power around him that Tynan was lost to it, and roared out his pleasure, lifting her hips to him as he spilled his seed, rocking deep, sweating and shaking.

In the blind aftermath, he fell against her, astonished and delighted—and in moments, ready to continue. He lifted his head, about to kiss her throat, when she shoved him, hard.

"You have your consummation. Now go."

He caught at her, bewildered. "What?" He'd thought she would be pleased. "I'd rather—"

She trembled with the aftermath, but there was power in her when she shoved him, an almost desperate strength. "I said go."

Fury struck through him and he pulled away violently. "So that's the way it will be." Angrily, he swept his shirt off the floor and shoved his arms into it. "I will have an heir from you, but once that's done, I'll not trouble you again."

"Perhaps there need not be another time, then."

"Aye, that'd be a lucky thing." He fastened his breeches, heat burning his cheeks and boiling his blood. "No wonder your lover left you."

Her voice was weary enough that it shamed him. "Please do not speak of that."

He hesitated, wishing to take the words back. It was not his way to be cruel, but he could not recall when he'd ever been so thoroughly humiliated. Perhaps it was best they leave it as it was. "Good night, wife," he said, and left her.

Alone in the chamber, Adriana curled under the blankets into a small, tight ball, her knees drawn up to her chest. She did not cry. Her shame was too deep for that.

But she could not avoid the waves of memory. The

Black Angel standing beside her on the steps to the bed, his naked chest gleaming in candlelight, his hair loose on his shoulders. The feel of his hands on her, gentle and strong. The sensation of his mouth on her breast—

She closed her eyes and covered her eyes. She would not think of it, would forget all of it.

But it was not as simple as that. Over and over she pushed the images away, replaced them with visions of the fields at midmorning, when fog still lingered in wisps in the deepest furrows. Or her dogs, running full tilt across the lawn.

Or Martinique. Lush and green and warm. Where she had been free. Where laughter had seemed the natural response to life, and music flowed from lips and hands and from the very trees.

It was Martinique that lured her, at last, into sleep. When she started awake, it was dawn, and she did not know what had awakened her. Lying still for a moment, she listened.

Horses. Coming fast.

Tossing the coverlet away, she rushed across the room, stubbing her toe in her haste to climb up to the embrasure. She flung open the heavy draperies. Below, on the road over which her husband had ridden, came two horses with mud-splattered bellies, and on their backs rode two men.

For a long, breathless moment she stared, unable to believe the evidence of her eyes. A blond man, hair fallen loose from its queue to spread in a glitter over his shoulders, rode a black horse, his woolen cape billowing out behind him. The other man, his hair a tumble of black curls, rode a bay.

A catch tightened her throat—joy and despair. Only one day late. Only one.

Then joy overtook all else, and Adriana flung open the casement, unmindful of the rain. Leaning out, she cried, "Julian! Gabriel!"

The dark man rose up in his stirrups and lifted one arm, his face breaking into a smile. "Riana!" He whooped madly.

She turned and scrambled down from the steps, leaving the window open in her haste. From the floor, she retrieved a wrapper and stuck her arms in it as she rushed out into the passageway, banging hard on the doors of her sisters' chambers as she went.

"Get up! Wake up!" she cried, and flung open one door after another. Her sisters sat up, poked heads between the curtains of their beds, blinking and tousled. "Get up!"

Phoebe said, "What is it, Adriana?"

She pointed, words deserting her for a moment. "Our brothers are home."

3

Adriana raced for the steps without waiting to see if her sisters followed, tumbling down the stairs in her bare feet, nearly flying down one set, then the next, and then the landing above the top floor. "Julian!" she cried as he came through the door.

She scrambled the rest of the way, and by the time she hit the ground floor, her brothers were rushing to meet her. Adriana, without thought, flung herself toward them, a sob breaking free at last as their strong, fierce, *dear* arms captured her, one fist against her ear.

"I thought you were dead," she cried, and buried her face tighter into one shoulder, then the other, smelling wet wool and the oil Gabriel used in his hair and the heat of their hard journey. Their hands grasped her, pulled her tight, and she wept in purest, deepest gratitude while they kissed her hair and held her close. A hundred memories, a thousand, rushed through her. "I missed you both so much!"

At last she pulled back, her heart pinched, to be sure it was not some dream or trick that her imagination played.

But there was Julian, a lock of blond hair falling free to brush his high-planed face, sunburned and more weathered than it had been. She touched his cheek and stubble itched her fingers, but in all, he looked well. Older, stronger. More powerful. Tears streamed down her face. "I missed you," she whispered.

He kissed her head, a smile at last breaking that graveness, and she turned to Gabriel, older than Julian by three years. Morning dew caught in the black curls of his hair, giving him a halo—a halo belied by the mischievous glitter in his pale green eyes. From his pocket he took a bouquet of barely mashed wild-flowers, plucked by the side of the road, and bowed as he presented them. "I did not forget," he said, for it had ever been Gabriel who remembered her love of flowers.

She laughed, but finally saw the hollows that made his angular face gaunt, the darkness below his eyes. She put a hand to his face. "Gabriel, are you ill?"

He shook his head, and Julian urgently took Adriana's elbow. "Are we in time? Did you marry?"

But before she could answer, shrieks and cries came from above, and the prodigal sons stepped forward to greet the other girls.

Tynan heard the flurry of cries and footsteps from the drawing room, where he'd taken his foul mood the night before, intending to drown his frustration in several bottles of port. To his disgust, port did not seem to be the answer. He finally gave it up and wished for tea, but did not want to rouse some weary servant after so long a day of work. He contented himself instead with the fire and remnants of the feast he found in the kitchen.

By morning he'd wound his way around his masculine embarrassment—he'd not ever left a woman displeased!—to the practicalities of the situation. The bond had been sealed, and his grim, cold wife wanted nothing more to do with him once he put a babe in her belly. So be it.

He had been dozing in the big chair when he heard the shouts, and then horses, then the tumbling of feet on the floors overhead. New guests, he supposed, without much interest, but stood up nonetheless. He'd greet them as lord of this manor, set the tone now.

But at the threshold he halted, his gaze snared by the vision flying down the steps. A wealth of thick hair tumbled over a body barely hidden by lawn nightrail and thin wrapper she'd scarcely managed to tie. Her bare feet were slim and white, and he'd glimpsed the slender ankles by candlelight the night before.

His wife.

Gone was the colorless woman bound up in black bombazine. Her skin glowed peach and white. Her eyes burned in her face. Her mouth was red and full. Had he been *blind* the day before?

Stunned, he blinked. Once, twice. Stared as she flew, graceful as a butterfly, into the waiting embrace of the two men at the door. They gathered her close and enfolded her in a fierce embrace, their faces hard and moved at once, and Tynan saw the rare, deep, unbreakable bond between the three. One blond head, one dark, and the tall, finely shaped woman between them.

He had one instant to absorb that these were her brothers, the exiles, come home too late to save her, before the other sisters appeared, one after the other, and a chaos of shouts and cries and greetings and hugs and kisses erupted. The slim black woman Tynan had seen the night before also appeared. Exotically attired in some bright fabric, she burst from the servant doors and piled herself into the mix, crying out in a mix of French and English and some language Tynan did not recognize.

Adriana stepped back, letting the woman in, and Tynan saw her wiping away the happy tears on her face, saw her cover her mouth in joyous disbelief.

And he realized that he'd not been at all blind the day before. Her features were clear and even, but not particularly remarkable, and her hair was very pale. Black had sucked all the color from her, and the stiff fabric had made her appear plump.

But now that hair hung loose, thick and very long, and the palest shade of saffron, a color so delicate it made him think of ethereal, fleeting things—the gauzy trails of spiders, the first soft rush of morning. In contrast, her unbound breasts swayed in earthy heaviness beneath the thin fabric, and her cheeks were flushed with the happiness of her brothers' return. Tynan, looking at her, felt an unwelcome stab of desire.

At last she seemed to sense his presence, and turned like a startled hare into the flame of his gaze. He raked her, head to toe, and lifted an eyebrow. Her narrow chin lifted, though he saw a flush spread upward from her neck. But instead of the arrogant toss of her head, the haughty disdain he expected, she stepped forward. "Come, my lord, and meet my brother, the *Earl*."

Sharp irony burned in those eyes. The irony that both had lost—Adriana her freedom, Tynan his hope of controlling an English estate. Coldly, he met her gaze, and leaned close. "A pity we consummated the marriage, is it not?" he said in her ear.

So close, he smelled the lavender that had enticed him the night before, and a lingering trace of their heated joining. His wish to put his hands on her swelled. He discovered he even liked the haughtiness that now flared, and the fierce loyalty that burned in her eyes. "Indeed."

They stood alone at the edge of the group. Tynan, acting purely on instinct, lifted a hand to the small of her back, sliding it down toward the voluptuous swell of buttocks. "A fine pair of *brothers*," he said. "But they cannot give what I can, wife."

He had the satisfaction of seeing her color rise before she tossed that head and gave him a thorough once-over, her delicate nostrils flaring with distaste. "I expect there are a thousand rakes in London who give what you do."

He blinked. Then, quite to his surprise, he laughed. "Not quite," he purred. "Not quite." He dropped his hand, freeing her.

"Julian, Gabriel," she said, stepping forward. "I would like you to meet my husband, Tynan Spenser, Earl of Glencove." Adriana tossed her head. "Tynan, this is my brother, Julian St. Ives, Earl of Albury."

The man turned cold eyes upon Tynan. In the arrogant tilt of his chin, Tynan saw a reflection of his wife's haughty armor. Albury's coloring, like Riana's, was very fair—that cool English beauty that so flattered women and often made a man look weak and pretty. It would be a mistake to judge Julian St. Ives so, however. There was steel in those gray eyes, a shrewd intelligence across the high brow, and character weathered into the jaw. He gave a curt nod. "How do you do."

Not to be outdone, Tynan lifted a brow. "Quite well, thank you."

"And this," Adriana said, gesturing, "is my eldest brother, Gabriel St. Ives."

"Man about town," Gabriel added wryly, and unlike his brother, held out his hand in greeting.

Tynan shook it, liking the faint irony of his comment and the directness of his measuring gaze. Gabriel was the taller of the pair, and owned the lean, ropy grace of a master swordsman. His hands were large and strong. Decisive.

Phoebe intervened, finally, pushing her way to the middle of the throng. "You've all greeted them now, let the poor men come sit and eat. Girls, off with you. I'll send Mary to help you dress."

Tynan stepped to one side. Adriana stood where she'd been, looking a bit stricken as she watched her brothers go. Then she caught Tynan's perusal and brushed by him, her thin gown swirling over the tips of his shoes. She pretended to ignore him, and Tynan chuckled to himself when she could not resist one last, piercing look in his direction as she began to mount the stairs.

To see if he was watching.

Oh ho, he thought, and gave her his most wicked smile, intrigued when she blushed and hurried up the stairs.

Phoebe, more sensibly attired than the other girls in a heavy cotton wrapper, her hair woven neatly into one long braid that hung down her back, ordered chocolate and tea, bread and butter and cheese to be brought to the dining room, sent the girls up to get dressed, tried to move Monique and failed.

Tynan watched it all from his post by the hearth, arms crossed over his chest, a certain restlessness in his shoulders and knees. He didn't know what he was waiting for until Adriana came back into the room, simply dressed in a shepherdess's gown, her hair hidden by a cap. A thin scarf, tucked into the edges of her bodice, hid her breasts.

She saw Tynan at once, but chose not to acknowledge him, going instead to stand between her brothers at the table, one hand on each of their shoulders as if to assure herself they were really here. Tynan found it rather touching, and was again intrigued by her need to ignore her husband. It was the sort of alert inattention that spoke volumes of her deep awareness of him. Perhaps things were not as grim as they'd seemed last night

Standing between her brothers, Adriana sighed, brushed at her skirts as if wiping something unpleasant from her hands. "Have you eaten?" she asked.

"Phoebe has seen to it."

"Good." Abruptly, she doubled her fist and pulled

back, hitting Julian in the shoulder, hard enough to knock him sideways. Then she turned, lightning fast, and aimed for Gabriel, who took the cuff on his back. "Why the bloody hell did you let us think you died?" she cried.

"Adriana!" Phoebe said, shocked.

Gabriel laughed, ducking another blow. "Ask Julian—'twas his doing. Ow! Stop that." He grabbed her wrist, but she wrenched free and hit Julian again. The blond brother, laughing, jumped up, captured her hands and wrapped them around her waist, hugging her from behind, his head against her hair.

"Poor Riana!" he said in a mocking voice, rocking her back and forth. "Safe and comfortable here at Hartwood, mourning her dear lost brothers, while they fought the seas and pirates and slave traders."

She halted, and Tynan saw the quick alarm. "Not slave traders! Not really?"

Gabriel sobered. "Yes, really."

Tynan simply watched them, his eyes narrowed as he absorbed the easy camaraderie between them. Here were deep bonds, invisible but powerful, and in the way of new grief, he suddenly ached for his own brother with a pain that nearly blinded him. Sorrow burned through him, stealing his breath, suffocating him with a fresh sense of loss.

He made to turn away, but somehow Phoebe was beside him, her hand on his arm. "You should have seen them as children. Wild, and Riana often as not the ringleader."

Bleakly, he stared at them, now grouped so Adriana could hear their exploits. "'Tis hard to believe she is the same woman who stood like a widow on those steps yesterday."

Phoebe laughed. "Oh, just wait. My sister has a thousand faces."

"Does she, now? And which is real?"

"All of them."

Grateful for the distraction from the threat of his grief, Tynan looked thoughtfully at his new wife. His gaze caught on the tender sweep of hair at her nape, the grace of a collarbone, the voluptuousness of her breasts, and he was assailed with a sensual memory of her fighting her own body last night, and losing with such violence. He thought of the tight-lipped ghost of yesterday, and the butterfly look of her flying down the steps to fling herself with such heartfelt love into her brothers' arms.

A thousand faces.

All his hopes now lay with this puzzling woman. He needed to win that loyalty she gave her brothers, needed the fierceness he glimpsed below the surface, needed that nearly bitter wit. And he thought, standing there with more heat in his veins that he would have claimed, that he knew exactly how to capture her.

He turned to Phoebe. "Send her to me in the library when she is free."

It was plain that Julian and Gabriel were exhausted, and once they'd eaten, Adriana insisted everyone leave them to go to their rooms and rest. There would be ample time to hear their adventures later. She walked with them to the foot of the stairs, somehow reluctant to part with them, even for a few hours.

Julian took her hand. "Riana, forgive us. We heard

too late, and came as quickly as we could. How long have you been married?"

She let go of a soft, bitter laugh. "One day." She wanted to add that she'd felt them coming to her, but didn't. "But do not think on that. I am just so very glad to have you back again."

Gabriel kissed her head, and she felt again his thinness as he leaned close. "Are you ill?" she asked, catching the front of his shirt to halt him so she could look at him closely in the bright light falling through the windows of the hall. The pale eyes were clear, and his color lacked the yellow tones it took on when he sickened, but he was extremely thin.

From behind, Julian touched her shoulder, and she looked around in time to see a silent message pass between the pair. "We encountered some rather . . . difficult adventures," Julian said. "Unfortunately, Gabriel suffered a bit more than I, but he's hale as ever now."

A ripple of unease touched her, and Riana frowned. "Do you swear?"

Gabriel smiled. "I swear it."

She forced herself to release them, step back. "Rest then, and I'll see you at supper."

"Get word to Cassandra," Julian said.

"Of course." She watched them climb the stairs, feeling an odd sense of loss. It surprised her. What in the world could she have lost? Her brothers were home, at long last.

Then it struck her—these were men. The brothers who had left her had been youths—Julian not quite twenty, Gabriel only a little older. They'd still worn the dewy flesh of the untried, the slim figures of boys.

No more. At twenty-five and twenty-eight, they were full-grown men with broad backs and thick stubble on their chins.

Men who'd seen more than they wished of the world, evidently.

Phoebe came out of the drawing room. "Riana, Lord Glencove asked me to send you to him in the library when you had a moment."

Tynan. Adriana nodded. "Thank you." Might as well be done with it. Smoothing her skirts, tucking a wisp of loose hair into her cap, she went to the door and scratched it. He called out for her to enter.

The room occupied an eastern wall, and was bright with morning. Tynan stood in gold-edged silhouette against one long window, facing the gardens.

"Phoebe said you'd asked for me," she said.

"Aye," he said without turning. "Please close the door."

There was something odd in his tone, and Adriana felt a small quiver of nervousness, but she did as he asked. Then, a queer anticipation leaping in her veins, she moved to the middle of the room, uncertain what to expect. She folded her hands.

For a moment he did not look at her, but kept his face turned toward the view of the bowling green beyond the window. Sunlight touched the crown of his head, kindling red-gold lights from the very dark strands. A rather spectacular effect, Adriana thought, and looked away.

At last he turned toward her and straightened, as if pulling himself from some faraway spot. "So, at last your long lost brothers are home."

"Yes."

"Which puts me in a strangely unbalanced position."

She frowned, puzzled. "I suppose."

He left the window and crossed the room, halting a few feet away, his hands loose at his sides. A flash of the way his belly looked—all gold candlelight and gold flesh, melting to a supple expanse—crossed her vision. She quelled it, took a breath.

"It seems I need you more than you need me," he said, inclining his head. "I find I dislike that imbalance."

"As I disliked it the other way yesterday."

"Indeed." He pursed his lips, frowned, made a little gesture with his hands. "I can think of little that can cause more misery than a man and a woman bound in dislike to a false marriage—"

Hope flared in her. "I agree—"

"But the fact remains, I need this alliance, my lady, and will require you to remain bound."

Hope died. "Oh."

He lifted his head. "However, I have thought of a proposition to ease both our consciences."

A stray finger of light shifted in that instant, and it fell on his face, illuminating the strange, high bridge of his nose, a flaw that gave his face a peculiar interest. He really was a most beautiful thing to look upon, she thought with a sense of resignation. "A proposition?"

"Aye." He took a step toward her. With a challenging expression on his mouth, he boldly lifted one hand and touched her cheek very lightly. "I think you are less unmoved by me than you would admit. And I admit freely," his finger trailed down her jaw, "that you . . . intrigue me."

Adriana swallowed, snared against her will by the rolling sound of his vowels, the depth of his resonant voice. And curse him—curse her wanton flesh!—the brush of his fingers kindled small shivers across the back of her neck. "Your proposition?" she said sharply.

He dropped his hand, lifted his chin. "Give me time to woo you, Adriana."

She snorted. "I am not, sir, a wooable female."

"Are you not, then?" A dimple appeared in his lean cheek, wicked and amused punctuation to his devilish smile. "But then you've have not heard my bargain."

She lifted her eyebrows skeptically. "All right. What is it?"

"Give me one hundred kisses, over one hundred days, to prove myself."

"Kisses?" She blinked, thinking she must have misheard. "I dislike kissing."

"All the better." Something glittered in his eyes. "No gamble at all for you."

"No." She stepped back, suddenly imagining herself trying to resist the taste of him, the feel of his breath over her chin, her neck. A sense of genuine panic rose in her chest. "A kiss is too intimate to share so capriciously."

"Ah." He nodded. "Intimate."

Adriana only nodded stupidly, thinking she had convinced him it was a foolish bargain.

"'Tis only mouth-to-mouth kisses that require intimacy. We'll have none of that."

"But where would you kiss me, then?"

A slow, seductive shrug, an even slower, more seductive smile. "Wherever it comes to me."

"No," she repeated breathlessly, "I cannot agree to such a bargain."

"But—" He lifted a finger, and Adriana thought of a faery king, come from the woods to woo her into an unholy life. "—At the end, if I've not been successful in capturing your heart, I would leave you in peace forever. One hundred days of misery, or thousands upon thousands of them?"

In spite of the danger, the idea of being rid of him held allure. "You would leave Hartwood?"

"Aye."

"And what of the financial arrangements we have made? My brothers' return does not solve that."

"Everything will be as we have arranged it—you will have the funds you require. I will—with luck—have gained the political influence I have come to achieve. I'll simply leave you. 'Tis not unusual that a husband and wife do not reside together."

That part was true enough. She narrowed her eyes, considering. If he did not kiss her mouth, she could most likely keep him at arm's length. "Very well. You may have your hundred kisses—though I warn you they'll do you no good." Dryly, she cocked her head. "It isn't as if I am innocent of such things."

A flicker, a darkness—desire?—showed on his face for a moment. In a low voice he said, "Indeed."

And for just a heartbeat longer he held her gaze, and she thought of the brightly embroidered edges of his cloak for no reason she could name. She did not look away.

He stepped forward. "I would like the first kiss now."

Before she even had a chance to panic, he captured her right hand and lifted it to his mouth. He brushed his lips, dry and light, over her fingers, then let her go.

That was all, a single brush of his lips over her hand, but Adriana found herself snared by a thousand details—the light breaking in red-gold arcs over the dark crown of his head, the slight tug of wool over his shoulders making a soft sound, the tip of his ear, almost pointed, like an elf's.

And with a faint sense of despair, she realized she'd been half hoping for more of a kiss than that. Much more.

4

Cassandra arrived mid-afternoon, windblown from her ride. "Where are they?" she asked without preamble when Adriana, spying her horse and carriage from the music room, had rushed to let her in.

"Asleep, I'm afraid. They'll be down for supper."

Cassandra took off her hat and gave it to a servant. "How do they look, Riana? Are they well? Did they give any explanation of where they were, why they didn't write at all?"

"They look well," she said, taking the questions in order. "Gabriel is very thin, but swears he's not ill. And no, they gave no explanation."

They moved in silent agreement to the music room, close by the front doors. It had been their mother's favorite room, and seemed to be the place they migrated when something serious needed to be discussed. A harp sat in one corner, dusted daily though no one played it; and a variety of instruments in cases stood along the south wall. Adriana liked the room for its greens and golds; for the wallpaper she had helped her mother choose when she was seven or eight—a pattern of pheasants and stylized fruit in a cheerful blend; and for the relative quiet. She often came here to read.

She perched on a settee now, and took up the sewing she'd put down, waiting for Cassandra's restless energy to dissipate on her turns through the room. Which it finally did.

"I thought them dead," she said, and suddenly turned from her pacing so quickly her skirts washed forward with a swish. "But that will wait. How did you find your husband?"

"What do you mean? You saw him." She shrugged. "His nickname is apt."

"You know what I mean, Riana. Was he gentle with you? Do you suit?"

A faint heat edged her ears. Leave it to Cassandra to rush in where others would look away. "Those are private matters."

Cassandra made a soft noise of impatience. "Well, I'd agree that one wouldn't wish to stand out in the streets and shout it around, but between sisters—who've shared much more—it seems a logical question."

It was true they'd shared these secrets with one another. When Adriana, dazzled by the first heady attentions of Malvern, had needed to whisper her secrets to someone, it had been to Cassandra she'd gone, knowing instinctively that this sister, unconventional even in smallest childhood, would not judge her. And when Cassandra, devastated by the private cloddishness of a man who'd swept her off her feet within weeks of her debut, had needed a confidante and advice, it had been to Adriana she'd gone.

Still, what had transpired between her and Tynan last night seemed to Adriana too new, too raw, too *private*. She summoned a smile that hinted of things she didn't want to say and lifted one shoulder. "He's skilled, and lacks brutality. I can bear him well enough."

Cassandra's eyes widened. "So that's how it is." She shifted, her face sober again in that lightning way she had. "I don't like him, Riana. He's too false for you. Be wary."

"Of course." Adriana waved a hand. "I am no fool."

"Good." Suddenly, she sat. "Where is everyone?

"Phoebe and Monique are plotting some enormous homecoming feast, and the girls were chattering enough to drive a magpie mad, so I sent them out riding."

Cassandra leaned forward, a posture of secretiveness. "There's more we should discuss, while the others are absent."

Adriana felt a stillness go through her. She put aside her sewing. "What is it?"

"The magistrate has learned of Julian's arrival. The ship docked three days ago, and some ratty consort of Malvern's mother happened to see our boys disembark." She paused. "There will be a summons within days."

"Where did you hear this? So quickly?"

Cassandra lifted her shoulders. "A gentleman called on me this morning to tell me. He came within moments of your messenger."

"I see." She took a breath, let it go. "Well, it is not unexpected."

"True." Cassandra stroked her palms together, her lips pursing as she watched her long white fingers. Then she raised her eyes. "The scandal will be resurrected, Riana, in every detail."

With effort, Adriana kept her expression blank, though she could not help the sudden, involuntary twitch of an eyelid. "Undoubtedly," she said. What else was there to say?

For a long moment, filled only with the sound of a clock ticking on the mantel, silence engulfed them. At last, Cassandra made an impatient noise. "Riana, honestly, do not let it cow you. Move to town. Dress in your finest, and lift your chin and—"

"And look down your haughty nose." The voice came from the doorway, edged with faint irony. "You do it so very well."

Tynan, of course. He stood there in tall boots and tight breeches that showed the length of his thighs, and that living wealth of hair was faintly mussed. Idly slapping his riding crop against his knee, he inclined his head. "Am I interrupting?" he asked, though it was plain from the quirk of his lips that he didn't particularly care if he was.

One could not say yes, of course, but Adriana was forming excuses for a private conversation, wishing to rid the room of that virile, heated scent that came from him—horse and coriander and male—but before she could speak, Cassandra leaped to her feet.

"Not at all, sir," she said, going forward to draw him into the room. She pulled her head back a little to look at him approvingly. "Her haughtiness is an excellent tool, I should think."

Adriana rolled her eyes at the congratulatory smiles they exchanged. Of course, they'd both think of brazening it out. An Irish rake in English society and a young widow who took pleasure in her collection of slightly outré and scandalous guests. "It's so easy for both of you," she said, and turned her head toward the window, gazing at the soft green day.

"What do you mean, Riana?" Cassandra asked. "We're cut from the same cloth, you and I."

"I'm not like you," she said quietly. She valued the opinions of others—perhaps too much. "I want pleasant afternoons spent in a tea shop, in the company of ladies. I want to shop for gloves and tsk over the antics of my children . . . and . . . take smug pride over my roses and play the harpsichord of a late evening." She turned. "I'll endure the scandal again if I must, but I'll do it from here."

Cassandra hooted with laughter. "Oh, Riana, you have such an imagination! Is this the lady fantasy? I haven't heard it before."

Piqued, Adriana drew herself up. "It's no fantasy, Cassandra. It's the life I was born to live."

Cassandra gave another hoot, slapping her hands down onto her skirts in a most unladylike fashion. A lock of her hair fell down and she brushed it away distractedly. "I've heard the lady pirate, and the lady adventurer and the lady explorer. This is the first I've heard of the Lady at Large in London!"

Adriana felt her cheeks burn. That was the trouble with sisters, she thought darkly. They remembered every stupid thing you ever said—and loved more than anything to drag them up again.

She couldn't bear to look at Tynan to see what effect this little hilarity was having upon him. No doubt he was as dazzled and admiring of Cassandra's beauty as he'd been on the steps yesterday. Adriana had clearly seen his hope that it would be her sister who'd be his bride.

A dozen responses rose in her throat, but in the end she couldn't utter any of them for the mingled embarrassment and fury in her throat, and she simply pushed by the both of them. "I'm going out for walk."

"Riana!" Cassandra cried. "Wait! I was only teasing you. I didn't—"

Adriana threw a murderous glance over her shoulder and made for the heavy oak doors. From a hook by the door, she grabbed her cloak, hearing Cassandra protest once more.

Outside, the fresh autumn air struck her face with its scents of leaf and mold and the promise of winter lurking in the shadows, and she dragged in a deep gulp of it as she strode across the green toward a path that looped around the estate.

"My lady!"

Adriana glanced over her shoulder to see Tynan, leaning into a little run to catch up to her. She picked up her pace; few could keep up with her long-legged stride when she wished to put them behind. And even those who could catch her—she glared at him from the corner of her eye as he came up beside her—would soon weary of her stony silence and energetic pace.

To his credit, he said nothing for the longest time, only walking beside her when vegetation would permit, falling behind when it did not. Adriana strode into the hills, ducking under low hanging branches and shifting her skirts automatically to keep them free of familiar catches. After a quarter of an hour, her skin grew warm and perspiration built on the back of her neck, and she was breathing hard.

But next to her Tynan kept up as easily as if they were out for a Sunday stroll. It was astonishingly annoying. At last she stopped at the crest of a hill to glare at him. "Are all Irishmen as hale as you?"

"Any that are as well-fed as I," he said. "Though those are few and far between." He looked around him alertly, shading his eyes for a moment, and Adriana was glad to see there was at least a sheen of perspiration over his brow. "It's rather remarkable, isn't it?"

Below spread the estate of Hartwood, the house and the stretches of lawn, and the hills rising gently all around. In the hazy distance was a glimpse of the village, just the church spire and the edge of the fields, fallow now that harvest was done. "Peaceful," she said. "Which is why I'm loath to leave it on a fool's errand."

"Your sister meant you no harm."

She tsked. "Do not presume to tell me the motives of my own sister, sir." She whirled and began to walk again. "If she had wished me no harm, she would have kept my secrets to herself."

A low, deep chuckle rolled from him. He bent from the waist gracefully to pluck a tall stem of grass and righted himself. "There is no more irritating human in the world than our siblings, is there? They know us all too well."

"Have you siblings?"

A perplexed shadow crossed his eyes. "I did. A twin brother."

A twin! The thought of two such faces in the world was a little unnerving. "Identical?"

"In face, but not in spirit. He was a much nobler man than I." A stile dividing a hedgerow stopped them, and Adriana watched the sorrow come on Tynan's face like the swift descent of a winter night. "Far more."

Against her will, Adriana wanted to know more, but he seemed to shake away the shadows, and turned his vivid gaze on her. "He despaired of what he called my sensual habits," he said, and lifted a wicked brow, flashing that dimple in his cheek with the effortlessness of long practice. "Shall I illustrate?"

Riana's lips quirked into a half smile before she could stop them. She held up a hand. "No, thank you."

He helped her over the stile and they walked in a peaceful silence to the spot Adriana had in mind, the deep shadows of an ancient tree, its trunk as wide across as three men. Below it grew a thick bed of tiny tangled daisies and grass. She sat, smoothing her skirts beneath her, and Tynan settled beside her, elbows resting on his uplifted knees.

"You'll have to go to London, you know," he said finally. "You can't send your brothers out there alone, when it was in your defense they acted."

"*Must* we discuss this?"

"Aye." He fell backward, taking his weight on one elbow as he looked up at her.

Adriana found her eyes sliding over the fall of his hair, thick and rich looking, barely caught by the thong he'd used to tie it back. A faint roar rose in her ears, induced by her embarrassment over the subject, and the whole made her speak sharply. "I don't see why."

"Well, for one, 'tis possible I might be able to help you, if you'll let me."

"You?"

For a moment he stared out toward the soft green view, and a faint hint of red stained the high plane of his cheekbones. He stood abruptly, brushed grass from his elbows. "Right. I am mistaken."

Adriana reached for him, and succeeded only in catching the hem of his coat, something she would never have ordinarily done. But now the roar in her ears was worsened by pride, and by embarrassment that she'd been rude to a man who appeared to only want to be kind. "Please wait."

He made a soft sound, a bitter whisper of a laugh. "For what purpose? Shall we sit here and think of more ways to humiliate each other? It seems we have already discovered the way to pain for each of us."

"No. No, I am sorry. I did not mean—well, I did. I meant to be rude because I was humiliated. The entire subject offers no end of humiliation for me, and—" She took a breath. "I apologize."

He gestured with one hand. "Let's walk, my lady. 'Tis often easier to speak when the feet are in motion."

She nodded, surprised when he held out one lean, long-fingered hand to help her to her feet. Accepting the gesture of sympathy, she took it, and had a fleeting sense of tensile strength, not only in his hands, but through the whole of him. "Thank you."

For a little while they followed the slim path that

led over the crest of the hill into a small copse of hardwoods. Again the simple act of moving seemed to dissipate the tension Adriana felt. She squared her shoulders. "It is not my usual way to indulge in insults. I do most sincerely apologize."

"Accepted." A beat of hesitation, then: "Will you tell me how it happened with your lover?"

"How it happened? I made a fool of myself with a rake, and when he put me aside, my brother killed him in a duel."

"Not that." He looked at her. "Did you fall in love?"

She felt his eyes on her face and lifted her chin. "I thought so at the time."

"And is it, perhaps, that wound that still lingers a little?"

"No!" Adriana exclaimed. She hated the tiny, knife-thin slice that went through her at his suggestion. "What pains me," she said clearly, "is the utter disregard I displayed for my father, or the repercussions my actions would have upon my family. I acted heedlessly, selfishly—and hurt a great many people that I love in that heedlessness."

"Mmm."

He didn't speak again for several long minutes, and Adriana found herself watching him. He walked tall and straight, with a certain jaunty set to his head. As they went along, he touched things they passed, trailing his fingers over the delicate head of a foxglove, across the bumpy bark of a tree, along the crumbling edge of a brick wall, left from some unimaginably distant time. And as he touched, he looked. Looked up to admire the fading leaves of an arching oak, to watch a sparrow sail through the blue sky, to glance back over his shoulder at something his fingers had not quite absorbed.

It was a curiously appealing habit, one he evidently carried on as he thought, for next he said, "I'm not entirely clear why your brother would face a trial. Men are killed in duels monthly."

"Yes." She sighed. "Unfortunately, Malvern was the son of the King's brother. His mother is . . . well-known to men at Court and in Parliament, and she's been quite insistent that the crime should be tried."

"Mmm. I see." He cast a single raised eyebrow toward her. "A pretty mess."

Riana suddenly imagined how it would go, the scandal sheets and the wags and the gossip at court. She squeezed her eyes shut and stopped, giving out a little moan. "Oh, God! I am so glad to have them home, but it has been so peaceful here—"

"St. Bridget!" he cried out, and took her arm. "What a selfish little twit you are! I'd expected better of a daughter of James St. Ives."

She looked up, startled.

His eyes narrowed. "Imagine what he'd think of you now! You're whining about scandal and embarrassment when your brothers have rushed home to try and save you from a marriage you evidently did not want. They slayed your lover at the risk of their own necks, and now again will face the repercussions of that act, and you snivel here about—frivolity."

It was not only her ears that burned now, burned red as berries by the feel of them, but her cheeks and forehead and chin. She yanked her arm from his grip and bowed her head in shame. He was right.

But she could not seem to find words to give him that, and only put her hands on her cheeks, faintly amazed when they did not seem hot.

Tynan stayed where he was and did not speak.

Finally, Adriana captured the racing of her heart, smoothed her skirt and turned back, lifting her chin. "You've a very sharp tongue," she said.

He had the grace to wince a bit. "Aye, too quick at times. I'd have said it more kindly if I'd stopped to measure my words," he added, his gaze direct, "but I'd have said it."

"It needed to be said."

"Will they hang?"

A quick terror pressed through her, and she raised her face to him. "I don't honestly know. It's more likely they'll be transported if they're found guilty." She swallowed. "Is that your wish?"

"I wish no ill on anyone, save the—" His mouth tightened and he halted. On his face Adriana again saw that fleeting, dark despair, and wondered what caused it.

Before she could begin to form opinions, he said gravely, "In this I offer my most earnest promise, my lady: I wish no ill upon your brothers. I will do nothing to harm their case, and all in my power to assist them, if you will but assist me."

Adriana met his eyes, searching his face for hints of duplicity. "I don't know why, but I believe you." She shook her head. "Though I cannot think what will be gained by my appearance in London. Seems it will only stir the gossip to a higher frenzy."

"'Twill serve them by reminding all you are no harlot, no scarlet woman, but a lady of good standing who was ill-used. It will show the true devotion that lives between you and your siblings." His lips pursed momentarily, and a shrewd expression came into his eyes. "And in truth, dear wife, I require your assistance in my own task."

In the distance a bell on the village church tower rang four times. Adriana looked up, startled to discover so much time had passed. "We must start back, or be late for supper." She lifted her skirts. "Come, tell me this task as we walk."

He joined her, lacing his fingers behind his back. "I have thought long on this today, and have devised a new plan."

"Yes?" She couldn't help smiling at his wish for prompts, and to her surprise, he smiled back as if in acknowledgment of his weakness.

"What did your father tell you of my plans?"

"Nothing, particularly. Only that you were ambitious."

"I've been thinking that with the right influence, perhaps I might locate a seat for purchase on the House of Commons."

"He did mention that. It's political power you wish to secure?"

A shrug. "Aye. What else?"

She considered. He was obviously well to do and did not need money. "But don't you already have a seat in the Irish parliament? Why would you wish to secure a seat in the English as well?"

"A new mountain to climb, I suppose." The words were light, and Adriana knew instantly they were pure fabrication.

"I see." They passed, single file, through a narrow bit of the path, and when he rejoined her, she said, "It is not an impossible task, though I doubt I will do much to further your cause. You keep assuming there is some value to my name, but all was erased—" She sighed. "—with the scandal."

"Leave that to me," he said, and smiled.

Perplexed, Adriana stopped for a moment. "What a puzzle you are." She scowled and moved on. "How came you to have such a fortune in such a beleaguered land, sir?"

"Well, I can tell you it isn't the land," he said grimly. "With the trade restrictions against our natural crops, linen and wool, we've had to be clever to find a means of feeding our people. My father built a glassworks that has grown quite profitable." He gave her a sideways grin. "I seem to have a knack for business. In the past decade I've built two more sites, and we employ nearly an entire county."

"Glass?"

"Aye, crystal and china. The very finest. I'll have some sent to add to your table."

Adriana realized suddenly that she rather liked him. Dangerous. "As you wish," she said, and determined to ignore him the rest of the day.

5

Tynan dressed carefully and simply for supper. His man, Seamus, had brushed his coat and put a burnished gleam on his boots. "Wish me luck, Seamus, old man," Tynan said, tucking Julian's ring in the pocket of his waistcoat.

"No good ever came of the English," the old man muttered.

"Not yet," Tynan agreed. But he whistled as he moved through the passageways. His rooms were in a spacious corner of the keep, and he took the narrow, winding steps to a newer wing, mulling his plan for this evening's meal.

A servant in the foyer directed him away from the simple room where the brothers had eaten this morning, and he entered a formal dining room. It was a dark room, a darkness exaggerated by heavy furniture in ebony and mahogany and even teak. Though long windows gazed toward the open expanse of lawns to the north, autumn was full upon them, and with it, an early sunset. To offset the darkness, embroidery in bright colors enlivened the seat cushions and sideboards, and an enormous chandelier blazed overhead, all the candles in it lit. The light caught on the cut crystal, the fine place settings, and the snowy white cloth. Everyone but Adriana had arrived.

"Good evening," Phoebe said warmly, coming forward.

He bent over her hand. "Good evening."

She smiled and directed him to a seat to the right of Julian, who nodded politely and without warmth. "Spenser."

Gabriel held the other end of the table, which had been much reduced in size for the small group. Monique sat to her son's right, a red-patterned turban covering her hair. As if she felt Tynan's eyes, she swiveled her proud head and gave him a slow, calm nod, accompanied by the faintest of smiles, as if she understood his surprise. She seemed to occupy a strange position in this house—he'd thought her at first a servant, but she came and went as she wished. He wondered which side of the stairs she slept on.

"So," Ophelia said, lifting a goblet of wine. "Will you entertain us with stories of your travels, brothers?"

Indulgently, Julian smiled. "What would you hear, my pretty?"

"Everything!" she cried.

"Wait!" Adriana sailed into the room, breathless. "Do not begin without me." She rushed to take her place, directly opposite Tynan, and he found himself dazzled once more by yet another face of his bride.

Tonight she wore ruby silk, pattered in some way to make the light move in swirls over the fabric. It fit closely over bodice and waist, revealing her smooth shoulders, and it was cut low according to fashion, so swells of white breast crowded into the square neckline. A single red ruby lay upon that abundance like a drop of blood. Her hair had been swept into an elaborate coiffure, laced with jewels, and her cheeks were flushed, making her eyes seem deep and smoky.

She looked, he thought, like a masterful courtesan, like a woman ready to tumble at a moment's whisper into a bed, into wild kisses and wilder embraces. A woman who would drive a man mad with her abandon.

Here was the face that had captured her lover—the ill-fated Malvern. Tynan would lay money upon it. No man could look upon her in this mood without feeling the same surge of pure lust that filled his loins in this moment. He remembered the soft, protesting sound she'd made as she fought herself last night, remembered the feel of that flesh against his palm, and he wanted like the very devil to squander the ninety-nine kisses left to him upon those breasts.

Phoebe, sitting next to him, said, "A thousand faces."

Tynan blinked and forced himself to look away. "Aye."

"Now," Adriana said, addressing her brothers, "tell us what happened to you after the uprising. We thought you dead! Where did you go?"

Julian smiled. "We sailed by night on a fishing boat, right out of their clutches."

"A fishing boat!" Cleo exclaimed, wrinkling her nose. "How ghastly!"

"Better than the alternatives, love. They'd have been happier with no less than our heads."

"How did you live?" Adriana asked.

"For a time," Gabriel said, "we simply wandered, taking whatever work we could find to put food in our bellies."

Julian held up his hands, callused and tough. "These hands have not known a gentlemanly day in three years."

"What sort of work?" Cleo asked. "Were you soldiers of fortune?"

"She reads too many novels," Cassandra said with a snort.

"As it happens, Cleo my sweet," Julian said, "we did have that chance for a bit. It wasn't quite the romance you might imagine, since we only defended a dairy farm, from soldiers from the colonies."

"And then, " Gabriel said, eyes shining as he smiled at his sister, "we lived with Indians. What do you think of that?"

"Savage *red* Indians?" Ophelia exclaimed. "Weren't you terrified?"

"Not savage," Julian said, and Tynan glanced at the Earl in surprise, for there was a harshness to his pronouncement. "Far more civilized than we in many ways."

"Careful how you say that, Julian," Ophelia said, aiming for a light tone, "we'll think you've gone native."

A heat and bristling rolled from Julian, distinctive as a perfume. Tynan narrowed his eyes, intrigued.

"Perhaps I have," Julian said. "Or perhaps I only wished to." He reached for his wine and drank it in a single gulp.

"Ah, but we left them soon enough," Gabriel said,

leaping gracefully into the sudden silence that threatened to engulf the table, "and had far more rousing experience—a shipwreck!"

His words had the desired effect. The occupants of the table swiveled their heads to listen to him give tale of the grand and terrifying adventure. Tynan watched Julian instead, who bowed his head under the cover of the shipwreck tale. His fists tightened and his mouth grew hard, and even his jaw grew rigid, as if he were fighting some terrible vision.

Adriana reached out and lay a white hand on the velvet sleeve of her brother. He raised his eyes to her, and Tynan saw the bleakness there. "You left someone behind, didn't you?" Adriana said softly. "*There* is the tale I would hear."

"No," he said harshly.

Her voice was soft. "As you wish." Her hand stayed there, on his sleeve, but she suddenly looked up and caught Tynan's gaze. For the first time there was nothing but the true woman, shining from the depth of those very blue eyes. Her mouth was sober, and he glimpsed again the sharp intelligence. And he had the sense that she welcomed his attention to this, that he, too, had glimpsed the burden on Julian's soul.

Tynan inclined his head ever so faintly, acknowledging her worry. Her gaze lingered one more brief moment, then she turned her head to hear Gabriel's story.

After a moment Julian regained his poise and pitched punctuation into the tale of shipwreck and adventure, and none would ever have known of the breach unless they'd seen it.

* * *

Adriana tried to keep her eyes from her husband during the meal, but as if he were a candle burning alone in a dark room, her eye was drawn to him again and again. In his dark coat and black hair, he seemed the very opposite of light, till one caught the flash of his white teeth or the glitter in his eyes or the sweeping gesture of a graceful, open palm. Each time she glanced his way, sometimes covertly, sometimes under guise of listening to a comment he made, it seemed she captured him at yet another dazzling moment—savoring a mouthful of braised carrots, fingering curiously the pattern on the silver, swirling his wine to smell the fragrance of it. He listened with intent and curiosity to the banter around him, but seemed to have little need to draw the attention of everyone, like so many men she had known. He was, it seemed, content to observe.

When the party moved into the music room after supper, it was no better. Adriana perched on a settee, tensely wondering if Tynan would sit beside her. He did not. Instead, accepting a glass of port offered by a footman, he sat in a hard chair across the room, directly in her line of vision. Her eyes strayed to the length of his thigh beneath close-fitting trousers, noting the simple, luxurious play of a long muscle when he moved his foot to brace it against the other knee. He lazily, slowly, sipped the port, and Adriana saw the delight in his face when the flavor hit his tongue, watched with a helpless sort of fascination as he lifted the glass again and inhaled the scent, his whole attention focused upon that glass and what it contained. Then he tasted it again, letting it linger in his mouth before he swallowed, that arching top lip drawing her eye.

At once alarmed at her staring, she shifted her attention to the family. Cleo, who had been practicing, took up the harp, and Gabriel tried his hand on the violin, laughing at first over his clumsiness. Soon enough he rediscovered the notes and fingerings, and Cassandra swirled up to take a seat at the pianoforte, one of several instruments at which she was expert. Like their mother, she was especially musical.

The music was sweet and lively and haunting by turns. Gabriel quickly found his pace, and Cleo leaned deep into the harp, her head cocked prettily. The notes entwined, and Ophelia began to sing a ballad in her sweet clear voice.

A ballad that was interrupted. Their butler, Duggett, appeared at the door, and not even the hands tucked behind his back could allay the worry on his face. "Lord Albury," he said to Julian. "You have a caller."

Julian scowled, and sent a glance toward Gabriel. "Who is it?"

Duggett hesitated only a brief moment. "The village magistrate, my lord. He insists he has most urgent business with you."

Adriana pressed a palm to the suddenly empty place below her ribs. "The magistrate!"

Julian stood. "Please continue," he said to the musicians. "I'll only be a moment."

Left to their own devices, the siblings would likely have trailed at least to the door, where they could overhear what transpired in the foyer. As it was, Gabriel took the lead firmly and swung into a lively favorite, a challenging piece from Mr. Clementi.

But Adriana, as the eldest daughter, had a right to join her brother, and she did so, lifting her chin haughtily as she went to the foyer. Horace Howser, the magistrate, was a small, red-faced man carrying a flat black hat. His brow, despite the cool evening, was dotted with perspiration at which he blotted with a snowy handkerchief. When he spied her, he bowed faintly. "Good evening, Lady Adriana. I do apologize, as I was telling your brother here, for interrupting a happy reunion, and especially for this unpleasantness, but I was told—"

"Please," Julian interrupted. "Just get to the business so we may return."

"Er, yes. Quite right." He twisted the brim of his hat in his hands, wiped his forehead once more. "I've been told to arrest you, sir, on charges of manslaughter." His face, already persimmon, deepened to a remarkable tomato shade. "Er, not that I'll be enforcing arrest, of course not, but I'd hoped you would spare me the necessity by agreeing to turn yourself in at London."

"Of course. It is not unexpected." Julian clapped him on the shoulder, cleverly turning the magistrate to the doors. "I'll send word we've arrived, and you needn't worry any more about it at all."

"Very good. Thank you. Good night." He bobbed his relief like a little fat duck. "Thank you."

And although the small man appeared much relieved to exit without his burden—arresting a lord had to loom as the most terrifying of provincial magisterial duties—Adriana felt that someone had yanked the ties of her corset another notch.

As Julian turned, he met her eyes with a forced smile. "You needn't look so doomed, Riana. We've known it would come since we arrived. Better to get it over with."

"I just did not expect . . ." She sucked in a breath. "I did not expect the summons to come so quickly."

"Nor did I," he admitted, and for a moment the gray eyes turned silvery hard. "But we'll set out tomorrow. Sooner tended, sooner done." He offered his arm and gave her a smile, lifting his chin in an exaggerated way to encourage her. "All that's to be done is to put a good face on it. We don't want to worry the girls, now do we?"

"No. Of course." She took his arm and let him lead her back into the room, but she perched uneasily on the edge of the settee, trying to breathe, while he made light of the summons to the others. In a moment Ophelia took up a ballad of lost love, as if to express the unspoken.

The melancholy tune triggered a wild emotion in Adriana. Not the lost love, only the sad, sad sound of the notes, a sound that reminded her of all the long days she'd missed her brothers. Now here they stood: safe and whole and unbearably dear, but only for tonight. In the morning they would depart for London, and their fate.

Between one moment and the next, a violent mix of thankfulness and regret rose in her throat and she stood up in a panic, excusing herself hastily as she blinked back tears. She slipped through the long doors to the east, out to a small promenade that lined that side of the house, and took in a great gulp of cool air, struggling to rein in the overwrought tears.

Too much. There had been too many surprises the past two days. That's all it was.

A booted heel on the stone promenade alerted her that she was no longer alone. "Are you ill, my lady?" Tynan asked in his soft brogue.

Brushing her hands over her cheeks hastily, she turned and smiled brightly. "Oh, no! I'm fine, thank you."

He lifted a thumb to wipe away the tears she'd missed. "Weeping for joy or sorrow?" There was in the gesture such gentle soberness, such unthreatening kindness, that Adriana felt the tension in her neck ease suddenly.

She sighed. "A little of both, I'm afraid." Shivering in the chill air, she crossed her arms and focused on the shadows of the hills surrounding them, and the heavy cloak of stars above them. "I am so grateful that they've returned home safely to us. It's been so very, very long. And yet, if not for my foolish actions, they'd never have had to flee at all." She looked at him. "How does one undo such a wrong?"

His voice was low. "I have no answer for that."

"An honest answer, at least."

"Do I strike you as a dishonest sort?"

She raised her eyes, and after a moment, shook her head. Rake or no, he struck her as a man who spoke his mind.

"A beginning, then."

Adriana heard a soft rustle, and then he settled his

coat about her shoulders. It was warm from his flesh and smelled almost overpoweringly of that distinctive scent of him, coriander and male and the faintest touch of something she could not name. "You'll be cold," she said in faint protest.

"Not at all," he said, offering his arm. "My blood is quite warm in the presence of so alluring a woman." His eyebrows rose. "I'd suggest if you'd like to be a help to your brothers, you'll leave that gown at home when we depart for London."

"This?" Adriana asked, looking down. "Is it too much?" She brushed her hand over the skirt, loving the feel of the watered silk. "I had not thought it any more so than most of my evening wear."

He made a nose, half laugh, half sigh. "Perhaps I'd best examine your wardrobe before we embark, then, if you're so ill-equipped you cannot discern the difference."

"I do not think that will be necessary." They strolled toward the gardens, and Adriana considered the matter of her evening clothes. Had she not admired the way the dress fit her, the way it made the most of her bust and skin? Still, he did not need to know that. Now that she thought of it, she ought to be embarrassed that she'd bothered.

No. Lifting her chin, she met his gaze. "All right, I knew it was a rather more flattering gown than some others I might have donned."

"Dangerously so."

She smiled. "Perhaps."

"I suspect you are a more dangerous woman than most credit you with."

"Ah, no," she said with a sigh. "Indeed, it is quite the reverse. Cassandra's little set think I'm marvelously heedless, when in truth what I said to her this afternoon is quite true: I only wish to have an ordinary life."

"Mmm."

She raised her head, and again she was impressed by his height. "You sound as if you do not believe me."

"No." He glanced down and grinned. "No. I rather fancy you more as a lady pirate."

She laughed. "You would!"

"That gown is more to the taste of a lady pirate than a lady about town."

"Perhaps." She smiled and inclined her head, unable to resist a small bit of banter. He'd raised her spirits with his attentions, letting her lose her regrets for the moment. "There is a bit of me that longs to be the pirate, I suppose. We do not entirely ever leave our childhoods behind us, do we?"

"If we are fortunate, we do not."

They paused on the edge of the garden, Adriana because she didn't wish to go into the depths of that scented darkness with a man who moved her far more than he should have. And perhaps Tynan sensed that, for he released her and captured his hands behind his back, standing a respectful distance from her.

"Pirates seem popular with the lot of you."

"I suppose they are. We were terrified of them when we were children—they were known to sail the islands, looting and killing and . . ." She did not finish.

Tynan lifted one arched, dark brow. "And ravishing unsuspecting women asleep in their beds?"

"Well . . ." She shrugged lightly. "At any rate, we found the tales of them romantic. Gabriel swore he'd known a famous one as a child, and wears a necklace the man supposedly gave him. He fed our imaginations with tales of dashing sword fights and women swooning for the virile criminals."

"And you, Adriana, did you swoon?"

"Oh, no!" She drew herself up and took a fencing stance. Swiping the air with an imaginary sword, she said, "I preferred imagining myself in trousers, with a red scarf tied about my head."

"Indeed," he said dryly.

"Is that shocking?"

He shifted, inclined his head. "No." The vivid eyes met hers. "'Tis only my rogue imagination that makes it so."

Realization dawned. "Oh! I'm sorry."

He laughed. "Do not be. It was a rather . . . delicious picture."

How did they seem to find themselves wandering this path over and over? She cast about for some way to shift the conversation.

"Are you a swordswoman, Adriana?" he asked.

She straightened. "A bit. My father was quite liberal when we lived in Martinique, and my brothers were mad for it. Gabriel is a master. No one can best him."

"And Julian?"

The lump of regret and worry that had landed in her belly at supper now returned. "He preferred pistols, always." She sighed and moved away a little. "I fear he is much changed."

"Aye. There is grief there."

"Yes." And she remembered now the darkness on Tynan's face when he'd spoken of his twin this afternoon. "You recognized it, owning it yourself, did you not?"

It was his turn to shift his face away. In his waistcoat and shirt, he presented a profile as lean and graceful as a cat, and Adriana found her gaze sliding with approval from the broad shoulders down his long back to the finely made hips. When she realized what she was admiring, she jerked her eyes back to his face. "It has only been months since my own brother died," he said.

"Your twin."

A nod.

Adriana clasped her hands below her chin, wondering suddenly if it were wise to follow this path now. He was dangerous enough—how much more so would he be if she learned the shape of his heart?

The sleeves of his coat brushed her chin, and without thought, she bent her head a little more so she could put her nose close to the wool, to breathe that scent in more closely. It was done without thought, the way she would pluck a rose to breathe its perfume, but Tynan chose that moment to turn, and Adriana knew her error in an instant. It was part of her failing that she could not seem to resist smelling, touching, tasting with vast enjoyment, and there was something about it that captured a man's attention.

Just as Tynan's sensuality over dinner had captured hers. A sense of danger rose in her, but with a wild rush of heedlessness, Adriana didn't move.

There was a sudden, taut attention in his form, a

poised awareness that needed no motion to express it. And indeed, he moved not an eyelash as he watched her slowly lower her hands until they were loose at her sides. His eyes were fixed hard upon her, on her face, and upon her mouth, and lower still, to the display of flesh above her bodice.

When she'd seen desire on him before, it had been edged with humor, with the teasing lightness of a rake who could always find another pair of lips to kiss, another beauty to warm his bed. But now she sensed a much darker edge to him, one that conversely alarmed and exhilarated her. She simply stared up at him, aware that her breathing had suddenly become shallow.

He took a step and then another, until he stood before her, a hand span apart, so close she had to tilt her head to meet his eyes.

It seemed he would only stand there looking at her for the longest time, while color rose in her cheeks and spread heat to the tingling tips of her ears. "When you appeared in this gown," he said at last, and his words were rougher than any she'd heard from him, "it came to me that squandering my remaining kisses upon your breasts would be well worth the cost."

Her breath disappeared entirely, lost in anticipation. The square of flesh exposed above her bodice seemed, suddenly, to be acutely sensitive, for she felt a cool breath of wind cross it, and mingled in that wind, the short burst of his breath. It seemed she could even feel his eyes.

He edged closer still, and his voice dropped to a low, lilting murmur. "But we said nothing of touching, did we, my lady? So my bargain is not broken if I simply—" He raised his hand and brushed his fingers over her neck. "—touch you."

Some voice in the back of her mind gave a thin shout. It urged her to move, to duck away, to run— run far and run fast. And yet she did not move. Her gaze caught on the spiked shadows of his lashes, shadows that hid his irises, and she thought absurdly of an enchanted rose thorn hiding some witched being.

But when his hands moved, so very, very lightly, she closed her eyes. Only the tips of his fingers brushed her, tracing the edge of her bodice, over the rise and fall of her breasts, then sliding upward, to her shoulder, the side of her neck. Light as a breath his fingers moved, to her jaw, her cheek, over the bridge of her nose. In his trail he left flesh rippling and tingling, as if she were imprinted with the reflection of her lust.

At last those skilled fingers edged her lips, one, then two, whispering over her mouth. A bolt of unbridled yearning struck her hips, and in alarm and shame Adriana jerked away, nearly stumbling on her skirts in her need to retreat. Only his strong hand, snaring her elbow, saved her from an undignified sprawl. "Don't," she cried softly.

"You are my wife!"

She fought free to free herself, but his grip was powerful. "Please." A wave of despair crashed over her, and with her free hand she covered her face. "I cannot . . . do not ask me to give that." Her voice sounded broken to her own ears when she begged, "Please."

Abruptly he released her, and Adriana had been pulling so hard she nearly sprawled again, but righted herself by stumbling a few steps sideways.

Then, acting on pure instinct, she lifted her skirts and ran. Ran into the cold shadows of trees, where the only dangers were lurking wild animals.

When at last her breath deserted her, she halted, leaning on a tree. The lining of his coat stuck to the perspiration on her back, and air touched the dampness on her chest and forehead. She stripped off his coat in furious haste, as if it was the thing that had cast a spell—not her own wanton senses. Even so, she could feel the burning imprint of Tynan's fingers, so light and skilled, moving on her flesh. She felt that if she looked in a mirror, the trail would be burned scarlet on her.

In despair, she cried out—then covered her mouth with her hand. Five years she'd been virtuous! Now, in twenty-four hours time, she was already falling to the temptations of a rake no better than the first who had seduced her.

No, that was a lie. Even in a day's time she sensed the difference between Malvern and Tynan, one a boy, the other a man.

Still, five years! Five years in a world of calm, where nothing untoward leapt from the shadows to lure her into a trap of her own hungers. But in all those years, she had not allowed a test. She'd hidden away here at Hartwood Hall, venturing out only to Cassandra's little salons once every quarter or so, and even then, only when she cloaked herself in invisibility, in the blacks and browns that were so unflattering, in fabrics that did not cling, in gowns cut to give the impression of pudginess rather than voluptuousness.

She had not allowed a test, fearing what now

proved true: that she was weak. That she seemed to have missed some essential moral imperative that other women held as a matter of course. For years she'd blamed it upon her childhood in Martinique, but her sisters had also lived there, and they did not struggle with such temptation.

No, it was not her childhood. It was not Martinique or the loss of her mother so young, or anything except a fatal flaw in her own makeup. She was a slave to the pleasures of her senses.

And where had it led? To the death of a man whose only mistake had been to cast her off. To the exile of her brothers, where both had undergone trials she would not have wished for them. To misery for her father, who had missed his sons until the day he died.

Regret burned in her for all that she'd done. Somehow she had to find a way to put things right again, to make it up to her brothers, her family. It was too late to make it up to her father, but perhaps he would see her good intentions from where ever his soul resided.

Feeling calmer, she pushed away from the tree and walked back toward the house. Her truest, deepest flaw was this heedlessness, and whatever it took, she had to resist it. She would not fall prey again. Tonight, some madness had led her to don this wanton's gown, but henceforth she'd become invisible. Tynan—no, Lord Glencove—had had no desire for her when she'd worn the invisible bombazine. If she donned such a cloak every day, he'd forget his desire for her. He'd wonder whatever had captured him for even a moment.

Breathing in the cold night air, she resolved to be the perfect, cool, moral wife to the Irish earl, so demure and proper she'd make a vicar's wife envious of her virtue. Her step picked up. Yes. It would even, she thought, give credence to the story Tynan said the public would need to believe if her brothers were to escape serious punishment—that she was an honorable and virtuous young woman of good family who'd fallen to the seduction of a notorious rake.

Yes. That would do.

When she returned to the house, she skirted the music room and headed up the back stairs to her own chambers, in order to arrange the details of her plan. There was a brown wool traveling coat that should do nicely for the journey to London, and a singularly unflattering gown of the same fabric. When she arrived in town, she would have some new things made. Maybe even something in that peculiarly awful shade of yellow that made her look as if she were dying any moment.

Heartened, she pursed her lips, feeling tension drain away from her. Brown, yellow, black, perhaps a few pallid pastels, just to throw off the game. And in them she would disappear, become invisible, and Tynan would tire of his wish to seduce her. And when he returned to Ireland, as he surely must, she would again be free.

After all, if temptation never presented itself, she would never have to grapple with her response. And if she never grappled, there was no danger of another fall.

Tynan watched her run into the shadows, then grimly turned toward the house, striding quickly to burn the heat from him. What a maddening female! Why did he bother at all?

As he approached the wide promenade that ran the length of the back of the house, a shadow broke from the deeper shadows clinging to the stone wall. Tynan halted as Julian strolled toward him, cloaked in that aura of tense danger that only a man who'd known battle carried.

Warily, Tynan eyed him, gathering clues. A bit foxed, he thought. And haunted by whatever he'd left behind. In the darkness, the hollows below his eyes were exaggerated.

Tynan took the offense. "Are you going to warn me that you'll kill me if I wound her?"

A slow, silent shake of his head. "I expect I'm only required to down one. Were I you, I'd take care with my sister herself. She's an excellent shot."

"Hmm." Tynan found himself glancing over his shoulder, a wee bit concerned for her in spite of himself. "She told me about the swords, not the pistols."

"She's better at swords. Deadly with a dagger." Julian lifted his glass, sipped from it slowly, lowered it again. Tynan waited, poised, unsure what this scrutiny meant. "I would ask your intentions."

"Intentions?" Tynan echoed. "I married her!"

"So you did. And I must ask why."

Why? Had he a sister, Tynan supposed he'd ask the same question. "Because your father asked it. Because I would like to secure political connections in England. Because it was time to take a wife." He shrugged. "Marriages have been made on worse."

"True." Julian raised his head toward the sky. "I

suppose we'll wait and see how you redeem yourself. And perhaps my sister, as well."

"Redeem." Tynan repeated the word very quietly, his nostrils flaring. His hands fisted at his sides and he forced himself to bite back the wave of anger the comment raised in him. "I've no need to prove anything at all to you, St. Ives."

The cool gray eyes noted the fists with a flicker. "Don't you?" He lazily lifted his glass once again. "I rather assumed this whole charade was for benefit of proving yourself."

As a charm against his anger, Tynan called up a memory of his brother, cloaked in his cowl, joyously celebrating a forbidden mass in a glen guarded by the burliest men in the village. He breathed in, thinking he could even smell the incense that clung to those black robes, and it gave him the courage to release his clenched jaw, to open his hands and let his fingers hang loosely at his sides. "I've no need to explain myself to you," he said, pleased at the faint hint of arrogance in his words. "And your sister has no need of redemption."

"In her eyes, she does."

Tynan raised a brow. "We're none without sin."

"Ah, but woman's sin lies more heavily upon her." Julian sounded inexpressibly weary. Almost to himself, he breathed, "How very little it has changed!"

Curious now, Tynan crossed his arms and leaned negligently on the stone balustrade. "This scandal," he said, "how severe was it?"

"Malvern was not only a rake, he was a braggart," Julian said, and his jaw tightened. "And my actions only inflamed it."

Tynan narrowed his eyes. Adriana and Julian each blamed themselves, as Tynan and his mother had each blamed themselves for Aiden's death. His mother had grieved so desperately she'd grieved herself into the grave, doubling Tynan's burden of sorrow.

Standing now with his wife's brother, he remembered his own resolve when he'd put her body down, and he reached into his waistcoat and drew out the ring. He held it out to Julian. "I bought it from a peddler."

"Strike me blind." Julian took the ring and narrowed his eyes. "You thought me dead, then."

"I did."

Julian swore again, in some wonder. "It was washed from my hand in that shipwreck we spoke of." He put it on his finger. "What are the chances it would arrive in your care?"

"Larger than you might think." Tynan lifted an expressive shoulder. "It washed ashore in Dingle, and a peddler found it. There's none for many counties who'd pay for such a bauble, or could afford the price he asked. I am known in my country, and it was delivered to me."

"And you knew the crest, and knew me dead. And saw all of this," he stretched out an arm, "as your own."

Tynan lifted one brow, and a shoulder to go with it, unapologetic.

"Does my sister know?"

"She does." Tynan saw no need for subterfuge here. "I needed me an English wife. And I admit the pleasure of being Earl of Albury in all but actual title would have suited me," he said. "But I'm willing to work to clear your name, if you'll lend your assistance to my purposes when you are cleared."

"Work to clear my name? You?"

Tynan lifted his head. "Are you testing me, sir?"

"If you've a temper, sir," Julian responded, "you'll never weather what's waiting for you in London."

Just so. "Will you help me or won't you?"

"That," he said coolly, "remains to be seen." He pushed away from the wall. "But I've one warning to offer: play the rake with my sister and I'll see you ruined. Not only here, but in Ireland, too."

Tynan clenched his fists. "We understand each other."

"Yes," Julian said coolly. "We do."

6

Adriana awakened with a strange sense of anticipation in her chest, and could not quite pinpoint the reason. It certainly wasn't the weather, which was cold and gloomy, threatening rain that did not quite fall. It could not be what awaited her brothers in London. In fact, thinking of that, she frowned. She ought to be feeling dread. Dread for them, dread for herself, dread all around.

But instead the slight, fevered sense of excitement clung to her as she washed and dressed, and directed her maid to pack the things she'd chosen last night.

"Not the red silk?" Fiona asked. "Nor the blue? The blue is so fair on you, milady."

"Only what I've set out, Fiona." She eyed the duns and browns and grays with satisfaction. Not a single, tiny splash of color among them. Perfect.

She bustled downstairs to have breakfast, the anticipation taking a little leap that faded all too quickly when she found only Phoebe in the room.

Nevertheless intent on good spirits, she said, "Good morning!" Laid out on the sideboard were kidneys and rashers, and piles of fluffy sliced bread and jam. Adriana filled a plate to groaning, her appetite whetted by the cool day and her eagerness to be on the road. She sat down with her sister. "Where is everyone?"

Phoebe's portion was far more modest, only a hunk of buttered bread and tea. "Julian and Gabriel set out very early. Cassandra went with them, to see to the house."

Adriana nodded. Not unexpected. "They won't go to the magistrate today, will they?"

"Oh, no. Julian said tomorrow would be soon enough."

Spreading her own bread thickly with strawberry jam, Adriana said lightly, "And Lord Glencove? Did he set out with them, too?"

"No." A faint, knowing glitter lit Phoebe's dark blue eyes. Adriana privately cursed the whole notion of sisters. "He's seeing to the coach and horses. He assumed you'd prefer a companion."

"I see." The anticipation in her lifted a notch. "Good. The girls are still abed?"

"As ever. Ophelia was still pouting late last night about being forced to stay home. Cleo is rather more understanding."

"And you? Do you mind staying behind?"

Her eyes widened. "Of course not! I loathe London."

"And there is the matter of a certain new vicar, after all," Adriana said archly. Knowing, after all, went both directions.

Phoebe colored faintly. "He is still only settling in. He'll need the assistance of the Ladies' Society to help. He's not even hired a cook yet."

The new vicar, a rugged man from the North, had arrived only last Saturday, to take over for the retiring man, who had married Adriana and Tynan. "Of course," Adriana said, and patted her sister's hand. "You've no interest at all in his broad shoulders."

"Riana!" Phoebe smiled slightly, but her calm had returned. "Not all of us think in such terms. And after all, the parish is overflowing with lovely, suitable young women."

"Of which you are one, my dear." Adriana put her hand on her sister's. "You're as lovely as any of them."

Phoebe smiled, shaking her head. "It's a very pretty lie, and I thank you." Done with the subject, she reached into her pocket. "I've had a letter from Leander. Would you like to hear it?"

"Of course." Leander was their cousin, raised with them from the time of his parents' death at six. He and Phoebe had been close to the same age and had become close during the terrors of the journey to and from Martinique. "Does he plan to pause in his wandering to visit us?"

"Not yet," Phoebe said with a smile, and put on a pair of spectacles, shook out the letter, and began to read aloud. It was bold and brash, a tale of adventures across India, filled with the sights and sounds and music of a distant land, a special sort of magic that belonged to Leander alone. Phoebe captured his tone of breathless, joyous excitement perfectly, and by the time she finished, they were both laughing.

"You read his letters beautifully," Adriana said.

Phoebe folded her spectacles and set them on the table, a faint smile giving her plain features a light-struck aspect of which Adriana was sure her sister had no awareness. "When I read of his adventures, I admit I sometimes wonder what it would be like to be Leander, to be male and filled with a spirit of adventure, and have the fortune to indulge it."

"But you do not even like to leave Hartwood, Phoebe."

"I know." She smiled, and gave a little shrug. "Still, one does wonder."

An authoritative booted heel sounded in the foyer, and Adriana felt the pleasantly simmering anticipation take a sudden, heated jump. Both sisters looked toward the door, and in strode Tynan—in a dark mood by the look of him. In place of the usual glint, there was only impatience in his eyes, and he was dressed for travel in that heavy black cape with its bright, embroidered edge, his hair tied back from that dark angel face. "Will you be wanting to leave today, my lady," he asked briskly, "or shall we brave the thieves and robbers along our way after nightfall, when we'll be ever so much easier for them to capture?"

Adriana shot her sister an amused glance. "I'm quite ready, sir. Let me fetch my cloak."

In good weather, on good roads, the trip to London could be accomplished in a bit less than two hours. On such a wet day, the ruts and mud would slow them considerably, adding at least an hour to the journey. Adriana pinned her hat in place, gathered a novel to amuse herself with on the way, and cheerfully bustled outside to the waiting coach. It was not quite the latest style, and the paint was appearing a bit faded, but Adriana had always loved the green plush interior and the well-sprung comfort, and she smiled happily in anticipation of a journey. Tynan waited with ill-concealed impatience as she kissed Phoebe, promised to write daily about developing events, and accepted a basket of food from Monique.

She allowed the footman to hand her up, then settled her skirts about her and put her book in her lap. Tynan climbed in behind her, and the door was closed tight. The coach, which ordinarily seemed quite roomy, seemed cramped with the length of his legs, the breadth of his shoulders, and that annoyingly pervasive scent of him, somehow exaggerated this morning by the dampness.

He flung himself back against the facing seat and peered out the window. Adriana looked out to wave with a gloved hand at Monique and Phoebe, who gave one last wave and hurried inside, out of the rain.

Then it was only the two of them in the rocking coach, the sound of the wheels and the clop of hooves and the patter of rain on the roof. "Bloody awful day for the coachman," Tynan commented.

"They'll be compensated, I assure you." His mood was dark indeed, she thought, and it somehow pleased her. She had suspected he had this brooding side—the Irish were famed for it, after all—and she found it was much easier to dismiss him when he glared out the window like a tomcat with his tail swishing. Men could be such children. She smiled to herself and picked up her book.

"What are you so cheerful about?" he growled.

Adriana looked up. "Why, I'm cheerful by nature, sir! And I do love being abroad of a morning, heading into town. I have not ventured far from Hartwood since my father died, and I find I'm rather pleased—no matter what the circumstances—to be off on a bit of an adventure."

"Mmmm."

"One might ask what's made you so ill-tempered." She said it lightly, edging the words with brightness, so he would know she laughed inwardly at him.

He only glared. One did not laugh at a cat, after all. "I loathe this journey. It bores me."

"I have another book," she offered, reaching for her bag, tucked beneath her skirts. She pulled out a bound edition of Voltaire's *Questions sur L'Encyclopedia* and handed it to him.

He glanced at it. "I don't read French."

"Ah. Well, then, take mine." She handed it to him.

Tynan took it, read the title, and she watched him attempt to hide his smile. *"Clarissa."* He lost the battle with his sense of humor, and he chuckled, the blue eyes lighting—finally—with that glint she'd grown to enjoy. "I assume you're reminding yourself of the evil intentions of rakes."

Adriana lifted her chin. "Exactly."

He returned the book. "I wouldn't want to hold you from your edification."

"I suppose you're one of those men who scorns romances in favor of those pompous tomes by Fielding and Defoe."

"And if I am, if I say that women have muddled the field of novels, and Richardson is an embarrassment?"

He'd begun in a slump, but with these words he straightened, as if warming to his subject.

Exactly as she wished. "Is that your claim or not, sir?"

"I'm an Irishman," he said with a lazy smile. "We're quite fond of romances."

"So you've read Richardson, have you?"

"Does that surprise you? I prefer the happy ending, myself. All these tragic endings . . ." Shadows flickered beneath the sooty lashes. "There's enough tragedy in real life for me, without seeking books with them."

She inclined her head. "Refreshing. Though I admit I do not picture you reading much at all."

A shrug, a restless shift in his seat. "I prefer to be busy at something," he agreed. "But my mother was often abed with various complaints. I often read to her."

Adriana felt a stillness press into her at the sudden vision of him sitting with his ill mother, reading. It made him seem too good.

"Her favorite," he said, and the word rolled from his tongue in that musical lilt, "was *Rasselas*."

"A very sad book indeed."

He shook his head. "She wept and wept over it. I can't think why a person would want to weep so."

A rut in the road jolted them roughly, and Adriana put her hand out to steady herself before she answered. "At times," she said quietly, her gaze fixed on the passing landscape, "it seems that's all there is to do. And it can be cleansing, in its way." She smiled. "But I suppose men do not have that freedom."

"No, I think not."

"Would it not be a relief, at times? Haven't you ever wished to howl and scream in grief or anger?"

The heavy lashes descended, hiding his reaction. "A man does not howl or scream. That's left to women."

Realizing the conversation had drifted into a realm that was rather darker than she intended, Adriana said, "So what is your favorite novel, then? Do you have one?"

"I don't care for novels, particularly. Laborious and too long. I prefer essays and humorists. Swift, for example."

"Of course." She smiled.

"And Shakespeare. Such pretty words—they roll in your mouth like some delicious parfait." He closed his eyes and quoted,

> *"And I serve the fairy queen;*
> *To dew her orbs upon the green,*
> *The cowslips tall her pensioners be:*
> *In the gold coats spots you see;*
> *Those be rubies, fairy favors,*
> *In those freckles live their savors."*

Adriana was captured by the rolling music of his brogue, snared by the obvious pleasure he took in having the words against that tongue. His closed eyes entranced her, and she found her eyes upon his lips.

"'I must go seek some dewdrops here,'" he continued. "'And hang a pearl in every cowslip's ear.'" He opened his eyes, grinning and clearly charmed. "'Hang a pearl in every cowslip's ear,'" he repeated. "I loved that as a boy."

She blinked, forcing herself to straighten from the rapt posture she'd assumed under the spell of his voice. God save her from his quoting the sonnets! "Well done," she said calmly. "It somehow does not surprise me you quote *A Midsummer Night's Dream*—the fairy queen and all of that. You Irish do have that longing for magic, don't you?"

"It's what ails you English," he returned, grinning. "Too much reason."

"No such thing, sir. Reason, order, industry—that's what the world is made of."

His laughter boomed out of him, robust and glorious. Adriana shivered at the sound, and found herself quite unable to tear her eyes from him.

"It isn't that funny," she said.

"I think," he said, with eyes glittering, "that you resist magic for fear of letting it sweep you away."

She raised her chin, smoothed her skirt. "Not so. Superstition is wearying beyond measure. My maid, Fiona, can barely take a breath without some ritual attached. She put rue in the corners of my chamber."

"Did she, now?"

"Yes! And there's a candle for this and a charm for that, and a special blessing to say when you cross a particular part of a road, and an uncursing to do when a villager cackles." She rolled her eyes. "She's quite gifted and generally a very intelligent girl, so I allow her to do what she feels she must, but I vow it would be exhausting to remember it all."

He raised an ironic brow. "How generous of you."

Adriana looked away, chastened. Why did he make her always feel as if she were some silly, vain woman? She wasn't, she thought fiercely, and pointedly looked outside, turning now to heavy forest on either side of the road. The rain blurred the view a bit, making it appear to be a dream world, smears of the darkest green of pine mingled with the sudden splash of yellow on birch and ash. A red vine spread across a hedgerow, and at its foot bloomed a stand of wild crimson roses, vivid in the gray light.

"I've never seen so many flowers as grow in this country," Tynan commented. "Especially in the spring, but even now flowers are everywhere, in every tiny waste place, on every wall, in every garden in every inch of the towns."

Adriana glanced at him, wondering at this pleasant comment after the sharpness of the previous one. Was he attempting to make amends, or had she been too sensitive? She scowled. She was spending far too much time trying to puzzle him out. Deliberately draining her voice of any but the most polite of tones, she answered, "I imagine Ireland as very lush."

"'Tis green," he said. "Moss and grass and shamrocks everywhere, even in the water. But not flowers like this." He gestured with that long-fingered, beautiful hand toward the forest. "Not a flower in every corner."

"You'll like the town house, if you care for flowers. There's a conservatory, stocked with all manner of them—orchids and roses and lemon trees."

"Who tends it when you're in the country?"

Adriana shrugged. "The servants do. Leander—that's our cousin—sees to it when he comes to London every year or two—he'll go roaring through with clippers and fresh soil and great fuss, then it's fine again until he returns the next time." She didn't add that she loved the place, that it reminded her most pointedly of Martinique, where Leander had fallen so madly in love with the science of botany. "And indeed, you'd find Martinique quite a splendor."

He inclined his head ever so slightly. "More flowers than England?"

"Thousands more!" She found herself lifting her nose, as if smelling them on the air. "At night, it smells of . . ." She shook her head. "There are no words for that scent in the night. As if all the finest perfumes had been spilled into the very wind."

The heavy lashes shaded his expression again, suddenly, and Adriana wondered what she'd said now.

But she'd spent too much time entirely on trying to read his every thought. Feigning a yawn, she tugged a blanket over her shoulder and settled back against the seat. "Oh!" she said blinking, "I believe I'm sleepy. You will forgive me if I nap a little?"

"Of course."

Tynan watched her lean back and close her eyes. He'd not seen her in this animated mood before, her eyes bright and alert, her expression filled with the light of intelligence. She'd drawn him into conversation, teased him lightly, been chastened when he teased her in return.

And every shade of emotion showed in her face, in her dancing eyes, on her mobile mouth.

That mouth. From beneath half-closed lids he allowed himself to admire that lush, fine mouth at leisure. The tips of his fingers tingled faintly, remembering the plump give, the resilient firmness of those lips last night. He remembered the heady eroticism of her breath soughing, moist and warm, over the heart of his palm, a hint of the pleasure to be found within that harbor.

Harbor. He sighed softly and made himself close his eyes entirely, though that was not the help he supposed it would be, since his imagination provided what his eyelids had blocked out. She had a mouth like a courtesan in the face of a saint—few men could resist the contradictions contained in such an arrangement. Few men could have resisted indulging the speculations he now entertained, speculations regarding the taste of that succulent lower lip, the flavor of that particular, exaggerated bow on the upper. Or fail to wonder what splendor lay within.

St. Bridget! He thought of Aiden, who'd resisted female flesh every moment of his life on earth—not, as he'd often told Tynan, because he did not hunger for them, but because he wished to leave them in their innocence.

Tynan allowed himself one more glance at that ripe mouth of his bride. His brother had never seen a mouth like that of Adriana St. Ives.

He shifted restlessly, focusing his gaze beyond the coach. His brother would also laugh at him in this, for he longed to kiss her—no, kiss was far too mild a word for what he wished to do with that mouth—precisely because it was the one line she had drawn. Contrary, his mother would have said. Aiden was the good twin. He, Tynan, was the wild one, the heedless one, the one who took glee in breaking rules only for the delight of getting away with them. Aiden had made an art form of living within the strictures of both God and man.

Aiden, Aiden, Aiden. His brother had been constantly in his thoughts this morning, and he couldn't think why. Soon after his brother died, memories of his twin had been so excruciating to Tynan that he had shut them off entirely. He went about his days like a man suddenly missing an arm or a foot. And then his mother sickened, and thoughts of her welfare pulled him out of himself.

Now, in the misty distance, he spied a gray church spire poking above some village square. Only the tower, ancient and graceful, showed. Tynan thought, irrelevantly, that Catholic hands had built that spire. Within, candles had burned for saints and the Latin was sung.

As his brother had sung it.

It was only natural, Tynan supposed, that he should find his mind lingering upon his lost sibling now that he'd landed in the midst of so many of them. He'd seen clearly the love that bound them, and was envious of it. His family was all gone now, and, with a peculiar sort of awareness, he realized he wished to begin building a new one. He wanted children. Children to run in wild packs over the Irish hills, heirs to learn his business and carry on his name; daughters to fuss over and marry off to strong Irish men. He wanted a family.

Across from him, Adriana had indeed fallen into a doze. Her mouth parted a little in sleep, and not gracefully. He thought she might snore if that hint of a rattle were any indication, and it gave him a stab of fondness.

Here was his wife, for better or worse, the woman who would get his children, but whom he would have to woo her to be a willing lover and then willing mother. He did not want the lives of those children poisoned by acrimony between the parents.

There was much work awaiting him in London. In his wild youth he'd spent much time there, cutting a swath through more women than he liked to remember; he hoped they remembered him kindly, kindly enough to assist him in healing the rift in his bride's heart, and assist him, too, in finding the prize he hoped to take back to Ireland: a seat in the House of Commons. It would require every shred of his wit, and all of his hale charm, and a woman—this woman—to guide him through the sometimes bewildering muddle of English social life.

And while he set about reestablishing his social circle, he'd take time to simply observe Adriana, discover her joys and sorrow, her weakness and her strengths. From knowledge alone came the prize of a woman's heart.

He'd won a good many hearts. Surely one more would be little enough to ask.

As he slid into a doze, his last thought was that he wanted this heart more than any other. And sleep overtook him before he could form surprise.

The journey took nearly three and a half hours, and by the time they arrived at the town house in Marylebone, Adriana was chilled through. It had not helped that after his initial willingness to chat, Tynan had been quite thoroughly asleep the rest of the way. Though, she thought darkly, climbing the stairs to her chamber on aching hips, she failed to see how he could have slept through the jolting last hour of the ride.

As if anticipating the state in which her sister would arrive, Cassandra had left orders for hot water to be brought up and a bath to be drawn immediately. Fiona, along with a handful of other servants and the bulk of their baggage, had not yet arrived. It would be at least another hour, certainly, and Fiona would be in worse shape than her mistress.

Adriana called for assistance from one of the cook's helpers in getting her gown off and the water poured. The trouble was, the girl could not seem to avoid staring. "Ye've very fine skin, milady."

Adriana nodded, and dismissed her. "Tell cook to send chocolate and tea and a big platter of cheeses to the drawing room in a quarter hour," she said. "And send someone to tell my husband, as well." Not that he'd need much refreshment after his restful journey, she thought.

She managed dressing by herself by donning a simple muslin. Not quite as muddy a shade as she wished, but one did work with what one had. Refreshed, she returned to the drawing room and found her brothers and Tynan already engrossed in a conversation—one that broke off abruptly as she entered.

"Telling secrets already?" she said lightly.

Julian rose quickly, and before he even spoke, she saw by his face that he'd come to a decision. "We were only waiting for you, Adriana," he said with rare formality. "I thought we might have tea first, but the day grows late. I'm bound to deliver you to Cassandra."

"And you?"

He let go of a quick, impatient sigh. "There's no

point in delaying, Riana. I know you hoped for an evening or two, but I'd rather be done with it."

"Oh." She sank to the divan, her skirts whooshing out beside her. Fear burned under her ribs once again. "Gabriel, too?"

The brothers exchanged a glance. "I doubt he'll be retained."

"But you will?"

Julian clasped his hands behind him, inclined his head, as if they were only discussing a minor investment or the price of peas. "Undoubtedly," he said. "But it will go quickly. For all that I fled in terror of Malvern's mother, time has shown me the folly of that action. I'll surely be tried by the House of Lords, and which of them will condemn me for a duel?"

"It's such an uncommon pursuit in London, after all," Gabriel said dryly, stroking the little beard he'd grown on his dark chin, and winked. "Never seen the likes."

Adriana looked from one to the other, trying to put on a brave face. Plucking at a loose thread on her skirt, she managed a light reply. "I suppose if all else fails, Gabriel and I will simply be forced to rescue you. I believe I still have my sword in some trunk hereabouts."

Julian bent to kiss her head. His long, strangely powerful hand cupped the back of her head and he murmured, "I knew I could count on you."

Adriana smiled, but bent her head for a moment, attempting to marshal her defenses as Gabriel stood and Julian moved toward the door.

"Spenser," Gabriel said, "we'd like you to accompany us, if you would be so kind."

Adriana glanced up at her husband, and discovered

a close, careful expression on his face as he looked at her. "Of course," he said smoothly, pushing away from his customary place against the mantel. Adriana saw that he'd washed and put on a fresh shirt, and his hair was brushed to gleaming, leaping life. Even in the rain-cool light of the drawing room, that hair shone.

"Coming?" he asked.

"Yes."

The carriage had been brought around, manned by two liveried footman, who handed Adriana into the coach. Tynan climbed in afterward, the only one among the three gentlemen who did not wear a hat, and settled next to her, as he should. Although she squeezed as tightly as she was able into the corner of the coach, there was no escaping the solid feel of his body along the length of her own.

And suddenly she remembered he had a kiss coming to him today. As if he'd spoken the threat aloud, she looked up at him, alarmed. "Will you be coming to Cassandra's . . . after?"

Mockingly, he smiled. "Do you wish for my company?"

"I'd like a report."

Gabriel reached across the small space and covered her hands with his own. "We'll be there, love." He winked. "All for one . . ."

Even Julian, a full-grown gentleman with worry on his brow, put his hand over theirs. "And one for all," they said in unison.

It might have been only a childhood game, but Adriana cared not at all. It cheered her. If the three of them acted together, they could not fail.

7

There were no other guests for supper at Cassandra's, for which Adriana was grateful. They took it in the cozy upstairs sitting room, surrounded with candelabra and a warm fire. The servants served the simple meal and left the wine on the table, and Cassandra dismissed them.

Adriana felt jumpy and restless, and managed only to pick through a few bites of food. Cassandra did her best to keep up a light patter of gossip and news, but it did not seem to help. Finally, she jumped up and paced to the long windows, going dark now.

"What is that you're wearing?" Cassandra asked, a wince in her voice.

"I've owned this gown for years. You've surely seen it before."

"Oh, indeed. At least a hundred times, and I've grown to loathe it more each time. That color is hideous on you."

Adriana only raised her brows.

"Not this again, Riana! The bombazine and now this dun? What are you about?"

"Nothing at all. I choose to remain invisible. Is that so difficult to fathom?"

"Invisible. Is that what that is? No, I'm sorry, it's far too remarkably ugly to render you invisible."

Adriana laughed.

Cassandra tore a small bit of bread into an even smaller piece, her eyes narrowed. "Why?" she asked finally. "I'm willing to be your ally in almost anything, but I fail to grasp your motive in this."

Adriana thought of Tynan's eyes, burning into hers in the garden last night, over supper earlier, in the hallway when she was half-dressed—

She crossed her arms. "You would not understand."

"Oh, I see." The words were acerbic. "Because I am not the beauty you are, Lady Lovely?"

Adriana made an impatient noise. "How ridiculous. It was you who nearly slew the man on the steps the day he arrived, not I."

"You *were* jealous!" Cassandra said with wonder in her tone. "As I live and breathe, that has to be a first!" She laughed. "I've waited all my life for a man to see me before he saw the glorious Adriana or even more glorious Ophelia—it's a good thing the child is so much younger or neither of us would have had a chance—and the only reason it worked that one time is because you hid yourself in that horrible dress!" She reached for another crust of bread, plucked a teeny piece from it, and popped it in her mouth. "You were jealous, weren't you?" She grinned impishly and tucked her knee under her elbow. "Please say yes."

Through this long, long speech, Riana had simply

folded her arms and waited for the end. Now she dropped her arms. "Yes. Terribly."

Cassandra sighed, as if reveling, then grinned. "I think you like him, your black angel."

"I don't know." She moved to the table, sat abruptly. A vision of him riding that great, black horse came to her, and more: the first, stabbing sight of him dismounting, all lithe perfection and gleaming black hair and dazzling charm. Oh, he'd made her heart stop for a moment.

Then that wounding, painful instant when he'd been unable to hide his disappointment that she, not Cassandra, would be his bride. She covered her face with her hands. "He frightens me."

Cassandra spoke softly. "Because he's beautiful?"

A dozen flickering images burned over her imagination, his supple, naked belly in the candlelight; the way he paused, touching everything, listening to everything when they walked; the sound of his voice, rolling around Shakespeare as if it were a spell of enchantment. She lowered her hands and met her sister's curious gaze. "Because I desire him," she said bleakly.

"If you wish to keep him at arm's length, sister," Cassandra said, "do not gaze at him with those thoughts in your eyes."

Adriana moaned and covered her face again. "You see what a quandary it is?"

"Yes." Cassandra's voice was grim. She lifted a broad-bottomed silver butter knife, turned it over, set it down. "God, you love so easily! When will you learn how inconstant the male race is, Adriana?"

"I said nothing of love!"

"But I know you." Cassandra sighed with impatience. "I remember Antoine. Do you?"

"We were twelve!" she protested. "He was beautiful and charming, and I was a romantic child."

"And that would be normal, but you—you had to steal away and let him kiss you. A stable boy!"

"It wasn't much of a kiss."

"But when Papa found out and sent him away, you pined for months, vowing you'd never love again!"

Adriana tried to hold back a chuckle, but she could not. It burst from her, rich as that lost childhood time. "Juliet never pined better than I! I was certain I would die." At her sister's glare, she straightened her face. "Sorry. You never did understand."

"Not him. Ugh." She gathered a breath, widened her eyes, and continued, "The point is, there was Antoine, then Henry—"

"Shipboard romance, nothing more," Adriana said dismissively. "Thousands of young girls must be smitten by boys aboard ship."

"But you wrote to him for a year, Adriana!"

"There was nothing untoward about it. He was a gentlemanly child—he only held my hand when I was seasick. If our affections had survived, he'd have been a perfectly suitable husband."

Cassandra set her mouth. "And how do you explain away Malvern, Adriana?"

She'd known where the conversation was leading, perhaps even wanted this brutal reminder, but it still felt like a fist to her belly. "Lust," she whispered. "Lust and sin and youth."

"But not *love*."

"No," Adriana said fiercely. "No, I only fell prey to an evil part of my nature. He charmed me, nothing more."

"Oh, Riana!" Cassandra reached over the table and took her sister's hand. "Look at me."

Reluctantly, she raised her eyes.

"I was there," Cassandra said softly. "You were smitten from the first day he spoke to you."

"No! I—"

Cassandra's fingers tightened. "He was beautiful and charming and kind. He brought you presents and pursued you as if you were Helen of Troy. You resisted him, for months—months! And he did not relent until you fell in love." She paused. "In love, not lust."

Adriana looked at the fire, clinging to her sister's hand as remembered emotion came back to her. That deep, almost spiritual feeling she'd had, the purest, most singular thing a young girl ever knows: first love. She nodded. "Yes," she said with difficulty and bitterness. "I loved him."

Standing, she moved away from the gentleness and strength of her sister's gaze and hand. "And I do not wish to make that mistake again," she said firmly. "But I have learned my weaknesses, Cassandra. And one of them is my own hunger. I will not have the will to resist him if he chooses to capture me. So I must make myself invisible."

"Ah! I see." Cassandra nodded. "I'm not certain he is that foolish, but I suppose it is not a bad plan."

"Will you help me?"

"Yes. We'll go shopping tomorrow." She smiled. "Phoebe would tell you to read sermons."

"She's virtuous. Perhaps I should." Adriana paused. "And perhaps you should be as alluringly beautiful as you know. Draw his attention away."

Cassandra pursed her lips. "Is that wise? If you truly desire him, that will cause you pain. I'd rather not be part of that."

"Who better, Cassandra?"

"Because we are sisters?" she asked, but both of them knew the truth.

"Because you will never be tempted."

Memory made a tight line of Cassandra's mouth. "There's truth enough in that."

The noise of a carriage and the low murmur of men's voices reached them. Adriana peered out the window to the street below. "Here they are." She pressed a hand to the spot below her ribs that felt suddenly hollow. "Cassandra, there is no possibility Julian will hang, is there?"

A half-beat of hesitation was all Adriana needed. She closed her eyes as Cassandra said, "No. But he may be transported. If it were anyone else he'd killed, but the son of a former mistress of half of Parliament, including the King's brother . . . if Malvern had not been the best friend of the Prince of Wales . . . if there—"

The voices came into the hallway below, and the sisters looked toward the sound. Adriana tried to hear some measure of the gravity of the situation, but only heard Gabriel make a jest, likely some form of gallows humor. Whatever it was, it brought forth a chuckle from Tynan. And then they were on the stairs and at the doors, and Adriana found she was holding her breath.

And as if they knew it, the men stood silent, side by side, no expression on their faces whatsoever. But in a flash Adriana saw how alike they were—graceful, as befitted the swordsman and horseman they each were. Gabriel had always been the tallest man Adriana ever met, but as they stood side by side, she saw that Tynan was taller by a tail. Tynan's hair fell in that thick, glorious swath down his back, and Gabriel's tumbled in a glory of curls women went mad for. Tynan's eyes were bluer than morning, while Gabriel's were that pale green that was so startling in his face.

But on two mouths she saw the lurking amusement at the torture their silence gave, and in two sets of eyes a glitter of laughter. And it was in this that they were so much alike.

Here were men who chose to thumb their noses at fortune. Who laughed at threats, and made a dance of sorrow. As long as she could remember, she'd loved best this quality about Gabriel—it balanced her too serious turn of mind, balanced the drama she found in every moment.

And of all things, it was the one quality she most heartily despaired of seeing in a man she was bound to resist. She glimpsed, suddenly, a flicker of that brooding darkness in Tynan's face, and worry leaped in her.

"Tell us!" she said sharply.

It was a room for women, not men, and they dwarfed the small, carved chairs they took. Tynan swept by Adriana, and she smelled the city night on him, smoke and river air and rain, and again remembered that he'd not taken his kiss today.

"There's little enough to tell," Gabriel said. His

mouth was grave now. "They did not detain me, as his second. Julian will be taken to the Tower, and will be tried by the House of Lords."

"When?"

"I don't know. Soon, I should think." Gabriel helped himself to a pear and bit into it. "Tonight I'll go about and see what I might hear. Unless you have some use for your husband," he said with a wicked grin at Adriana, "I thought he might come with me."

A ripple of relief washed through her—if he were out, he would not claim his kiss—and she spoke quickly. "He's a man. Since when do men ask permission of their wives?"

"It wasn't permission," Tynan said quietly, all too close. His breath whispered over her ear, and Adriana repressed a shudder. "Only a polite understanding of the pleasure newlyweds often take in each other."

Adriana winced, blushing. "Do you mind?" she said, glancing at her siblings.

"I do." He took her hand and stood abruptly, tugging Adriana up with him. "Excuse us. I require a word in private with my wife."

She yanked discreetly at his hand, trying to pull away. She suspected his motive here, and feared that hallway and his strength and the strange tension she felt about him tonight. But he held fast to her hand and she could do nothing to free herself without causing a scene. Lifting her chin, she allowed herself to be drawn into the passageway, all too conscious of her sister and brother exchanging a speculative glance.

The hallway was dim, with only a single candle spluttering in a sconce, and against her will, Adriana felt anticipation. His hand, dry and strong, nearly engulfed hers, and she liked the heat of it, the smell of night in his coat, the look of his long, glossy hair falling down his back.

"What is so private?" she asked.

He turned and faced her. The small light from the candle caught on one high, arched cheekbone and on the tiny bristles of beard on his jaw. A sudden, hard wish made her want to put her hand there, feel that prickle and his firm jaw against the heart of her palm.

One side of his mouth quirked. "Do you have some other use for me tonight, wife?"

Adriana made her face blank. "Of course not."

"I thought you might be a little . . . lonely, your first night in town, perhaps a little melancholy over your brother." It was half-teasing, half-serious, unexpected tone, which unsettled her.

He had not let go of her hand, and Adriana realized she'd not made a move to take it back, either. She did so now, hastily. "I will be fine."

"There is much for me to learn in these places. And I suspected you had no use for me, since you have your novel's Lovelace to keep you company."

Drat him! Adriana couldn't help but smile. "True."

"I suppose I must claim my kiss now," he said, and eased ever so slightly closer to her. "I've been thinking all day on where best to land it."

She swallowed, a hard pulse beating in her throat, and raised her eyes. "And what did you decide?"

He lifted a hand and touched a single finger to the center of her brow. "Here."

And somehow, she did not move as he took one

step closer, lifted his hands, those big, graceful hands, and put them around her head. They covered her ears, creating a sense of envelopment. Slowly, he bent his head and very deliberately pressed his mouth against the place on her forehead, that spot he'd primed so simply with his finger.

He did not hurry. It seemed a thousand years between the moment he first began to bend and the instant his warm lips touched her flesh, and another thousand—filled with a rushing sort of dizziness—that his mouth stayed there, moist and hot, burning into her head—that he lingered. Her nose brushed his chin, and the prickles of beard sent a ripple of something straight through her middle. His hands did not move, but she felt his thumbs against her cheek and thought of them on her mouth last night.

By the time he let her go, Adriana knew her skin was flushed the color of wine, and again the imprint of his hands and lips lingered on her flesh, echoing with tingles that it seemed should be visible.

As if it were nothing, he stepped away again and asked calmly, "Do you ride?"

"What?" her voice seemed to come from very far away.

"I would like to ride tomorrow. Perhaps you would accompany me?"

She found her wits and pushed away from the wall, where she seemed to have slumped. "Yes. That would be fine."

"Good."

They rejoined the others, Adriana wondering faintly where her mind had gone. How would she resist if he did this every day? She threw an alarmed and pleading glance at Cassandra, who took one look at her sister's face and leaped into action. "Will you deliver me to an acquaintance on your way?" she asked.

"Of course."

"I'll fetch my wrap then. We'll let Riana off first, shall we?"

Gabriel glanced at Adriana quickly, but remained silent. She did not miss the way he stroked that tiny strip of beard between lip and chin, but there were some things a woman could only share with a sister. Gabriel would simply have to wonder.

Tynan found Gabriel an agreeable companion. No, more than agreeable, for the man possessed a zest for living and a rueful mockery that belied a piercing intelligence. Tynan supposed most people liked Gabriel for the same reasons—certainly Adriana was devoted.

And yet it was still a surprise to discover the level of greeting that awaited Gabriel at a coffee shop called The Stag and Pointer, where they got out in a mist that was hourly leaning more toward rain than drizzle. A bow-fronted window showed a glow of red and yellow lamplight within, and the shadows of men in conversation—none of which differed from the coffee shops Tynan had frequented on his early visits to London. Some catered to a literary crowd, others to the theater, others to the idle sons of the nobility.

The Stag and Pointer attracted another set entirely. Tynan ducked under the door, blinking in the heavy smoke of pipe and cigar that hung like a gray blanket in the room. As he glanced about him, he was startled to discover a middle class lot, clerks and shopkeepers by their dress, and among the ruddy English faces one would expect in such a place, there were many others—foreign faces. Black faces. One man, small and round in the waist, with a fringe of grizzled gray hair springing from his balding pate, was so black that his skin shone in the light, and Tynan stared in surprise at him for a moment. He'd never seen skin of so dark a hue. The face would be lost in the darkness but for the graying goatee surrounding his mouth and the brightness of his eyes.

It was this man who caught sight of Gabriel first, and he came to his feet, an expression of utter disbelief on his mouth. His hands braced themselves against the table, as if the old man thought he would faint away without it. The others at the table, many of them black, though none so dark as this one, turned to see what had caught his attention, and it was one of these who said, "St. Ives?"

Another cried out, "Gabriel!" and nearly overturned a chair in his haste to make his way across the room. As he approached, Tynan saw that he was quite young—not much more than fifteen or sixteen, his face still bare of beard. And without any self-consciousness at all that Tynan could perceive, he hurled himself into Gabriel's arms. "We thought you dead!"

And then there were a dozen men, all colors, who surged forward, speaking all at once, asking a hundred questions, a thousand. Gabriel took a hand here, gave out a smile there, a clap on the back, never seeming to

mind the close press of the youth who gazed at him
with something akin to worship.

With the finesse of a diplomat, Gabriel guided them
all to places, signaled to the barkeep, settled the youth
at his left, and at last came to the old man. "Jacob," he
said with gravity, then winked. "I have missed our
debates, old man."

"Have you brought me tales of the New World?"

"Tales enough for a month of drinking," Gabriel
promised, then turning, somehow drew Tynan forward. "You must meet my brother-in-law, Tynan
Spenser."

The faces were not particularly welcoming, but
Tynan gave a nod, thinking of the men in his village
pub, put off by the clothes of a gentlemen. He did not
blame them, and would not push where he was not
welcome. Instead he took his place, and a pint of ale
and became a shadow, observing only.

Gabriel was obviously popular with them, this crew
of seamen and merchants and foreigners, and the mantle sat easily upon his shoulders. With the skill of a
great statesman, he absorbed their interest and turned
it back to them, seeking answers to their feeling over
Julian's arrest.

By the time they returned home, past midnight,
Tynan felt both disturbed and excited. Here was a
world he had not even dreamed existed, one that
threatened the fabric of life as he'd known it, but
offered promise of a new one. While their opinions
boded ill for Julian, Gabriel seemed unconcerned
about it, and Tynan took his cue from him.

But as he entered his own chambers and removed

his neckcloth, loath to disturb the snoring Seamus, Tynan half smiled as realization dawned upon him. Beneath Gabriel's pretty manners, beneath his elegant tongue and the glitter in his eye, lay the very serious and pointed heart of a reformer.

Tynan could not say why it pleased him so, but the warmth of it lingered with him as he slept, and clung to him the next morning, when he awakened long before the rest of the house stirred.

Restless, driven by the evening's revelations, he went abroad. His journey took him to the East End, through neighborhoods of mansions abandoned to immigrants from all over Europe and the east. Here there was already much activity as dockworkers and fishmongers set out to work, and as he walked, Tynan heard the mingled accents and languages of a dozen cultures. In the genteel areas there was, so early, a kind of rarified silence, broken only by the odd horse or milkmaid crying out her wares. Here, no such silence reigned, and the air smelled sharply of the river and dung, and cabbage and fish.

And here he found a church. Grime stained the old stone, but within there was a thick smell of beeswax and mildew, and incense. Tynan paused for a moment, feeling vague tensions bleed away under the familiar and comforting mingling of scents. Mass had only just begun, and he took a place near the rear, where he would not be noted.

Not that any would note him particularly, another Irish laborer come to a weekday mass. He kept a set of clothing for the purpose, ordinary workman's clothes: a pair of rough brown trousers he carefully did not wash too often, a clean but wrinkled linen shirt that once had belonged to his father, a rope belt, and scuffed boots with a hole near the toe. His hair gave him away as a gentleman—it was too neatly kept and too clean—but he left it unbrushed and stuck an ancient hat atop it, pulling it off only when he came inside. For a day, he'd left his beard unshaved.

It was a dangerous ruse he played, especially here, with so much at stake. His seat in the Irish parliament hinged entirely on his rejection of this faith, and all he hoped to gain could be negated in a single instant if he were caught practicing what all thought his family had given up forty years before. He had told himself he would not come here, not with the chance of being seen in his workman clothes by someone in the town house.

But his conscience had not allowed him to forgo the ritual if it was at all possible to pursue it, particularly when he was certain to be attending services with his wife at some point. He came for Aiden. For his mother.

Tynan knelt alone, his hat clasped between his hands, his head bowed as the priest sang out the ancient Latin, and let relief and a certain joy fill him. While his brother and mother had lived, religion mattered little to him. That had been Aiden's province— the passion Tynan spent on women and wine and song, his brother had spent on the church. Aiden had gone away to France to study for the priesthood— secretly, of course—and Tynan had gone to work with vigor in business. Over and over Aiden told him that they both served God and their nation, each in their own way, and Tynan had cheerfully believed him.

The sweet sorrow of the liturgy rose seemed to fill the entire church, up to the wooden beams. Filled him. The great irony for Tynan was that he'd learned to find joy in the church only after those who would have loved seeing him sit here were taken from him. But here, he could be close to them. Here, he felt he could sense the spirit of his brother. Here, he could almost imagine he was his twin—called to a noble struggle, willing to sacrifice all for the good of God and his nation.

But only by defying it. It was the small, secret thing he could do. His brother had been murdered for his faith. Tynan would practice it in his absence.

Adriana stirred slowly, caught in the pleasurable world between sleep and wakefulness. A sense of anticipation crept into the blurriness, nudging her like a small child: *Wake up, wake up! We have much to do!* It was such an odd, unfamiliar nudging that she was reluctant to surface entirely and find it was only the lingering edge of a dream. Instead she burrowed more deeply into the warmth of her down coverlets and let the outside world remain mysterious a moment longer.

But it was the very feel of those coverlets that made her sit upright, tossing the thick warm weight from her in a rush of genuine excitement. Cold, rain-washed light fell thinly through the unshuttered top half of the long windows that completely lined one wall of the room, but the very sight of the windows themselves, their casings painted a pale aqua to match the walls, gave her a leap of happiness.

London!

Tossing the coverlet aside, she shivered into her woolen robe and put her feet into waiting slippers. Too eager to pause even the moment it would take to put a light to the waiting coals, she rushed across the carpeted floor and flung open the middle set of shutters.

It was wicked of her to be so filled with excitement over their arrival in the city when it was such a dreadful errand that brought them here. She thought of Julian awakening in the Tower, and a little of her exuberance bled away.

But not entirely. After a deep sleep in her good bed, Adriana could not help the sense of eager anticipation she felt as she peered out the window. There, two stories below, were the streets of London, already alight with movement, peddlers calling out their wares, horses clopping, a bright green carriage with a gold crest. Across the street a maid scuttled back from some errand, a brown-wrapped package under her arm, a black umbrella protecting her from the drizzle. A man and a boy set up a stall. A man in worn trousers and a shapeless hat hurried toward the south.

London!

She could not wait, not another breath, to be out there, in those glorious streets. She flung open the door that connected to the small maid's quarters where Fiona slept. The girl, newly hired only a few months before, slept on, curled deep in her pillow, only the top of her red head showing against the snowy linens. A calico cat with a gold nose curled on top of her hip, and Adriana petted his silky head before flinging open the shutters. "Up, you lazy girl!"

"What?" Fiona blinked, then remembered herself and scrambled out of bed, blinking widely. She curtsied and mumbled an apology, pushing the weight of her hair out of her face. "Sorry, milady . . . I don't—"

"Never mind all that. Get dressed quickly and come help me. We're here! I am most impatient to be out." She swirled back to her own chamber.

To her credit, Fiona appeared almost immediately, and inside a half hour Adriana was rushing through a cup of tea while she waited for a footman to finish some small errand for the cook so he could accompany her. She heard him returning and put her cup down in a clatter, reaching for her gloves.

But it was Tynan who stood in the door, looking flushed and windblown. He did not wear his usual black, but breeches and coat of a rich blue with an embroidered waistcoat beneath. A color that—and she was certain he knew it—pointed out the dazzling shade of his eyes. "Good morning!" he said heartily. "Are you off on errands so early?"

She nodded. "I'm awaiting a footman to accompany me." She lifted her brows. "I expected you to be abed well beyond this," she said, picking up her cup again. "Gabriel never rises before noon when he's been out to the coffeehouses."

"He is yet abed," he said with a shrug. "At heart, I'm afraid I'm a provincial sort—up with the dawn, to bed with the cows."

Provincial was not the word she would have chosen to describe him in this high good humor. "I see." Afraid of giving herself away, she frowned in the general direction of the door. "I wonder where Peter is."

"Were you particularly needing his assistance, or would I do in his stead?"

Adriana looked at him in alarm, trying to think quickly of a lie to account for her need for a footman. Not only did she fail to imagine a good excuse, she failed to come up with anything at all. "No," she said finally. "I thought I'd walk awhile, perhaps look in on Julian. I'm afraid it won't be terribly exciting."

He grinned at her, that rake's grin filled with good white teeth. "'Tis always exciting to escort a beautiful woman. It seems a shame to be abed when the whole of a great city awaits."

"Yes!" Adriana exclaimed before she remembered she was to keep her distance. But she couldn't think how to withdraw it. "I do love London," she admitted.

He offered his arm. "Then I say we shall explore it together this gloomy morn. We'll have it all to ourselves."

Adriana was lost. Not even imagining how Cassandra's mouth would tighten if she observed her in this moment could give her the strength to turn down the invitation. She took his arm and they set out, protected from the soft drizzle by a great black umbrella.

❧ 8 ❧

They walked, agreeably silent, to a crossroads that led to a cluster of shops Adriana especially liked. It was early yet, but already there was more to see in twenty paces than Adriana would see in two thousand at Hartwood. She walked with her head up, her eyes wide open, her heart drinking it all in: the bookseller with the day's most popular titles on display in the window, the bakery with its heavenly scents, the coffee shop, just opening for the day, the greengrocer and flower sellers, the ragged children running errands for pennies or a crust of bread, the dogs snuffling in alleyways, the derelicts lurching along, smelling of river and sweat.

She resisted the urge to chortle aloud at the pleasure of it. Resisted, too, the wish to babble about it to Tynan as she might have to one of her sisters.

But whatever could be said against the man, Tynan had repeatedly proved himself to be quite perceptive. "What a light step you have this morning," he commented. "It was my impression you came to visit your sister quite often. Is it such a novelty to be here?"

"I used to visit once a quarter or so, but I have not done so since my father died. And when I am a guest of Cassandra, I feel compelled to follow her schedule." She spared a smile. "She is not an early riser, I'm afraid."

"So I gathered. 'Twas near ten when we set out last night."

Politely, she asked, "Did she accompany you?"

He glanced at her. "She rode with us to her destination, as you saw."

Adriana ignored the stab of jealousy that went through her at the thought of Tynan and Cassandra together in the coach under a moonlit midnight. Well, not moonlit, exactly, since it had been overcast then, as well. But—

"She flirted with me," he said.

Adriana looked up. "It's her way."

He chuckled. "No, it is not. She was grim and determined, and it was quite painful to observe." He pulled his arm close to his body, pressing Adriana's hand into his side. "If she's part of your defense, my dear, I'd suggest you must give her instruction in the finer arts of flirtation."

Abashed, Adriana managed, "Whatever do you mean? I have no accomplishments in that arena."

Directly in front of them the owner of a tea shop opened the door with a broom in hand, releasing the warm, yeasty scent of freshly baked bread. The woman was as square as a box, with a square, broad face. She smiled expansively. "Come in and warm yourselves. I've fresh hot cross buns and clotted cream—a lovely breakfast for a gloomy morning."

Adriana would have moved on, but Tynan tugged her toward the door. "I've a weakness for hot cross buns," he said, flashing his rakish smile at the woman.

Under the force of that smile, Adriana noticed the woman could not help lifting a hand to smooth her wiry gray hair. "Right this way, milord," she said, bustling into her establishment with her head high. "A fine spot for you, right here by the window, so's you can watch the world pass."

"Thank you," Tynan said, gesturing for Adriana to settle. "Tea and buns for both of us, then."

"Right away."

He sat down across from her, and Adriana saw the humor in his eyes as he leaned close. "I believe taking tea in a London shop was one of those things you were longing to do?"

In that instant Adriana felt her world shift. In part, it was attributable to his extraordinary beauty. That rich head of hair, the perfection of his dark eyebrows and sooty lashes making his eyes so startling, the breadth of his shoulders under his blue coat. It was partly the quality of his good humor and his wish, for whatever reason, to give her a little of the fantasy he'd overheard that day in the music room. She didn't want to fight him this morning. She still—for all that she was past twenty—felt young. There were a young woman's wishes in her breast, the wish to be admired and flattered, the wish to engage in stimulating conversation with a man so beautiful he nearly hurt her eyes.

But most of all it was the desire to relax her guard, have an adventure, be herself.

It had been so long! In that instant when Tynan smiled at her across the table in the sweet-smelling, warm tea shop, she felt a tight knot of herself suddenly unfurl, stretch, come out of hiding.

"You have a good memory, sir." She inclined her head and gave him a wicked smile. "Though this is not proper tea, it will do nicely." She glanced discreetly over her shoulder and lowered her voice. "And I rather think the ladies hereabout most earnestly wish they were in my shoes, and I a dead fly on the floor."

She startled him. The surprise swept quickly over his brow and mouth, then was subdued under a pleased lift of his chin. "There's the difference," he said. "Such a subtle glance, a teasing bit of a smile—there's the mark of a woman accomplished in the art of flirtation."

A small warning told her she was entering the territory she'd vowed to avoid, but she quelled it quickly. "I did send Cassandra out to flirt with you."

"She did her best," he said with a regretful wince.

The proprietor bustled out with an enormous tray of buns and tea. "Here we are," she sang out. "A little of everything for this cold morning." Her flushed pleasure was all for Tynan.

And he did not disappoint her. He bestowed the best of his smiles upon her. "Excellent," he said with enthusiasm. "I've not seen such a lovely spread in months." He admired the food for a single, respectful moment, then lifted his extravagant gaze to the woman herself and sighed. "Thank you," he said with a heartfelt depth of sincerity.

The woman fair floated back to her kitchen, and

Adriana heard her singing a moment later. She turned to Tynan, who was cheerfully piling sugar into his cup, humming something under his breath. Feeling her gaze, he glanced up. "Is there something amiss? D'you want something else?"

"No," Adriana said softly. "This is lovely."

"I am very hungry," he said. "And the one thing I'll give your English bakers are the pastries. I had to have my tailor let out my waistband when I was here last."

"You'll be a fat old man, then, won't you?" Adriana, too, was hungry. She spread a plain bun with clotted cream and jam, carefully, with the exact mix of color and balance she liked, building anticipation for the pleasure that was to come. It was as lovely as she'd hoped and she made a soft sound of approval.

He chuckled. "And you'll be stout as an old peasant. But what use is a waist, I say."

Adriana dripped a little jam on her chin and caught it, laughing. She lifted her cup in a mock toast. "To a fat old age, then."

He raised his cup as well. "But not too fat to ride a horse."

They both gave full attention to the feast for a few moments. Adriana enjoyed the view through the window, carriages and horses and foot traffic beginning to thicken as the morning ripened. The drizzle had halted for a moment, but the strange yellow fog that sometimes hung about the city in the autumn seemed to be creeping in around the buildings.

"Did you enjoy your outing last night?" Adriana asked after a moment. "Discover anything interesting?"

He sipped his tea, as if considering her question. "It was not what I had anticipated. Gabriel has an unusual set of friends."

"Well, his circumstances are not the usual."

"True. And yet he seems to exert a great deal of effortless power among them. They roared in welcome, but he seemed to take it in stride, getting down to business very quickly to learn what the mood in town is over Julian's arrest."

"And?"

"'Twas a middle class crowd," he said slowly, "merchants and seaman and the like. A good many of them are foreign." His eyes narrowed slightly. "They're quite radical, some of them. It was . . . impressive."

Adriana sighed in frustration. Gabriel had always attached himself to political reformers—and with good reason, she supposed. The current world was not particularly friendly to his interests. "But what did they say of Julian's case?"

"They were relieved to see Gabriel was not charged. But they were also pleased that Julian was." He said it plainly, without apology.

"Pleased? Why?"

He made a dismissive gesture with one hand. "The general spirit seemed to be that it was time that peers of the realm were punished with the same laws as ordinary men."

Adriana frowned. "I suppose that's not unexpected, but he will be tried by peers." Her scowl deepened. "But surely Gabriel stood up for him?"

"What do you think?" Tynan's mouth quirked in a wry smile. "'All for one . . .'"

"Did they listen?"

"Aye. Your brother has a rare gift for oratory."

She laughed. "So he does. My father vowed if Gabriel ever took it into his head to lead a revolt, we'd all simply have to lay our weapons down and let him have his way."

His attention sharpened. "Really." It was not, precisely, a question.

"Planning a revolt?" she asked lightly.

He blinked, and the thick lashes erased the alertness in his eyes, so when the sweep was finished, he was only good-humored Tynan, flirt and rake and exuberant companion. "Of course. It's what all earls most dream of."

She laughed as she was meant to do, but carefully stowed away this hint of his darker nature, sure there was more to Tynan Spencer than he wished the world to know.

Rather than return to the house, Tynan hired a carriage to take them to the Tower, bearing a package stuffed with the good Mrs. Tingle's hot cross buns and a package of loose tea she was persuaded to sell.

But even before the carriage pulled up at the gates, it was plain there was some activity within the walls. A crowd was gathered around the gates, and judging by the noisome hissing and booing, a criminal of some disrepute was going to the gallows today.

Adriana stared at the crowd in horror as they passed, then resolutely brushed it away. Julian would not end there. He would not. If she had to crawl through the moat and scale the walls herself, she would not allow him to hang. "I wonder what the criminal has done," she said.

"Probably killed his sister's lover," Tynan answered calmly. She stared at him in pained astonishment. He looked at her and grinned.

"You're a beast."

"Aye."

Still, she could only imagine how Julian must feel about the spectacle, and was doubly glad they'd brought presents to cheer him. She prayed his windows did not overlook the hill.

At the gates, however, a burly guardsman refused them entrance. Adriana, stricken, put her hand on his liveried arm. "But he's my brother, and a peer of the realm." She gestured to the package of buns. "I've brought him presents to cheer him while he's incarcerated."

He was unmoved. "I'll deliver them to him."

Adriana took a breath to mount a second protest, but Tynan took her arm, shaking his head minutely. She sighed heavily and allowed herself to be led away. He signaled to the carriage to wait and followed as Adriana marched toward the river. "Where are you going?" he asked at last.

Only when her next steps would have dumped her into the water did she turn and halt, staring up at the windows of the immense, rambling structure. "Where would they hold him, do you suppose?"

Tynan shook his head, eyeing the vast, rambling estate with its dozens of towers. "Haven't a clue."

"The White Tower is comfortable, they say. They

would not put him in a dungeon." She paced to her left, frustrated by the few windows she could actually view from there. "Let's just stand here for a little. Perhaps he'll look out and see us and be cheered a little."

"Adriana—"

She glared up at him. "What will it hurt?"

He shrugged. Lifted a hand.

Adriana stared very hard at the buildings, imagining that she called to her brother in her mind, just called his name. If she concentrated very hard, perhaps he would sense her presence, just peek out for a moment and be cheered.

She thought of him in a round gray room, with perhaps a desk and a bed. It would be cold and damp. Anxious, she said, half to herself, "I should have penned a note to cheer him, too. It never occurred to me that he would not be allowed visitors." A wrench of despair suddenly pinched her heart. "God, Tynan! We *must* get him out."

"This serves nothing," Tynan said, taking her arm firmly. "Come, let's find some amusement, and this evening you can pen him a long letter, which I will see delivered in the morning."

Still oddly reluctant, Adriana stared at him miserably. "How long do you think he'll have to be there?"

"None of us know the answer to that question." His voice was gentle.

She allowed herself to be led away, back to the carriage. When they were under way, Tynan said, "Since there is naught we can do for your brother today, I would like to begin my campaign."

"Your campaign?"

"Aye." He adjusted his sleeve just so. "We'll be wanting to entertain and be entertained. I believe," his gaze flickered over her gown, "perhaps our first stop will be the dressmaker's."

"Entertain?" She frowned at him. "Tynan, you seem to continually overlook the fact that I have no command in Society—and will have even less once the scandal is resurrected."

His expression was calm. "Leave that to me."

"If you have standing on your own, I'll only be a hindrance to you."

"No," he said. "It will be in my favor to have rescued a English damsel with a scarlet past." He smiled down at her. "You are an asset, Adriana. Believe me."

She closed her eyes, imagining herself hosting a supper to which no one came. Or worse, one in which the guests cast speculative glances at her behind their hands. "I cannot entertain," she said quietly. "Please do not ask that."

"You must," he countered firmly. "And remember, 'tis not only for me you're going to act." His eyes took that coldness she had seen there so rarely. "But your brother, in that tower."

Adriana met his cold gaze with one of her own. In his impeccable coat, with that devastatingly beautiful face and wicked charm, he was the very picture of a gentlemen who meant to charm all of Society. But he did not know how it would be, and evidently had no intention of resting until he had his way. With a shrug she said, "Very well, if you wish to entertain, we will do so. But I am correct in this."

"I'm willing to gamble." His gaze flickered again

over her gown. "And I will do anything to see the end
of that . . . that . . . color."

She sighed. It seemed the fates planned to thwart
her at every turn. "As you wish. But you needn't come
along. I've already made arrangements to shop with
Cassandra this afternoon."

"I think not," he said. "I trust her less than you."

Tynan was quite satisfied with the progress of the day,
in spite of the way Adriana ran hot and cold with him,
her moods mercurial and dizzying. One moment she
flirted openly, the next she hid behind the haughty chin
or tried to disappear into the dullness of her cloak. The
sights and sounds of London excited her, and she could
not keep the shine from her eyes—but the thought of
her brother in the Tower sent her into darkest despair
and regret. Her laughter was quick and deep, and it surprised her that he made her laugh so often—which
made him want to see her laugh even more.

Mercurial.

He did not think he'd ever known a woman who so
fascinated him. The quickness of moods might have
tried the patience of another man, but he enjoyed the
challenge of countering the dark moments and gloried
in the bright ones.

The moments he most enjoyed were those when
her guard slipped the tiniest bit and he caught a flicker
of desire on her lips, and in her eyes a swift glimpse of
hunger as her gaze flitted over his hand or his mouth.
She liked his hair, he thought, and wondered how to
use it to further his cause.

But slowly. There was no rush in this. He wanted her, all of her, when she came again to his bed. Wanted her willing and whole, with all reserve gone, and all the passion that lurked in her set free and focused without reserve upon him.

At the dressmaker's shop he sat in a comfortable chair and nodded or gave a scowl to the choices of fabrics and designs presented to him. Nay to the pale blue muslin and printed pinks and sunny yellows. Too pallid for her.

At last the dressmaker began to comprehend his wishes. While Adriana stood still in the middle of the small room, Madame bustled into the back and returned with two bolts of fabric in her arms, and she was followed by two assistants also carrying heavy bolts.

"Set them there," she fussed, and with a quick gesture tugged out a long length of deep maroon, patterned with stripes in cream and ivy-green. It was a simple sort of fabric, but the color and pattern draped over Adriana's body like a breath, and brought forth the color of her skin and hair and eyes.

Tynan inclined his head in consideration, and as if to urge him to approve, the dressmaker tugged the fabric tight against Adriana's body, showing the fullness of her bust, the smallness of her waist.

"Aye," he said. "That one."

They settled on several others, and then the dressmaker shooed Adriana into the back to be dressed in a particular style. While she was gone, the dressmaker smiled. "She is hiding, that one." She winked. "But you will see, my lord, what a magician I am!" She clapped her hands. "Hurry, girls!"

Tynan heard a cry rise in the back room, Adriana protesting—loudly—and he grinned. If she disliked it so, he would almost certainly approve. He crossed his arms in anticipation.

But even the protest did not prepare him for the vision of her in the gown she wore when she emerged. The fabric of this model was only a poor grade of muslin in a greenish shade, but it did not matter. The lines, too, were unusually simple—fitted long sleeves and a square neckline cut low, and a waist fitted all the way to the hips.

Tynan was a worldly man. He'd lost count of the women he'd had, much less the ones who'd caught his eye for a moment or two, but in this simple, poor fabric model of a ball gown, Adriana put them all to shame.

It was, in part, the revelation of just what a glorious shape she hid beneath her badly made gowns—the beautifully lush breasts, the small waist, the surprisingly voluptuous swell of hips. Her arms were neat, her neck long and alluring.

But it was her skin that made him ache and shift, and wish there was no one else in the room. Skin as clear and smooth and perfect as a bowl of fresh milk, skin that glowed with an inner light, almost luminescent in the bright room.

He wanted to shed his shirt and press his chest to that silkiness. He wanted to lick it. And as he stared in pleasurable anticipation, letting his gaze swoop down her neck, glide over her collarbone, swell over that abundance of breasts that were near to spilling free— oh, lovely thought!—he noticed that her breath came faster than it should.

He lifted his gaze to her face, and there, in the company of the dressmaker and her assistants, in a public shop in a public square in the middle of London, their eyes locked. In hers, Tynan saw reluctant arousal, awareness of his perusal, haughtiness and need, all in a whirl. Her nostrils flared faintly, and she suddenly sucked in a deep breath and looked away to let it go.

The dressmaker, oblivious or polite, rushed forward with a new bolt of fabric. "Now in this you must trust me, my lord. We've said no pink, but this is—" She flung the edge of the fabric over Adriana, draped it close, tugged it close to her form. "—is different, no?"

"Ah," he said.

He did not know what name to put on the stuff, but he knew what it made him think of—fairy wings. Gossamer and pale. The color was pink, but only the faintest possible shade, the last moment of sunlight on a winter day.

Nor did he know why it gave her skin so much more luminosity, so much more power. Against that breathy shade, her lips darkened to a hot berry and her eyes glowed vividly blue, and Tynan, unaccountably, wondered if her nipples were pale or dark, rose or cinnamon.

He swallowed, surprised at the fever of his thoughts. With a wry smile, he nodded. "Yes. That one, definitely."

Adriana looked mutinous. "I shan't wear it," she said.

He grinned. "Oh, yes you will."

The door to the shop suddenly swung open, halting any reply she might have made. Tynan glanced up, curiously, and saw a woman of some wealth, attended by a footman. The matron wore an enormous hat trimmed with feathers and fruit, and her wig was so tall she had to duck under the doorway. Her face was aging, but Tynan could see the beauty she must once have been.

Adriana made a curious little noise, and both Tynan and the matron turned to look at her—which was evidently exactly what she did not want, in spite of the noise, for she was struggling to turn away, while Madame struggled just as intently to make her stand still so the gossamer fabric did not tear.

"Well well," the matron drawled, "if it isn't the Lady Adriana."

Pinned where she stood, Adriana looked down, turned her head as far as she was able.

But the woman was not about to be deterred. She moved with the practiced glide of a woman who knew her power over men, her skirts bobbing on their panniers in a way that made a man wonder what lay beneath. "I hear your brother is in the Tower, my dear. What a pity."

Still Adriana did not respond. She seemed to be shrinking into herself, as if willing herself to disappear, and Tynan wondered if he ought to go to her rescue. Instead he waited to see how it would unfold, looking for clues to the scandal, and to Adriana's heart.

"Have you come back to London to whore around a bit more?" the woman inquired.

Adriana's head snapped up and Tynan saw the blaze of fury in her eyes before she shifted, pushing the dressmaker—shocked into muteness—away. She turned away, head high, and carried herself with dignity into the changing rooms.

Having lost her primary quarry, the woman turned to Tynan. "Is she your slut now?"

He stood, and his height put her immediately at a disadvantage. "She is my wife," he said in a low, dangerous voice. "And I'll thank you to hold that evil tongue."

"Oh, how divine!" she cried. "A bloody Irishman." She gave a mean laugh. "Who else would have her?"

He raked her with a cold gaze and tucked his hands behind his back, glancing toward the dressmaker, whose face burned with the horror of this scene. "What shrews old, faded women become in the presence of youth and beauty," he said smoothly.

Leaving the shrew to splutter, he moved to confer with Madame. "Do what you must to have the gowns ready posthaste," he said, and tucked a guinea into her hand. Raising a brow, he smiled. "The ball gown first."

"Ball gown!" the shrew cried. "As if any door will be open to you!"

Tynan gave her his best, most wicked smile. "Oh, I think you'll be surprised." He exaggerated his accent, rolling the r's and the lilt. "I've prettier manners than you, and an ever so irresistible smile." Lazily, he crossed to her, letting his eyelids drop suggestively, letting his eyes scrape over her powdered bosom. He knew his power, and it lay in sex, a subject he suspected this witch knew all too well. "I'll be welcomed."

She glared up at him. "Not if I have anything to do with it."

He shrugged lightly. "Do your worst." Adriana, garbed in the mustard cloak, joined him, and he put his arm about her protectively. To his surprise, there was a tremble in her shoulders, and she kept her head lowered. "Good day," he said, and departed with a slow, precious dignity.

On the street he turned Adriana to face him, leaving his hands on her shoulders. "Why didn't you slap her?"

Now that there was no need to control her expression, Adriana's face collapsed into misery. "That was Malvern's mother." She lifted those deep blue eyes. "Now do you see how it will be?"

And Tynan, for all his bravado in the shop, did see. He would have to work quickly. "Let's get you home."

She nodded, an expression of such defeat on her face that he could not bear it. More than anything, he wished to take her into his arms and hold her quiet and close, to ease this shame—but in this public street, with the sting of insult burning still, he thought it unwise. Instead he took her hand and placed it on his elbow jauntily, keeping his other hand over hers.

Adriana retreated to the conservatory when they returned home. A long narrow room that ran the length of the building on one side, it housed an enormous collection of plants, most of them tropical specimens that Leander had gathered on his travels. There were exotic flowers and vines climbing posts, and greenery with enormous leaves. Many of the plants she remembered from Martinique, for while most of the children had taken shells and rocks as mementos, Leander had spent two weeks carefully settling various slips and cuttings in pots. He spent the entire ocean voyage hovering over the collection and worrying about it, but nearly all had survived.

Adriana's father, indulgently, had the plant house built as a surprise for the youth. Now many of the specimens that had made that journey were almost a decade old and dripped blossoms from the ceiling, and cast shade on sunny days.

It was one of Adriana's favorite spots. It smelled of earth and dampness and hints of sweetness from the flowers, and the agreeably dense warmth of the air made her forget her troubles in ways she never quite understood.

This gloomy afternoon, she carried a box with her. It contained the pages of her journal and a freshly sharpened pen, as well as ink, a set of watercolors in cakes, and brushes. Hidden from the world behind an overgrown pot of fatsia japonica, sat a wide wooden table, painted annually to keep the moisture out. It was here that Adriana settled. The glass walls rose from the ground to a point far above her head, and on such a cool day, condensation covered the panes, effectively blocking out the world.

She sat still and breathed the comfort of the air, closing her eyes to steady herself on the fragrance of times past. Times that were easier than these, sweeter. The mingled scents triggered memories—she and Julian and Gabriel running down a stretch of sparkling white beach, dashing in and out of the turquoise surf, the sky blue and endless above them. They'd been wild then, wild and free, and they'd all believed it would last forever.

The tight knots along her spine began to ease at these memories, and encouraged, she tossed open the mental box that contained her days there—she always imagined memories as being stored in neat trunks with careful labels on them—and let them spill into her mind.

The birds were something she'd never stopped missing. Birds with wildly colorful feathers, and musical and strident cries, birds like flying flowers. And her bedroom on the plantation, with its polished floors and gauzy curtains and the mosquito netting around the bed. An airy place.

Thoughtfully, she took out her paints and brushes, and wet the little cakes. A flash of blue, across the top of the thick paper, a triangle of bird wing, with a tipping of white.

There had been dangers, too, of course. Deadly insects lurking in hidden places, beautiful snakes with fatal teeth, poisonous creatures washing up on the sand. Even the unlikely, fantastic threat of pirates had some basis in reality.

But happiness had reigned for the children. As those gilded memories came back to her, she sketched them out in little patterns of watercolor, amusing herself with shape, soothing her tumult with repetitive motion.

At last she was calm enough to write her thoughts in her journal. It was a rigorous requirement she set— she wrote every day. She did not require herself to record details of daily events necessarily, but an emotional and sensory history.

Tynan played the hero this morning. I can't bear to put the details down just yet—perhaps I'll never be brave enough. We met up with Malvern's mother at the dressmaker's and—it was horrid. Tynan shielded me, hurried me away, would, I vow it, have slapped her himself. I admired the control he had over his anger, which boiled in his eyes, and I fear that anger would be an awesome thing to witness if he let it go. Perhaps that is why he holds so tightly to it, why one only glimpses a tail of it now and again.

He is such a puzzle! I find myself watching him from the corner of my eye, drawn over and over and over again to something . . . something I can't quite grasp.

Perhaps, if I am honest, it is in part his beauty. His hair and his eyes, of course, and that aggressive and graceful arrangement of features. But also the irregularities that take him from merely beautiful to breathtaking. His nose is rather too large, and the bridge is high and a little off center. It gives the whole a much more interesting aspect.

And I like his hands, so long and lean and graceful. He uses them in conversation with a fluency that makes one think of the men of the Continent—it is more expansive than an Englishman would indulge.

But there are many beautiful men. About Tynan, there is more, some internal quality that's most extraordinary. I sometimes wonder what it would be like to live in his mind—I suspect there is, within him, a grand, wild garden, exuberantly overrun with some extravagant flower—foxglove or those tall pink things that grow on rooftops. It storms there, in his garden, for I've seen the darkness cross his eyes, sudden and fierce— and just as quickly spent. He is relentlessly good-humored. Even when he's wounded, he's quick to twist the moment to something wry.

And that makes him appear to be shallow, but he is not.

He is a puzzle. And he makes me think, all too often, of what sort of landscape is my mind, my soul. I think I have been walled inside a garden of my own making these past five years, protected from without, and fearful within. In my garden, things are carefully arranged, with nothing too untidy, and nothing too bright, and the door safely locked.

I am frightened of what will happen if I fling open

that door. I am afraid of the storms that could sweep me
away. I am not brave enough anymore.

A footstep on the stone floor made her hastily close
the book and put down her pen. A dark head appeared
over the tops of an extravagant orchid, then Gabriel
came into view, carrying a single yellow rose. "I suspected I'd find you here," he said, and presented her
with the flower. "May I join you?"

Adriana lifted it to her nose and smiled. "Of course.
We've had little time together since your return."

He settled across from her and flung out his long
legs. His breeches and stockings were immaculate, his
hair tamed and combed back to a long, curly queue. As
had become his habit, he stroked the tiny strip of beard
on his chin and then raised those pale green eyes to her
face. "Spenser said you met Malvern's mother this
morning."

"Yes."

"And it did not go well."

"No."

"Riana, look at me."

She sighed and raised her head.

He took her hand in his and earnestly leaned forward. "You must not allow her to shame you." His lips
quirked. "Especially not her."

Adriana smiled a little. "A case of the pot and kettle,
I'm sure."

"Pot and the ashes of the fire, more like." He
snorted, then shook his head. "The world is not all
England, Riana. You were freed in the Islands—don't
allow this world to put you in chains."

She swallowed, an ache in her chest. "But this is the world in which I must live."

"Is it?"

And in this, she was clear. "I loved the islands, Gabriel, but I cannot live there now. I am too aware of the injustice. This world may be flawed, but at least there are laws against men owning other men." She took a breath. "And I cannot leave the family."

"I know." He moved his thumb over her fingernail meditatively, his gaze fixed on something far away. "Julian bore it better than I, the separation. I was homesick every moment we were gone." He gave her a wry smile. "I'm afraid I do not have the heart of an adventurer at all."

In her mind's eye she saw him as he'd been that morning in Hyde Park, horror on his handsome face as blood seeped into Malvern's coat. She thought of his thinness now, and the hints of great trials. "Were you really taken by slavers?"

The faintest ripple of pain crossed his face and he closed his eyes. "I was."

A pain cut through her heart. "Did they hurt you?"

He tightened his hand around hers, raised his eyes. "Not anywhere that won't heal." He touched his heart. "I'm whole, where it matters."

She let go of a choking little laugh. "It certainly puts the matter of a being cut in Society into perspective!"

"Indeed." His grin was quick and wry. "But in truth, I suppose you must attempt to conquer that society. For Julian's sake."

"I tried to see him today, and the guard would not let us in." A heaviness settled low in her chest. "What can we do, Gabriel? Tynan said the spirit was against him last night in the coffeehouse."

"With them it is only the anger of the working man against the nobles. Not so much to worry about." A troubled expression crossed his brow, and his fingers went to that small strip of beard on his chin.

"But?" she prompted.

He took a breath. "But it seems there is some strong feeling about dueling. Even among those who should know better, there's talk of . . . making an example of Julian."

Stung, she breathed, "Oh, God."

"We won't let him hang, Adriana. That much I promise you. I've an appointment with a barrister in the morning, and have sent some of my friends out to see what they might learn about the source of this hanging mood." He clasped her hand. "You must not worry."

"You must give me something to do, Gabriel. I'll go mad if I have to sit in this house, wondering and worrying."

He seemed to consider a moment, then nodded. "I will think of something. In the meantime the guards can be bribed most days. And I'm sure Julian would welcome your letters—as many as you'd care to write."

From any other man, Adriana would have felt the words a mere balm, a way to soothe the spirits of a child. She trusted Gabriel to keep his word. "Thank you," she said. Then, determined they should not spend all their time enshrouded in gloom, she lifted her head and pasted on a smile. "What are your plans now, Gabriel? Will you take a wife and become a merchant and raise a bunch of fat children?"

"I think not," he said. "No wife or children for me. There are too many other things to claim my attentions—and no promise that any of them will ever provide me with a reliable living."

"Oh?"

"I am writing, Riana." His pale eyes were very serious. "And I am afraid I have married my cause." With a rueful lift of one heavy brow, he said lightly, "To free the slaves in all the world."

Taking her cue from his light tone, she said, "Well, it should certainly keep you busy." But she felt some sorrow that such a tender man would not take a wife. "At least I shall not be forced to share my flowers with some other wench."

He laughed. "Just so." He stood, tugging her hand. "Come, let's find ourselves some dinner. I've supports to gather, revolutions to seed."

Adriana shook her head. "I'll stay here. I must write to Phoebe."

For a moment he did not loose her hand, but gravely gazed down at her. "Are you all right, Riana?"

She smiled. "Yes."

There was doubt on his mouth, but in the end he said only, "Very well," and left her.

Tynan returned to the town house well after dark, eager to share with Adriana the course of the afternoon. He peeked into the dining room and the parlor, but she was nowhere about. Finally, the butler directed him to the conservatory. It was tucked behind the kitchen, reached only by a single, unassuming glass door off the dining room.

In the daytime it was likely a splendid place, Tynan thought, entering the close, scented dimness. Candles burned softly in one corner, and he headed in that direction, calling out her name. "Adriana? Are you here?"

She peered around a large potted palm. "Here."

"Ah, good!" Jauntily, he joined her. "I have good news."

"About Julian?"

He should have thought of that, that her first concern would be her brother. "No, I'm sorry."

"Oh." She gestured for him to join her at the small table. Across its top were scattered small, botanical watercolors, along with her brush and paints and a jug of water. She lifted one to give him room. "What is it, then?" she prompted without much interest.

"May I?" he asked, pointing to one of the paintings.

She lifted a shoulder. "I have no true talent at it, but it . . . occupies my thoughts."

Tynan frowned at the ennui in her manner, but picked up the drawings, several of them. The paintings were simple in form, strokes suggesting a shape, a flower, a leaf, the details suggested with subtle color graduations. "I disagree with your assessment," he said. "I like these very much."

"Thank you." There was no joy or pride in the words, and restlessly she picked up a brush and poked it in a small cake of green. Dabbing it on the paper, she said, "What is your good news?"

His senses prickled suddenly. "Have you been here all day?"

She raised her head. Nodded vaguely. "I told you it is my favorite place here. I often spend my days here."

"Have you eaten?"

A faint frown pulled her forehead. "I'm not hungry. But if you are, I can call for—"

"No." He waved the offer away. "It was not myself I was thinking of." Abruptly, he knelt in front of her. "I hope you haven't been in here brooding all day."

Her mouth tightened a little, and she picked up the brush, put it back. "Not brooding. Just thinking."

"Come," he said, "let's have the cook make us a platter of cheese and fruit, at least. Some wine, perhaps?"

"No, thank you," she insisted, and with effort met his gaze. She smiled, very falsely, as if to prove she was quite well.

He'd known her only days, and in that time she'd already shown herself to be changeable from one day to the next, one *moment* to the next. He could not say why this particular face disturbed him, called warning to his nerves, but he was a man who valued his instincts. Without thought, he stood and reached for her. "Come here, Adriana."

"What?" she said with annoyance, tugging hard against his grip on her arm. "If this is about your bloody kiss, I would much rather we wait."

There were blue shadows on the fine flesh below her eyes, faint but true, and he shook his head. "No kiss, I swear it."

Still she resisted. "What, then?"

Instead of playing this game with her, Tynan simply bent, picked her up easily, and turned to sit in the chair he'd taken her from. He wrapped his arms tightly around her, trapping her arms against her body, holding her close against his chest as she struggled. He chuckled and put his mouth close to her ear. "Please, lady, wiggle a little more. It's most . . . enjoyable."

She ceased immediately, and as if the fight was all she had left, her entire body went lax—legs and arms and the rigidness of her neck and shoulders. Her head fell on his shoulder. "Why are you doing this?" she said without interest.

"Comfort," he said simply, settling her more closely against him, and rubbed her arm, her back. "I wanted to do it earlier, but the street didn't seem quite the place." He tilted his head and put his cheek against her hair. "You were wounded, and I could do nothing to stop it."

"I was so humiliated," she whispered.

"Aye." He held her closer, pleased on some low level at the fit of her in his arms. Carefully, he did not allow arousal. He closed his eyes and stroked her back. She leaned against him limply, her head on his shoulder, her hands in her lap, for a long, long time, as if she had no will to act on her own.

And though he had begun in innocence, to comfort her, he was a man and she was a most desirable woman, a woman who had occupied far too many of this thoughts these past few days. He found he could not quite shut out the plumpness of her right buttock nestled against his member. He could not avoid breathing in the scent of her hair, that faint lavender

scent that never failed to make him think of her fighting her body so hard on their wedding night. Against
his cheek her hair was silky, and a lush breast pressed
against his upper arm.

A soft, strange mood overtook him. Gently, he
moved his cheek against her hair, found one of her
hands and slid his fingers through hers, taking pleasure
in the slim coolness, in the slow way she let her fingers
fall against his, not protesting, perhaps even joining.
She was not small or light, but his legs were strong and
he did not mind the weight, the fullness of her, an arm-
ful of woman.

And in time she, too, seemed to shed her tense
reserve. Almost absently, she turned her face slightly
against his neck, and he thought he heard her breathe
in and sigh, felt her breath fan over his ear. Her thumb
moved lightly on his hand, the most reserved
response, and in reply he stretched open that hand,
and their index fingers touched, met, pressed, then
each finger in turn. Fingertips to fingertips, then whole
fingers, and at last, palm to palm. He thought of Shakespeare, "Palm to palm is holy palmers' kiss," but did
not speak the words aloud, content instead to let their
hands speak what words could not say. Their fingers
slid together, making a clasp, then slid apart in exploration, and back together.

One hand, dancing, and his cheek on her hair, and
her nose turned to his neck. So little, but his breath felt
shallow over it.

He didn't know how long they were so lightly
joined before he lifted her hand to his lips and pressed
a kiss to the center of her palm. He did not hurry, for

he liked the ghostly brush of her fingers against his face, liked the tautness of her body as arousal moved in her, loved the taste of her flesh. He lingered, touched the tip of his tongue to the skin—

She bolted. Scrambled off his lap, out of his arms, shoving at him like a wild animal coaxed out of the darkness to eat from his hand, only to skitter away in terror over some unrelated noise. "Cad!" she cried, backing away from him. "I keep thinking you're different, and then I see you're just the same."

And this time his anger—that red beast he'd never controlled as well as he wished—rose in him. "As if I act alone!" he cried, leaping to his feet. "You gaze at me, you respond to me, you want me—and then push me away. D'you think a man has no pride?" He stepped close, backing her into a table. "D'you think I don't go away and wonder where I've gone wrong every time? I'm no lover ready to scorn you—I'm your bloody husband, and the law tells me I can have you if I wish. Now, if I wanted it."

"I would never forgive you."

"Aye," he said tightly. "Which is why I'm giving you this time. But you made a deal, and you need to be thinking of that when you're off feeling sorry for yourself all the time."

There was fire in her eyes now, sparks and fury, and in some part of his mind, that not devoured by thwarted need and anger, he was glad of it. The part consumed by desire noted the way her breasts moved over the bodice of her gown—magnificent flesh!—and the part consumed by anger made him reach up and touch that flesh boldly. He put an open palm over the lushness, touching fabric and flesh at once as he stared down at her, his jaw hard. She did not flinch or make some move away from him, but only stared at him, daring him to make her hate him. Cross that line.

"Today in that shop, I thought of this breast and what it will taste like," he said, his voice low. He scraped his fingers over the place where the nipple rose. "I thought of the color and of putting it my mouth, and making you cry out."

Still she remained utterly still, her eyes dark with fury, but there was desire, too, and the flesh he stroked and coaxed so boldly was rigid in response, as rigid as his own flesh. He leaned close, his mouth inches from her own, and he scraped his nail lightly over her gown, over that sensitively erect nipple that so wanted his touch. She quivered a little, lowering her eyes. "You want me, Adriana. You ache for my lips on this place, the soothing heat and the depth of my mouth—" Slowly he stroked, brushed his fingers over the bare flesh above her bodice, then back down, and to his dark satisfaction, she made a soft noise of protest. "—here."

Her mouth was a breath below his, so close he could have blinked and taken it. But he did not. "I'm willing to wait till you're ready to tell me that."

Abruptly, she tossed back her head, a blaze burning in her eyes, and she covered the hand that covered her breasts, holding him there. "As you've already seen, my lord," she said in a low, fierce whisper, "I am well named the Slut St. Ives. It is no large task to kindle the wanton heat that burns in this body." Her breath came quickly, lifting her flesh more tightly into his hands, winding tighter that coil of need in him. "But while I was young then, and foolish, and let my passions hold the day, time has taught me wisdom, too. You may well find me in your bed, and find me wild, but you will never claim anything more than that." She shoved his hand away. "Leave me now, my lord."

For a long moment Tynan only stared at her, seeing just how deep the wound went for her. A pulse in his sex insisted he take her, and his blood pushed so quickly through his body that he was nearly dizzy with longing, but he willed himself to step back. "You will, one day, come to me, Adriana." He lifted his chin. "Mark me."

Before he could make any move he might regret— more than those he would already rue by morning— he strode away, buttoning his coat as he went to hide himself from the servants. At the door he thought better of his retreat and turned.

"My lady," he said deliberately, "in the morning we will ride. In Hyde Park. And on Friday next, we will attend a ball hosted by the Duchess of Sherbourne."

She could not hide the stunned amazement that announcement brought. "How on earth did you manage that?"

Stung pride made his tongue sharp. "Some women enjoy my attentions."

That haughty chin rose and a cynical smile curled her mouth. "Oh, I'm quite sure of that."

He left her. Left the conservatory and called for the carriage to take him to the coffeehouse Gabriel liked. At least one member of this infernal family was agreeable.

⋆　　⋆　　⋆

Adriana had not the strength to move after Tynan stalked away. Her hips were weak and her hands shook, and she simply slid down and sat on the floor, staring with a kind of stunned horror at the candles which flickered in a draft and caused reflections on the panes of glass around them, echoing over and over. In this pane the flames were thin and long, in that one, short and blurred, in another, perfectly reproduced. Like her past, echoing in the present, sometimes skewed, sometimes clear, always flickering.

And in spite of those flickers of the past, she could not keep the moments with Tynan at bay. They replayed themselves in her imagination without her leave, illuminating one moment and another: his head on her hair and his hands on her back; the feel of his fingers lacing through hers, slow and sweet and arousing; the smell of his neck, which had tempted her too much.

And more: his mouth, hovering so deliberately close to hers as his hand touched her breast; his fingers on her breast, on the bare skin; his thumbnail so erotically scraping over her nipple. With a cry she covered the place with her own hand, wanting to rub the sensation away.

Today, in the shop, when his eyes had been so full and deep and frankly admiring, had she not wanted to stand before him without the cloak of fabric, stand naked and see that approval turn to deepest need?

She clenched her fists and pressed them to her eyes. Last night Cassandra had worried about her penchant for falling in love. What she had not told Cassandra was that she'd burned for those boys of her youth. Burned, night after night, imagining Antoine's kiss. He'd had a mouth that was shaped like a bow, full beneath, slimmer above, and the flesh was dark red, his teeth so white against it that she could not sleep at night for thinking of the contrast.

She had imagined kissing him so clearly that she was sure the truth could not be as lovely as her imagination. But when she had at last tasted that sensual mouth, taken her first taste of the forbidden, her girlish imaginings had evaporated in a sudden puff. His mouth had been a thousand times more. He'd been afraid at first, afraid to kiss a noble girl, afraid of being punished. But once he began, once she responded with such enthusiasm, he'd lost his fear. They kissed and kissed and kissed, at every opportunity, for months, until they were unhappily discovered and the boy was sent to a neighboring plantation. She'd missed him for a long time.

No, not him. His kiss. The feel of him.

Then there had been Harold, the boy on the ship, who had not ever managed to kiss her, but held her hand and expressed himself that way, touching and touching and touching her fingers, her palm, her wrist. In its way, it had been as erotic as Antoine's kiss.

Adriana pressed her fists more tightly to her forehead, resisting the last. Malvern. *Everett*. It had been his want of her that had been so inflaming. A handsome courtier with powerful relatives and elegant manners and bearing who had chosen her from all the women in the London. The power had gone to her head.

And now her first test, and she was failing again. It did not matter if he was her husband—in fact it was somehow worse. What woman lusted after her husband? It was the very height of foolishness, especially when that husband was such a rake he had earned a nickname of his own. A name no doubt given him by women like the Duchess, who would honor him in spite of the scandals. Had they been lovers?

Was she going to meet his lovers everywhere? How many women did a rake enjoy? How many would have known the sight of his flat, supple belly by the light of a candle? How many would have known the skilled touch?

God, was she jealous?

With a moan, Adriana pushed her hands through her hair. Love or lust? Which had she felt with those boys and Malvern? Which was stirring in her now?

And which was more dangerous? Lust, by its very nature, burned through to cinders in time. Love would not. If it was lust kindled in her now, then the fates had sent her a test she was bound—for her own self-respect—to resist.

If it was love . . . She closed her eyes. If it was love, her doom was sealed forever, for not only would love lead her to fall to her passions, but she would also be left with her empty arms when his lust burned through. It was impossible to imagine a greater humiliation. For what would they say then, the wags and gossips? She could hear them all too clearly: "Poor Countess Glencove, so quick to love, so quickly left behind."

She winced, her eyes closing tight. No, that she could not bear.

She wanted a child, and would give that much of herself at the end of his foolish time of kisses. She would get herself a baby or two and play good wife to him when he required it, but for the rest, she must remain aloof, safeguard her heart and her passions.

But now, hiding still in the conservatory, she saw she'd been playing a foolish game, pretending, like a maiden, to resist out of shyness. She was no blushing virgin, and Tynan was right about one thing: she had to stop thinking like one. She had to go about with her chin upraised, with her haughtiest expression. She was a countess, the daughter of an earl, the wife of a man who was going to go far if his energy were any measure. She was also, she knew, beautiful.

Women would cut her. The men would not.

And for Tynan, the reverse was true. In women he'd find his allies. In men, resistance. In that, the match was brilliantly made.

She stood, brushing off her skirts. Yes, she would ride in Hyde Park in the morning. And she would go to the Duchess's ball in the gown he'd chosen.

As she gathered her paints, she considered that perhaps she ought to simply invite her husband to her bed, as well. It was the mystery that appealed to a rake, wasn't it?

But the very thought made her hands shake. No, she was not ready for that just yet. Not until she was stronger, until she had learned to rein her emotions more firmly. Not until she could sleep with him and reveal nothing at all of her own feelings would she cross that line.

✦ 10 ✦

As she drank her first cup of chocolate by the window of her bedroom, staring out at the dreary, wet day with a sense very like disappointment, a knock came to Adriana's door. Before she could call out entrance, her husband strode in. He was dressed to go out in a redingote and tall boots, and his expression was quite grim.

Adriana started to rise. "I'm sorry. I thought that the weather would prevent our riding. I have not—"

"Sit down." He took a hand from behind his back and revealed that he was holding a sheet of paper. His mouth in a hard line, he glared at the page, then slapped it on the table before her. "I felt I should be the one to show you."

Reluctantly, Adriana looked down. And all the blood in her body seemed to abruptly drain out in a rush. Her ears buzzed, and she put a hand on the table, suddenly sure she would faint.

Tynan caught her hand and said fiercely, "Breathe."

She sucked in a great breath and the faintness ebbed. Squaring her shoulders, she forced herself to take another look. It was a crude, satirical drawing. She'd seen scores in her life, political and scandalous; they were distributed on street corners and slyly tucked into the storefront windows of the printers who issued them.

But she had never been the object of one before. "It's so . . . vulgar," she said at last. The sketch showed a woman leering, lifting her skirts so high her garters showed. One breast nearly fell out of her bodice, and her hair was askew. Behind her lay a dead man, and around a corner peeked a lascivious-looking man. And behind him came a black face and a noble with a smoking gun. A tag line read: *Round Two?*

"Mmm," Tynan said, sweeping it up. "Flattering, too, wouldn't you say?"

She wanted to smile, but found it impossible. Her chocolate roiled in her stomach and she feared very much she would be sick. Pressing a napkin to her mouth, she shook her head. In sudden horror, she looked up at him. "Will it hurt Julian, do you think?"

He tucked the awful thing in his pocket. "I'll go out and see what I can discover on that score. The weather is too poor for our ride anyway."

She nodded dully.

For a moment more, he lingered, then—perhaps, she thought, because they had parted on such an uneasy note the evening before—he simply said, "Good day."

She did not rouse herself to watch him go. He had to be as horrified as she was. Odd that it made her feel so bereft.

By the time she emerged from her chamber an hour

later, neither Tynan nor Gabriel were anywhere about to keep her company. Resolving to avoid the trap of hiding and feeling sorry for herself that she'd indulged yesterday, she sent a note to Cassandra. Her sister returned regrets. *I have a most important engagement this afternoon,* she wrote. *Tomorrow, dearest.*

There was nothing to do. She read for a while, but found she could not sit still long enough to do the novel justice. Her attention kept wandering. Each time a servant passed in the halls, she wondered if they'd seen the cartoon, and could not bear to raise her eyes and see the hurriedly covered shock on their faces.

Finally she took out her writing box, stationed herself by the stove in the conservatory, and wrote a letter to Leander.

> *I am enjoying, this very moment, your collection of flowers. There are a good many in bloom; the roses, of course, and some others. My favorite is a yellow orchid with tiny brown spots on the petals. I am sure you would correct me in the correct Latin name if you were here. You must come soon for a visit, you know. You and Julian and Gabriel could trade adventure tales.*

The letter occupied three-quarters of a very quiet hour, during which a solid rain began to fall, casting a chill through the rooms. She fetched a warm shawl and put new coal on the fire, then wrote to Ophelia and Cleo, together. In this one she described the dressmaker's shop and the assistants and the French dolls and the gowns she'd ordered, knowing how much they would enjoy the vicarious pleasure of it. She left out the confrontation with Malvern's mother, of course. She ended with a cheerful postscript: *We are invited to a rout at the Duchess of Sherbourne's mansion. I shall wear the pink silk.*

She sealed both and gave them to a footman to be posted.

And still there was nothing to do. Around her the house echoed with silence, broken only by the murmur of voices from the kitchen or the absent humming of a maid as she went about her chores. Out in the street the world hurried on, and for a time she stood by the window of the parlor, looking out. She wondered where her brother and husband were, what exciting business engaged them; she imagined them in some bustling spot, with voices and newspapers and plenty of debate.

At home at Hartwood she would have gone out for a walk. The idea made her faint with terror today.

If she had been born a man, where would she be in this moment? Certainly she might have spent her morning engaged in correspondence, but it might not have been with family. Perhaps she would have been a scholar or in the church or engaged in politics.

No. She wrinkled her nose. Cassandra would have been the scholar, Phoebe in the church. It was impossible to imagine Ophelia as a man at all—she was so very suited to womanhood. Cleo? Cleo was as yet unformed, her interests colored by Ophelia's gentle frivolity.

What would she herself have loved? Adriana wondered. Adventure. Travel. Perhaps she'd have bought a commission and sailed the seas. Or built an import trade.

From the doorway the housekeeper asked, "Would you like some tea, milady? It's right cold this morning."

Drawn from her thoughts, Adriana turned, absurdly grateful for the small kindness. "Yes, Mary. Thank you."

She was bored. And lonely. It was too quiet here, and she was too afraid to venture out for fear of meeting yet another member of society who would cut her.

The idea bloomed naturally: What if she did not venture out as herself? What if she went out as a servant? Borrowed a gown from Fiona and pretended to be a housemaid running an errand for her mistress? She could buy a mutton pie for her lunch and eat it on a bench under a sheltering tree, with perhaps a little cider to wash it down with.

Or—a logical extension of her thoughts this morning—why not a man?

Well, there was one practical consideration. She wondered quite seriously if she could bind her breasts tightly enough to hide them. First she would try the servant's gown.

Why not? With a little chuckle she hurried upstairs to find Fiona, and found her darning a pair of much mended socks in the anteroom off her bedroom. "Fiona, I have a wicked plan, and need your help."

"Wicked, my lady?"

"Well, not *that* wicked." She plucked the socks from her maid's hands. "These are worn through. Throw them away and I'll see you have ten new pairs by day's end."

The girl's hazel eyes grew shrewd. "And what crime am I committing to get them?"

Adriana laughed. "No crime! I only—" She glanced over her shoulder and hurried to close the door before she continued. "I want to borrow your clothes. Some dress you keep for days off?"

"My lady, I have only two, and they are very poor."

"Let me see."

Plainly thinking her mistress had lost her wits, Fiona put down the darning and opened the small wardrobe in the corner. She took out a simple blue wool with a white collar. It was worn but generously cut. The other was also wool, this one the color of a good claret, and obviously Fiona's best. A little lace adorned the skirt and sleeves. "This suits you," Adriana said. "Put it on. I'll wear the blue. When you're ready, come help me dismantle my hair."

"Yes, milady." She did not quite dare look askance at Adriana, but her expression showed some alarm.

"We'll not do anything dangerous, Fiona," she said. "I promise."

She was quite transformed, Adriana thought, admiring herself in the mirror over her dressing table. Fiona was of a size, and the gown fit well, though she had to scramble for shoes, finally deciding on a pair of leather slippers she wore when the weather was fine for gardening. Fiona brushed out her hair and pinned it in a simple knot at the nape of her neck, then draped a large woolen shawl around her shoulders and pinned it at her waist.

"Will I do?" Adriana asked.

Fiona frowned doubtfully. "You look like a lady dressed as a peasant," she said sadly.

"Surely not!" She scowled at herself in the mirror.

"Do not stand quite so straight," she said. "Let your shoulders go, and your hips. Only ladies have to walk so straight, the rest of us have to work too hard— we've got to be free to move our bodies."

"Oh!" Adriana took a breath and shook her shoulders. She thought of childhood, of running along a beach with her brothers and of climbing trees. The tension left her hips suddenly, and she turned. "Better?"

Fiona's expression said not.

"Very well, then." She stripped off the shawl and put it in Fiona's arms. "I'll return in a trice."

She did not bother to rifle through either of her brothers' or her husband's things. They were all too thin to accommodate her bust. Instead she marched down the passageway to her father's room and pushed open the door.

The smell of him—leather and horse and powder— struck her with the force of a whip, cutting deep into vulnerable flesh. Stunned, she only stood in the doorway for a long moment, a sense of fresh loss upon her. The windows were shuttered, leaving the room dark and cold, and she felt strangely reluctant to enter. He'd not lived in these rooms for more than five years, not with any regularity, anyway, and her memories of him here all came from the days when she'd been presented at Court. Before he grew ill. Before she met Malvern. Before the duel.

She closed her eyes and leaned on the door frame for a moment, allowing the sense of her loss to fill her for one moment. She had genuinely, deeply loved James St. Ives. Unlike many fathers of her acquaintance, he'd never held himself distant from his children. He'd involved himself in their affairs—sometimes with maddening results—and arranged things to make them happy when he could. He talked with them, and listened, and wanted to know who they were. His loss had left her numb for months.

Somehow, she had forgotten him in all this upheaval the past few weeks, but it had been his hand that pushed it all in motion, hadn't it?

For the first time, she wondered what his purpose had been. What had he seen, particularly, in Tynan Spenser, to cause him to select the man from the scores he knew on some level or another? And Tynan himself had said that the Earl was most specific about which daughter he should wed—Adriana.

To the room that smelled of him so insistently, she said aloud, "What were you thinking, Papa?"

But of course there was no answer. Remembering her purpose, she went first to the windows and flung open the shutters, then marched to the wardrobe and pulled out a handful of coats. More of that rich smell came with them, along with dust that made her sneeze, twice.

The Earl of Albury had favored a dandy's colors—apple-green and bright yellow, satins in rather exuberant stripes, and sleeves heavy with lace. Perfect. She chose the green coat with gold buttons and a finely made shirt of lawn with cotton lace that would drip well over her knuckles. Before his illness, he'd been stout, so there was no trouble finding a waistcoat roomy enough to hide her bosom. Breeches to match, white stockings flocked with gold, and a pair of shoes with buckles. The whole was only a little outdated.

Finally, from the stands on a table, she chose a wig imported from France, made of natural auburn hair dressed in a queue. Gathering it all up, she closed the door carefully behind her and rushed back down the hall to her own chamber. Fiona stood up as Adriana rushed in with a happy squeal. "Not even my sister will know me when we're finished here," she cried.

The maid widened her eyes.

"Oh, don't worry," Adriana said. "No one will catch me out."

The girl helped her bind her breasts with a length of linen, and while Adriana pulled the shirt over her head, Fiona brushed the coat vigorously. They stuffed more bits of linen into the too-big shoes, and Adriana pulled on the silky gold and white stockings.

By then even Fiona grew a little giddy. "I've always had a yen to do this meself," she confessed, helping Adriana into the coat like a true valet. "But you're tall. It helps you." She took up the wig. "Sit down, milady."

They'd carefully pinned her hair into a circle around her head, and as Adriana sat, cocking her head in a faintly mocking way, she was deeply pleased. She didn't at all look like a woman, but a young man with too much time on his hands and a stipend to waste. In the servant's gown, she'd appeared only a slightly altered version of her youthful self, not at all invisible, as she'd hoped.

But now Fiona settled the wig on her head and the dark hair erased the last bits of Adriana. It made her skin paler yet, and took some of the brightness from her lips, putting the focus instead on her eyes, making them brilliantly blue, like the promising eyes of a rake.

She raised a brow and drawled, "Strike me blind."

Fiona could not halt a delighted little giggle, which she tried to catch back with her hand. Then she stepped back and made a little curtsy. "Milord."

Adriana even felt different as she rose. Taller, leaner, stronger. She liked the illusion of night-bred pallor the dark hair gave, liked the way her mouth appeared not flirtatious in a pout, but disdainful. Experimentally, she walked across the room, checking the fit of the shoes—and oddly, the sense of them being too large was a help. She set them down with more authority than she used in everyday life. From a casket on her table she withdrew a small bag of coins, which she tucked neatly in her waistcoat pocket. "Well, what do you think now, Fiona?"

"Very good."

"I suppose I have to venture out alone now," Adriana commented, admiring herself. "Wouldn't want your reputation harmed." She rolled her eyes. "Not that I can do it more damage than has been done simply by being my maid." Then a practical thought made her frown. "How am I going to get out of the house like this?"

Fiona grinned and fetched the hooded dun cloak from the bed. "Keep your head down till you're well away, and none will think to question it."

Adriana resolved to reward the girl richly upon her

return home this afternoon. She donned the cloak and tied it tight beneath her chin, tugging the front low to cover the edge of the wig. "Come with me, and play lookout."

The conspirators tiptoed to the door, where Fiona peeked out and waved her hand for Adriana to follow. They hurried down the hallway and paused again at the top of the stairs. Fiona held up her palm and they waited for Peter, one of the footmen, to move away. His footsteps faded toward the kitchen and Adriana clutched Fiona's elbow tightly for a moment. "Wish me good adventure," she whispered.

Instead Fiona said, "Be careful."

Adriana rushed down the stairs and slipped out the door. For several blocks she kept her head down against the steady drizzle, keeping her cloak close around her. Nearby a butcher's she ducked into an alley and shed the cloak, leaving it on a protruding nail for some lucky washerwoman to find. Although the color pained everyone, it was warm and in good condition, and it pleased her to think someone would get use from it.

Loosening her shoulders, letting her arms swing free by her side, she strode out into the gray day. The clothes were surprisingly warm, and the hat she'd tucked under her arm kept the worst of the rain from her face. For the first few blocks, she was very conscious of her masquerade, afraid at any moment that someone would look at her in shock and surprise and point a finger.

But the clothes themselves seemed to cause a shift in her. Very quickly, she was striding along in the too big shoes, her arms swinging loosely, the coat billowing out around her thighs. As she walked, without any particular sense of destination, she thought again of Martinique and her brothers and their games of pirate on the beaches and in the forests. In those days, Adriana had thought nothing of donning a pair of breeches and a shirt stolen from a brother. If her mother had lived, she would have likely made Adriana behave in a more ladylike fashion, but her father had been more indulgent.

She found a jaunty little bounce in her step, and to go with it, she created a story for her male persona. She was a cousin to the St. Iveses, since anyone who knew the family would see the resemblance. Given the preponderance of mythological names both her mother and her sister—Leander's mother—had bestowed on them, she ran through the choices in her mind, and with an ironic smile settled on Linus. Linus St. Ives, just come from India, a younger brother to Leander.

Linus, she decided, was a rake and a notorious gambler with uncanny luck. These guineas in her pocket now were winnings from the faro tables last evening, and she was anxious to waste them appropriately.

But first, something for Fiona. She ducked into a haberdashery and purchased ten pairs of good woolen stockings, but it did not seem enough to repay the maid's goodness this morning, so she ordered several lengths of ribbon in various colors, then spied a thick velvet in the same shade as the girl's good dress. "Give me that one, too," she said. Her voice was deep enough that she didn't need to alter it much, but to be sure, she roughened it ever so slightly. The man behind the counter seemed to notice nothing amiss. "Very good, sir," he said, and pointed out some silver buttons. "Maybe she'd like those as well."

Adriana waved a bored hand. "All right."

Duty discharged, she emerged from the shop with a wild sense of freedom and lifted her head to admire the streets that were hers for the day. To do with as she wished. Tucking the package wrapped in brown paper under her arm, she set out to see what she could see.

In Barclay's coffee shop, less than a half mile from where Adriana surveyed the world, Tynan hunched over the scandal sheets and pamphlets he'd collected this morning. Although the coffeehouses boasted of egalitarian mixing, there were certain differences between the various establishments. The Stag and Pointer, which Gabriel frequented most regularly, had evolved from a medieval tavern. It crouched between worlds; the City and all its political glories on one side, with the town's most crumbling tenements on the other. Its clientele reflected the mix, drawing the politically minded from the darkest neighborhoods. Barclay's, situated toward the West End and the more fashionable areas, attracted idle young lords who came to boast of their amorous and gaming exploits to other bored and wealthy young men who would inherit grand estates and titles . . . someday.

Tynan did not particularly care for the crowd here. He'd learned, as a young man, to ape their ennui, but he found their idleness appalling. Even at twenty he'd been industrious, building on his father's modest success in glass manufacturing, seeking new methods of generating capital and more efficiency, which could, in turn, be returned to the workers and the business, creating work where none existed. He'd come to London in those days to learn what he might of the ruling class. He'd learned well, learned to affect the good-humored boredom, the lazy witticisms required for membership.

He'd also availed himself of the abundance of females—widows and actresses and bored wives—and the other extravagances available to the men of his class. He'd been quite young, after all.

Now he came here to reestablish connections he'd made in those days, to feel out the political possibilities that might exist for him, and to reinforce the notion that he was a mindless fop who'd do no harm in Parliament.

But this noon he sat alone, scowling away any overture that came his way. He drank coffee and grimly surveyed the papers he'd collected this morning, from the crudest to the most wittily elegant, all gleefully exploiting this choice gossip.

The drawing he'd shown Adriana had told him this was bad. Much worse than he'd originally understood.

The collection showed him just how bad it was—and with a burn in his gut, he found it centered most intently upon the wife he'd taken. In various levels of crudity, she was shown tearing off her clothes, lifting her skirts, chasing a pack of men with her tongue hanging out.

And in spite of himself, he was shocked.

He supposed he'd thought it a simple matter of a rake seducing a naïve young virgin. The scandal sheets and lascivious tone of the drawings suggested that Adriana had been a more than willing participant. Was that true, or had Malvern's mother been busy?

"Spenser," said a voice at his elbow. "You're famous this morning, man."

He glanced up to find John Stead, Baron of Cheveley. Always gaunt, he now wore the hollow-eyed, pasty look of an opium addict. "Stead," Tynan said without interest. The man loathed him and made no secret of it, for Tynan had unwittingly stolen away an actress for whom Stead had conceived a desperate passion. "Enjoy it while it lasts," he added. "There'll be something to take its place next week."

Stead leaned a shoulder against the high back of the booth. "I don't think so." He crossed his arms lazily over his chest. "The trial starts Tuesday next, y'know. I'll be sitting with the House of Lords. Wouldn't it be a shame if we voted to hang?"

Tynan made his eyes cold. "A shame," he said, quelling the quick fear the words triggered in him. Then, recovering, he added, "Though not so much to me, since I stand to—" He broke off, his attention snared by a figure passing before the window of the shop.

"Excuse me," he said quickly, and leaving everything where it lay, pushed by Stead and rushed outside.

A thin youth in an apple-green coat and a black hat strode up the heavily trafficked street. He would have sworn the face belonged to his wife. Surely she had no more brothers?

Urgently, he pushed through the throng. The green coat disappeared around a wall. Tynan broke into a trot, ignoring the strange glances cast in his direction. He rushed around the corner and barreled into a stout matron in a black cap who upbraided him smartly with a sharp slap of her cane to his back. "Mind your manners, young man!"

"Sorry," he said breathlessly, peering over her shoulder. The green coat was gone. Although he followed for a bit longer, it was plain the figure was lost.

St. Bridget, he prayed soundlessly, don't let her be that much of a fool.

11

Adriana thoroughly enjoyed her day. She strolled boldly through the streets of London, stopping when she wished to browse the shops and stalls, nodding to gentlemen, smiling at ladies. She ducked into the infamous Child's to warm her hands and drink a cup of coffee, a shiver of cold fear and reckless excitement burning together on her spine. The men about paid her little mind when she picked up *The Spectator* and hid her nose behind it. The coffee was strong and hot, and after perusing the political news for any word of Julian's trial—there was none—she was on her way again.

By late afternoon the drizzle had stopped, but a cold wind came after it, cutting through the wool broadcloth to her very bones. After so long a day of walking, she was tired in a pleasant way, her spirits much improved. What cared she for the gossip of society? How could they touch her if they could not even see her?

It was a heady feeling indeed, and although she knew it was also made mostly of bravado, the relief from worry and shame was so deep she embraced it entirely. She was loath to give it up, to return home to the silence of the conservatory, the boredom of writing more letters.

For a moment she wondered about the possibility of calling on Cassandra, but her sister's note had made plain that she was engaged for the day. Idly, Adriana wondered what task held such urgency, and she realized with surprise how little she really knew of the details of her sister's town life. Cassandra might entertain lovers all day, or act on the stage, or be engaged in some other scandalous lifestyle that she knew nothing about.

Not likely, Adriana thought, smug in her own daring adventure. Cassandra had always been exceedingly cerebral. It was a great deal more likely that she'd found a commission to translate some Greek or Latin obscurity for the popular press. Adriana had read some of Cassandra's previous work, and her sister did have a flair, though Adriana could not imagine anything more dull.

The autumn sun began to sink by just past three, bringing new urgency to her need to decide what to do. It would be sensible to hail a carriage to deliver her a few blocks from the town house, but though she passed two in the rapidly chilling fall gloaming, she did not raise her hand.

And as if she'd known all along where she meant to end up, she turned into a narrow, old street near the City walls and paused uncertainly, disliking the sudden change in the spirit of the neighborhood. These were not at all the friendly streets she'd browsed today.

But there, housed in an ancient inn with half-timbered walls, was a sign announcing THE STAG AND POINTER. It stood between a bookshop and a tobacconist's. The bow-fronted window glowed with a cheery orange light.

Gabriel's haunt.

For most of the day she'd carefully steered clear of any of the places she might meet her own set, or anyone who would know her. It was not difficult—it had, after all, been five years since she'd been abroad in London, and her face had changed in that time. She knew people saw what they wanted to see, too, so they saw a handsome, effeminate youth of good family.

The temptation to make Gabriel laugh was too great to resist now, and she headed purposefully toward the cheerful window, carefully keeping her eyes averted from the pamphlets and cartoons posted in the window of the bookshop. If Gabriel was not here, she would depart immediately and return home.

And besides, she was curious.

The room was hot and large and not nearly as dark as she had imagined, for tallows guttered in sconces all around, and oil lamps lit darker corners. There were not many people about at this hour of the day. A pair of merchants ate a supper of mutton pie and ale, and a cluster of middle class youths bent over something, their cups shoved aside.

"What can I do for you, sir?" the proprietor asked from behind a corner bar. He was a tall black man with golden freckles. "We've mutton pie tonight."

"I'm seeking an associate of mine," she said in her huskiest tone. "Gabriel St. Ives. Have you seen him?"

"I have." The dark eyes were measuring, but evidently he found nothing amiss. "I'll give your name."

She settled with an elbow against the counter. "His

cousin, Linus St. Ives. And bring coffee," she added. Carelessly, she removed her hat and put it beside her, turning with what she hoped was idle curiosity to scan the other patrons.

No one at all seemed to notice her. A very good thing. The tightness in her shoulders eased the slightest bit.

From a room at the back, Gabriel emerged. The gold embroidery on his coat gleamed even in the darkness. The proprietor came behind him.

And after him, Tynan.

He saw her at the same moment she saw him, and at the rage in his eyes, Adriana very nearly bolted. She stood up, a tremor deep in her belly, and schooled her face to maintain the sleepy, lazily alert expression she realized in that instant she had taken from her husband.

"Linus," Gabriel said, holding out his hand. "So good to see you here."

Adriana gripped his hand. "Gabriel," she drawled, nodding.

"I haven't had the pleasure," Tynan said.

Gabriel's nostrils flared with amusement, the only betraying sign as he turned. "Of course," he said smoothly, "this is my cousin Linus St. Ives."

Adriana extended her hand. "Just in from India."

Tynan's hand enfolded hers, hot around her cold fingers. His thick lashes hid whatever expression might have shown in the low light, but she didn't need to see anything to sense the danger rolling from him. "How do you do."

"We were about to have some supper, Linus," Gabriel said. "Join us, will you?"

"Be honored."

Gabriel led the way back to the room from which they'd come. Adriana had assumed they were participating in a meeting of some sort, but although the room would have held a dozen, they were alone. The roof was low, held up by dark timbers, and a mullioned window looked toward what appeared to be an herb garden. She spied the rain-silvered fronds of an overgrown lavender. Within, candles supplemented the last dying rays of day.

Gabriel gently closed the door and turned to Adriana. "What possessed you?"

At the same moment, Tynan exploded, "Are you mad? Do you want to ruin your life, and mine with it?"

Her feminine self might have been cowed by their tone. Oddly, the young man she'd been all day only lifted a brow. "I was bored. Stuck in the house without a companion or a task. I thought I would lose my mind." She lifted a shoulder. "I tried one of Fiona's gowns first, but this worked better."

Tynan's eyes burned a hot blue against his dark face. She noticed for the first time that he looked drawn, and a wisp of hair had come free from the queue. "I saw you, walking past Barclay's this afternoon," he said, his mouth tight. "I knew it was you in a moment, though I couldn't catch you." He picked up a handful of pages and flung them across the table at her. "Have you seen what they're saying?" His lilt grew more exaggerated. "D'you have any idea?"

Stung by this abrupt intrusion of reality after her escape, Adriana shoved them back at him, sending papers flying into the air, onto the floor. "And haven't you learned yet that I do not care? Didn't I warn you?"

He slammed his hands down on the table and leaned over it, fury plain on his handsome face. "No! You've never given me the tale, only hints, and in those you make yourself so innocent, Riana! Bad luck, bad timing. A wolf stalking you."

Every word fell like a razor against her heart. She stared at him, more wounded by his rejection than she could possibly have imagined. His eyes burned with censure, and she looked down at the scattered papers.

Mutinously, she picked one up, and spoke in a low, mocking imitation of his Irish lilt. "Wounds your pride, does it, Lord Glencove?" She felt Gabriel's hand on her shoulder, but shrugged it off. "Maybe you shouldn't have reached so high above your station, then."

With a soft cry, she scraped all the papers into a pile and grabbed them, tearing them into pieces. Gabriel reached for her again, but she flung all the bits of paper at Tynan and whirled away, ready to stalk out.

Gabriel stopped her, putting an arm out to hold the door closed. Burning with humiliation and an anger wilder than any she'd ever felt, Adriana slammed the flat of her palm against his lower arm, hard. But he didn't budge. A hand came up and pressed against her neck. "Riana," he said quietly.

She raised her head. "All of you can do anything you wish, and nothing ever happens. How many lovers do you suppose Malvern had before me? A dozen? A hundred?" She turned. "How many did you have, Lord Glencove, when you were sowing your wild oats in town?"

The men exchanged a glance, an unreadable, manly

expression that professed ignorance. She gritted her teeth. "I had *one.*" The cursed tears welled in her throat and she frowned to force them back. "One," she repeated. "It was foolish. I was heedless and headstrong, but I think I've paid *enough.*"

"You have," Gabriel said gently. He put an arm around her shoulders, and gratefully, she rested her forehead against his chest. "You should never have paid at all."

He was so familiar, even after such a long time away. So familiar and dear. She leaned against him, as she always had, her hand gripped around his strong swordsman's arm, her forehead against his chest. And from him, from the brother who'd allowed—nay, encouraged—her in every endeavor, she drew strength. After a moment, she took a breath, blew it out, and straightened.

Tynan slumped in a chair, that loose lock of hair making him seem somehow vulnerable. It fell, dark and glossy, across his cheekbone, drawing attention to his uncommon nose. For the first time since he'd ridden so dashingly into her life, he looked . . . defeated. As if he felt her gaze, he raised his head. There in the aquamarine eyes, so clear and troubled, she saw regret.

But he did not speak, only looked away, a ruddy color coming into his cheeks, and Adriana realized that she, too, owed an apology. She'd forced one from him often enough. With a sigh, she took the wig from her head in a single gesture and stood there as herself. "Tynan, I spoke in anger. I apologize."

He nodded. "As did I," he said wearily, and rubbed a hand over his face, then dropped it. "Come," he said.

"I think it's time I heard the story of Malvern, whole and unvarnished. Can you do that?"

Adriana hesitated, then nodded. If he meant to be married to her, he might as well hear it. "It's not particularly pretty."

He gave her a wry expression, then looked to the scattered, torn paper on the floor. "So I gathered."

"The man will be bringing a supper soon," Gabriel said. "Put the wig back on. He's discreet, but it's better to go by the book when we're able." He cleared his throat. "They've set Julian's trial, Riana."

"When?" She fixed the wig, tucking hair under it where it had come loose.

Gabriel reached up and straightened it a bit, and tucked a stray wisp of blond into place. "Tuesday a week. It seems your husband met up with an enemy of his who gloated over it. He threatened to vote for hanging."

"I'll lie," Tynan said grimly. "Tell him that I stand to inherit if Julian hangs."

"Inherit?" Adriana frowned. "You know that's not possible."

"What difference, if it tempers his desire to hang your brother."

"Have you any other enemies we should be appraised of?"

"None I can think of."

A knock sounded, and a servant entered, bearing a platter of cheeses and meats and pickles, along with a fresh loaf of brown bread. Gabriel asked him to bring ale, and they occupied themselves with the food until he returned. When he had again departed, closing the door behind him, Tynan prompted, "Tell me of Malvern."

Adriana glanced at Gabriel, who gave a slight nod. She plucked out a chunk of cheese and took a bit of it, then began. "It was the first year I came to London, five years ago. I was presented to the King and Queen. Malvern was there."

She told the story simply, hesitantly at first, then with more courage. Malvern, glimpsing her at Court, had pursued her relentlessly for months. Each time she attended a rout or a ball or open days at Court, he appeared. He flattered her, charmed her, professed love upon sight.

For a moment she paused, examining an olive as she remembered all of it. "I resisted very prettily for the longest time," she said, "but he was very . . . persuasive."

"So he led you down a merry path, did he?"

Adriana glanced at Gabriel, who gave her a secretive little half smile, his tongue firmly in his cheek. "Well, not exactly," she said, and closed her eyes. "I was . . . headstrong."

"Were?"

"Am." She raised her eyes. "I am headstrong. Perhaps it was losing my mother so young. Perhaps it was Martinique. I let my senses carry me away." She paused, unable to look at either of them. "And once the breach was crossed . . . we . . . I . . . ." She winced. "I lost my head."

Tynan listened without expression as she talked, at first hesitantly, then with more certainty as she told a tale much like he'd expected. A debauched rake intent on having his way with a young virgin. Malvern had pursued her relentlessly for months, appearing at every rout and concert, finding ways to discover where she would be every moment.

But even as he listened, Tynan found his attention more on Adriana herself than upon the tale. It was odd to look at her in a wig and coat. As much as he disliked admitting it, even to himself, she mocked men very well in it. The dark wig gave her a pallor much as the black bombazine had, and underscored the shadows beneath her eyes, making her look the young rake who spent too many nights gaming and drinking and wenching. Somehow she had managed to hide her beautiful breasts beneath a buttoned waistcoat that was too large for her.

The biggest surprise was the way she had shed all the small, betraying gestures of a woman, the delicate nibbling of a corner of bread, the graceful tilt of a head, the careful, self-aware mannerisms of a sex that were constantly examined. As if the coat carried some magic, Adriana moved with long strides and her gestures were wider, and she bit with gusto into the meat, tearing into it without self-consciousness.

It was only her hands that would betray her. They were long and white and graceful, so delicate of bone that they could only belong to a woman. He did not know why, but found himself oddly moved by the sight of them, draped in lace, moving so beautifully as she talked. He did not think he'd ever noticed them before.

She paused in her tale, closed her eyes, and continued. "I will not lie to you, Spenser," she said quietly.

"When at last I fell to his charms, I no longer cared for the opinions of the wider world. I thought only with my senses."

"Did you believe he would marry you?"

She peered into the distance, face sober. "No," she said, and met his eyes.

A pain, one for which he could not find a source, burned in him at that. "I see."

She sighed. "You asked for the story. If I am dishonest, what point is there?"

He nodded. "How long did this go on?"

"A few months." She reached for Gabriel's hand, and he gave it easily.

Again Tynan felt a sense of loss for his own brother, and he was glad, however he felt about his wife, that she had her brothers to stand for her.

"And there it went very sour. He was not content to simply move on. First, he cut me very publicly, to embarrass me, I suppose. And then he—"

"And then he bragged," Gabriel said. "Julian heard him and called him out."

"And killed him," Tynan concluded.

"Yes," Adriana said.

Silence dropped, a very loud silence, it seemed to Tynan, echoing as it did with that very dramatic season five years before. He could not look at them.

It pained him to imagine what his mother would have made of all this, and what Aiden would have thought of this story.

He wrestled with his shock over marrying such a woman, and with the shame of finding he was not as forgiving as he'd always believed. If, by some miracle, he found a seat in the Commons to buy, how could he hold up his head in the company of those men? How could he sit at the head of a table full of guests, and wonder what lay in the minds of the men as they looked at his wife?

Ah, pride. A deadly, deadly sin.

"If you wish to annul the marriage, sir," Adriana said quietly, "I would not stand in your way."

He jerked up his head. She reached up and slid the wig off, as if removing all masks, and met his eyes with composed dignity. "I would prefer it to the grim prospect of sharing my life with a man who holds me in contempt."

He did not speak immediately, and suddenly all the confusion of the day's events cleared away. "No annulment," he said. "On the contrary, Lady Adriana, I was blessed to have fallen into your realm, so I might be taught the smallness of my own nature." With as much dignity as he could muster, he rose. "Excuse me."

He left them without looking back, walked out of the room and out of the shop, into a night as cold as winter on the sea. Through the dark streets he strode, remorse in his heart, strode past small fires burning in dark little squares, past alleys that would have made a much larger man tremble in fear. He sometimes heard the scrabble of footsteps and half hoped a thief or cutthroat would dare tackle him, for he would welcome the relief of a physical scuffle.

But instinct was well-developed in these mean streets, and they scented the brooding disturbance in the gentleman, and faded away into the shadows.

The church doors were open, and Tynan blinked as

he stood in the back for a long moment, his face tingling back to life as it warmed. For a moment he wondered at the wisdom of his instinctive push to come here, only fully realizing he'd come dressed entirely as himself. Anyone might have seen him.

But before he could go, a parishioner left the confessional, pulling a shawl over her head. Tynan took her place.

"Forgive me, Father, for I have sinned," he said in a hoarse voice. "It has been a year since my last confession."

Adriana waited, reading in her chamber, until she heard Tynan come in. Relief washed through her at the sound of his voice in the lower hall, and she flung a warm wrapper around her shoulders and crept out to meet him.

He went directly to his chamber, and she went quickly after him. At the closed door, she paused, her heart in her throat, to arrange her freshly brushed hair over her shoulders and pinch color into her cheeks. Then she raised a hand and knocked.

His voice was muffled. "Enter."

Adriana eased the door open. His back was to her as he shuffled through a handful of mail. "My lord?"

He whirled, obviously surprised. "Is there something wrong?"

"No." She swallowed and clutched her hands together. "I only wanted to thank you."

A soft, derisive sound came from him, and he tossed the mail aside. "You owe me nothing." Still without looking at her, he shed his coat, absently pulled the thong from his hair. It spilled free over his shoulders and down his back, a glorious shawl that framed his shadowed face with such power that Adriana felt it almost as a blow. "Go to bed," he said gently. "We'll ride in the morning, if the weather is fine."

She twisted her fingers so tightly they hurt and took a step toward him. "I came," she said, and her voice wavered enough it embarrassed her, "to give you your kiss."

He raised his head, and Adriana saw the pain cross it. A wave of something ached in her chest at the sight of his vulnerability, and she moved to stand before him. "I thought, considering the day, that you might want one particularly."

"You are too generous, my lady," he said roughly. His eyes burned, the green and blue almost lit from within. "And I do not, tonight, deserve your good opinion."

She lowered her eyes, afraid of showing too much. His hands hung loosely at his sides, and she took the left, nearest her, in both of her own. "Then allow me to kiss you," she whispered. With gratitude in her heart, she pressed her lips to his fingers, then put his hand on her cheek. "Thank you," she said, then dropped his hand and moved away, hoping he might call her back.

He did not, and Adriana walked to the door before she turned. He stood exactly as she'd left him, his hair loose and shimmering in the candlelight, his hands loose at his sides, his eyes . . . stricken. "Good night," she said, and closed the door.

12

As if Nature had a stake in the ride, the morning was clear and bright, free of the noxious yellow fog or even a wisp of cloud. It was the sort of crisp, clear autumn day that made every Englishman proud to be one, the sort that would draw every cranky dowager and young buck and tittering debutante out from their stuffy drawing rooms and into the sunshine.

Adriana was ready. She'd sent a footman around to Cassandra with a note, begging a habit to wear, and she admired herself in it now as Fiona put the finishing touches on her hair. The habit was a vivid, deep turquoise, with a demure neckline but a close fit through the torso and waist. To afford comfort on the hunt, the skirt was wide and simple, and Adriana thought it would do very nicely. She finished it with a hat in the same turquoise, trimmed with dyed ostrich feathers that plumed behind her.

Tynan had already breakfasted and left word he'd meet her in the stables. She strode outside with a sense of purpose, her crop in hand, and met him leading the horses out.

And as if he'd had the same impulse as she, he was dressed gloriously himself. Gone was the somber black. He wore a vivid green coat and breeches, with a beautifully embroidered waistcoat. His leather boots were highly polished, and a tricorn hat sat on his head. Spying Adriana, he paused for a moment.

And here, now, was a shift between them. It was nothing she could name, but as their eyes met across the yard, a shimmering pleasure filled her. There was admiration in his face, and a shared sense of purpose, and, finally, a kind of camaraderie that had been missing till now.

He swept off his hat and bowed low. "I see we're both adorned for battle." His grin was rakish and irresistible. "Well done."

With a haughty smile, she inclined her head and flipped open a fan. "Weapons ready."

He extended a hand, and she took it, allowing him to assist her. Then he mounted his own horse, that fine black gelding he'd ridden into Hartwood that first day.

"What, no ribbons in his mane this morning?" Adriana asked lightly.

"'Tis better in some settings not to be too Irish," he said, and winked. "Though he's fine enough for a king of Ireland, wouldn't you say?"

"Indeed."

They set off at a mild pace, taking a winding route through the forest of tall, clean town houses clustered around the squares that sprung up every quarter mile or so. The streets were already thick with traffic, peddlers and servants, chaises and carriages of every description, dashing phaetons, and well-bred horses and pairs of young ladies in broad hats trailed by bored footman.

Adriana breathed it all in, raising her eyes to admire the newly turned bright gold of leaves against a brilliant sky, reveling in the clatter of horses and carts on the uneven streets, the harsh calls of peddlers crying their wares. She even enjoyed the odd mix of horse and bread scenting the air.

"Such glorious weather should assure the park will be crowded," she remarked.

"I expect you're right, Countess." He guided his horse around a pothole and then looked at her. "We've one chance to set the spirit here. Can you brazen it out?"

"I'm ready."

The blue eyes sharpened. "Can you pretend to be madly in love?"

Adriana frowned. "Why?"

He set his mouth, and reined in at the edge of the long, wide expanse of green that was the park. "Listen closely, my dear, and do not mistake my meaning."

She nodded, reining in beside him.

"Everyone here will have seen some version of the scandal sheets by now."

"You don't say."

He looked away, as if considering his next words. Adriana found herself admiring the strong, clean lines of his face, a softness in her chest.

"The only emotion you must not show here is shame," he said finally. "I tried to force that on you yesterday, and you forced it back at me, and your way is better. They'll feed on shame like crows."

"I understand."

"Good. And we'll give the impression of a love match for the same reason. You didn't marry an Irishman because no one else would have you—"

She didn't know why, but that made her smile. "Even though it's true."

"And I did not come to you with hopes of a seat in Parliament, but because I was smitten by your allure." He lifted a brow mockingly. "It does your reputation no harm to have captured the *heart* of a rake."

"I see. Especially one with such a nickname."

"Ah!" She would have sworn it was discomfort that made that bar of color seep into his cheekbones. "I didn't realize you'd heard it."

"Oh, yes. The Black Angel." Adriana said it with relish. Unable to resist, she leaned in close. "Are you really so close to heaven, my lord?"

His lashes dropped in that alluring way that he had, and he raised a brow. "There are those who've made their comparisons."

Adriana laughed. Spying an open carriage coming their way on the path, she leaned in and put her hand on his shoulder as if unable to resist touching him. "Remember, Spenser," she said clearly. "I am only *acting* the coquette today." She lifted a gloved hand to his cheek, "To impress the dowagers like these passing us now." Slowly, she caressed the hard cut of his clean-shaven jaw, staring into his eyes. "They're taking down every detail as we sit here."

"Excellent," he said, and took her wrist and put her hand on his chest, his eyes glittering merrily as he pressed her palm close, presumably against his heart. "I do admire your hat, my dear."

Adriana blinked and put her other hand on her own heart. "I vow that embroidery on your vest is the finest I've seen. What is that pattern?"

"Celtic knotwork," he said, and gravely bent his head to her hand, planting a kiss on her knuckles. "The girls in my village have found a market for it."

The carriage passed, and Adriana could not halt a chuckle. "Oh, that should do nicely."

"As a start." He took his reins and Adriana followed. "By the way," he said as the horses began to walk. "This bit of playacting does not cancel my kisses."

"Oh?"

"That is a private matter between us."

A ripple passed through her, but Adriana nodded. "As you wish."

As expected, the park was full of those out to take in the fine weather. Adriana braced herself to be brave as she recognized the crest of a family she had known in the past, but her mouth went dry.

"Steady," Tynan said quietly, and stretched out a hand. "Tell me who these people are as we pass."

Relieved to have a reason to look away from the open coach, Adriana smiled brightly and falsely at her companion. "You mean you aren't acquainted with everyone in town?"

"Hardly."

"They are the daughters and wife of Lord Meecham. The young woman is Lady Meredith, who should be married by now and is not. The mother is plain by her pinched mouth—see how she scents my approach?"

"Look at her," Tynan ordered. "And smile."

"I cannot!"

He gripped her hand tightly across the space between their horses. "Do it."

She raised her chin and fixed her mouth in a smile she hoped was at least supercilious, and turned her head. It was faintly possible to do it only by blurring her vision over the icy stare of Lady Meecham, then over the curious and avid gaze of the daughter. The son, a baron of some lesser estate, caught her eye. To her amazement, he winked.

They passed and Adriana let out a breath, taking her hand back to flip open her fan and wave it urgently. "I shall faint if I'm required to do that around the entire promenade."

"No, you won't."

And she did not, of course. Tynan teased her and made jokes about hats and headdresses. To those with whom he was acquainted, he nodded, but did not stop, even when some of them clearly would have done so, curious about his bride.

In contrast, none of Adriana's former acquaintances appeared to feel compelled to do so much as acknowledge her. Those who gave her the hostile gaze of judgment were preferable to those she'd known who looked right through her, as if she were invisible. Her cheeks burned, but with Tynan at her side, it was not difficult to keep her head up. If she flagged, he nudged her, or made some droll comment on the occupants of the carriage.

As they neared the bridge crossing the Serpentine, a voice cried out, "Adriana!" It was the voice of a woman, and it startled Adriana so much that she tugged too hard on her reins and the horse nearly reared. She glanced behind her, but the sun was full in her eyes and she could only see the shape of an open curricle until it pulled even with her.

"Margaret!" Adriana cried.

"I'm so glad to have caught you! Are you in town long?" Tall and sturdy, with a plain, intelligent face, Margaret Harding was a school friend who'd been presented at Court the year before Adriana and generally acknowledged to be a poor catch. She'd surprised everyone by landing a handsome earl who was smitten with a woman who loved horses and dogs as much as he, and Adriana had heard they were happily raising dozens of spaniels, horses, and children on the Earl's sprawling Dorset estate.

Margaret rode alone this morning, unattended by any but a friendly black spaniel who put his shaggy paws happily on the side of the carriage and barked a greeting. Adriana chuckled. "Hello to you, too."

"Behave yourself, Loki," Margaret admonished, slapping the dog heartily on the flanks. "Where do you stay? May I call?"

"Of course. We're here for at least a month or two." She gestured toward Tynan. "May I present my husband, the Earl of Glencove, Tynan Spenser. This is Margaret, Countess Uppingham."

Tynan gave her his most charming smile. "Delighted."

Margaret beamed and dipped her head. "The pleasure is mine." With a quick glance around her, she said, "I must say, the pair of you are quite brave. The scandal sheets are brimming with the gossip this morning."

"Bound to happen," Tynan said with a shrug.

"Indeed," Margaret said briskly. "Richard is quite in an uproar over it all. A peer on trial for a duel! Whoever heard of such a thing?" The dog barked at an approaching horse, and Margaret shushed him again. "I'll call this afternoon and we will speak of all that we've missed, shall we?" She took up the reins. "And there's a concert tomorrow evening at Vauxhall. I remember how much you loved music. Shall we attend?"

Adriana started to refuse, but Tynan said smoothly, "Splendid idea. I adore concerts."

"Still in St. George Street?"

Adriana, unsettled with the speed of the engagements, nodded, then waved as Margaret cheerfully drove away.

"Not entirely without allies then, are you?" Tynan said with a smile.

She blinked. "I suppose I am not."

He leaned close suddenly. "That witch is arriving from the left. I'd know that monstrosity of hair at ninety paces. I think you should kiss me."

And for one wild moment, tempted by the dancing light in his eyes and the heady pleasure of the day and the surprise of discovering a friend in town, Adriana very nearly did just that. At the last moment she ducked her head, putting her gloved hand up over his mouth. "Not even for this masquerade will I kiss you, my lord."

He did not immediately straighten, but leaned as close as he dared, considering the beasts upon which they rode and whispered. "You will," he promised.

A shiver rippled down her spine. Yes, in all likelihood she would. But not yet.

Not yet.

* * *

After an hour, Tynan could see the strain mounting on Adriana's nerves. Her mouth looked tighter and her shoulders more rigid, and at last he declared the exercise over. Leaving the park at the west end, they rode slowly toward home, speaking little. They passed a little band of men passing out pamphlets on one corner, and by the cries, they were protesting labor practices of some sort.

As if they reminded her, Adriana said, "Gabriel told me you have a cause."

"Did he, now?"

"He did." She looked at him seriously. "He would not say what it was."

Good man, Tynan thought. He had been right to trust Gabriel. Carefully, he said, "I've told you, more or less. I wish to buy a seat in Parliament. Cromwell is a monster, I'm afraid. 'Twould suit me to influence things in regard to my countrymen."

"I don't understand."

He sighed. "What do you know of Irish politics, Adriana?"

"Little," she admitted. "Only the very skeleton, I suppose."

Tynan took a moment to consider what to present and how, without giving away his own, private struggle. "You needn't know much of anything but that your country has oppressed mine in every possible way the past three hundred years. Through taxes and export restrictions the land has been reduced to a most abject brand of poverty. In past years there've been some concessions made, but only because the people rioted in Dublin."

"Concessions like your glass manufacturing?"

"Aye. And some straw power in the Irish parliament that is meant to allow us to govern a bit on our own, though in practice, that has not yet been realized."

"So you've come to influence your land by serving in our government."

"Aye."

"There's nothing so mysterious in that."

"Not if you're a sensible person," he agreed. "But 'twould likely not do my cause any good if those who'd grant me the sale of a seat in the House of Commons knew my true motive." He raised a brow. "Better they think I'm a rake without a single brain who simply wants to play politics and likely won't show up for a vote in ten."

Surprise and delight mingled on her face, and for a moment Tynan was struck most forcefully with her dazzling beauty. "Tynan, that's brilliant!"

He inclined his head. "Thank you. One is certainly happy to meet with the approval of one's spouse." He paused. "Such folk as your friend would be an asset as well."

"Margaret? Yes, she would be. Or at least her husband."

"Will you invite them to dine with us?"

"Yes," she said without hesitation. "It would be my pleasure." Carefully, she looked away. "I have not thanked you for all you've done, Tynan, for me and my family. We were in the most dire straits before Julian returned, and I've been ungrateful when you were nothing but generous." They drew even with the stables. Tynan smoothly dismounted and went around to help her down.

But there, he paused, caught somehow by the halo of light that glazed her blond head. The blue of her habit caught in her eyes. When she gave him her hand to allow him to assist her, Tynan felt the past hour rush through his nerves, the teasing, the playful touches, the light flirtation, the subtle, powerful play of attraction between them.

All of it had kindled his quiet, constant desire for her, and now it swelled. When she dismounted, he did not let her go when she made to take her hand away.

Unalarmed, she turned. The blue eyes raised to his, eyes bright and clear, and unlike most of the women he'd known, these burned with knowledge, with a lively, enchanting intelligence. Her cheeks were flushed with exercise and he could smell the heady mix of sunlight and a clean breeze wafting from her hair.

And as if she did not know it was there, he saw yearning on her face, a yearning betrayed by the slight, convulsive tightening of her fingers over his own, of the slight flare of her nostrils. Her gaze slid to his mouth and back to his eyes, as if to utter a request she could not voice. If he had wished, he could have bent to taste those lips at last.

Instead he only let the moment stretch between them. He held her hand loosely, and his other hand touched the bend of her waist, and he let his own wish show on his face, but he did not move closer.

And in that long, suspended moment, he grew curiously aware of everything around them. The smell of hay and dung from the stables, the clatter of a harness, the lazy rumble of bees drinking the last of the season's nectar from bedraggled flowers in the garden.

He spoke from the heart. "You are a very beautiful woman, Adriana. It was a pleasure to be seen with you."

Her breath caught; he saw it in the quick swelling of her breast against her bodice. "Thank you," she said.

He forced himself to simply let go and offer his arm to escort her inside.

Even so, he was unable to quell the foolish, boyish leap of his pulse when she took it, when she smiled, almost shyly, at him.

Ah, Aiden, he thought. Do you see her? Do you approve?

❖ 13 ❖

When Tynan returned from his round of social calls, he found a note from Adriana waiting for him, and immediately went out again, to Cassandra's town house in Gerrard Street.

He was shown by Cassandra's servant to the downstairs parlor, where the sisters and Gabriel were assembled, their faces telling the tale even before he noted the untouched tea trays. Their grim expressions were out of place in the light, airy room. Painted in pastel tones, and boasting exquisite plasterwork highlighted with gilt, it invited a person to let go of a held breath, settle back, forget the troubles of the day. Long rectangular windows faced the back garden, adding to the light and airy feeling. A surprisingly conservative room for the famed salons, Tynan thought.

"Spenser," Cassandra said coolly from her place on the delicately made sofa. "Please sit down. Much of this concerns you."

He looked toward Adriana, hoping for some clue, but her eyes were shadowed, her mouth tight. With a sense of unease he slipped his coat from beneath him and perched on an upholstered chair. "Pray," he said, "what news could have given you such grim faces?"

"I have been informed," Cassandra said, her hands woven tightly together in her lap, "that there is a contingent among the House of Lords who wish to make an example of Julian." She jumped up and paced behind the sofa, the taffeta in her skirts rustling noisily. "I suspect Mrs. Pickering is behind it."

"Mrs. Pickering?"

Adriana answered. "Malvern's mother."

"Ah." He narrowed his eyes. "How is it she wields such power as to turn a body of men against their own? She's well past the courtesan's age of influence."

"She has a curious effect on men," Gabriel offered. As if to occupy himself, he picked up his cooling cup and stirred a lump of sugar into it. He glanced at his sisters and back to Tynan. "Talents particularly appealing to men of certain . . . tastes."

Tynan thought of the horrendous pile of hair and the shrewish voice, the strident tones of her voice, and could not imagine what any man would find appealing about her. Except . . .

He blinked. "Ah."

Cassandra swished in a circle, paced to the wall and back again. "There is no way to know what number she has influenced, until the vote."

"Which would be a disaster for Julian, should the votes go the wrong way," Tynan said. He scowled. "Surely they would not hang him."

"Doubtful." Cassandra crossed her arms.

"But not entirely certain," Gabriel added.

Adriana made a soft, choked sound, and looking at her, Cassandra said, "Likely if he's guilty, it will mean transportation."

Adriana's face was drained of color, and Tynan felt an odd, deep pang. He wanted to move close, take her hand, give her courage, but she wore that invisible and definite cloak of distance he'd grown to recognize. She would not welcome it. Now she wiped her palms against each other, as if they were unclean. "There is more, Tynan."

He raised a single brow. "Yes?"

Gabriel put his cup and saucer down. "I have heard from Richard Stuart. He has decided not to sell his seat in the Commons."

Tynan felt Adriana's tight gaze on him, and he held carefully to a neutral expression, but the news hit him hard. "I see."

"Oh, you'll find another," Cassandra said briskly, bustling back to settle uneasily on the edge of the sofa. "If not now, within a year, the scandal will have died down and someone short on funds will leap on the chance to profit from his unpopulous seat." She arched a brow. "Who knows? Should Julian be transported, perhaps you'll be a lord in practice if not truth, and won't need the Commons."

"Enough, Cassandra," Gabriel said, rising. He looked at Tynan and cocked his head toward the door. Work to be done.

"You have a very low opinion of me indeed." Tynan stood, stiffly. "I must go. Riana, will you do me the honor of accompanying me?"

Startled, she blinked, and against the paleness of her

face, her eyes were huge, aggrieved. Her hands fell to her skirts and she nodded. "Of course."

Cassandra, evidently regretting her sharp words, followed the trio to the foyer. "What will you do?"

Gabriel lifted a shoulder. "We must find a way to influence the vote, I should think." He tugged on a pair of gloves. "See what you can accomplish among your set."

A servant brought their cloaks, and gave Adriana one Tynan had not seen, of a dark, rich blue. "An improvement," he commented. "What did you do with that awful mustard-colored thing?"

The faintest glimmer of amusement lightened the dark expression. "I left it in an alley yesterday."

"Good riddance."

Gabriel nodded at Cassandra, and the trio stepped into the cold evening. "I've an appointment I dare not break," he said. "Will you take the news to Julian, and I'll meet you there?"

"But we can't—" Adriana began.

"We can." Tynan handed her up into the waiting chaise. "Leave it to me. Mere Irishman I may be, but I've a way with prison guards." He nodded at Gabriel and climbed in behind Adriana.

Dark was falling, and Tynan realized he was quite famished. "Shall we visit the tea shop and take him some buns? I'm quite hungry, and I noticed you did not take your tea."

"If you like."

He gave directions to the coachman, deciding in an instant to sit beside her instead of across. There was a curious pleasure in feeling her arm against his, in the sight of her skirts squishing up to his thigh. Spying her gloved hands, the fingers worrying each other, he reached over impulsively and took one in his own. "You must stop fretting so, Riana," he said.

"I'm terrified, Tynan." She closed her eyes tightly. "I had no idea it could come this." A little breathlessly, she said, "We were both, Julian and I, foolish in our way. But it isn't as if this has never happened before!" She looked at him. "I can't bear the thought that he might hang for this."

He tightened his fingers around hers. "He will not hang. We won't allow that to happen."

She straightened a little, blowing out a breath as if to steady her nerves, and nodded. "And what about you? Does this man's refusal thwart your plans? Have you another option?"

"I'll not lie to you—that seat means the world to me, and I am sorely grieved to have lost it over this. But your sister spoke the truth: in a year's time, this scandal will be over, and there'll be some seat for me."

"Still, it will go easier for you if you press for an annulment," she said with quiet dignity. "No court would deny it."

A pain pierced him. "Is that what you want? For me to walk away and leave you to all this?"

Her lashes swept down. "No."

And as if the word were some honeyed balm to the just inflicted wound, his heart lifted absurdly. With a subtle shift of his body, he faced her, and took her chin in his free hand, lifting it toward him. She kept her eyes downcast for a moment, then took a breath and lifted the long, dark lashes.

"Nor I," he said quietly, and cupped that pale cheek in his hand, drawing warmth from it. In the wide, troubled eyes, he saw a wild mix of gratitude and sorrow and even . . . tenderness.

Which lead to a wave of tenderness of his own. He leaned close and put his forehead against hers, respecting her wish that their mouths should not kiss. "We'll stand together," he said.

Her fingers tightened almost painfully around his. "Tynan, you are too good. I pray no more of my past sins tarnish your plans. I do."

His heart ached in that moment, ached with an emotion he dared not examine too closely. He was nearly relieved when the chaise pulled to a halt and the coachman tapped on the roof. "Here we are!"

"Come," he said, as lightly as possible. "Let us feast on hot cross buns and clotted cream, then take some cheer to your brother." His smile was grim. "Doubtless he needs it as badly as we do."

She smiled. "Worse, I'm sure."

Adriana suspected it was a hefty bribe that bought them entrance to the Tower. She waited in the chaise, the package of warm buns in her lap, and peered out the window, made faintly apprehensive by the damp seeping into the air from the Thames and the sight of the forbidding walls of the old fortress. The waters of the moat eerily reflected the cold light of the moon.

Tynan came back. "We're in, love." He helped her down and offered his arm, and Adriana took it gratefully. A wet gust of wind, laden with fallen leaves and small bits of debris, slammed them suddenly and she winced away from it, turning her head into the shelter of Tynan's body until it passed. He lifted a hand, protecting her face, his own head bowed against it.

In the strange way of sexual appreciation, Adriana found herself suddenly and acutely aware of him. Even with the sharp fingers of wind buffeting them, she noticed a thousand details—the crook of his arm, taut above and below her hand on his elbow, the protective way he pressed her hand close to his ribs and put his long, graceful hand up as a shield for her face. In some odd way, she sensed the whole of his body in relation to the whole of her own, limbs and torso, shoulders and hips, and knew that he sensed the feeling between them, too. With a swift intensity, she ached for his hands to be on her, exploring her body as she longed to explore his, in the silence of a room lit only with a brace of candles, a long night's exploration of shared pleasure and discovery.

When the gust died, as abruptly as it had begun, Adriana lifted her head, a liquid sense of hunger in her belly and breasts. His hand, hitherto a shield only, came in and touched her flesh, slid down her neck, rested against her shoulder. In the darkness his eyes were shadowed, unreadable, but his mouth parted ever so slightly, and she saw the flare of his nostrils as he leaned in. She raised her chin, ready to meet that kiss, that mouth, at long last—

"You coming in or not?" cried a voice from the gate. "I ain't got all night!"

Tynan jerked his head around. "We're coming." He dropped his hand and urged her forward, and Adriana, trembling faintly, moved with him through the gates and into a dimly lit street. Along the walls were windows, most with glass, but not all, and behind them was the guttering, uneven light of cheap candles. A shadow loomed at one, and Adriana looked hurriedly away, fearful suddenly of what she would see. As if the ghosts of all those held here over the centuries lingered, the air was immensely cold, even when they were led across an open courtyard and past the ghostly gray White Tower to another farther on.

The guard led them up a tight, medieval stairway and to a heavy locked door. "Ye can't stay long," he said, and opened the door for them.

"Thank you," Tynan said.

Adriana entered first, and made a sound of dismay before she could catch it, for her brother was truly not himself. His hair, unbrushed and unbound, lay in a tangle down his back, and his face and hands were none too clean. He'd evidently been dozing with his head on the table, for he looked startled and confused, and an impression in the shape of his ring marked one cheek. He'd not shaved in several days.

"Adriana!" he said, and became aware of his appearance, smoothing his shirt front and touching his hair. "How did you get in?"

She did not stand on ceremony. "God!" she cried, and flung her arms around him, pressing a kiss to his head. "You are despairing, Julian! Do not despair." She stepped back and showed him the package. "Look what we've brought."

"And more," Tynan said, taking a bottle from his coat.

"Port?" Julian said in surprise.

"Aye." Tynan shrugged and turned away, settling himself on a three-legged stool in the corner.

"And look," Adriana said. "I even thought to bring a pot of clotted cream." She put the small pottery crock on the table. "It's even cold, still. We paid for the pot, and I swear the woman would sell the shirt off her back to my husband." Her hands fluttered. "Have some—"

Julian snared her hands in one of his own, and she was relieved beyond measure to see the smile on his mouth. "Adriana. Please sit."

She closed her mouth and nodded, doing as he asked.

"I have no visitors," he said calmly, taking a bun from the package. "So there's been no call for me to—" He shook his head. "Open that, will you, Riana?" He pointed with his chin at the bottle. "I apologize for my appearance. I'm half mad with ennui. If it weren't for the direction of my window, affording me a view of the street, I'd be full insane now."

"What can we bring you?"

He shook his head. "You've done well." As if to illustrate, he bit into the bun and savored it, then washed it down with a swig from the bottle. "It will only be another week. I spent longer in the hold of a ship."

Adriana's eyes widened. "The pair of you had quite a lot of adventures!"

"We did at that." He ate heartily for a moment. "Tell me, what news of outside?"

Tynan answered. "It's that very news we've come

to discuss." His tone was grave enough that Julian lifted his head and waited. "There's a move afoot to make an example of you."

"I see." Julian lowered his eyes, then gave a nod. "Malvern's mother, I suppose?" he asked Adriana.

"That's what they say." She gave him a puzzled look. "Though she certainly has lost her beauty. Gabriel said men of certain tastes still find her appealing?" She looked from Julian to Tynan. "What does that mean?"

The men exchanged an alarmed glance, and it annoyed her. "Oh, please. What do you think you're protecting me from?"

Julian chuckled. "There are things you'd rather not know, my dear."

"No, there isn't." Seeing that Julian would not answer, she looked to her husband. "Will *you* tell me?"

Oddly, a bar of color showed along his cheekbones. "Later."

"For now, let's change the subject, shall we?" Julian spread a bun with cream. "Amuse me with something besides the tale at hand."

"Well," Adriana said lightly, "I have had an adventure of my own."

"Indeed?"

Across the small room, Tynan chuckled. "She did."

Adriana, pleased by this small encouragement, spun out the tale of her outing in men's clothing, deliberately enhancing the more amusing aspects, exaggerating her voice and putting on a bit of a swagger when she told of entering Child's. As she'd known it would, the story made Julian smile, then laugh.

"And what possessed you to do it at all, Riana?" he asked, down a quarter of the bottle and considerably more mellow by the relaxed set of his shoulders.

Momentarily at a loss, for she did not want to tell of the satirical drawings, she glanced at Tynan. Smoothly, he said, "It was a dare, I'm afraid. She won."

In that moment, with that easy lie, Tynan Spenser stole her heart. She gave him a beatific smile.

"She never could resist a dare," Julian said.

"Is that so?"

As if this reminded him, Julian turned to Tynan. "I have heard tale of your brother, Spenser."

Adriana would have sworn Tynan paled, but she could detect nothing unusual in his voice. "Have you, now?"

Julian lifted the bottle, drank deeply, put it down. "In a letter from a woman in your village, as it happens. She told me of his untimely death."

Adriana felt the mood in the room shift. Both her brother and her husband were lazily alert, eyes hooded but sharp, bodies sprawled but wary. "And how is it, Lord Albury"—there was quite a roll to that R, a sure indication of Tynan's ire—"that you came to be writing to a woman in my village?"

"I was checking on you."

"Ah." A bitterness came on his mouth. "And have I passed your inspection, my lord?"

"I'd say so." He lifted the bottle. "If you hadn't, the port would have done it for you."

Adriana had the sense that they were discussing more than it appeared, and a needling of sharp curiosity stuck her. With effort she kept her mouth closed and simply looked between them, trying to gather clues. Tynan's face was uncommonly passive; even that mobile mouth was still. Julian wore not an expression of triumph, as she might have expected, but one of deep speculation.

The guard unceremoniously opened the door. "Long enough," he growled. "You've another visitor. These two have to go." In the shadows of the tiny landing, Gabriel's gold-embroidered coat glittered.

"So soon?" Adriana protested. "We've not—"

Tynan took her arm smoothly. "We'll be back, if we can."

Understanding him immediately, Adriana said, "Oh." With as much grace as she could gather, she bent to kiss her brother's head. "Do not despair, Julian. I think of you every moment."

He nodded, rising to extend a hand to Tynan. "Thank you," he said simply. And then, inexplicably, "I suppose it never hurt a man to be prayed over."

"True enough," Tynan said.

Julian winked at Adriana as she passed, and gave her arm a quick squeeze. With a heart considerably lighter than it had been, Adriana went down the stairs in silence.

During their short tenure a fog had rolled into the fortress from the river, bringing with it a smell of fish and salt. Stepping into the courtyard, Adriana shivered and tugged her cloak closer to her. "This is an evil place," she said. As if to underscore her words, a raven flew out of a hidden spot by the walk, crying out in harsh censure. Adriana, startled and repulsed, huddled close to Tynan, grasping his coat with a small cry.

He looped a strong arm around her shoulders. "Aye," he said. "I'll be as glad to be gone."

But even with the brace and warmth of his arm around her, the walk seemed very long. The miasmic fog, the flutter of heavy wings in hidden places, the spluttering light at barred windows all spoke of despair and death.

When they were safe in the chaise and clopping home through the dark streets, she felt guilt at her sense of relief. Julian would not be in that evil place if not for her heedlessness. Margaret said this afternoon that she needed to make amends in order to overcome her guilt. How could she possibly make amends to Julian for all he'd suffered? Or Gabriel, who'd been taken by slavers?

Come to that, she could *never* make it up to her father, who died believing his sons had been killed in an uprising in Martinique.

Staring out at the darkened streets, she sighed, gloom once again enveloping her. There was no way to make it all right again. The task was too enormous.

Then a thought made her frown and she turned to Tynan, also lost in his own thoughts. "What power does Malvern's mother hold?"

He made a soft noise of amusement, and cleared his throat. "There are men who like to be . . . shall we say . . . dominated."

"I don't understand. Say it plainly."

"All right." He touched his lips. "There are men— and women, too—who prefer to be tied up, even beaten. Abused, I suppose, though they do not view it that way."

"Oh." Adriana's eyes widened as she thought of it. "And she is the sort of woman who does the tying?"

"That's what they say."

"Well," she said without embarrassment, "that does make certain other matters a little more understandable."

"He did not abuse you?"

"Malvern? Oh, not at all." She shook her head. Thinking of the cryptic discussion between her brother and Tynan, she inclined her head and asked, "Tell me of your brother, Tynan. You never speak of him at all."

"What would you hear?"

"I don't know. Whatever you wish to tell me. What was he like?"

In the darkness, he turned to her and smiled. "In memory, I make him into a saint, but he was not that. He was headstrong and stubborn, like my father."

She chuckled. "Nothing like you, of course."

"Well, we did share that quality, though my mother said I was tenacious in the way of a cat, sneaky, while Aiden was a bull, barreling through anything in front of him."

"Did he marry?"

"No. His devotion was . . . complete." A more ragged edge roughened his voice. "In the end, it cost him his life."

She wanted to know how he'd died, but it was not the sort of question one asked. He would volunteer the information if he wished for her to have it. Instead she asked, "How long has it been?"

"Less than a year."

"You must miss him dreadfully." Without thinking, she reached for his hand, and he accepted her touch, turning his hand over to meet her palm to palm.

"That I do," he said.

"It must be difficult for you to watch me with my own brothers."

"No," he said clearly. "It is a joy."

The quiet, simple statement, rolling from him on that lovely Irish lilt, suddenly seemed to Adriana to sum up the whole of this man who'd come to her so abruptly, disturbing her safe, careful life in unexpected and unwelcome and startling ways. But at the heart of all of it, she knew why her father had liked him. He was a man of honor, a man of his word, and there was a very great river of kindness running through him. She tightened her grip. "Thank you for all you've done."

"And welcome you are," he said, and a hint of teasing crept into his voice. "I am quite certain you'll find a way to repay me." He lifted her hand and pressed a kiss to her inner wrist. "Will you not?"

She yanked her hand away. "Why are men ever thinking only of one thing?"

He laughed. "Do you not think of it, Riana?" He shifted, and settled an arm around her shoulders. An instant bolt of awareness spiked through her, shooting down her spine and into her belly, and it annoyed her. "Weren't you thinking of kisses outside the Tower?"

His breath whispered over her earlobe, across her jaw, and she closed her eyes. "A moment of weakness only."

"Not weakness—anticipation."

Anticipation. The scent of him enveloped her, and her flesh remembered suddenly the taut moment outside the Tower. The sense of awareness and connection flooded her now with an almost unbearable power. She closed her eyes as he touched her neck with his nose and, with a free hand, loosened the ties of her cloak. She tried to think of some word to stop him, but here in the dark, alone with him as the carriage rocked them side to side, she could not summon a single one.

"I think of kissing you all the day," he murmured, his hand sliding under the woolen cloak to light upon her shoulder. The tips of his fingers were cold and she shivered. "I think about where to land each one I am allowed. Should it be your ear?" He drew a line around the edge of it. "Or, perhaps, your throat?" All four fingers slid from her chin to her collarbone, light as feathers, and a shudder coursed down her spine, though she forced herself to remain still.

His voice deepened to a luxurious caress, the lilt rising and falling and rolling into her ear as his delicately wicked hands followed his narrative. "I wonder to myself which place would drive you mad? Here?" His fingers drifted over her breasts, slipped beneath the demure scarf she tucked into the bodice and, in a sudden gesture, pulled it free. She caught her breath, and knew he could tell she was aroused—her breath was hurried and shallow, and his hands were upon the upper swell of her breasts, so he could feel that. One finger edged along the lowest edge of her bodice, nearly upon her nipples if he but knew it, and she closed her eyes.

"Ah," he said, and he, too, was aroused. She heard it in the new huskiness in his voice. "There."

In the dark, rocking closer and closer into the circle of his arm, the cradle of his body, Adriana let go. She did not stop him when he tugged her close and bent her into the curve of his arm. She did not halt him when he brushed the fabric of her cloak away and bent his head over her breasts and pressed his sensual mouth to that low, low place just above the corner of her bodice.

She did not halt him. In fact she found herself arching toward him as his tongue came out and seared a line along the edge of that bodice, one side to the other, drawing a line across both breasts. Nor did she protest when his lips moved, and moved, and moved again, pressing hot, open-mouthed kisses over her breasts and her throat and back down. His hair brushed her chin and she made a soft sound, and as if he knew what she wished, he reached behind him and pulled the tie from his hair. It spilled free over his shoulders, around his face, scattered across her throat and touched her breasts.

She raised her hands to it, taking a handful and letting it spill over her arm, silky and rich and gloriously sensual, and it was this, his hair, that sent her reason into some dark closed place and allowed the fullness of her sensuality to spill forth. She touched his hair and his head, trailed her fingers over his eyelids and let him kiss her palm, her wrist, her fingers.

And when he hauled her into his lap, when her hips pressed hard into his member, she shifted more fully, pressing closer, and he groaned in deepest pleasure.

But even this did not make him into a wild beast, as it had often done with . . . others. Instead his head came up, and his hands, and he clutched her closer, putting his mouth against her throat while his hands tugged at her sleeves, tugging them down over her arms, pulling her bodice lower, lower.

Her breath caught at his intent and for one tiny moment she felt reason begin to invade as her breasts, pushed high by her corset, spilled from the top of her dress.

But his mouth was too quick for the protest to last. Those elegant lips, those deft fingers, captured her, and his fluid tongue, his gentle teeth, his suckling mouth fell to their carnal task. Her hands tightened in his hair and her breath left her, and she let go, let herself fall into the unimaginable pleasure of his swirling and teasing and scraping. A pressure built in her abdomen, and she found herself aching for more, for his tongue in her mouth and his—

The carriage rolled to a halt, and they ceased, frozen in place. She was sprawled over his lap, her breasts exposed, her arms trapped neatly at her sides by the dress. His hair spilled over his shoulders, mussed by her hands, and there was a glazed, lazy expression on his face that she knew was reflected on her own.

He acted quickly, tugging the cloak tight around her, smoothing back his hair and setting her beside him before the footman had even jumped down. With a quick grin at her, he said, "How many kisses did I spend?"

Her body still pulsed and there was something wicked about having her breasts naked beneath the cloak, but no matter how she struggled, she could not quite get her hands in place to fix it. "Help me!" she whispered insistently.

He let go of a wicked laugh. "Must I? It's ever so erotic to imagine that cloak slipping the tiniest bit."

"Tynan!"

"Pretend to sleep," he said as the door handle moved. "I'll carry you in."

There was no time to do anything else, so she complied. He swung her easily into his arms and managed the step to the ground with no trouble. "She's exhausted," he said jauntily. "I'll just take her up to bed."

Bed. She tensed. Was that what they were going to do now? What else had she expected?

"Keep your eyes closed," he murmured. "There're footmen all about."

It felt like her cloak was slipping, and with that covert, hidden part of her, she hoped it was. She hoped he was tortured by a glimpse of flesh he could not touch, to pay him back for this game. With a wicked little wiggle, she managed to get her hands in place to make *sure* a small glimpse of something showed.

"You're a wicked thing," he said on a harsh exhalation as they climbed the stairs. "And I vow you have the most beautiful breasts I've ere seen."

He reached the top and Adriana opened her eyes. "Are we out of sight?"

He shoved open her bedroom door and put her down and pressed her against the wall. "Aye, we are." Even through her skirts she felt the aggressive thrust of his member, and with a fierce sound he bent and put his mouth against her neck, sucking hard as his hands went under the cloak to touch her breasts. "How many kisses have I spent, Riana?" he breathed.

"A dozen at least."

"Too many for one night." His fingers teased her nipples to aching points. "But I must spend two more."

She knew she should reign herself in, but it was impossible. Her blood boiled with want of him, with the glory of the feelings he roused in her when he bent and opened his mouth over her right breast, lingering with heat and swirling tongue. "One," he whispered, pulling away, and moved to her left side. "Two."

He stepped back and covered her carefully. "I must save the rest."

"Must you?"

A wicked, wicked smile made his eyes glitter. Anticipation," he said, and before she could react, he slipped into the passageway and closed the door behind him.

Adriana, senses in a delicious uproar, slumped against the wall and closed her eyes.

Anticipation. She smiled.

14

Vauxhall was one of the many pleasure gardens scattered through the fashionable neighborhoods of London. Many of Adriana's former acquaintances had forsworn Vauxhall in favor of the more genteel Ranelagh, but she much preferred the former. The arches and promenade, the graceful statues and benches, the well-tended gardens themselves, all pleased her. But it was the music hall itself she most enjoyed. A high-ceilinged great hall with elegant plasterwork touched with gilt, it had, in fact, inspired Cassandra's parlor.

Under that arched roof gathered all the classes of London—a mark against it in many eyes, but a great benefit in Adriana's. It seemed to her criminal to limit music to the upper classes. One of the great beauties of life was music, and she felt it should be offered freely to all. And here, it was.

One of her gowns had been delivered earlier that afternoon, and Adriana wore it arrogantly, holding her head at a proud level as she and Tynan made their way up the promenade in the early dark, looking for Margaret. She knew eyes followed her—the deep blue velvet with its overskirt of gauze made the most of her extravagant figure, and the deeply cut bodice, even without the necklace of sapphires that had been her mother's, would have drawn attention.

In fact, she'd been appalled at the display, and had come down with a length of fine gossamer silk tucked over her shoulders and breasts. Tynan shook his head, smiling the faintest bit, and with a single, bold gesture tugged it out. "You're no blushing maiden, Riana, but a married woman in the full blossom of her beauty." His eyes had skated with dark appreciation over her flesh. "Wear it proudly. Haughtily."

As she walked down the promenade, it was not difficult to hold her head proudly, and it was Tynan who made it so. Dressed in an immaculate suit of midnight satin, the waistcoat again embroidered with the Celtic design that was so unusual, he was by far the most elegant and attractive man in the park. Women dipped their heads to gaze at him discreetly behind their fans, and young girls openly stared. Tall and lean, his eyes glittering with that hot light, he winked at one, smiled at another, caused a whole crowd of girls to giggle wildly as he passed.

And in her matching midnight dress, blond where he was dark, round where he was straight, lush where he was lean, Adriana thought they made a startlingly handsome couple.

Margaret had a box, and waved madly to them from it when they entered the building. Adriana waved back and would have gone straight to her, but Tynan held her back. "First we must be seen," he said, then leaned close as if whispering some intimacy.

"And remember how desperately in love we are."

Adriana smiled seductively up at him. "No woman here would fault me," she said sincerely. "You're the most dashingly handsome creature to have graced these walls in a decade."

His eyes glittered. "Am I, now?"

"You are." She flipped open her fan and inclined her head. "Though I suspect your conceit already informed you."

He laughed with genuine amusement, the sound ringing out as bold and robust as the man himself. Adriana caught on the sight of those big white teeth and felt a ripple of need go through her. To have those teeth on her flesh . . . !

Tucking her arm more closely to him, he led their promenade. "This will not be easy," he said, nodding to an acquaintance. "Hold steady."

And in a quarter turn it was plain this was much more difficult than a ride in Hyde Park, for there was no height from which to peer down at the hostile. And there was no buffer of wind and sun to protect her from the murmuring that began to rise around them, most of it inaudible, some of it less so. She heard "Malvern" and "duel" and "trial," and at last, "whore." Her face flamed, but Tynan had heard it, too, and tightened his grip.

Leaning close, he whispered, "Shall I kill him for you?"

She managed a small smile. "There's been enough of that, hasn't there?"

"Ah, perhaps." He glanced over his shoulder. "Pity. I would have enjoyed it, I think."

The incident made her remember another night, and with horror, she realized they should probably not have come. Not here. Urgently, she said, "Tynan, there is something you should—"

A man moved into their path and stopped. Adriana's heart squeezed as she recognized him—John Stead, Malvern's foppish second the day of the duel in Hyde Park. By his stance, he was more than a little drunk, and his eyes carried a feverishness Adriana found alarming. "Well if it isn't the merchant and his whore," he drawled.

To her surprise, Tynan said in a genial voice, "Stead. Have you met my wife?" Only then did Adriana see the hot color staining his cheekbones. "But I suppose you'll be jealous of my good fortune again, so you'll excuse us."

"I'll look forward to seeing your brother hang," Stead said to Adriana. There was no doubt he was very drunk, but the words struck horror through her anyway.

"Ah, but you'll not wish to vote that way," Tynan said, clapping Stead on the back. "Did I neglect to tell you the title will then be mine?"

The piggish eyes narrowed. "Is that so?" he drawled. Taking out a box of snuff, he cocked his head at Adriana. "Wasn't it here that you indulged yourself with Malvern in a box? I believe I was even here that night."

Adriana flinched, catching the quick, unguarded wound in Tynan's eyes. She looked away. "Honestly, darling," she drawled, "must we bore ourselves with this worm?"

"Certainly not." He made a move to go around.

Stead shifted slightly. "I'll take her when you're fin-ished with her, Spenser," he said. "Times a man doesn't mind leftovers."

Adriana felt the furious tenseness go through Tynan's body, and she countered with a strength of her own while pressuring his arm, that they move away. There was an odd long moment when she was gripping his upper arm, pushing with all her strength, and he was just as steadfastly pushing back.

"Do not respond," she said to her husband fiercely as she managed to move them along, despite Tynan's resistance. "He hopes to draw you into a duel to make Julian look bad. You may kill him ten times when this is done, but not now."

Abruptly, Tynan he relaxed. The color on his cheekbones remained, hectic and dangerous, but in every other way he appeared to be the perfect, light-hearted rake. He even managed a laugh, and glanced over his shoulder, then leaned close. "Do not think this is finished, Adriana," he said. "In this moment, I could cheerfully choke the breath from your pretty neck and not even blink with remorse. Do you under-stand me?"

"Very well," she said, spirits plummeting.

He had no memory of the music, only a sense of taut heat and the shattered brilliance of jewels reflecting the light of candles, and a burn in his chest that would not ease, a burn made of anger and hatred and humili-ation.

And desire. For Adriana burned, too, like a torch in

the darkness, her skin pale and pure against velvet, her throat draped in sapphires that fell in stars over the rise of her breasts, her hair swept up but catching all the light in the box as if she wore a halo. Her back stayed straight, her chin high, and for all his fury at her, he could not help but admire that strength of will.

Until last night, he had not seen how much like Julian she was. Both of them so icy and passionate by turns, those cool eyes reflecting far too much of what lay inside the mind. Tonight, as Julian had last night, she fought despair. It hovered in a pale mist over her too-bright eyes, and he'd added to it by responding to Stead's insinuations.

He shifted as a melody was sung by a tiny woman in a tiara, her voice three times as large as she. He could not halt himself from imagining another night, and his wife entangled in passion, making love in the shadows of some box here. It was not uncommon, of course. The boxes were deep and dark, and facilitated that sort of thing.

But Adriana would not even kiss him. Her own husband.

It seemed each time he looked about, there were more eyes fixed upon him, and he imagined pity on those English faces. Pity that he'd made so poor a marriage when he had so much to gain with his wits and his riches. Pity that he was saddled, not with the Venus of the town, but a soiled—

A tiny voice, *her* voice, echoed in him—that she'd only taken a single lover, when the rakes in these halls could never count high enough to encompass all of theirs.

Not even his own.

But he was not here to challenge all the world's views, he thought. He'd made a bad match here, one that would cost him all he hoped to gain. In the bargain, he'd made himself look a fool by insisting they appear to be in love—so now he looked not only misguided but imbecilic.

And wouldn't they laugh if they knew the truth—that he did not even avail himself of that wealth of sensuality, that lushness of figure and looseness of passion!

God, he could not bear it.

Abruptly, he leaned over to whisper to Margaret, "Will you see my wife home safely? There is business that requires my attention immediately."

"Of course." Her eyes were troubled, and she patted his hand.

It was churlish of him, but he left Adriana without a word, leaving her to wonder.

To ache, a little, as he did.

In her chamber, hours later, Adriana allowed Fiona to help her undress, reverently handling the blue velvet. Then she scrubbed the cosmetics from her face and Fiona took down her hair. Adriana stared dully at her reflection and thought of the start of the evening, which had begun so promisingly. Tynan, looking so dashing, with that pride in his eyes—pride that she was his wife, pride in her beauty and her obvious sensuality . . .

And then those very things had caused him to turn

away. She thought again, with the hollow sense of loss, of him leaving her so abruptly, his jaw tight, his eyes cold. And to her horror, tears welled up in her eyes.

She snatched the brush from Fiona. "Thank you," she said. "That will be all."

The girl lingered a moment, the worry plain in her eyes. "Miss—"

"Leave me."

She hurried out, and Adriana stared with fury at her own face, seized with an urge to scratch it, scratch her throat and cheeks and mar them irrevocably. If the scars were savage enough, she'd never worry again about the temptations of the flesh, now would she? She'd never face again the deep, thudding pain of that haughty rejection of a man who suddenly found himself soiled by her.

With a cry, she flung the tortoiseshell brush at the mirror. It crashed into the glass with a satisfying noise, and she was somehow pleased when a fragment flew out and nicked her lip. As the shards fell in a silvery heap to the dressing table, she touched her tongue to the spot and tasted blood. Bleakly, she slumped, and the terrible fury left her as suddenly as it had come.

A knock came at the door. Wearily, Adriana called, "Come in, Fiona." She stood. "You'll see I am unharmed."

But it was not Fiona. It was her husband, his neck-cloth sticking out of his pocket, his wavy hair mussed, his eyes dangerously alight. Warily, she took a step back. "I did not expect you tonight," she said mildly, raising her chin.

He closed the door behind him very deliberately. A stir of fear moved in her, one that took a sudden surge as he came into the light and she saw that he'd most definitely been fighting. A red bruise marred the blade of his cheekbone, and she thought she saw another at the edge of his jaw. The sight of his wound dredged up the most peculiar wish to tend him, and she hated herself for the weakness. She laced her fingers together tightly.

"Have you ever expected me, Riana?"

She didn't know how to answer him, and did not know how to manage him in this mood. "Are you drunk?"

"Unfortunately, not as drunk as I wished. It is my failing that I cannot tolerate the stuff long enough to truly obliterate anything. I only—" He touched his face. "—end up fighting."

A dangerous brightness lit his eyes, the green glowing amid the blue like some eerie faery light. "So have you come to beat me?" she said.

Tynan blinked. "No." He looked over his shoulder at the dressing table, then lifted a hand. Adriana flinched when it came close to her face, but he only used the tip of one finger to touch her lip. "You've already done that."

It brought back the whole horrendous evening, and she turned away, shame washing through her again, along with a pain she couldn't—wouldn't—name. With her back to him, she said, "Then what do you want?"

He took her arm, not gently, and turned her around. "Look at me," he said roughly. "I'll not fade away from lack of acknowledgment, as you seem to think your past will."

She yanked away from him violently. "Leave me!"

"Not this time, Adriana." He snared her, looping an arm around her body and dragging her next to him, and in spite of her fear and anger, she felt that familiar pulse rise in her, a thrilling, rumbling excitement. She hated herself for it, that she could still want him when he'd behaved so very badly.

She put her hands against his chest, half protesting. "Tynan, you're angry. We'll talk in the morning."

"No, Riana, I am not angry." His other hand curled around her neck and he shook his head. "I'm half mad with jealousy." His thumb moved on her neck and he looked there, as if there was some message he read. "And desire." His lashes, thick black curtains, rose. "I've come for my kiss."

"Please," she whispered, shamed that it would come to this, that she would find herself so very inflamed over a man who had humiliated her only hours before. "Do not insult me this way, Tynan. I can't bear it tonight."

"Insult you? You misunderstand me," he said in a low voice, bending closer and closer, until his breath fed her own. "I mean it as the highest of all compliments, that I cannot sleep another night without tasting your lips."

If he had been violent, she might have found the will to resist, but he was not. It was not gentle, either, but hungry—desperately hungry, and as rich as anything she knew. With a pounding heart, Adriana felt her will give way, and she dizzily gave herself up to the long-buried need to do just this, to open her mouth to his, to taste the richness of whiskey and caramel on his lips, to feast on the slow, restrained, but yearning way he kissed her lips, just her lips, then her tongue, and back to her mouth.

"Oh, God," she whispered when he pulled away for an instant, and her hands were somehow on his face, on that lean and beautiful jaw, feeling the sharpness of his high cheekbones and the hint of whiskers along his upper lip.

And as if her soft whisper was the blow that broke the dam, he grasped her face and captured her close and kissed her again, this time with no restraint in his wildly probing, devouring hunger, no restraint and no grace, only reckless passion. She kissed him back, too, able finally to express all the sorrow and rage and joy and despair that had hurtled through her these past weeks. She grasped him closer, putting her hands in his hair and rising on her toes, and pressed her body into the length of his.

She felt tears on her face, and could not halt them. As he kissed her with such deep need and deeper regard, she felt a sense of the world expanding all around her, inside of her, as if she stood at the door of her closed garden and saw a wild, open field beyond. She fancied she smelled fresh mown grass and a wind bearing the freshness of the sea, and all of it was simply Tynan.

Tynan.

She had dreamed of his lips and kiss, but had never imagined his big hands could be so gentle while his mouth was so rough, that there could be such a sense of holiness in the way a man touched her.

And when he broke away with a soft cry, she clutched his jacket and pressed her face into his neck, unable to speak the rush of feelings in her. His strong arms came down around her back, and she felt his lips on her hair, and for a long time they simply stood there, both of them wounded and heartsore, drawing strength from the other.

It was he who spoke at last, spoke quietly into her hair. "Forgive my fit of temper tonight, Adriana. I was cruel and you did not deserve that."

"No, I did not," she agreed. With a strength she did not know she had, she pushed away and lifted her head. "That's twice. I forgive this time, but not a third."

His face was sober as he nodded. He brushed a lock of hair from her face. Then, with an effort, he stepped back. "Good night, then."

Stunned, Adriana watched him cross the room, and the words were out before she could halt them. "Will you not stay?"

"No," he said roughly. "When it is time, you will come to me. That act I leave to your will."

Adriana watched him leave and the door swing shut with a sense of . . . what? Astonishment. Frustration. And below all that, a sweet, pure kind of song that made her feel as tall as a cedar, as wise as a queen. With a dizzy pleasure, she crossed her arms around herself and spun around in a circle, feeling her hair fly out from her body and the heat he'd roused on her skin.

And she knew exactly what to do. To Tynan Spenser, who was man enough to apologize and man enough to walk away from coercing her, that hot-tempered but very gentle man who had so many layers she wished to explore, she would offer the only gift she had.

Tynan dismissed Seamus once he'd assisted him with his boots and coat. Shirtless, he poured water into the bowl and washed the grime and fight from him, wincing a little at the bruise on his face. Ruefully, he leaned into the mirror to examine the place, shaking his head at the foolishness of expressing his roiling emotions with his fists, like a boy.

Bloody terrified, that's what he was feeling. He'd come to England intending to be sensible and make things move, and what was he doing? Bloody falling in love with a woman too many would call a whore. His mother, God rest her soul, for one.

What about Aiden? Tonight he ached for his brother's calm wisdom, his ability to see through to the heart of a matter. Would he, too, condemn Adriana as a whore?

And suddenly Tynan knew his brother would not. Staring into the dim reflection, he could almost imagine it was Aiden staring back at him, with that quirky bit of smile on the edge of his mouth. Absently, Tynan raised his hands in the prayerful gesture his brother had often employed, increasing the illusion that his brother stood on the other side of the glass, and he imagined the conversation.

She's lovely, Tynan. And strong. You came here knowing there was a scandal.

"Aye," he said quietly, crossing his arms on his chest as himself. "I didn't know how bad it would be. How can I hope to manipulate a House full of men to my favor, when they're all thinking of the sex I'm having at home and wonderin' how long she'll be faithful?" He scowled. "And the English are so bloody polite they'll never say a word straight to me, they'll just chuckle in their clubs all night about the—hell!" He broke off at the impossibility of it all. How could he do this? How could he love her and marry her and still do anything at all for his country and to avenge his brother?

He closed his eyes. It was impossible, all of it was impossible. He should have stayed home to fight these battles, instead of chasing across the seas on this mad plan. He did not belong here.

And Adriana did not belong in his world. He could not ask her to don that mantle.

Do you love her, then?

He glared at the mirror, seeing in his own face the truth. "She's a good woman, too, you know. Such a pleasure to sit and talk with her, to listen to her laughing. She loves her family, and she'll love her children and they'll never be afraid to be too loud. She won't turn my daughters into little dolls, either. And she'll have a lot of strapping sons—that's a woman made to bear plenty of children, mark my words, and never weaken from it."

And in his mind's eye his brother smiled. It was the smile they shared that had always shaken folk. There'd been those who'd said no man with such a wicked smile should ever be a priest, that it was the smile of a rake. And in Tynan it had been. His brother's charisma had been turned to higher service.

Listen to your heart, Tynan.

But what portion of his heart? That which told him he'd not find her like again in this world?

Or the one that lived to serve his people, his land?

Or that which told him that a true love would not ask so much of a woman as he would end up asking. Too much—

A scratch came at his door, and he called out entry, watching in the mirror as the door opened and Adriana came in. His heart slammed to a stop for a moment, until he saw what she wore—a hooded cloak. In confusion, he turned. "Where are you going?"

She closed the door and lifted her head. "Only here." She took a step forward, then halted, and he sensed a little uncertainty in her. "Were you speaking to someone?"

He did not even consider a lie. With a gesture toward the mirror, he said ruefully, "The ghost of my brother. In my mind, if nowhere else."

A troubled expression crossed her lovely face. "You must miss him unimaginably. When I thought Gabriel and Julian were dead, I felt a part of me had been cut off."

"Aye." He rubbed his ribs, and wondered what had brought her here. "Why are you wearing that?"

"Oh. Well." A blush, deep and painful, covered her face, and she backed away. "I'd thought . . ." She took a breath and lifted her hands to the hood, pulling it off. Below, her hair was loose, and she'd woven flowers into it, flowers plucked from the plants in the conservatory. They were twined, red and yellow and white, into the silky, endless length of it. She gave him a faint, apologetic smile. "But I see that you have matters of . . . or thoughts . . . I'll come back another time." She turned toward the door.

"Riana," he said softly, suspecting her purpose. "Why have you come?"

She turned back, clutching the cloak close about her, furthering his taut, earnest wish that what he suspected might be true. "You've given so much, Tynan," she whispered. "I wanted to give . . . something . . . back.

"Have you come to make love to me?"

She raised her head. Nodded. "You see, I have often kissed and I have had a wild affair, but there has never been the luxury for me to . . ." She hesitated, and he thought he could see, in the dim light, a rise of color in her cheeks.

Tynan lost all sense of his own breathing as she squared her shoulders resolutely and met his gaze. But her speech was broken airily by the rush of her breath when she said, at last, "No man has ever seen . . . all of me." She pulled the cloak from her shoulders and let it fall. "It's all I have to offer you."

And Tynan, in that moment, was lost. He felt momentarily faint at the sight of her, the clear perfection of her uncovered flesh, from the pale, broad forehead to the creamy shoulders, and made a soft sound. Her breasts were magnificent, full and high, crowned with deep rose nipples. Her belly swayed in toward the small light square of hair at the base, and her hips were wide and womanly, a lush swell above long legs and thighs that were not slim. He did not breathe as he filled his eyes with the gracefulness of her limbs, all of it gauzed with the flower-studded frosting of her hair.

She took a breath, and her breasts rose with it, making him most gloriously dizzy. "I most earnestly wish to make love to you, Tynan," she whispered.

And still he could not move. His hands felt awkward and too large at his sides; in his loins and chest, and a pulsing dizziness at the back of his head, his need of her battered him. He was afraid to step forward. As long as he was still, he remained in control.

He gathered himself, closed his mouth and raised his eyes to hers. "You are," he said in a voice raw even to his own ears, "the most beautiful creature God ever made."

And without a single other thought, he moved to her and fell to his knees to put his arms around her waist and kiss her smooth belly. Her flesh seared his own bare chest, and she made a small noise when he stood and kissed her mouth with all the need he'd kept pressed down. The fullness of her breasts pushed into his chest, and her hair brushed his arms, and her mouth was wild as an Irish dawn. He drank of that nimble tongue, smelling the exotic flowers she'd woven into her hair, and she kissed him joyfully in return, open and free, her arms twining about his neck, and even that brush—the flesh of her arm against his bare shoulder nearly made him cry out.

He swung her into his arms and put her on the bed, kissing her face, her eyes, feeling her hands on his back and chest. His hair suddenly fell around their faces, and she made a soft, pleased sound that broke through his stunned good fortune. He lifted up at little and grinned. "You like my hair," he said.

"Oh, yes." A glitter came into her eyes, too. "And you like my breasts."

He slid an open palm down from her shoulder, at last touching that wealth of flesh. He shifted his gaze to what his hand encompassed. "I like every part of you, Adriana. Within and without."

Her expression sobered and he thought for a moment there was a sheen of tears in her eyes. It pained him that any woman with such a gift for passion, the thing men sought beyond all others, should have been so foully treated. And by him, too.

"'Tis rare," he whispered, "to find such a beautiful woman with so sharp and quick a mind. And you—" He shifted so his hands could give proper homage, so he could begin to rouse her as she'd been roused in the coach. He curved his palms to fit her breasts, a tight hunger in his loins at the way they spilled over even his large hands. "You have passion, too." Reverently, he bent to kiss the upper swell, and ached at the softness. "There is naught on God's earth as soft as a woman's breast," he whispered.

And then there was no more reason in him. He touched the border of her nipple with his tongue, edging around the circle with a lost sense of excruciating anticipation, then touched the roused tip and at last took it all the way into his mouth with a low groan. Her back arched, and he felt her hands go to his hair, and she was pulling at him, dragging his lips to her own. "Kiss me, Tynan!" she cried.

He did, gladly, and there was a depth of intensity, a wildness of spirit in the joining of their mouths, that he found himself lost in the kissing for a long, long time, felt her lostness, too. There was sweetness and hunger and even relief in it, as if their lips had been carved from a single block of clay and now molded in recognition one to the other.

He took her breath into him, smelling the heat of her flesh and the nectar of flowers, and the length of her arms around his bare shoulders, the softness of her naked breasts against his chest. And it all struck him as unbearably precious.

But he'd been waiting for her a long time, and the pressure of his passion grew pointed and irresistible. He stroked her body. Her back. Her breasts, her waist, her legs, and felt her sinuous movements under his hands, and gloried in the stroke of her strong hands along his own body, felt her pushing away the offending cloth of his breeches.

And at last they were both as God had made them, flesh to flesh. He closed his eyes to feel the slide of her thighs against his own, the press of her belly, the whisper of her arms, the brush of her hair, shuddering when she arched closer, her breath hurrying over his shoulder, and opened her mouth on his neck, her mouth urgent, erotic.

This time there was light enough to see her as he shifted, and there was willingness in the shift of her hips, and there was a cry when they joined, such a deep and guttural and pleased sound that was both of their voices lifted and mingling, that he paused at the power growing at the base of his spine. She opened her eyes to look at him. "Kiss me," she whispered.

And he did as she asked, so their lips and tongues tangled as their bodies moved in ancient rhythm, until the movements were too violent and need overtook them. Tynan ached to make it last, this wonderment, this strangely sacred joining, but his body betrayed him and he went rigid, his hands too tight on her shoulders, and he knew it, his mouth hard against her neck. Even as the fury of his own passion ebbed, hers grew, and urgently he lifted his head and kissed her with all the fury of feeling in him, feeling teeth and bruises and never minding because her release was wild, wilder than his own, such a violence of reaction that he wondered how she could have lived with it inside of her. And still pulsing, he let himself down against her, pressing the whole of himself into the whole of her, his Adriana, his beautiful wife, and kissed her until they could not breathe.

For a long time Adriana drifted in a wilderness of sensation. Tynan's sleek body pressed against hers, the smell of his hair against her face, the weakness of her muscles, all trembling. He moved away long enough to pull the coverlet over them and held her close, his big hands smoothing her arms and back, his cheek against her hair.

And somehow there was no need of words. When her body ceased its shivering, he slid down to kiss her gently. And again. Kissed her softly, kissed her expertly. Sometimes it was only their tongues, sliding between relaxed mouths in the most delicate of dances. Sometimes he suckled at her lower lip, then her top, inviting her to do the same. Some were tiny brushes of their mouths. Some held teeth.

And while they kissed, their hands moved, exploring, learning the contours of the other's body. She trailed her palm down his side, over his hip, over his shoulder, loving the supple heat of his skin. His hands skimmed over her breast, her hip, her leg. And after a time his fingers slid between her legs, and his mouth plied hers, and he coaxed from her another orgasm that nearly equaled the first. At which time she rose and came back with a cloth to wash him and showed him that she, too, knew a little of this game by pleasing him with her mouth.

She loved the look of his long limbs, the taut belly and scatters of hair. His legs and chest were covered with dark hair as silky as that on his head, and his member lived in a nest of curls she liked almost as well. His hips were high and firm, as she had expected, and when he left her once to tend to nature, she greedily admired the long back and hips with a new level of arousal and knowledge. It seemed to her, looking at him, that the heavens had been very kind to create this thing called man.

At some point she lay lazily against his shoulder. "Tell me about your home, Tynan. You speak little of Ireland."

He stroked the curve of her elbow. "I try to think of it as little as possible."

"Why?"

"I am not truly at peace anywhere else," he admitted. "I was thinking this morning of the clean fog that comes off the ocean, not this yellow cloud that chokes the breath from a man."

She smiled, somehow pleased that at least one small portion of her original vision of him had been correct. "So you are a country man at heart."

"Aye." Absently, he brushed his toes over her foot. "You'd not believe how lovely it is, how wild. Sometimes it seems possible to see the old kings ride over a hill, or glimpse a fairy dancing in the shadows of the forest." He turned his blue-green eyes on her. "I sometimes think my blood comes from that ground, and when I'm too long from it, I begin to weaken."

She frowned. "Are your people Irish all the way back? How are you my cousin, then?"

His smile was wry. "Ties go in both directions, love. 'Twas some connection between your father's father and mine. I don't know what. My own family has been on this same land for two thousand years." One side of his mouth lifted into a teasing grin. "And sure, I'm the son of Aonghus Og, you know."

"And who might that be?"

His big hand curled around her breast, and his teeth flashed in his dark face. "The god of love, who has four birds around his head that are his kisses. Haven't you seen those birds flying around me?"

She laughed. "The god of love is Dionysus."

"That's my name, too." He yanked her hips close to his. "Sure and the women faint in me arms, breathless for want of me."

Her lids fell to half mast as her own desire rose again. "And maidens tear away their clothes to dance with you on the light of the full moon."

"I've no patience for maidens," he said, bending close to her lips. "I've a gift with the rest."

She loved him for that, and met him eagerly when he showed her, thoroughly, and there was no need for more speech. Only hands and kisses and flesh and limbs, moving one against the other, drunk on the pleasure and sensual alignment that had been brewing between them since that first night.

Somewhere in the darkest part of night, they fell asleep entwined. Adriana slept deeply, somehow safe in the circle of his arms. She dreamed she was in a garden of exuberant flowers, where birds sang freely, and it was this image in her mind when she awakened to find him gone.

There was light in the room, the yellowish light of a foggy dawn, so thin and ghostly she did not see him immediately. A little confused, she looked around and finally spied him, sitting in a chair in the gloom, his head bent into his hands. It was a posture of such abject despair that she did not immediately speak, alarm lighting in her heart. He wore only his breeches, and his hair spilled down over the hands that held his head.

When he shifted, making a soft sound like a groan of regret, she closed her eyes to pretend sleep once more, but her heart raced with worry and regret. What had she done to give him that expression? Where was the joy that had lain on his beautiful face last night?

She heard him move, and the bed bent under his weight. It seemed natural she should awaken at such a disturbance, and she tried to appear as if it happened naturally, slowly blinking open her sleepy eyes.

He bent over her with a grave expression, and without a word, bent down to kiss her fiercely, enveloping her with arms and lips and legs, her body still wrapped in the coverlet. "What is it, Tynan?" she whispered, wanting to comfort him.

"Nothing," he said roughly. "Everything. Let me hold you."

And she did, gave herself up to his mute sorrow. But unlike the playful and joyful ways they had joined through the night, this time there was deep soberness, a hunger that went far beyond the simple need for physical pleasure. It was as if he meant to bind her to him, bind her with his kiss and his excruciatingly gentle hands, and when he was in her, when they were as close as it was possible to be, he raised his head and looked at her with those shattered eyes. Adriana, her breath held, lifted her hands to brush and hold his hair from his face, offering silently her promise that she would do what she could, no matter what burden he carried. And as if it broke his heart, he made a broken noise and kissed her, and his movements grew intense, and they were lost, splintering together into whatever the future would hold for them both.

For good or ill.

15

In the morning, Tynan left to make calls. Adriana found
herself moving more slowly, and her thoughts returned
again and again to the moment when she'd awakened
to see Tynan, obviously aggrieved, with his head in his
hands. And when he came to her after that, there'd
been an almost desperate flavor to his embrace, as if
they would not have much time together.

It did not make any sense. What was he hiding from
her? She did not suspect him of lying, but at the same
time, he was careful about what he revealed, and this
morning Adriana felt she urgently needed answers.
She thought Gabriel knew some of it, but he had not
come home the night before, and she didn't relish the
idea of waiting around all day for him. Though before
last night she had begun to care about Tynan Spencer,
now her heart was in mortal danger, and if she needed
to pull away, it was best that she should know as soon
as possible.

Julian, she thought. He'd spoken of writing to
someone in Tynan's village; perhaps he knew something.

*   *   *

She recognized the guard at the Tower gates and gave him her best smile. To her surprise, he blinked as if dazzled and waved her through.

The morning was dark with autumn, and fog clung to hollows within the walls, but Adriana did not let the atmosphere distract her this time. She walked quickly and climbed the stairs to Julian's cell with a sense of purpose.

"Good morning," he said without surprise when the guard let her in, and then poked his head into the package she carried. "Ah! You're a gem."

"You don't seem very surprised," Adriana said with a smile, untying her cloak. His hair was neatly combed back from his face, and there was soap left on his jaw from shaving. Fondly, she reached up and wiped the last of it away.

"I saw you coming across the green." He took her cloak and set it on the bed, only then turning to her with a frown. "What's different about you this morning?"

She looked away, the night's journey swelling in her memory. "I don't know what you mean." Settling in the second chair at his rude table, she took out a loaf of freshly baked bread and buttered a slice. "You look well," she commented.

One side of his mouth lifted, one of the quirks of expression she had missed. In many ways, he'd always been terribly sober, and this slight wryness was as twinkling as he ever got, but she welcomed it. "You've a glow, sister," he said, and winked. "Your husband must be wooing you well."

To her amazement, Adriana blushed, and the blush made her chuckle. She batted his hand away when he would have touched her neck. "You've your secrets. Leave me to mine."

"All right, then." He broke off a hunk of cheese. "You must all be quite worried about my state of mind. I saw Gabriel last night, and your husband departed only an hour ago. Now you." A faint frown crossed his forehead. "Is it so worrisome? The pair of them will sidestep direct questions. You'll tell me the truth. Is it bad?"

"I don't honestly know, Julian. Only what they've told you." She inclined her head. "We'll be attending a ball at the Duchess of Sherbourne's at the end of the week. I suspect Ty—that my husband has plans for that."

Julian examined the cheese with narrowed eyes and took a bite, his body loose and calm. "They won't hang me, Riana. Our father commanded too much respect."

"But transportation? Surely you've had enough banishment."

A shadow crossed his face. "It does not matter. If I am transported, Gabriel can see to the girls as well as I, and I have faith in your husband's goodwill."

That lingering despair plucked at her. "What did you lose in the colonies, Julian? Or is it *who*?"

He shook his head, that pensiveness making a mask of his whittled clean face. He nearly spoke, then lifted a shoulder and leaned back in his chair. "No one. Nothing."

Clad as he was in a simple shirt, untied at the throat,

his chest showed, and Adriana glimpsed a mark at his collarbone. In surprise, she leaned forward. "Have you a tattoo?" she said, half delighted, half surprised.

He put a hand to the collar, as if to pull the shirt together, then gave her one of his rare smiles, and instead pulled the sides apart. A strangely appealing zigzag ran from shoulder to shoulder, just below his collarbone. "I also pierced my ear, but Gabriel seemed to think a gold earring was too much the pirate if I meant to stand trial in the House of Lords."

She laughed heartily. "I am quite jealous, you know. I was thinking the other morning what life I'd have chosen if fate had made me a man, and it was a life of adventure I would have liked."

"Yes," he agreed. "It would have suited you." He sobered suddenly and put down his cheese. "Tell me, Adriana, how you like this husband of yours."

She took a breath, folded her hands in her lap. "Actually, it is Tynan who brings me here. I have begun to wonder if there are secrets about him that I should know."

"Secrets?" Julian spoke as if the word bewildered him, but Adriana knew her brother well, and he could not hide that sudden intensity that lit his eyes, turning the pale gray to a hard silver. "I'm not sure I know what you mean."

She stood up, paced to the window and stared out at the Thames, wondering how to phrase her vague feelings. Finally, she turned. "I think he is, at heart, a most honorable man. It's like steel in him, a core of truth and strength that's very rare." She frowned. "But I sense, often, that he does not reveal everything to me."

Julian was still for a moment. "Perhaps you should give him time to reveal himself as he sees fit."

"I am falling in love with him, Julian," she said quietly. "That frightens me. If he has some terrible secret, I feel I should know before my heart goes beyond the place I can reclaim it."

He only looked at her. Measuring.

Adriana moved back, sat in the chair. "I think you know some of it. I would very much like answers."

"It isn't my place to tell you."

She made a sound of protest. "But I am your sister. He isn't your blood! I am."

"True. But I am a gentleman, and I took pains to discover what I could in order to put my own mind at ease, and in doing so, put him at a risk I did not understand." He lifted his hands, prayerlike, to his lips. "I do not wish to add to that risk."

She closed her eyes, truly afraid now. She couldn't think what secret would put Tynan at danger in any way, unless he were a murderer or some other criminal. "What danger, Julian? I don't understand."

He took her hand in his own. "This much I can tell you, Riana. He may ask more of you than you are willing to give, not because he is cruel, but because his task is much larger than he. Only you will know how much you're willing to give." He took a breath. "And, honestly, the girl I knew would not have been willing."

She snatched her hand away, stung to the very quick. "I am not that girl any longer. My life did not freeze when you left. I continued to live, day in and day out, and I grew up." Lifting her chin, she said, "I was a foolish, vain girl, Julian. I know that. But I *was* only a girl."

His lips quirked. "And I was a headstrong, idiot boy, and Malvern only a selfish little twit who probably did not deserve his fate, either."

"Does your conscience pain you on that count, Julian? I never thought to ask."

"It does," he said without emotion. "But one cannot travel backward, only forward."

"True." The tension between them had eased, and Adriana found she wished to stay a little. "Have you any cards? Would you like to play?"

"I do," he said. "And I would."

By the end of the day, Tynan was weary of wearing a mask of joviality, weary of the small talk he was forced to indulge for the sake of politics. Politics! All the petty maneuverings and flutters and favors made him impatient. There were times he despaired, imagining himself required to attend not only the sessions of the Irish parliament, but the English as well. He feared he'd drop dead of sheer boredom.

And yet, even for a man of action, there was no other path, save that of pure revolution, and he did not wish to choose violence to meet his ends. Too many of his own would die.

Only the thought of Adriana lightened his step as he came into the town house and the maid directed him to the plant room. He loosened his collar as he went, thinking with longing of less restrictive clothing, less foppish, less likely to be marred by the work of a man engaged in an honest day's work. The thought felt sour in some way, and he scowled as he came into the scented, humid room.

Adriana had not heard him enter, and he captured the instant of observation close: her blond head bent over her watercolors, the slope of a white shoulder contrasting against the rich ruby tone of her dress. There was some sadness about her, caught in the soberness of that lush and wicked mouth. A jolt of surprising hunger struck him, and without a thought he covered the distance between them and placed his hands on her shoulders, putting his mouth against her nape. She startled a little, but the ripple of reaction in her arms gave him the reward he'd sought. He closed his eyes, feeling a kind of relief.

She leaned into him and he circled her silky throat with his hands and pressed a kiss to her brow. "I've ached all day for you," he whispered, and put his hands lower, lightly resting on the upper rise of her breasts. "How will we manage dinner?"

With a strange graveness, she lifted his hand to her mouth. "Tynan, if I ask you questions, will you answer them?"

He stilled. "What questions?"

She turned and raised troubled eyes to his face. "What is it that haunts you? What secret do you keep?"

He shifted his body away from her, hid his face by examining the blossom of a vine curling up the girders. "I—" he broke off, realizing he did not wish to lie. He closed his eyes and turned to face her. "I have spent this day engaged in wearying discussions of all sorts, and longed only to come back here to you. I will reveal all that I am to you, in time. But allow us this little stretch of peace first. Can you?"

With a troubled expression, she rose. "Are you a murderer?"

He could not halt a small burst of laughter. "No. I am not violent and I have no mistress." He reached for her, a wash of dizziness on his spine as her scent filled his head. "Those things I promise," he whispered over her lips, and kissed her, knowing it was her weakness.

And it was as it had been the night before, a thick explosion of something carnal and yet deeper than that, enveloping them completely and mindlessly, and no more was said of his secrets at all. Not that night, or for several more.

With the trial looming so close, there were, suddenly, a great many things to do. Adriana and Gabriel met with barristers and others who helped them devise a strategy for the trial. On many things, they all agreed. Others, such as whether Adriana would be called to testify, were hotly debated. Gabriel was adamantly against it, insisting there were many others who could be called to tell the truth of events.

One afternoon, fresh from a rather heated session with the barrister, Adriana linked her arm through her brother's. He wore crisp blue satin, and the fabric was cool against her fingers. "You needn't be so fierce on my behalf," she said. "If I'm called, I'll manage."

"I won't have you dragged through it all again." His expression hardened, stubborn, and Adriana was reminded forcefully of their father.

She grinned at him. "You look so much like Papa when you set your jaw that way."

"Do I?" It pleased him.

"Yes. Stubborn idealism."

"When I was small, he was like a god. I wanted to be just like him. And then he went away for such a long, long time, and though Mama tried to excuse him, I was quite angry." The pale green eyes flashed with humor. "Then he came back and brought me so many sisters and even a brother!"

"Lucky you."

"Lucky you," he returned. "Who'd have taught you of pirates and swords?"

Adriana laughed, leaning into him fondly. The day was cold but bright, and the streets were full of traffic and noise and scents. Gabriel, so tall and graceful, exotic but obviously a gentleman, attracted attention wherever he went, and she basked a little in the shield he offered. Dressed plainly, with a hat to hide her hair, no one bothered with a second glance. "I did love pirates. I thought you'd grow up to be one."

He laughed. "Perhaps I have!"

"Ah! And what are you apt to steal?"

"Liberty," he said, lifting one heavy dark brow with a quick grin. "What say you, lady, will you take up your sword and join me?"

"My sword is a bit rusty these days."

"Well, then we shall have to practice. Will you spar with me?"

Happily, she lifted her head. "Yes! Oh, it would be fun! Will you come now? I've spent so little time with you, Gabriel."

"Of course now," he said, mockingly pulling up his chin. "One must always be ready."

"One for all . . ." she said, laughing.

They were in the back garden, warmed by their exertions, when Tynan found them. It was the sound of their shouts and laughter that drew him. A wide expanse of lawn butted up to the house, with doors to the conservatory and the back sitting room, and he went through the parlor.

At the sight that greeted him, Tynan paused, smiling. Gabriel was in his shirtsleeves and satin breeches and a pair of tall boots, polished to a gleaming shine. Adriana had shed her day dress in favor of a man's shirt and a simple skirt, and her hair was pulled back from her face into an untidy knot. They sparred joyfully, sister and brother, one so dark, the other so fair. Watching them, Tynan was struck by two things.

The first was that Gabriel was a remarkable swordsman, his rapier an extension of his athletic grace. He made a dance of it, thrusting and swinging back, tricking Adriana with sly feints and ruses, laughing broadly when he succeeded.

But while he enjoyed the company of Gabriel, who had somehow become his friend these past weeks, it was naturally Adriana who drew Tynan's eye. She, too, laughed and danced and thrust, obviously regaining a skill that had grown stale, and he saw yet another face of her—here was the wild child, the one who'd played happily with her brothers in a tropical world that retained its power to make her eyes grow soft even these many years later. Her expression shone, full of life and joy and exuberance, and he thought with an odd pinch of the woman he'd first encountered, bound up in black bombazine, hiding herself away.

Crossing his arms, he chose to stay back a little, puzzling over the seemingly endless facets of this woman. What about her brother brought out this side of her? This playful woman who cared little for fashion or vanity, who wiped sweat off her brow with a sleeve, attracted him violently.

Gabriel seemed to make her remember, with great pleasure, the adventurous side of her personality. It was to Gabriel she'd gone to share her adventure of dressing in men's clothing, he remembered.

And who brought on the woman in black bombazine? The contrite, sorrowing woman who was ashamed of her passion? Was that Cassandra?

He crossed his arms. No, with Cassandra, she seemed to be striving for some standard of proper behavior as defined by society, which struck Tynan as a little odd, since Cassandra obviously cared little for the opinions of the vain and shallow set. She was too intellectual to be satisfied with that.

Phoebe? No, not her, either. Phoebe was kind and good and would never make judgments.

With a shrug, he stepped out into the garden, thinking perhaps Adriana simply punished herself. He would have to see what he could do to prevent that. "Ho! Swords!" he said.

"Spenser," Gabriel said with a nod. "Will you spar?"

He settled on a bench. "I'll leave that to the two of you." Lifting a wicked brow at Adriana, he said, "'Tis a

pleasure to see a woman embrace a sport without wilt-
ing and whining."

Adriana, flushed, laughed. "No whining here. On
guard." She feinted toward him, a smile quirking one
side of her mouth. "We've uses for your ilk, mate."

The lovely, smoky blue of her eyes held a mischievous light. "D'you now?" he drawled.

Gabriel sat beside him, panting, and gave him the
sword. "She's worn me out," he said with a grin. "Your
turn."

Tynan stuck it in the ground, point down. "I've
other ways."

Adriana sighed in exaggerated annoyance. "I was
just regaining my arm!"

"No, my dear, you got your arm back an hour ago."
Gabriel shook his head. "If it weren't for me, you'd be
the best swordsman in England."

"I am the best *swordswoman*." But she gave it up and
sat on the bench with them, and they traded tales of the
business they'd all undertaken. Seated between them
in the crisp autumn day, Tynan almost forgot the loss
of his own family in the pleasure of finding a new one.
Covertly, he touched her fingers, and with a secret
smile she took it.

Adriana found herself loath to pursue the question of
Tynan's secrets, for the golden spirit of this time
seemed too precious to invade. And so she let it rest,
undisturbed, thinking she would somehow breach it
once the trial was done. There would be time enough
then.

Behind closed doors, in the garden of his world, she discovered that he devoured her with the same intense and curious devotion he expended upon everything else. He seemed to never tire of discovering some new way to please her, and he was as eager to accept her own more shyly offered but no less enthusiastic attempts to please him.

She discovered that he teased unmercifully and laughed with great gusto, and that there was no more beautiful sight in the world than his eyes, glittering with pleasure and humor and appreciation when he was buried deep within her. And nothing more moving than his sober mouth when he slept, unaware of her gaze. His world, the garden of his mind, truly did bloom in greater vividness than did the rest of the world's, though the storms, it was true, were fierce and battering. Sorrow could flash over him, turn him darkly brooding for long hours—and it seemed to her only natural that such a thing should be true. How could there be a capacity for joy without an equal capacity for sorrow?

In those first breathless days, she allowed nothing to intrude to spoil her pleasure. She did not ask herself if she was in love with her husband, simply allowed herself to feast at the banquet he offered. He, too, seemed content to drink of the cup that she offered.

On Thursday morning Cassandra appeared at the door to the town house as Adriana was taking her breakfast. A footman showed her into the dining room, and Adriana rose immediately, alarmed by the loose wildness of Cassandra's hair and the shock on her face. "What is it?" Adriana cried.

Cassandra wordlessly waved a letter, and Adriana snatched it from her. It was in Ophelia's unformed hand. The words were to the point: *Phoebe was thrown from her horse and she is in terrible pain. You must come.*

Adriana raised aggrieved eyes. "Nothing else?"

"No." She swallowed. "We must go to her now."

"Of course." Adriana found her mind frozen, captured in a hurrying circle of *what if? what if? what if?* With a bitter sense of regret, she thought of the letter she had begun on Sunday and did not finish.

A fall from a horse could lead to a long and agonizing death, or only a simple bruise. What did terrible pain mean? She pressed a hand to her ribs, feeling breathless, and gulped in a lungful of air. It only helped marginally. She nodded vaguely. "Right. We must go. I'll leave word with the servants. Gabriel and Tynan must stay. The trial . . ."

"Yes."

She thought, too, of the rout tomorrow evening at the Duchess's invitation, and felt deeply torn. Tynan needed for her to be on his arm and would be terribly disappointed if she did not return. Hastily, she found ink and pen and paper and wrote a note to him, promising she would return by evening the following day if at all possible. She gave instructions to the servants, and gave another note to a footman to take to the dressmaker. The ball gown was to be delivered this evening, and Adriana wanted to make sure nothing had gone awry.

Then she and Cassandra, both silent and grim behind faces they attempted to arrange into calm masks, were flying toward Hartwood. Thanks to the recent, steady rains, the roads were in miserable condition, and after two hours they were still only halfway. Adriana's nerves were screaming.

"I can't bear it if anything happens to Phoebe," she burst out at last.

Cassandra leaned forward and took her sister's gloved hands in her own. "Do not worry just yet. Ophelia is prone to drama, you know. Phoebe as like as not is abed with a headache and bruised derriere, no more."

"Yes. You're right, of course."

"At the very least, there is no point in fretting now, whilst we still have miles to go." She settled back, and before she spoke again, Adriana saw the sharp glitter in her eye. "How is your husband?"

"Very well." She folded her hands, kept her face blank, and countered with a probe of her own. "And what has occupied you so deeply that you cannot even spare an hour for your sister?"

"Oh, Riana, is that how it has seemed to you?" True distress marked her tone. "I did not think—"

To Adrana's surprise, a buried flare of anger now blazed up in her chest. "How else could I have taken it, Cassandra? You well knew what I would face in London, and it was even worse than any of us anticipated. And yet when I sent notes around, you had no time for me. It was only when news came about Julian that you deigned to see any of us."

Cassandra lowered her eyes, and—most unlike her—went very still. "I did not mean to desert you," she said quietly. "I'm only . . . engrossed in troubles of my own." She pressed her lips together and raised her head. "I'm not able to speak of them, not now, but I swear, Riana, I did not mean to leave you so alone. Will you forgive me?"

Again Adriana realized how little she knew of her sister's life. Always she had been a most private person—but nothing ever stimulated Adriana's curiosity like an intriguing secret. "Can you not even hint?"

"No." There was no broaching the word. "I am assisting a friend, that's all. And I cannot speak of it, or chance risking my friend's life."

"Oh." Adriana blinked, then lifted a shoulder. Lightly, she said, "I do not particularly forgive you, since the fate of your sister should have mattered more to you than the fate of a friend."

Cassandra rolled her eyes. "Yours is a matter of pride, not your life. Forgive me if I cannot give homage to your vanity."

"Vanity?" Adriana narrowed her eyes, thinking of the look in Tynan's eye at the coffeehouse the day she'd dressed as "Linus." He'd been appalled at the level of the scandal. "Have you actually *seen* any of the scandal sheets, sister dear?"

Cassandra looked down her nose, the morally superior one, the sure one, the one intellectually so far above their trivial desires for social acceptability. Adriana itched to slap her. "No."

"When you return home to your safe tower of intellectual superiority, Lady Cassandra, perhaps you will prevail upon one of your lackeys to procure them for you. I do believe I've starred in a satire from the nastiest pens and most talented hacks in most of London." She inclined her head, a bitter edge to her words.

"My personal favorite showed me with my skirts above my head—by my own greedy hands, mind you—and twenty hands all reaching for that which was exposed. I suppose it was an offense to my vanity, you're right. Now that I think of it like that, I'll simply not bother my empty little head about it any longer."

"Oh, Adriana! I'm sorry!" Her sister bent forward, contrite.

Adriana jerked away. "Do not touch me, Cassandra. I would not want you to be soiled with my shallowness." To her horror, she promptly burst into tears.

Cassandra flung herself across the chaise and wrapped her arms around her sister. "Forgive me, Riana, oh, please. I'm so sorry. You are so intense and wild and sensual, you scare me to death." She clutched her closer. "I'm so sorry."

Adriana hunched away from her, squeezing as close as she was able to the side of the carriage. A draft chilled her neck and the side of her face, and still she leaned away from the fierce arms of her sister, who was abjectly sorry, and Adriana knew it. Somehow, she could not simply let it go—the wound had gone deep, not just Cassandra's cavalier dismissal of what had been one of the most difficult challenges she had ever encountered, but the fact that Cassandra had put someone else ahead of her family, at a time they most insistently needed her.

The power of her anger was surprising and appalling. "Cassandra, please," she said, lifting a hand against her. "I am truly wounded just now and cannot—"

Cassandra pulled away, stiffly. "You will not forgive me?"

"There is nothing to forgive," Adriana said quietly. "You must serve your own life, as I must."

"Riana, what must I do? I am truly sorry to have been so selfish!"

"Nothing, Cassandra. Do nothing." She relented a little and took her sister's hand. "I forgive you. But I admit I am hurt in a way that simply needs—" She wiped her face. "—to be left alone for a little."

"As you wish." Cassandra moved to her own side of the carriage. Both of them fell silent, staring out at the wet landscape. The trees had lost their leaves now, and Adriana thought it looked dreary. She wanted to go back to London, to the conservatory. To Tynan, who made the world bloom no matter what the weather.

Just the thought of his face eased her heart a little. Last night he'd come in late and a little tipsy from drinking with Gabriel, and had been particularly demonstrative. There was about him such a passionate gentleness that it made her hips a little weak even to remember. Softly, she smiled, thinking of how lovely it was to kiss him, and meanwhile she absently stroked her face with her glove.

"Oh, God, Adriana!" Cassandra said. "Tell me you're not thinking of him right now."

And this was why she'd avoided Cassandra. The avoidance had gone both ways. "Let's not speak of that. I'm sorry I was so evil just now."

"Oh, we will talk. Have you fallen in love with him?"

Adriana let her hands fall to her lap and looked directly at her sister, who bristled all over like a porcupine, disapproval making her back a stiff rod, her shoulders oddly fragile in their bitterness. "I don't know," she said honestly.

Cassandra let go of a little cry of frustration. Melodramatic, Adriana thought. "Have you learned nothing?"

From a place deep within her, Adriana spoke with sudden clarity. "Yes. I have learned not all men are of the ilk of Malvern and your husband. Some are kind and good and honorable." She paused. "Julian, for example. And Gabriel."

"There's the trouble. Our father and our brothers left us expecting too much." Genuine pain showed in her dark brown eyes. "They did not properly prepare us for the world as it is."

"Oh, but they did, don't you see? They gave us a powerful standard of goodness, to which few men can measure. Therefore, we do not settle lightly, and demand the best."

"And I suppose," Cassandra said dryly, "that Lord Glencove is such a man?"

"I don't know," Adriana said slowly, honestly. "He might not be the best of husbands. He will, I am quite sure, be tempted to the arms of other women." She smiled with regret. "They do fling themselves in his path. But his heart is true to those things he believes. He is a man of honor. And great loyalty, I think."

"How can he be true of heart and faithless to his wife, Adriana?"

"Is the only measure of a man's goodness his ability to be a true husband to a wife he marries for political gain? I did not agree to marry him for any noble motive, as you well know. I traded my help for his funds to save our family. If we are able to find some harmony along the way, is that such a bad lot?"

"Yes!" Cassandra cried, and in her fierceness, took Adriana's hands tightly in her own. "Think of Papa and Mama. Think of him with Monique. Think of that laughter, that passion. How can you ask for less for yourself?"

A vision of Tynan's eyes, glowing green and blue with that light of passion, rose before her, and a depth of emotion she did not care to identify washed over her. "I have found what I want," she said quietly.

"Oh, look at you, Riana! I know that look. It's the lust in you that makes you assign high motives to men who please you physically. Good sex does not equal true love. I have no doubt Spenser is a magnificent lover—he has that air—and I'm sure you've quite enjoyed him." Her eyes went hard. "But do not give away your heart."

"You have not heard a single word I've said, have you?"

"I've heard your delusions. And I'm telling you to keep yourself safe."

"I do not wish to be safe," Adriana said, and the sense of freedom the words gave her was like a marvelous bird taking flight. "I am far more satisfied with reckless joy."

"What of your little fantasy, Riana? That fantasy of growing roses and taking tea with your friends?"

She shook her head. "You knew when I uttered it that I did not mean it. I was allowing my fear to cow me." The giddy sense of recognition and joy in her was impossible to measure. "I will not live that way, hiding and fearing and ducking. They've already done their worst to me."

"Have they, Riana? Have they really?"

But Adriana did not answer, understanding at last that Cassandra, who seemed so wise and brave and free, had built a wall of her own, just as she herself had. With her salons and scandalous company and bluestocking ways, she appeared to be worldly and experienced and in control. But she only maintained that control by rejecting any hint of emotion. No love, no passion, not even anger or joy were allowed entrance to her garden.

The coach hit a rut and flung them dangerously out of kilter for a minute, eliciting from the sisters small cries of distress. Across the carriage, their hands met and clung, in case all was lost.

Then the driver gained control, and through the windows, Adriana saw the dear, golden walls of her childhood home. Where Phoebe lay, hurt by her fall. Suddenly, all the petty hurts shrunk to nothing. "Cassandra, let's not fight. You mean the world to me, you know."

"And you to me," Cassandra said, and hugged her.

Adriana swallowed the sharp rise of apprehension as they stepped out of the carriage, ducking their heads against the rain. She offered a vehement prayer to the heavens, "Please let her be all right!" then they were hurrying up the wide stone steps.

The door was flung open and Cleo stood there.

"Oh, thank God you've come!" she cried, and burst into tears.

At the sight of her, Adriana's heart pinched violently. Cleo's hair hung in tangled curls down her back, her gown was soiled across the front, and her eyes were swollen with weeping. Behind her, Ophelia appeared, similarly disheveled and distraught. Cassandra and Adriana hurried up to meet them.

"How is she?" Adriana asked, unfastening her cloak and tossing it off. "Where is Monique?" She could understand the girls falling apart, but not Monique.

"She has a fever!" Ophelia cried, with all the unfairness of such a fate in her voice. "She tells us what to do and we do it, but Phoebe needs you."

The two elder sisters exchanged a glance. "I'll see to Monique," Cassandra said.

Adriana nodded. "Go have some tea made for us," she said to the younger girls. "Wash your faces and hands, and we'll have tea as soon as I've seen Phoebe. Has the doctor come?"

"He saw her early this morning. But this fever has stricken the entire village and he's on his rounds. He'll be back later."

"Ophelia," Adriana said in her most sensible tone. "What did he say about Phoebe?"

The girl's eyes filled with tears, and she shook her head. Cleo spoke. "He said he cannot tell what damage there is until the swelling has gone down. She broke her leg, but it is her back that is the worry."

Her back. "I see." Gently, Adriana touched an arm of each sister. "See to our tea, my dears. And wash your faces. It will make you feel better."

Ophelia nodded, and Cleo flung her arms around Adriana's neck. "We have been so lost without you, Riana! We missed you terribly."

Pierced, she hugged her back, and then gently moved toward the stairs.

The house seemed unnaturally quiet as she moved down the halls—the pall of illness. What fever? she wondered. And wasn't it always the way that things came in bunches—no, in threes. Things came in threes. With a ripple of superstition, she worried about the third one.

She sighed, trying to brush the thought away. Fiona was having a bad effect on her mental processes. Still, she could not quite quell the worry about it. Julian's trial—

No. She would not think of it. Squaring her shoulders, Adriana swept into Phoebe's room, and halted.

Her sister lay deathly still in her bed, her dark hair loose on the white linen pillowcase. A young maid jumped to her feet. "Lady Adriana! She's been calling for you."

"Riana!" Phoebe opened her eyes and held out a hand.

Relief, cold and shattered, swept through her. "Oh, Phoebe, you terrified me. How are you?" She clasped her hand, used her other hand to touch her brow. "Does it hurt terribly?"

Phoebe managed a wan smile. "It is not nearly as terrible as the girls made it sound, I'm quite sure." The smile faded. "Still, it is bad enough."

The young maid dragged the chair over for Adriana to sit and hold her sister's hand. "I'll nip out and see about some tea," she said.

Adriana nodded. "Can you tell me what happened?"

"My horse shied. I've no idea why—but I managed to pull him back under control, and he bolted again, and put his foot in a rabbit hole. I was thrown off." Her fine dark eyes were full of sorrow, and Riana saw there was a blue and yellow bruise along the right side of her face. "He had to be put down, you know."

"Oh, I am so sorry." She stroked Phoebe's hair. "And you? What damage is there?"

"My leg is broken, but it's properly set." A sudden ripple of pain contorted her face, and her fingers closed convulsively over her sister's. "It is . . . my back that aches." She closed her eyes, going pale, and Adriana felt real fear. But Phoebe opened her eyes again after a moment and said, "It is not broken, however. I'm sure it will heal."

An unaccountable sense of dread filled Adriana. But brightly she said, "Of course it will. Rest now, my dear. I'll sit with you as long as you like."

⚜ 16 ⚜

Tynan returned to the town house at mid-afternoon, whistling cheerfully under his breath. The day had gone very well and he had a dinner engagement for himself and his wife slated for this evening. A dinner, he thought, jauntily taking the steps to the front door, that might at last net him the Commons' seat he pursued.

John Marsh, Marquess of Cockfield, had sought Tynan at Barclay's coffee shop, and without preamble said that word was Tynan wished to buy an open seat. The price was high—seven hundred pounds—and Tynan suspected the Marquess was offering the local seat in order to raise funds, but that suited him fine.

So it was with no small amount of dismay that he read Adriana's hurried note. Alarmed, he found the housekeeper. "What do you know of this?"

"Only what she said, milord. The Countess and Lady Cassandra hurried out of here mid-morning like the devil was after them."

"Have you seen Mr. St. Ives?"

"Not since yesterday."

Torn, Tynan paced. There was naught for him to do with Phoebe, and though a part of him wished to join Adriana, he could not afford to miss this chance this evening. He would have liked having her with him much better, but it would not do for him to miss this dinner, especially if events conspired to prevent them from attending the rout at the Duchess's.

No. He could not afford to miss either. He would have to attend both, even without his wife.

But as he stood before the long windows that looked toward the back garden, he thought of her fencing with Gabriel there, thought of her laughter and her hair, thought of her white breasts and the low cry she made when he came to her, and he did not want her so far away. He wanted her here, wanted her on his arm, his lovely, intelligent wife.

A creeping sense of doom edged into his mind, and he pushed it away fiercely. When he could not longer avoid it, he would tell her the truth—that they were not, under the Catholic laws that bound him, truly married. That in order for their marriage to be true, she would have to convert.

And not only convert, but hide that conversion.

What a tangled mass of lies politics had forced on his life! His father, forty years before, had ostensibly converted to Protestant, had taken a public oath renouncing his faith. He'd done it to safeguard his lands, and since no Catholic could hold property of any sort, to safeguard the small holdings through the county on behalf of his neighbors. It was not uncommon, but that did not make the act any less subversive.

He pinched the bridge of his nose. He had no inkling of how Adriana would receive the news. She did not appear to be particularly devout, one way or the other, but it was a large step, a conversion. And a dangerous one.

He was not entirely sure he could ask her to take that step.

And not for the first time, he wondered at the motives of his benefactor, the elder Earl of Albury, James St. Ives. Why had the man written to him, specifically? What had the Earl had in mind when St. Ives requested his consideration of this marriage?

The Earl had known of Tynan's political aspirations. It had, in fact, been St. Ives's wise tutelage that provided the clarity of his decision. If he bought a seat in the English parliament, he could influence the vote on his own land. Perhaps he could even begin to influence other things, over time.

Still, by the time Albury had written to Tynan, Adriana's fate had been sealed. The brothers were missing, the earldom in danger of being lost. Had St. Ives somehow imagined he would petition and be granted that seat?

Highly unlikely, Tynan thought, even given the tenuous connection between the families.

With a physical shake, he put the thoughts aside. The motives of a man now dead were likely never to be uncovered. And he had much to do. In the meantime, Gabriel would want to know the news about Phoebe.

But he had no luck finding him, and returned to change for his dinner engagement. Lord Cockfield and his wife were agreeable and quite understanding about Adriana's absence. The lady, a round woman with merry brown eyes, teased him a little. "I had so hoped to meet her, you know. She must be very beautiful indeed to have the gentlemen"—she said the word with great irony—"in such a tizzy."

Tynan laughed and bowed over her hand. "She is the star of my heavens," he said extravagantly.

She laughed. "Bring her to me when you can."

He promised he would. The three shared a companionable dinner with free flowing wine and a full complement of courses, and afterward he retired with Lord Cockfield to his study, where they downed another bottle and Tynan underwent a subtle grilling about his politics. It amused him to lie so boldly, but the plump lord was so eager for his funds that it wasn't even much of a struggle.

By the time he left, the deal was very nearly sealed. Whistling cheerfully, he decided he was not at all in the mood to return to the town house if Adriana was not there, and set out for the Stag and Pointer, where he found Gabriel at last, engaged in a vigorous debate with a black scholar with whom he disagreed most heartily and with great enjoyment whenever they met. By the grinning men surrounding the two, they'd been at it for a while.

The scholar, with a skin so shiny dark that Tynan had stared—rudely and with astonishment—the first time he'd seen him, smiled now. "Ah, my rescue!" he cried, getting to his feet. "Lord Glencove, you must take your brother-in-law far from me. I'm too old to spar with the likes of him."

Gabriel turned. "Tynan! Join us."

Tynan was a bit in his cups, but he saw Gabriel was far beyond that, for all that his oratory had been perfectly and incisively executed. Hectic color burned in his cheeks, and his eyes were over bright. There was despair beneath the brightness. "Let's have a bite," Tynan said, gesturing toward an empty table.

Gabriel's friends, who'd obviously formed a protective circle about him, gave Tynan understanding glances and moved away. The scholar clapped Tynan briefly on the shoulder as he left. "He's heard a bit of bad news, I think," he said quietly.

Tynan nodded. Settling across from Gabriel, he motioned to the barkeep and ordered the shepherd's pie for two. Though he'd eaten himself, he would keep Gabriel company.

"You heard about Phoebe, then," he said cautiously.

"I did." Gabriel swallowed. "And my mother has a fever. I'm here drowning my fear that the third curse will be my brother."

"Is there any news?"

"No." Gabriel wiped a hand over his face. "Nor will there be till Tuesday."

Strain showed on the man's mouth, and in his shoulders, held at an aggressively straight angle. With sudden inspiration, Tynan said, "Forget the pie. Let's go to your sisters."

Throughout the day, Cassandra and Adriana took turns sitting with Phoebe and Monique, and managed, finally, to calm them, and then begin to teach the younger girls how to manage a crisis. "You cannot accomplish everything all at once," Adriana said quietly to Cleo as they returned to Monique's room, bearing fresh towels and cool water, "so you take one thing at a time, and complete it, and move to the next."

"We were quite lost without Phoebe and Monique."

"I know. But if you wish to manage your own household one day, you will have to keep your head in an emergency."

Soberly, the girl nodded. "How are my brothers?" she asked.

"They're very well." She opened the door and found Monique shifting with some annoyance.

"I am weary of this bed!" she cried in her French-accented English. "Let me out of here."

"Not today," Adriana said breezily. "If you'll behave yourself, perhaps tomorrow."

Monique gave her a dark look. "How are my boys? How is Gabriel? He wrote me a letter that Cleo read to me, full of the gossip." Pulling her deep bosomed torso up, she added, "Does he have a woman?"

"Not that I've seen." She thought of Gabriel's words, that he would not take a wife. "I think he is simply too busy. He did tell me he's loath to ever leave England again, so at least we'll keep him close by."

"Ah. He said that?"

"Yes. He's quite busy, and Lord Glencove said he's enormously popular with everyone."

A fleeting sadness danced over her eyes, then disappeared. "He'll make the most of his talents, you'll see."

"Of course he will." She opened a copy of *The Castle of Otrano*. "Where did you stop?"

"Page one hundred ninety-one," Cleo said, and yawned mightily. "Mama, can I crawl up beside you?"

"*Oui*, child."

Worn by the drama, the fourteen-year-old curled up around her mother, the roses and dusk skin seeming all the more youthful against the white counterpane. In minutes she was fast asleep, her mother's arms locked around her. Adriana read for a long time, until Monique, too, drifted into sleep, then she marked her place, put the book aside, and tiptoed across the room.

At the door, she paused, oddly moved—and strangely, missing her own mother. Though Monique would gladly have made room for her, Adriana left them alone, cuddling, mother and daughter. And out in the passageway she wondered if she might one day have a daughter of her own.

She was unexpectedly weary. The long day and the cold weather, on top of her lovely but not so restful nights, had drained all the energy from her. Dutifully, she checked on Phoebe and found her resting comfortably after a dose of laudanum, then without so much as a block of cheese, she made her way to her sacred, special place—that bedroom under the eaves of the old part of the manor.

With more than a little gratitude she saw that a fire had been lit and her covers turned down, a footwarmer in place below the coverlet. The same young maid who'd been waiting on Phoebe now waited in a chair for her. She'd evidently been nodding off in the chair, for she blinked owlishly when Adriana spoke her name. "Jenna. You may go to bed, child."

"I'm supposed to help you," she said. "I'm sorry I fell asleep."

Was the manor so shorthanded? "Where are Jean and Minna?"

"Minna's down with the fever. Begging your pardon, milady, I'm not supposed to speak of Jean."

"Ah." She turned to offer her laces to the girl. "I'd wager it has to do with a handsome blacksmith, but you needn't break your vow of silence. I'm sure I'll hear of it somewhere. Help me off with this, and then you may go."

The girl did as she was told and would have lingered to assist her into bed, but Jenna nearly swayed on her feet, and Adriana dismissed her, making a mental note to see to more help.

She brushed out her hair, donned a long warm woolen nightrail, and with a jaw-cracking yawn fell into bed and almost immediately into sleep.

Laden with little gifts, and more than a little drunk, Tynan and Gabriel arrived at Hartwood quite late to find the house mostly abed. A brace of candles burned in the music room, and someone kept watch in one of the upstairs bedrooms that faced the road, but aside from the young footman who gave them entrance, everyone else seemed to have retired.

It was Cassandra, looking pale and haunted, who emerged from the music room. "Spenser! Are you mad? You might have been killed making that trip in the dark!" She saw Gabriel behind him and cried out. "What were you thinking?"

Gabriel only stood there, blinking in the warmth. "I spent too many years never knowing how any of you were. I had to come."

Tynan put aside his parcels. "Where is my wife?"

"Asleep. And I'd advise you to let her continue. She's exhausted."

"Is that right? When I need your advice, I'll ask it." He walked toward the stairs. "Will you take me to her, or must I rouse some weary servant?"

"Oh, you'll respect the weariness of the servants but not the lady?" Cassandra didn't bother to hide her hostility, and Tynan narrowed his eyes, remembering how she'd glared at him from the very first moment. He recognized that this was her true face—she did not like him.

And therefore there was no point in attempting to placate her. "My wife"—he emphasized the word subtly—"will not mind it."

With a twitch of her skirts, she huffed and picked up a brace of candles. "This way."

"How is Phoebe?"

"She is in no danger of death."

"But?"

"The rest we will not know for some time."

"I'm sorry."

"So am I," she said harshly, and stopped, gesturing toward a staircase that wound into the stone tower. "Second door to the left. Beware the ghosts."

And leaving him to make his way in dark, she took the candles and moved back the way she'd come. Undaunted, Tynan carefully made his way up the circular stairs. It was indeed very dark, and very cold, but he'd not shed his coat, and the wall gave guidance. The stairs opened into a short passageway, and here there was enough light coming through the window at one end for him to make his way to the second door.

He scratched, but there was no answer, and he entered quietly. A fire burned in the grate, casting soft red illumination into the room, and from an embrasure set with a double set of mullioned windows, the softness of cloudy night came in. The bed was an enormous four-poster hung with brocaded drapes, and he thought of the night he'd first made love to her, in a medieval room much like this one. It seemed a very long time ago.

She slept on her belly, her hair and the top half of her face the only things showing, and he resisted the urge to kiss her. Instead, he disrobed quietly, and shivering, slid under the down-filled counterpane, moving across the cold expanse of bed to the warm island of her body, and very gently took her into his arms. Without waking, she flowed into his embrace, sighed heavily and settled hard on his shoulder.

With an odd sense of relief, he too fell asleep, holding her close to his heart.

Adriana awakened with a snug sense of well-being. Tynan's body cradled hers from behind, his long arms looped around her, his knees tucked into the crook of her own. His breath, steady and deep, brushed her nape.

Then she realized where she was—in her bed at Hartwood Hall, in her nightrail, buried under the heavy feather counterpane. He, quite obviously, was naked.

In gentle wonder she turned, and Tynan, still deep in sleep, let her go, pulling the cover over his bare shoulder and burying his face into the pillow. The sight of him, so beautiful, in her bed when she had not expected him, gave her a wild sense of gratitude.

Have I fallen in love with him?

Had she? She probed the spot in her chest that held him, and found it deep and wide and soft, pleasure and joy and . . . what? Her gaze caught on his slightly crooked, aggressive nose, such a refreshing flaw amid the graceful lines of cheekbones and jaw and eyebrows. From that broad forehead sprung his thick hair, dark but touched with those hints of copper when the light was upon it. His hand lay on the pillow next to him, and she reached up with her own, touching his fingers and palm lightly, letting the emotion pour through her—love.

Love that made her lean close and press a kiss to his brow, gently. Love that rested easy in the cradle of her heart. Love that made her wish to travel to his wild Irish world and see what he'd seen through his boyhood. Love that made her want to bear children that had his eyes.

Love that made her wish to be the one holding his hand when he died, or having him hold hers while she slipped away. If he had a mistress . . . it stung, that thought, and she scowled.

"Such a sour face," he said, touching her cheek.

"When you discover you want another woman, can you promise to make it several and never just a single one?"

He gave her a quizzical smile. "What?"

"I think I can bear the idea of several women, but I'm afraid a single mistress will make me a terrible shrew."

Rising up to his elbow, he looked down on her. "How many shall I have, then? Is twenty too many?"

"You're teasing me."

"I am." Idly, he untied the laces of her nightrail and put his hand flat between her breasts. "Why would I take a mistress when I have a wife who so suits my passions?"

"For now I do. But we're new lovers."

He lowered his lashes. "Will you have lovers, too, Riana?"

"No."

"Then I will not take them, either." He met her eyes soberly. "We'll be faithful, one to the other."

It pierced her. "Are we to remain married, then?"

"Aye," he said roughly, and she caught a hidden worry, quickly erased, before he kissed her. "Aye, that suits me."

She breathed in the scent of his hair, closing her eyes. There was pipe smoke in the length, and a hint of port. "How did you get here?"

"Gabriel and I came together, late. He was in a state, worrying, so I brought him." He straightened. "About our agreement, now. When all is settled with your brother, I will wish to return to Ireland." He paused. "There are things we will discuss then. And you may choose to stay here or come with me then."

"I'll go with you, of course."

"You may not," he said.

Perplexed, she touched his chest. "What is it?"

"Let's wait till the trial is done, shall we?" He lifted a rueful brow and pushed his hair from his face. "How is Phoebe?"

Frowning thoughtfully, she didn't answer immediately. "You've frightened me now, Tynan."

His mouth showed no hint of humor, and his hand strayed, brushing over her jaw. "I meant to."

She thought suddenly of him the first night they'd made love, sitting alone in the dark with his head in his hands. "Is it about your brother?"

"Partly." He took a breath. "Now, you have to trust me. It will be better to wait. And I do not mean to appear callous, but can you leave Phoebe safely in the care of the others, just for this day and night?"

"The ball."

He nodded. "If you must stay, I will make our excuses, but it would be very good for my cause to go. And it will not hurt your brother's cause any, either."

"I understand. There is little that can be done for Phoebe today. We'll not know what damage there is until she is able to walk again, and that will be many weeks yet."

"All right. Then let's be on with the day." With his usual energy, he leaped up, shivering in the cold, and reached for his trousers. Adriana rolled to her side to watch him, smiling at the long smooth line of his back, the working of muscles in his shoulders.

"Can you spare even a few moments, sir?"

He bent over and kissed her, his hair falling around her face. "You're a lusty wench."

"So they say."

He chuckled. "We'll celebrate tonight."

17

The dress had arrived while they were at Hartwood, and when Adriana went upstairs, she found Fiona simply standing before the creation with her hands folded reverently over her apron. The maid looked at her with misty eyes. "My lady, this is a queen's dress!"

Adriana blinked in awe. It lay across the dark coverlet on her bed like something fashioned from the wings of fairies or dragonflies. Letting go of a breath of approval, she moved across the room to put a palm on it. "I cannot wear this," she said with some sorrow.

"What? You must! They'll all swoon in envy, they will."

Which was exactly the problem. The fabric was one shade from her own skin tone, and it was shimmering, diaphanous—a froth of nothing in so innocent a hue. She closed her eyes. "I cannot."

With her mouth set, she whirled, stomped to her door and went to find Tynan. She came upon him in the drawing room, frowning over a letter that he hastily folded up when she appeared. "Tynan, the dress will not do."

"Is there some mistake?"

"No. It's too wicked. It's terrible. I cannot appear in such a dress."

His smile broke, devastating and knowing. "It is meant to be utterly wicked, Riana."

"You do not know what they will say."

"Oh, but I do," he said softly.

"What you think it was to be and what it actually has become are—"

Reasonably, he said, "Have your maid help you put it on. We'll decide."

Adriana sighed and waved a hand. "Whatever you say. You will see."

Tynan's smile faded as she bustled out, and he took the letter again from his jacket. It came from his steward, who warned him of raids that had been made on neighboring counties, Protestants against Catholics, and the law all on the Protestant's side. A young man, hotheaded and outraged, had been beaten to death. He'd left a wife and small child.

The raids, warned the steward, were coming closer. He feared what would happen when they got to the glassworks.

Tynan pinched the bridge of his nose, torn in two directions. Tonight he hoped to cinch his aspirations toward a House seat. Julian's trial would begin Tuesday. If all went very well, he could depart London by Friday next.

But some presentiment of danger warned him that he could not leave it so long. What if the raids progressed before he was able to make the long journey? It took several days even in good weather and no storms to block his ferry crossing from Holyhead to Dublin.

And if there was such unrest, he would be very unwise to take Adriana with him, as he had planned. Which would mean leaving his confession even longer. Tension drew up his shoulders and he shifted to loosen them.

He heard her step outside the door and carefully tucked away the letter. Time enough tomorrow to decide. He turned, hands clasped behind his back, and waited for her to appear.

She strode in, as if to weight her form with a man's sturdy walk. But nothing could have marred the perfect marriage of that dress to that form. She halted, nostrils flaring. "You see? It is impossible."

"Au contraire," he whispered. The gown was made in some light, airy way of such fine fabric that it appeared to float over her body, curving itself around her lush breasts, swirling around her belly and hips. She looked like a goddess. No man would be able to think clearly while she walked a room in that dress, which was exactly what he'd hoped.

And yet it was Adriana herself who gave it the greatest dash. Her long neck held her pretty head at a defiant angle, and wisps of hair, loosened in her struggles, brushed her oval face. Against the paleness, her eyes burned like sapphires, dancing and alive and bold. "'Tis perfect," he said.

"It is not," she replied, and he realized he had missed, at first, the fury in her stance. "It makes me into a whore, and I will not wear it." Her eyes shimmered with tears. "And you are a pig, and I cannot believe you would have put me on display like this." She shook her head. "You're just like all of them, aren't you? You cannot see *me* for all of *this*." She gestured angrily at her breasts, at her body.

"Riana! No, that's not—"

"Perhaps I should attend as Lady Godiva," she said coldly. "I've the hair for it."

"Riana—"

She stepped away, shaking her head. "Why would you do this?"

He scowled, exasperated. "Because everyone in that room is expecting you to enter with your head bowed in apology and shame. Because they'll be wanting to look down at you." He stepped closer. "When you appear in this gown, like Venus, they'll be cheated of pitying you or disdaining you."

She made a sound. "No, they'll hate me instead."

"Hate you? No. Envy, perhaps. Lust, almost certainly. Not hate."

Wavering, she raised those dark blue eyes and bit her lip. It was an almost painfully vulnerable expression, and he told himself he must be very alert tonight, to protect her. "I'm frightened," she said quietly.

"It won't be easy, Riana," he said seriously. "But we've the Duchess behind us, and the arrogance of the gods to go with us." He put his hands on her arms and deliberately admired the fall of the gown over her breasts and hips. "And remember, 'twill be your husband who is most anxious for the evening to be at a close."

She nodded. "All right."

He kissed her forehead. "All will be well, Riana. I promise."

To her amazement, Adriana was able to nap—and quite deeply, waking only when Fiona shook her late in the afternoon, to take her bath. Even then the sluggishness of the nap clung. The hot, scented water was no real help, and she nearly drifted off again while she was soaking.

Fiona sent for strong, milkless tea, and as she dried Adriana's hair, patiently squeezing the water out, then combing and brushing it before the fire, Adriana drank her tea and very, very slowly, as if emerging from a chrysalis, grew more alert.

Now that she'd had some time to let the notion sink in, she realized Tynan was right, as ever. Society did wish for her to hang her head in shame. If women were allowed the same freedoms as men, there were a great many men, after all, who'd stand to lose quite a lot. Abruptly she asked Fiona, "Do you ever wish you were born a man?"

The girl made a snorting sound. "What woman has not?"

Adriana laughed, and suddenly the chrysalis broke entirely. She couldn't have said, just then, what it was that had fallen away, but there was a new buoyancy in her as Fiona and she worked together on her costume for the evening.

And a costume it was. She thought of Tynan, teasing her about being the god of love. "Who is the Irish god of love, Fiona? Do you know his name?"

"Aonghus Og?" she asked. "Sure, and I do."

"Who is his consort?"

"His lover, you mean?"

Adriana nodded at her.

"Well, let's see now. That would be Cáer."

"What is she like?"

"He dreamed of her and went to find her." Fiona combed through Adriana's waist-length hair. "Ah, milady, 'tis fine hair you have, that much is true." She paused a moment with the hair in her hands, as if trying to imagine what to do with it.

"Who was she?" Adriana prompted.

"Cáer, the one he dreamed of, was the daughter of the king of the sidhe. You know the sidhe?"

"No." She had been looking at the girl in the mirror—one brought without question to replace the one Adriana had broken—and now turned. "Who are they?"

"You'd call them the fairy folk, but in our land they're as dangerous as they are beautiful. And Cáer was the daughter of their king, who had other things in mind for his daughter, as fathers so often do."

Adriana chuckled. "So what happened?"

"Cáer took the body of a swan, but so lovestruck, so smitten was Aonghus Og, that he knew her straight away and carried her off to his castle."

"Was she glad to have him?"

"Well, now," Fiona said, a hand on her hip, a hint of a smile on her wide mouth, "what girl wouldn't want the god of love?"

Adriana laughed, full-throated. "Tonight, Fiona, I must be as beautiful as that swan girl. Cáer?"

"But of course you must," the girl said quietly, "since you up and married Aonghus Og himself."

Adriana only smiled. "Come, we must hurry if I am to be ready in time."

An hour later they stood back to admire their handiwork. Taking a nervous breath, Adriana stood tall and inclined her head. "Might I pass as a daughter of the sidhe?"

Fiona's eyes shone, and she clasped her hands to her mouth in pleasure as Adriana turned in a slow, graceful circle. "'Tis just as well we are not in Ireland, or they'd think you one of their own and steal you away."

Adriana smiled. Her hair was piled loosely on her head, with curls and wisps drifting free, as if blown there by a soft wind. Into it Fiona had pinned small jewels of many colors, so the various fires of garnets and emeralds and sapphires flashed as she inclined her head. The dress, which had seemed so daring this afternoon, still seemed to be made of dragonfly wings, barely pink, as if dawn and moon had met and loved. The craftsmanship was so exquisite, the cut so perfect, that it glossed her, covered and revealed and hinted with every tiny breath, every simple shift of a finger.

Around her throat she wore a single, enormous white diamond. It was not a jewel she'd ever worn, but a diamond seemed the only possible pendant for such an airily colored gown. It had also been a gift from her father to her mother, and would serve, if the evening proved difficult, to remind her of who she was, and of those to whom she owed her allegiance.

With a rush of excitement she turned and grasped Fiona's hand in her own. "Thank you, my dear. You've

quite transformed me." Earnestly, she bent and kissed
the girl's cheek. "This night has loomed like a monster.
But you've given me the tools I needed."

"I've spit in an eye once or twice," Fiona said, and
flushed. Then she stepped back and flung out a hand.
"Aonghus waits, Cáer."

"And you—the evening is yours. I suspect I shall
not need your assistance removing my gown."

Tynan paced in the drawing room just off the foyer.
He'd attempted to eat a little earlier, but the food had
sat ill with him, and he contented himself with a measure of medicinal brandy. It steadied his nerves a bit,
though it did little for the hollowness in his belly.
Later, at the ball, he would have a supper.

He could not think why he felt so agitated this
evening. There were matters of importance riding on
the events of the rout, to be sure, but nothing that
could not be addressed in some other way if this did
not proceed as he hoped. He paused before the broad
windows, staring sightlessly at the reflection of a candle in the dark glass. Society would not make a pariah
of Adriana forever.

Or perhaps they would—what difference would
even that make? His lot would be easier, would
progress more quickly, perhaps, if he gained the seat
he hoped to buy. But if he did not, they would return
to Ireland, return to his estates there, and he would
continue creating work for his tenants and others in
the county, struggling in the Irish parliament to affect
change before more bloodshed erupted.

Such reasonable thoughts, but still his spine was tight with tension, with a superstitious and unwarranted sense of dread, a sense of impending disaster. Phoebe and Monique, one hurt, the other sick with a fever, had been two—he waited for the third. And this afternoon he'd intended to go out to purchase a new pair of gloves, but had opened the door to find a magpie on the step. It turned, unafraid, and cawed at him.

His mother would have taken to her bed for days over such a bad omen. Aiden would have blessed the house with holy water. Tynan, who insisted a man's luck was what he made of it, roared at it and stomped out on the porch, glaring after it as it flashed, black and white, into the heavens.

Dread.

And the letter he'd received tugged at him. He worried about violence at the glassworks. Worried about the ill feelings whipping higher and higher, as they had more than once in his lifetime, until the people were belting out their rage upon one another.

"Milord?"

He turned. Adriana's little maid, with her thick, thick hair bound into a heavy crown on her head, poised nervously at the door. "Milady Cáer is ready."

Though the girl was outwardly the very picture of humble servitude, he did not miss the sparkle in her eyes. And he could not halt the sudden, fierce pleasure that swelled in him as her meaning donned. "Thank you, Fiona," he said. He stepped into the foyer and halted, dumbstruck.

A thousand faces, Phoebe had told him, and he thought he had seen them all by now—the nonde-

script wallflower on the steps the first day, the butterfly sailing toward her brothers, the siren at dinner that
night, the hoyden sword-fighting, the mischievous
wench in men's clothing.

As she came down the stairs to him now, he saw all
of them, and more. The butterfly danced in the many-
colored jewels winking in the siren looseness of hair
piled so that it appeared ready to tumble free at the
slightest touch. There was a hoydenish roll to her hips
and mischief on the tiny smile curling her lips, and
even a hint of the wallflower afraid she would not
please in the shyness he caught in her eyes.

But most of all she was devastatingly desirable. It
seemed so small a word to capture the essence of the
way she looked, he thought, his breath caught high in
his chest. Candle flame cast an aura of gold about her
shoulders, kissed the swell of breasts beneath fabric
that caught the light in wicked and not so wicked
ways, revealing now the shape of a thigh, a breast, the
dip of her waist, and then just as quickly hiding all. She
moved like a queen, graceful and straight, but there
was no halting the natural roll of her hips, the elusive
but unmistakable sway of heavy breasts barely contained in the airiest of fabric, the elusive but definite
strut of a woman who'd known the flesh of a man and
counted it a delicacy.

She met his eyes and glided toward him, the depth of
dark blue knowing and hinting of laughter. "Will I do?"

And although he had joined with her before, his
imagination gave him the most startling vision of her
hair tumbling free over her shoulders as he pulled up
those gossamer skirts. He imagined himself beginning

at her knee and tasting the flesh up her thighs, imagined the heat and pleasure he could give. He imagined how the fabric would dampen with her sweat, how closely it would mold her temptress's body.

He was most arrestingly aroused, simply by looking at her, and he raised his eyes to her face. "Cáer." He finally moved, feeling slightly dizzy, and took her gloved hand, lifting it to his face. "I will not even be able to look at you," he murmured, and to illustrate his meaning, pulled her to him with one hand.

And that only made it worse, because her eyes widened as he rocked his hips against hers ever so lightly, and beneath the fine fabric her nipples appeared. A hint only, and only because he knew to look. For a moment they only stood together, breathing each other's breath, before Tynan said, "I suppose we shall both have to beware revealing our desire."

She smiled. "Speak for yourself."

In that moment his fear doubled, tripled, and he found his hands gentling on her arms. Cautionary words made their way into his mouth but were never spilled, for in that instant he raised his head and saw Fiona standing in the shadows, an expression of warning in her eyes.

So he only bent and kissed his wife, one time, to see him through till evening. And it was in his heart, if not on lips: *I love you.*

He fancied he could taste the same on her mouth.

In the carriage, Adriana sat next to Tynan as they traveled the short distance to the Duchess's fashionable address. Both of them were silent, and after a moment Tynan reached over and took her gloved hand in his own.

It was Adriana who spied the house first. Towering four floors, the pillared mansion was built of pale brick, and every window blazed. Oil lamps, hung from posts at three-foot intervals, cast a festive light over the walk where carriages queued up to deposit their glittering contents. Silks and satins and velvets swirled into the flickering light, and jewels danced. Laughter and chatter perfumed the cold night.

Without speaking, Adriana gripped Tynan's hand more tightly. Her stomach roiled so violently she put her other hand to her mouth. She thought of all the people within, all the knowing looks that would be cast over her, all the speculation that would go on behind the men's eyes, and she shrank back in her seat, making a little cry. "I cannot do this, Tynan," she said in a small voice.

"'Ah, but you can, lass," he said gently. More gently than she deserved. "Where's that haughty chin now?" Two fingers touched her jaw and pushed up. "Think of Julian."

But she noted the brooding darkness in his face and was not reassured. "What if this only sets more of them against us all?"

"Never," he said. "Remember, Adriana, that you are not only beautiful—you are charming and intelligent and amusing. Dozens of those women have done far more than you did, and simply had the good luck to not be caught. They do know that."

Impulsively, she leaned forward and pressed a fervent kiss to his mouth. "Thank you," she breathed.

"Shall we?"

He helped her from the carriage, and offered his arm, and Adriana smiled up at him. "One for all."

His eyes tilted up at the corners. "Aye."

And then there was nothing to do but go forward. Breathlessly, Adriana clung to his arm and told herself this was a game. A game in which she was the daughter of a king of the sidhe, and the man on her arm the most compelling creature on the earth, the god of love.

When they entered and were announced, there was a soft, rippling hush on the breath of the assembled dancers, but it rippled from one side of the vast ballroom to the other, so it never did seem as if it stopped the room. Adriana knew her color must be high, but she tilted her head and forced herself to meet the gaze of those who looked up at them.

And as if the pair of them created a fairy glamour, she saw only admiration in the faces of the people below. One or two turned a head away with pursed lips, but it was men who did it, men she suddenly realized, who had likely been influenced by tales from Malvern's mother.

On the women's faces she saw expressions ranging from mild amusement to blazing smiles. One glared and turned away, trying to turn her daughter's attention, but the young woman refused to move, and catching Adriana's gaze, she gave her a faint bow.

Then the next group was introduced. Tynan and she were swept forward, to present themselves to the Duchess. Adriana had never seen the elusive and famous widow, but had heard tale of her beauty for many years, so it was a surprise to see a woman in her sixties, very plump but somehow saucy, holding court from an oversized chair. She had ropes of white and black pearls entwined in her elaborate coiffure, more pearls around her neck and wrists, and a stunning purple silk gown.

Tynan drew Adriana forward. "Your Grace, may I present my wife, the former Lady Adriana St. Ives, now Adriana Spenser, Countess of Glencove?"

Adriana curtsied prettily and rose to find the Duchess's twinkling eye upon her. "Why haven't we seen you at Court? I knew your father. You look nothing at all like him, thank the heavens."

Adriana grinned.

"But you take after him in other ways, I think. That adventurous spirit. Gemini! The man could never be still. I was sorry to hear of the uprising. He took it hard." The Duchess waved her fan. "But all's well that ends well, eh? Your brothers are home, safe, and you've snared yourself this dashing husband."

"The fortune was mine, Your Grace," Tynan said.

"I believe it was." The Duchess turned her gaze to the group behind them, dismissing them, and they moved away. Adriana let go of a breath, and found her hands were trembling slightly, but the overall sense of relief made her giddy.

"Well, Aonghus," she said airily. "I believe there are some ladies who long to dance the minuet with you. And my task here is plain."

"Save me a dance," he said, raising her gloved fingers to his lips. "Remember, I'm smitten with you, and a besotted husband shall dance with his wife, however gauche it appears."

"Beware Malvern's mother," she said, spying her in the crowd.

"And Stead," he countered, cocking his head toward the man, standing erect and ill-tempered by a potted palm.

"I will." She looked at him full on, allowing her love to shine in her expression even if there was no courage in her to express it aloud. "Thank you," she whispered.

They parted, each to the tasks they'd set for themselves. Before Adriana moved past two groups, she was snared by a woman in yellow satin. "Lady Adriana! Or is it Countess?"

Lady Julia was Margaret's sister, and her smile was knowing and bright. "Countess," Adriana said with a smile, accepting a glass of ratafia as she joined the small knot of women clustered beneath a torch that showed off their jewels and figures in the best light. One, a tall slim brunette Adriana did not recognize, turned her back. Seeing this, a second woman also turned away, and they departed haughtily. Adriana looked at Lady Julia and most subtly lifted a shoulder.

The encounter set the tone for the evening. There were those who shunned her, and there were those who did not. Once the dancing began, she was much in demand, and she forgot those who wished her ill.

And to her amazement, she discovered she was quite adept at the political byplays she needed to engage. Light banter came easily to her, and she was able to guide nearly any opening to her own ends. She found her husband was respected, and to her surprise, rather feared for his great intelligence. It was nothing specific that was said, only hinted at. She would have to remember to tell him that his face of unrepentant rake was no longer working for him. Anyone who spent more than an hour in his company could not help but see the fierce intelligence and prodigious energy underlying his rakish face.

On one question she met no success. None were willing to let any hint of their feelings about Julian known. She worried over it a little as she helped herself to a plate of supper, sugared plums and sliced roast beef, still pink at the center, and pickles and sardines.

"May I assist you?" Tynan said, coming up beside her.

"Only to fill yourself a plate and join me."

Leaning close, he whispered. "I would so like to join you."

Adriana laughed. A night of triumph, she thought with satisfaction. All would be well.

18

Much later, Adriana made her way back to the ball after taking time to blot her face and breathe some of the cold night air. A little giddy with ratafia and power and the promise of Tynan's hands and lips, she laughed softly to herself, remembering everything to tell Phoebe.

It was quiet and cool along the balcony that ran the length of the back of the house, and she smoothed a lock of hair into place, mentally composing the letter in her mind.

If he'd made a single noise, she had not caught it. Her first sense of danger was a fierce, bruising hand on her arm, and an alarming strength that pulled her nearly off her feet. She opened her mouth to scream, but a hand clamped over it before she could make a noise. She smelled an odd, sweetish odor along with a powerful note of port, and knew immediately it was John Stead.

Fear burned her. She shoved back with one elbow and connected with ribs, but although his breath whooshed from him, he did not let her go, only dragged her backward into the shadows and swung her around so her face was to the wall, her arms trapped in one single hand. It was a painful position, her neck at an odd angle, the cold wall against her chest, and she held still for a moment, trying to gather her defenses.

"If you scream," he said, "they'll all come running, and I'll make it look as if you were my willing wench." His hand was hard against her mouth, and he bent close to bite her shoulder. Adriana shuddered in revulsion, closing her eyes in an attempt to stem her panic. One shoulder was shoved painfully hard against the corner and his body held her in place, her wrists easily captured in one hand at unnatural angle. "And your brother will almost certainly be transported, if not hanged."

He said, "Help me here," and Adriana thought he was speaking to her until another set of hands were on her wrists, pulling them up over her head. Only the hand over her mouth kept her from slamming her face into the wall.

"You've no idea how long I've awaited a chance to revenge myself on your husband," Stead said, and most shockingly, shoved his hand into her bodice. She made a protesting cry, and he ground hard against her hips, though he didn't seem to be particularly aroused.

Think! She went utterly still, thinking to take him off guard, but he only took it as further invitation, his nasty hands groping at her crotch beneath her dress. The other man laughed, and another hand rubbed her breasts, and Adriana fought the revulsion they brought out in her.

For one long, endless moment, she endured it,

some part of her weeping at the indignity while the other wanted to curl up in shame and another screamed in a shrew's voice that she deserved it. Deserved it. She'd asked for this by flouting Society and taking her own lover, and by harnessing her sexuality to be used as a tool to gain her brother's freedom and her husband's will.

And then something wild broke in her, an anger so clean and hot and true that it lent her the strength of a hundred men. With a roar, she flung her body backward, using her skull as a weapon. With a jarring impact, she connected with Stead's face, and before he could react, she bit down with vicious strength on the hand over her mouth.

There was a noise, a growling sound of rage she recognized as coming from her, and she heard her dress tear, but it didn't matter. The hold on her wrists loosened, and she swung her head back again, and her elbow when she wrenched it free. A blow struck her head, and tears filled her eyes at the pain, but she did not cease her determined struggle. With elbows, with feet, with every part of her body, she fought back, and only when she heard footsteps did she let go.

The footsteps had been running away—Stead's accomplice. Abruptly, she was free, and turned with a savage growl. Stead backed away, holding his bleeding left hand in his right.

"You'll never touch another woman like that again," she said in a low voice. A voice so deeply angry and low that it shook.

Unrepentant, he sneered, "What will you do, have your brother call me out?"

Which of course was impossible and he knew it, and as if they'd been momentarily stunned into silence, all the places he'd touched her—hurt her—suddenly stung all together. Her arm and breast felt bruised by his brutal hands, and her wrists, and a spot burned on her cheekbone, where she had been scraped against the wall.

"No," she said quite clearly, raising a hand to her face. "I rather think my husband will manage this one for me. Be at the sycamore at Hyde Park at dawn." Her heart swelled as she said that, and not in a way that was pleasant. Cold fear invaded her at the thought of that misty dawn five years before, but she did not reveal it, only manipulated him into the one condition that was critical if this were to succeed. "Shall he bring the pistols or will you?"

He laughed wildly. "A duel. How utterly splendid! But as the challenged, it is my right to choose the weapons, and I choose swords."

She managed a shrug of deepest ennui. "As you wish. It shall please me to watch you die by any method."

With arch manners, he bowed. "Till dawn, then."

He moved away, whistling, and only then did Adriana shatter. She managed a handful of steps on legs that trembled violently, but then was forced to lean hard against the balustrade and carry her hands to her face, breathing deeply, fighting tears of humiliation. She gritted her teeth against collapse, steeling herself on gulps of air.

The cold steadied her after a minute, and she looked at herself, trying to take stock. The gown had torn a little at the bodice, and she could feel wisps of hair loose around her face, and there was no doubt the sign of tears on her cheeks. She could not return to the ball in this state. Nor could a single soul be allowed to see her this way. Wildly, she looked over her shoulder, trying to think of some solution, and she spied a set of glass doors that led to an upper bedroom. With any luck, she could find a cloak and wash her face, then summon a servant to fetch Tynan for her.

The doors opened at her touch and Adriana slipped into the dark within, silently closing the door behind her. The room was blessedly silent, although she could hear the sound of the music beyond. She paused for a moment, catching her breath, then attempted to move forward, and barked her toes against a chair. Wincing in pain, she squeezed her lips together, bending down to rub them.

The inner door burst open, spilling a rather tipsy male voice and a low, knowing laugh from a woman. The two tumbled into the room before Adriana could think what to do. The woman carried a candelabra, and she halted instantly when she saw Adriana. "What are you doing here?"

The man was vaguely familiar to her, but Adriana did not know the woman. Her black hair was loosened, as if she'd just come from a fresh embrace, and Adriana blushed as she realized the pair had likely retreated here to make love. Self-consciously, she touched her hair, and wondered how badly her gown was soiled. "I must have drunk too much ratafia," she said. "I could not remember the way back."

"Mmm." The woman waved the man away, and

with a scowl at Adriana, he backed into the hall. The woman closed the door and took up the candelabra, carrying it over to the table near where Adriana stood as if rooted, her toes still stinging.

The woman narrowed her eyes. "You're the one in the scandal sheets." The violet-blue eyes, so startling against her black hair, were frank. "Were you really as bold as they imply?"

Adriana considered her options and decided this woman, whether her motives were good or ill, was the only chance she had in this moment. "Not quite," she said with a sigh. "But bad enough."

"Was he worth it?"

"Is any man worth that?"

"Some might be." She poured water into the basin and dipped a cloth into it, then gave it to Adriana and gestured to the mirror over the washstand. "Your face is bruised."

Adriana moved, bending to see the damage wrought by Stead. "Dammit!" she cried, and realized she was not alone. "I'm sorry."

The woman smiled. "I don't think it was that glorious creature you're obviously so besotted with who did that. I suspect his hands are much more . . . delicate."

"It was not my husband." Adriana blotted the scrape on her cheek where blood welled out of a hundred tiny cuts, and saw that she would have a remarkably black eye by morning. Her glorious gown had torn in a short diagonal line between her breasts, too, and it made her furious. "But since I'm going to kill this one, it doesn't matter. He won't bother anyone else."

The woman laughed. "I'd like to see that."

Adriana turned. "We have not met."

"No," she agreed. "We do not travel the same circles, I'm afraid." But she did not offer her name. Instead she asked again, "Was your lover worth all you've suffered for him?"

Underlying the words was a plea, and Adriana countered with a question of her own. Looking at the door, she asked, "Is he the reason you ask?"

The woman crossed her arms. "Perhaps he is."

Adriana put the cloth down, and everything that had transpired over her involvement with Malvern rushed over her imagination. She thought of the first time he'd kissed her, and how the world seemed to shatter in its steps, remembered the first time he made love to her, with such skill and slow perfection, so she was not frightened, only desperate to meld with him. She thought of the headiness of those months just after, when he appeared so content with her and the fiery passion between them. "I thought so at the time," she said slowly.

"And now? If fate wiped your slate clean, would you do it again?"

Adriana thought of the duel that terrible morning, and the loss of her brothers and all that had transpired since. But most of all she thought of Tynan, bending his head to so sweetly drink of her lips, and the look in his eye when he joined with her.

"No. I caused my family terrible sorrow," she said at last. "And I don't know, even now, how I will put it all right again. But—" she touched her mouth "—I have found my own true love now, and wish I'd not given myself away so lightly before."

The woman, not much more than a girl, really, moved to the wardrobe and took out a cloak. "Wear this. Go to your left when you leave this room, and you will find a staircase that leads to the garden. There is a wall in the gate that will take you to your carriage."

Adriana put it on. "Thank you," she said simply, accepting her dismissal.

At the door she halted. "Will you tell my husband that I've gone?"

The woman nodded, her face sober.

Adriana paused, feeling she'd left something undone. "I am going to kill him," she said. "The one who did this. At Hyde Park at dawn." She slipped out, closing the door gently behind her.

The woman's directions had been sound, and she found the waiting carriage with no trouble. The footman, alarmed, handed her up and tucked a blanket around her. "Go in and find my husband," she said. "Tell him I am ill." Abruptly, she reconsidered. If he saw her in this condition, nothing she could do would halt him from returning to the ball to kill Stead. That could not happen. "No," she said. "Tell the coachman to take me home. Tell my husband I will see him there."

At home Adriana struggled out of her gown on her own, washed her face and hands, and examined her body carefully for marks. The bruises appalled her— the brand of fingerprints around her upper arm, a red mark where her hipbone had struck the wall, the black eye and scrape on her cheek. And, across her breast, the dark imprint of rough fingers. It made her furious, and she clung to that fury, for she would need it.

But it made her dizzy to imagine Tynan's reaction. She'd seen, in bits and pieces, the anger that lurked in him. He'd told her more than once that his temper was his greatest vice. A temper roused by his enemy's hands on his wife, kindled all the higher with protectiveness and jealousy—she sucked in a fearful breath. No. He could not be allowed even a hint of knowledge until she had finished it.

And how would she keep him from her when he came home? He would be angry that she'd left him at the ball, and perhaps worried. Could she darken the room, receive him without light, into her bed?

But then how would she slip out at dawn?

No. She could not see him until after the duel.

From without, she heard the approach of a carriage and four. With urgency, she donned a wrapper over her nakedness, pinched out the candle, and rushed from the room.

"Oh, God, let him forgive me for this!" she whispered as she padded barefoot down the hall and into her father's room, closing the door behind her. She listened carefully, hearing him enter and speak with a servant. Then his feet on the stairs, two at a time. She ached at that urgency, and the happy way he said her name when he got to her door.

Then, with a sense of utter disaster, she remembered the dress she had tossed on her bed in her rage. The beautiful dress that had been soiled.

And torn across the bodice.

She wanted to rush out of the room, explain everything, explain her absence and the tear, explain why she'd left him alone at the ball. Explain. . .

But to save her brother, and herself, and Tynan, she forced herself to sink down on the floor in the dark of her father's dusty room. She clutched her knees to her chest and ached too deep even to weep. Here was her chance to make amends—to all of them—perhaps the only one she had. There was nothing for her to do but accept it.

Even if it meant losing her husband.

Tynan smelled the distinctive odor of a candle just pinched out as he entered Adriana's chamber, and with a grin he moved to the bed. He'd been more alarmed than anything when first the girl with the enormous eyes, then his footman, had delivered the news that Adriana was ill. He wondered, with a pierced heart, if someone had been cruel to her and she was retreating.

But no matter—they had accomplished much, and if her courage gave out at the end, she'd earned that right. His fingers were untying his neckcloth as he called her name softly in the darkness. He tossed it off and started on his shirt, anticipating the fulfillment of his involved fantasies. "Adriana," he called, and suddenly worried that she might really have taken ill. The whole village had been ill with a fever, after all.

He touched the bed.

Empty.

Dread rose in him, that dread brought on by the cursed magpie on the doorstep this afternoon. There was a flint and matches on the bureau, and he lit the candle with a shaking hand and turned.

Empty. The bed had not been touched. But there, across the foot of it, was the gossamer gown, flung there in a tangle. He smiled, suddenly realizing she had likely gone to sleep in his bed. Picking up the gown, he let a wicked scenario roll out in his mind. He'd ask her to put it back on, and then he'd take it off.

But she was not in his bedroom, either. Flummoxed, he sat on the edge of the bed and put the candle down. The dress slithered over his thighs in a whispery rush, and with a pang he picked it up and held it to his nose, smelling the notes of her skin in the fabric.

He lowered it again, feeling foolish. And saw the tear at the bodice.

His whole body went cold.

Adriana was afraid to sleep, for dawn was not so far away. She waited until she heard Tynan leave again. Going where? she wondered, but could not linger on the thought. A little later there were again footsteps on the stairs, and she identified the lighter step of Gabriel. She breathed a little easier, knowing he was here.

She lit a candle in her father's room and riffled through his clothes once again. This time she did not bother with frivolity, with anything but clothing in which she could move easily and that would keep her warm. In preparation for kicking off the too-big shoes, she donned a pair of woolen stockings, and to afford freedom of movement, she bound her breasts with a strip of linen, then fastened her sleeves carefully. Over the simple linen shirt and brown woolen breeches, she donned a long waistcoat that left her arms free and would help keep her warm when she shed her coat. In it, she tested feints and swings. Perfect.

She would not wear a wig, which could slip and blind her. Instead she wove her long hair into a single long braid and tucked it inside her waistcoat. When she was ready, she made her way silently down the halls to Gabriel's chamber and scratched on the door to gain admittance, hoping he was not asleep. His low voice called admittance, and Adriana slipped inside.

He sat at his desk in his shirtsleeves, his long hair tied into a queue at his nape. He put down his quill when she came in. "So, it's true," he said, and there was a weight of weariness in his voice that gave her pause. "You're going to duel."

She moved closer, into the light, so he could see her black eye. "I am."

Gabriel lifted a hand, as if to touch the place, and muttered, "Bastard." His mouth tightened. "I suppose it is impossible to persuade you this is madness."

"Yes." She lifted her chin. "I spoke in anger when I challenged him, and perhaps it *is* a fool's errand, but as the hours have passed, I can see that Fate has put me here to fight for myself. It may be madness, Gabriel, but I can see no other way to put all this right. If I'd allowed Tynan to see this—" She shook her head. "And then we'd all be lost, wouldn't we?"

"Allow me the honor, then, Adriana. You know there are none who can best me at swords. I'll unhand him and be done."

"No." She lifted her chin. "When we were children,

I asked you once if you minded that your race would prevent you from inheriting what should have been yours as eldest son."

Gabriel's face stilled. "I remember."

"And you said God must have had a reason for making you as you were. God gave me, mere woman"—the words were heavily ironic—"two strong brothers to teach me how to fight for myself. And yet, what have I done? I stepped back and let the pair of you take the punishment that should have been mine." She paused. "It's time I fought my own battles."

For a long moment he only looked at her, the uptilted green eyes very sober. "So it is." He smiled, and kissed her forehead. "I won't let him kill you, and I won't let you kill him." He crossed the room and took up his sword, which he carried back and held out to her on open palms. "Allow me to present you with my own weapon, my lady."

"I'm honored, sir." She smiled at him. "You can't be my second, you know. He would insist that you fought in my place. But you will come?"

"Of course."

She glanced at the window. "In an hour, then."

Deliberately, she set out on her horse, riding astride as she'd learned in childhood. The predawn air was light and cool, and stimulated her dull senses. She delivered a note to Cassandra's butler, giving explicit instructions that the note was not to be given to her sister until first light, but then it must be done.

Then, head high, she rode for Hyde Park.

*　　*　　*

Tynan was half mad with a mix of emotions he could barely untangle—worry and jealousy and fear mixed with anger and a sense of betrayal—and all of them were underscored by the sense of impending doom he could not shake. He could not find Gabriel, and Cassandra's butler insisted the woman was not in, nor had he seen her since early evening.

He decided Adriana must have gone to her sister for comfort. And since there was nothing else for him to do, Tynan sought comfort of his own. Knowing it might come to this, he'd tucked his servant's garb into a cloth bag, and just before dawn he stabled the horse, changed his clothes, shivering in the cold morning, and set out on foot for the church where the old priest sang an early mass every morning.

As he made his way through the dark but stirring streets, he found himself fingering the carved wooden rosary beads in his pocket. They had belonged to Aiden, and Tynan kept them safely hidden away, for when he held the beads that his brother's fingers had worn nearly smooth, he felt Aiden's presence more clearly than at any other time. And as he walked, he probed the foreboding he felt, trying to find some cause for it. Julian? What could have changed his fate? No. Could it be Phoebe's injuries were more serious than they knew? Perhaps.

Within the church he dipped his fingers in the font of holy water, and was about to move into the comforting, if cold, interior, when an urgent sense of warning made him halt. The foreboding was so powerful, so intense, that he whirled in his tracks and ran from the church. *Adriana.*

Adriana.

Bewildered, nearly strangled with the sense of worry, he ran back the way he'd come, covering the distance to the stable in minutes. Without bothering to change his clothes, he tossed a shilling at the stable boy, mounted and rode into the street.

Overhead, the sky was beginning to lighten, the horizon all around edging into palest light. His spine ached with the pressure of urgency, and he paused, like an animal scenting the wind, and sent up a prayer to protect those he loved, to any saints that might be listening. His prayer was meant for all of them, the whole wretched St. Ives family, who'd somehow slipped into his affections without his notice.

The beads were wrapped around his wrist, the crucifix against his palm, and with an idle thumb he rubbed the martyred body of Christ. These warnings had come on him often as a boy, footsteps on his grave, as his mother called it. He'd known when Aiden was in trouble, had known, by the thrust in his own chest, when his brother died. This felt much the same, only diluted and more confusing because of it. He'd once asked his mother why God bothered to send warnings of doom if he himself could do nothing to avert it. His mother, cloaked in her faith, had shushed his question without answering it.

Perhaps she'd had no answer. Tynan had still never found one. He fought superstition and his worrisome belief in omens with rational thought and purest logic and the square, solid intelligence of a good businessman. Since seeing that damned magpie the day before, however, his rational side had been buried beneath his fears—and had opened that side of him to this sense of warning.

But only his rational mind could give him answers. Sitting on his horse in the run-down street, he looked at the sky and fingered the beads and let possibilities come to him.

The torn dress . . . the way it was flung on the bed, as if in anger. The strange look on the footman's face when the man came to tell him Adriana had gone home alone. The wide, sorrowful eyes of a woman he'd never met.

Dawn crept over the sleeping buildings, and Tynan, with that strange, intuitive leap that had made him a fortune, remembered Adriana fencing with Gabriel in the back garden.

With a growl, he spurred the horse and raced toward Hyde Park, praying he was wrong.

His horse was blowing by the time they hit the edge of the lawns, and he halted to listen for voices. Only silence and the ragged cry of swans afloat on the Serpentine came to him.

Swans.

He turned the horse and a figure emerged from the trees. Gabriel, standing straight and tall, holding up a hand. In his black cloak and high boots, he looked a pirate.

"Where is she?" Tynan asked harshly.

Gabriel caught the horse's bridle in his right hand and looked up. "If you'll give me your word as a gentleman that you will not interfere, I'll lead you to her. Otherwise, I must hold you here."

"Are you bloody mad?" Tynan acted in fury, kicking upward to loosen Gabriel's hand. Before Gabriel could make another grab, Tynan kicked the black gelding into a full run through the trees.

Leaves, damp with dew, slapped at his face and arms, and as he broke into a clearing, Tynan spied the assembly on the grass. A crowd had gathered, making a circle for the pair to face each other in the gray-blue light of dawn.

As he rode closer, he saw with an almost violent sense of relief that only Adriana had arrived thus far. Perhaps the whole spectacle could be prevented. Blind and deaf to anything but the sight of his wife, looking small and too thin in her father's clothes, her hair tied back in a long yellow braid, he made a move to dismount.

So he did not pay attention to the horsefalls thudding up behind him, and the blow across his shoulders knocked him clear. He sailed from his mount and struck the ground. The wind was knocked from him as he landed, but nothing else gave way. Before he could roll and stand, however, the force of a body was atop him, pinning him to the damp grass.

"Sorry," Gabriel said in an agreeable tone, "but I'm afraid my sister has gone through a great deal of trouble to prevent you from sacrificing yourself to this cause, and I am compelled to assist her."

19

Adriana was nonplussed at the numbers gathered to witness this fight, women as well as men, dressed nattily. None spoke, and they kept a respectful distance as she paced and glanced at the sky, and forced herself to maintain the calm that had enveloped her as she rode here.

At last Stead and his second arrived, and Adriana had a split second to observe that Stead was distressingly sober before he raised his eyes and saw that his opponent was not to be Tynan Spenser, his loathed enemy, but Adriana herself.

"You can't be serious," he said.

"Oh, I am, sir. It was my honor you insulted, so it shall be me who puts it right." She wished now she'd asked Cassandra to be her second. She wished to shed her coat to illustrate just exactly how serious she was, and it would put her at a disadvantage to toss it on the ground.

She unbuttoned it anyway, as Stead unbuttoned his own. She shed hers when he shed his. A woman, heavily cloaked, came forward to hold Adriana's coat, and she lifted her head to give thanks. The enormous, black-fringed violet eyes met her own, and Adriana only gave her a nod of thanks to the woman who had assisted her at the Duchess's ball. With dismay, she realized her hands were shaking.

Considering this course of action last night, Adriana had been absolutely certain it was the right move. Now she felt intimidated by the onlookers, and a cowardly fear of his greater size and reach, and her own brazenness. In that instant she wavered, on the verge of conceding defeat.

As if this showed on her face, the woman said quietly, "For all of us."

Adriana lifted her chin and took up her sword.

Stead tossed his head. "Well, then, since you've no men to take up your cause, let's just make this sweet and swift and be done with it." In a most ungentlemanly way, he thrust his sword toward her, as if to tear her blouse.

The anger she'd nursed through the night now rose afresh, and with savage joy she let everything come back to her: Malvern smirking when he sent her away, the chatter and talk in the streets, the ugly drawings. And more. As she lifted Gabriel's sword, she felt his strength and laughter, his deadly skill, fill her. She let Martinique, that wild, exotic place that had so shaped her life and her world, enfold her.

And she thought of her love, of Tynan, for whom she also fought today. "On guard," she cried, and thrust.

And they were engaged. Stead quickly saw his opponent was no girl playing dress-up, and they settled in to a deadly serious fight. A thrust, a parry, a block and a strike point to Stead, one to Adriana. In moments they were sweating. Adriana heard only her own breath, and the clank of metal to metal. Her being narrowed to this, to deflecting the slit-eyed ferocity of Stead's hatred, to giving vent to all she had endured. He cut her, high on her left arm, and the sleeve grew sticky with blood. She thrust and caught his side, only a glancing blow, but enough that he stumbled backward momentarily, and then she rushed her advantage home, dancing forward on quick feet. But he recovered with a swift upswing, and Adriana found herself very nearly without a sword.

But she, too, parried, and they were off again. Weariness weighted her arms after a time. Her shoulders burned with effort. Sweat prickled on her scalp. Her breath grew ragged and she fought to avoid the slightest sign of retreat. Stead was tired too, and with a blunt animal cry made a murderous thrust toward her belly.

Adriana swiveled sideways and simultaneously thrust her own sword, and in one sickening moment she felt the sword sink into flesh. A low dark murmur went up from the onlookers, and Gabriel was somehow grasping her arms, pulling her backward as Stead wavered in place, cold shock on his face.

He put his hand on the place and pulled it away, staring in disbelief at the blood on his palm. "It appears you have bested me," he said, and fell.

A surgeon rushed forward with his bag, and there was a sudden commotion, people dispersing quickly. Adriana dropped her sword, and all at once her entire body began to tremble, hands and knees and hips.

She raised her eyes to Gabriel. "Did I kill him?"

"Only if we're exceedingly lucky. I saw it go in—it was flesh only."

And as if to give weight to the words, the surgeon helped Stead to his feet. Adriana reached for Gabriel's hand to brace herself, her trembling increasing. Was this reaction? she thought wildly. Exhaustion? If she fainted now, like some swooning maiden, it would bloody ruin everything.

"Gabriel," she whispered, "hold me up. I fear I am going to faint."

He made a motion with one hand, but Adriana was only aware of gritting her teeth against the encroaching fuzzy blackness at the edge of her vision. She inhaled deeply, but it only made her more light-headed. Gabriel, behind her, was the only point in the world she could find, and she felt him holding her as the world spun. She kept her eyes open, staring hard at a world narrowed to a small slit as she breathed in and out very slowly, willing herself not to faint, to make her watery body remain upright.

Then into that narrowed world haloed with that fuzzy black came Tynan, but not Tynan, dressed in a peasant's garb, his grass-stained shirt open at the neck and an expression of unholy fury on his face. She reached for him, grateful, no matter how angry he was, to see him.

But the motion jolted free the pain that she had not until that moment acknowledged, a wave of slightly nauseating pain from her shoulder to her wrist, and in surprise she looked down and saw that her entire sleeve was soaked with crimson.

Blackness engulfed her vision. Strange, she thought, feeling herself fall in slow motion, she'd always thought fainting would be like sleeping, but it wasn't. It was fuzzy and confusing and it made her head ache, but she was distantly aware the whole time. Aware of her body simply refusing to support her, of strong arms catching her, of the cold, damp grass below her when she was stretched out. She was amazingly dizzy and there was an odd sort of buzzing sound in her ears, or maybe only her head. She felt the sleeve being ripped away and heard a low, Irish curse.

She turned her head slowly and opened her eyes. "Tynan," she whispered.

But he did not smile. Did not kiss her, as she hoped. He raised his heavy curtain of lashes and revealed only the same anger she'd seen a moment ago. She'd wounded his pride, she thought vaguely. "I had to," she said. "Don't you see?"

Gabriel's hand smoothed over her head. "All's well, Riana, but we've got to take you to a surgeon. Can you sit up?"

With his help she did so. And there, kneeling before her was the woman with the extraordinary eyes. A long black lock of hair fell out of her cape as she flung the coat around Adriana's shoulders and pulled it tight. "Well done," she whispered, and squeezed her hand.

Then she was gone in a swirl of skirts.

"Who is that woman?" Gabriel asked.

But Adriana only shook her head. "I don't know."

Then Tynan was lifting her in his strong arms, and even though she knew he would not welcome it, she put her hands on his face and kissed him, hard on the mouth. There was nothing he could do to stop it, and she felt the rigidness in him as he stiffly resisted, but then he was kissing her back, fervently, before he drew away.

"This will not be so easily solved as that," he said, and lifted his chin, shutting her out.

The surgeon had to be roused from his bed, and he muttered furiously about modern morals when he saw the dueling victim was a woman. But he gave her brandy and stitched her up neatly.

Outside, Gabriel took their horses, and Tynan put Adriana in a carriage and climbed in behind her, bringing with him his grim, bristling anger. It stung more than she wished to acknowledge, even through the cocoon of exhaustion that was spinning ever more thickly about her.

She leaned back, putting her head on the wall, and resolved not to beg him for his forgiveness. He knew the facts as well as she.

It was he who broke the silence as they rocked along the streets, now coming alive with full morning. "You might have let me know where you were." The lilt in his words was doubled. "So I didn't have to wonder all night if you were dead."

For that she truly was sorry. With an effort, she raised her head. A lock of hair fell in her face and she brushed it away. "I do apologize for that, Tynan. I feared what you would do if I told you what had happened."

"Ah." Bitterness edged the words. "It was all right if I worried myself half sick. It was all right if you made a bloody fool of me in the eyes of all the men in this town." He lifted a brow. "It was all right as long as you did what you felt needed doing."

During the long hours waiting for dawn, she had expected him to be angry with her. She had certainly anticipated that his pride would be wounded. But there was more here, something she could not in her depleted state quite decipher. "I did not mean to hurt you, I swear it."

"You don't ever mean to hurt anyone, do you, Riana? But you do what you like and never think."

"I cannot fight with you now." She sighed, shaking her head. "You can't have had much sleep, either. We should sleep, and then things will be clearer."

"You are not listening, Adriana. I do not intend to wait around while you get your beauty sleep so you can restore yourself to cause more damage in the lives of the people around you. I've never met such a selfish creature."

That one sailed home, an arrow piercing her straight through the heart. And out of fear of revealing how much power he had to hurt her, she reacted with anger. "If standing up for myself when a blackguard like him had the nerve to put his hands on my body without my leave is selfish, then so be it. But I'll wager here and now that no man in London will dare try it again."

"Perhaps you can tease them into it, Riana, and you'll duel weekly to the accolades that will no doubt pour down upon your pretty head."

"What a plague! Do you hear yourself? Men think

nothing matters but their own blessed pride and their tender little hearts and their desires." She clenched her jaw. "You're all so focused on every tiny little thing that you don't have time or room in all that preening manhood for a spare thought for the wishes of your wives and daughters." She slammed her hand down on the bench seat, the full swell of it coming into her chest now. "What is it that you want, Tynan? Some sweet little creature to flutter around, pampering you and hanging on your every word? Someone you dress up, like those French dolls you took to my sisters?"

His jaw was set so hard it drew the cords in his neck, and his hand lay in a tight fist in his lap. "Are you quite finished?"

"No!" she cried. "I have hidden my face for five years out of shame. I've ducked and tried to avoid facing all of it. I regret hurting my father. I regret that my hotheaded brother saw fit to kill the fool, and that they felt they had to leave. But would any of that have transpired if my name were James instead of Adriana? If I were a lord instead of a lady?"

And still his face was unmoved. Adriana felt a cracking inside, for she saw that she was fighting now for the man she had truly fallen in love with. Earnestly, she leaned forward. "You know it would not have, Tynan. You know it. And you know in your heart that you do not wish one of those proper little dolls to love. That you would never be happy with one of them." She reached for his hand, and touched, on his wrist, a string of beads. He jerked away abruptly.

She stiffened. "I see." She leaned back, feeling the ache in her arm, the weight of no sleep on her spine.

He tucked the beads in his pocket and bowed his head for a long moment. In spite of everything, she wanted to put her hands in that thick hair, wanted to press a kiss to that crown. He let go of a breath and raised his head. The anger was muted, replaced with pain. "Adriana, perhaps this is as good a moment as any for me to tell you what I have hidden."

"No," she protested. "Not like this. Not when I am so weary and you are so angry."

"Blast and damn!" He caught sight of something beyond the coach, and bolted toward the door, his hand on the catch. Before the vehicle was even fully stopped, he'd hurtled out, crying out a name.

Adriana stayed where she was, peering out the window to see what could have caused such a reaction. A tall, sturdy, black-haired man, travel-stained but prosperous enough in a striped broadcloth traveling costume, stood on the stoop, and Tynan rushed up to him, putting his hands on his arms urgently.

Without taking her eyes from the pair, she moved to the door and let the coachman help her down. "Come in and my butler will pay you," she said, worry rising at the cry that came from Tynan at whatever news was delivered. She was not quite equal to a run, but moved as quickly as she could. "What is it?"

He turned, and an expression of utter defeat was on his face. "The glassworks were burned to the ground. A dozen men were within." He bowed his head. "I must go."

"Oh, Tynan," she whispered, and put her hand on his arm. "I am so sorry. Of course you must. I'll come with you."

"No." That cord on his jaw showed once again, but he put his hand over hers gently enough, and his eyes had lost their bitterness. "I want you to go to bed. Now." He swallowed. "And you must stay with your brother, else all this will be for nothing."

Julian. She closed her eyes, torn exactly down the middle. But she nodded. "It will only be another few days, then I will come."

"I'll write to you as soon as I arrive, giving instruction."

Dread filled her, but mindful of the scene they were causing by standing out in the open this way, she only squeezed his arm and ducked her head. "Do not leave without bidding me farewell," she said, suddenly urgent.

He nodded.

"Your word, Tynan."

"You have my word." He nodded to Fiona, waiting to bustle her within, into a steaming tub of water.

Inside, the girl clucked over her bruises and the wound, and rubbed healing salve onto all of them. Then, wrapped in a flannel gown that seemed insufficient to warm her, Adriana crawled into her bed, ordered the fire stoked and chocolate brought to her. But before she could even properly adjust the pillows into the nest she so enjoyed, she was flat out, dead asleep.

Tynan, too, needed a bath and a rest and a hot meal. He settled for a shave and a wash while Seamus readied his bags. He'd left Thomas Flynn, a manager at the glassworks, in the dining room with a plate of eggs and rashers and a pile of snowy white bread from the ovens of the cook, one Mrs. Josephine Moody, whose talents in the kitchen could go a long way to healing almost any ill a man could face.

But before he joined Thomas, Tynan sat at his writing desk and took out a quill and pot of ink. He sent Seamus down to eat his fill, too, before they left.

In the silence left behind, he wrote: *Adriana—I could not bear to wake you.* He paused, his chest hollow, and tried to think what else to say. That he was angry, but with himself? That her actions had shown him the falseness of his own?

That he could not ask a woman he loved with such depth to take on a life that would be so much more difficult than the one she'd won for herself here?

Some part of him knew it was only despair putting such dark thoughts in his mind. That warning of doom had not been over Adriana at all. He had known it when the duel ended and his nerves only screamed the louder that the doom still lay ahead, and here it was. The glassworks burned, the Catholics within turned to corpses. All of his own work, all the hopes of the men he'd employed, dozens of them, gone in the flames of hatred.

In that moment when Thomas had given him the news, Tynan realized how vain his journey here had been. Vain in every sense of the word, vain because it had been pride that led him on a fool's errand, vain because it was his arrogance that made him believe he could overturn hundreds of years of ill-feeling simply because he decided it was time.

He belonged to Ireland, and there he would go. There he would spend his fortune. He'd put his hands and heart to work there, spend his fortune doing what he could, spend his political intelligence helping to build a true freedom from the straw Irish parliament.

The times and his obligations required that he maintain his lie, and it grieved him a little. But too many others would be hurt if he declared himself Catholic—he would lose his own lands, and all the lands he held in his name for the Catholics in his county. For Aiden's memory, he wished he could declare himself boldly, but he'd been given a task, and serve it he would. God knew his heart.

Grieved and lost, he picked up the quill and wrote quickly. Then he sealed it with his ring and carried it to Fiona. "Do not wake her," he said. "Give it to her later."

Fiona took the note with a troubled expression. "Begging your pardon, milord, but she'll be most sorely grieved if you do not tell her yourself. It was the last thing she said before she slept."

He closed his eyes. "I cannot wake her and still do my duty," he said with more frankness than was proper. As if to shake it away, he pressed a false smile on his face. "You made her a beautiful Cáer."

She fingered the note. "Thank you." She bobbed mechanically.

"Where is your home, girl? May I take your people some news of you?"

Her eyes flew open. "Oh, yes, milord!" She paused. "If you wouldn't mind, I've some stockings to send my sister. In County Meath?"

"Aye. Fetch them. I'll wait."

She scurried down the hallway and up the stairs at the end. Tynan stood outside Adriana's door with his hands linked behind his back, staring at the handle as if it would turn itself. Like a cat, he thought, and scowled.

He opened the door and entered silently. The smell of her hung in the air, lavender and toilet water and a hint of musk that was the alluring natural essence of her skin. At her bedside he stopped. She lay on her side, her head buried in the pillows, and her breath was so deep as to be nearly invisible. A scrape marred her cheekbone, and a purple and yellow bruise radiated from it, creeping over her eyelid, joining with the blue circle of exhaustion below. The sight gave him a physical pain, and abrupt violence rose in him again.

As it must have in her. He only imagined what had transpired. She had experienced it.

He smiled. And triumphed.

Here was the unadorned, unhidden face of Lady Adriana St. Ives. A woman whose passion showed in the fullness of her red lips and that bruised eye; whose laughter would mar the smoothness of that flesh with lines. Here was the lady, in her prim nightrail with tiny ribbons at the collar, and the hoyden, in the bandage around her arm. A thousand faces, Phoebe had said of her sister. But all were one woman, and the changing light only brought out unseen facets.

He thought of his wish that she should bear him children, and it pained him most of all that he was leaving that vision here on these shores. For he would have liked the way she bore them, in her belly and in her arms, and with that bossy voice. He would have liked planting them, and watching them grow. He would have liked holding his wife's hand at weddings.

But now she had regained her courage, and by morning she would be as celebrated as she'd once been scorned. She would be free to choose a more suitable husband from dozens of proposals, and host her sisters' presentations to Court, and take up the life of a proper English lady.

He half smiled. Not proper, perhaps. But English certainly.

As if she sensed his presence, she stirred, making a soft sound of pain. Very gently, the Black Angel, whose heart had remain untouched until now, bent and pressed a kiss to the head of the woman who'd stolen it entire.

And then he left her.

20

Adriana rose out of sleep by degrees, a sense of disturbance on her. Before she opened her eyes, she tried to
remember what it was, what worrisome thing she had
to face, and a host of confused possibilities presented
themselves. The trial? The ball? For a long moment
she could not even think what day it was, or what she
was to do, or what bed she'd awaken in.

Tynan.

She bolted awake, her whole body protesting with
varying levels of screams as she forced herself to sit up.
The light was low and cool in the room—perhaps
early evening, she thought, or a cloudy noonday. Who
could tell? With effort, she flung back the coverlet and
moved to the window, her hair spilling free, wavy
from the braid she'd worn.

Absently, she put her hand over the sore, bandaged
place on her arm and folded back the shutters to discover a cold, thick rain, and traffic that told her it was
at least not morning.

Lightheaded, she turned to call for Fiona and spied
the letter on the dresser. Her name was scrawled across

the face of it in that bold, hurried hand she had not seen since he arrived at Hartwood Hall. She halted, knowing it meant he'd already left, that he'd broken his word to her. A crushing sense of loss burned in her.

But the room was cold and her feet were bare, and delaying the inevitable would not make it disappear. Mouth tight, chin high, she marched across the room, plucked up the missive and broke the seal.

My dear Adriana,

No man (or woman) can serve two masters, and that is what I have tried to do these past months. It was my own recognition of that fact that angered me this morning. In your integrity, I saw my own lack. In your willingness to fight to the death for what you believed, I saw I have only gone half measures. In your full-throated devotion to your duty, and your desire to make an accounting of your mistakes, I saw that I have run from what I must do more often than I've accounted.

Which leads me to a confession you are owed. A confession I should have given long since, one I must deliver in this way because I cannot bear to watch your face as my lie is exposed.

I cannot write it in a letter that might go astray, for much rests on my ability to maintain this fabrication. Go to Julian. He knows the truth. Please accept my apology for it in advance. I am most sincerely sorry.

It is time now for me to take up my own sword. I will await word on the method you choose for annulment of this marriage, for I wish to leave you free to pursue your own dreams and goals without the hindrance of a husband you chose in a moment of desperation. The

funds, of course, will be yours to dispose of as you wish.
I consider our bargain well-met, and release you from
any further obligation to me.

And at last, I will say only that you have enriched
my life and leant a clarity of vision I had lacked till
now. I have no regrets over our time together, and hope
only that I have been of some help to you as well.

Most sincerely,
Tynan Spenser

Adriana sank down in her chair and closed her eyes, as if to erase what she'd read. She sat there, breathless, holding it loosely in her hands. At last she raised her eyes to her reflection. Her face was bruised and weary, but in her eyes she saw the light that had been lost. On her mouth she saw strength where once there had been weakness.

More than life itself she wanted to go after him, pack her bags and collect her maid and set off on a chase behind him, to convince him that her love was true and clear, and would weather whatever he thought threatened them. She thought of his face when he kissed her, thought of the unbearable tenderness in his eyes when they made love, thought of his easy laughter and zestful approach to living, and she knew she could not let him go so easily.

But whatever faced Tynan and whatever she faced herself were nothing in comparison to what Julian faced two days hence. Because her brother acted on her behalf, because he needed her now, she would stay. She would testify if necessary. She would stand up for him and for herself.

And then she would go to Tynan.

First, she had to see Julian.

Winter hung with frosted threat in the day, and despite her layers of clothing, Adriana was cold. Beside her, Gabriel shivered even through his greatcoat, and Adriana glanced up at him. Below his dark hat, his face was shadowed, and she glimpsed revulsion on his mouth. "Are you freezing?"

He shook his head silently, his gaze trained on the looming structure of the Tower. Ravens circled and landed, sailed off the ramparts and squalled in the dark day, lending gloom to the already threatening structure. "I hate ravens," he said. "So many ravens can't be good luck."

"I think that's the idea," Adriana replied grimly.

"Wait here," he instructed, and moved forward to talk to a guard in red and blue livery. Money exchanged hands and Gabriel waved her forward. She linked her arm through his elbow as they passed the gates and moved into the quiet walk beyond.

"It's better by day than it was by night," she commented, but it gave her the same creeping sense of despair it had the first time. "Oppressive. Julian will have nightmares for years."

"Ah, there are darker things in his memory than this," Gabriel replied.

She raised her head. "Will the two of you ever share the full scope of those adventures?"

He looked down, a sad smile on his elegant mouth. "Honestly? Not likely. I've no doubt you'll hear most over time, but never all. And do not try to dig out Julian's sorrow. He'll grieve a woman he met there forever, and it will be better to leave him to nurse that place alone."

"Will you tell me, Gabriel?"

"Perhaps." Then, as if he knew he'd grown too serious, he gave her a lively smile. "Buy enough port and I reckon I'll spill most anything."

At the foot of the stairs Gabriel halted. "Do you wish to do this alone?"

"No. Please come."

So together they ascended the narrow, circling stairs, feeling the damp and cold seep in through the walls. The guardsman unlocked Julian's door, and Adriana was relieved to see a coal fire burning on the grate. The room was drafty, but no more uncomfortable than many of the medieval rooms at Hartwood. And Julian himself appeared in good spirits, his long golden hair combed back from his freshly shaven face.

"Adriana, Gabriel!" he cried, and jumped up to embrace them, kissing his sister, punching his brother, and Adriana felt herself letting go of a breath. "What news have you brought me?" His brows beetled, and the effect was the same as ever: it lent his fair face a dark and dangerous angle. "What happened to your face, Riana? Did your husband beat you?"

She and Gabriel exchanged a glance and both laughed. "We've quite a tale to tell," Gabriel said, and launched into the story of Adriana's encounter with an enemy of Spencer, and her subsequent duel.

Julian looked disconcerted at first. "Why didn't you let Spenser or Gabriel duel on your behalf, Adriana?"

She sighed and even resorted to rolling her eyes in exasperation. "I wanted to fight my own battle, and I did. Enough, please?"

He shrugged, and Adriana pressed on. "I've come for another reason, Julian." She took out the letter from her husband and gave it to him. "What lie did he tell?"

Julian read the letter and his face emptied of all expression. The gray eyes were mirrors when he looked at her. "Did he return to his estates?"

Gabriel supplied the answer. "He has had periodic news of unrest during his sojourn here. Yesterday, a man brought the news that his glassworks had burned to the ground."

Julian glanced at the letter and nodded. He gave it back to Adriana and tucked his hands behind his back. "It is not my place to tell you."

She narrowed her eyes. "You will tell me this time, brother. I asked before and will not ask again."

"Do you wish to use his lie to remove yourself from the marriage?"

A pang of sorrow burst in her heart, and she put a hand over the place. "No! What could be so terrible that I would toss it all away?" Troubled, she looked down at the letter, at the scrawl of his handwriting over the page, and felt bereft.

"He is Catholic," Julian said.

For a moment Adriana waited for the rest, but when her brother only regarded her steadily, she cried, "That's all? He's Catholic?"

Julian nodded. "But it is more than you think, that choice. And if any learn of his affiliation, he will lose everything."

Still, Adriana could not quite take it in. "That is the secret. The whole secret," she repeated. "He's Catholic."

"Yes."

She made an exasperated noise and looked at Gabriel, who had a secretive smile on his mouth. "And this was so dreadful he could not tell me? And he left me, thinking I would reject him over that?"

Now Gabriel spoke, and his voice held the round vowels of his lecturing style. "We spoke of the question you asked me about race last night," he said.

She nodded, frowning.

"The question of his religion goes much deeper than simply what customs you will indulge as his wife. Imagine instead that Tynan is of my own race, and going to him, standing by him, meant you were also transformed. The struggle you will face is that difficult."

It was difficult to admit to such private feelings, but Adriana raised her head and met his eyes. "I was prepared to endure him only," she said at last. "And instead, he stole my heart."

"Can you stand with him, always? Take care in your answer, Adriana. He has endured much. He has given much, and will be asked to give more. His wife will be asked for the same courage." Julian bent his head and looked at his hand. On his third finger was the ruby ring that bore the family crest. "I was prepared to hate him on your behalf, and find I have grown to admire him deeply. I have not seen how you matured these past five years, Riana, but the girl we left would not be equal to being his wife."

She swallowed, stung. "Thank you ever so."

Gabriel took her hand. "You have been in here, Julian, but I've been out there. She is no more a frivolous, vain,—" He grinned at her puff of indignation. "—self-centered child. She has grown into a woman with courage and honor."

Julian seemed to take that into account, and then he inclined his head. "Then you must go to him."

She scowled. "Thank you for your permission, oh lord of mine, but I'd already intended to go to him as soon as the trial is finished. I do not need your instruction to make my choice to follow my husband. I only came to discover what secret so pains him."

"You needn't stay, Adriana. I would not ask it of you."

Gabriel grinned, that rakish, mischievous grin. "Oh, but I think she shall, brother." From within his coat he took a thin sheaf of papers. "For she's become a hero."

"What?" Adriana saw what they were and moaned. "Oh, not more satires!"

Julian laughed aloud, and behind her Gabriel joined him. She snatched the papers from Julian's hand and glared down at them.

"Madame Chevalier! Madame D'Artagnan!" Julian said, and laughed again.

Adriana gaped. There were three drawings, and all were equally flattering. In one, more skilled than the others, she was drawn straight and tall, her long braid suggested, her feminine curves downplayed, her sword arm graceful. And her opponent was sketched as a lascivious sort, eyes bulging. The caption read, *The lout learns a lesson.*

But Madame Chevalier, in spite of its greater crude-ness, pleased her ever so much more. It showed her as an avenging angel, a woman dressed in man's clothing and wings, her hair streaming out behind her, and a small army of women, some in various levels of disha-bille, descending from the heavens behind her. Adri-ana's sword was set to strike down a cowering crowd of terrified rakes.

She, too, laughed in delight. "This is priceless!" she cried. "I wonder who drew it?"

"The style is not familiar to me."

Gabriel frowned. "It is not signed, but I recognize the style. Whoever it is has a taste for radical politics."

Still smiling, Adriana imagined framing the thing, for the sheer pleasure of remembering that morning. And then a brainstorm took her. "I have an idea!" she cried, and grasped Julian's arm. "I know how we can put this all to rights."

The morning of the trial, Adriana carefully adorned herself. "Be ready, Fiona," she said as she patted the last curls of her hair into place. "I do not wish to delay until morning."

"Yes, milady."

The carriage arrived to take her and Gabriel, dressed as finely as his sister in wig and powder and the finest of morning suits. "Madame," he said, handing her up into the carriage with a wicked glint in his eye.

"Sir," she replied archly.

There was a crowd gathered before Parliament, of course. Adriana wondered if her mysterious satirist was among them. Gabriel had asked about with no luck; the artist was very careful.

As Adriana stepped out of the carriage, a cry went up, and startled, she paused, looking out. The crowd waved and called to her, "Lady Chevalier!" and some even tossed ribbons and flowers toward her. A man's handkerchief, starched and monogrammed, stuck to her sleeve, and a velvet ribbon landed across her shoulders. Instinctively, she took the standards and kissed them, grinning and waving back at them.

Gabriel offered his arm, suppressed laughter making his eyes starry and liquid. "What a fickle lot," he murmured. "One day harlot, the next heroine."

"Heroine is ever so much more enjoyable."

Within, however, her nerves came back. It was a thin crowd of Lords who gathered here today, but in their wigs and sober faces, she felt intimidated enough. In the spectator's boxes she spied Malvern's mother, her mouth pinched in a drawn face. She intended to win here today, no doubt.

Gabriel leaned over to whisper, "None of her lovers are here!"

She scanned the crowd and discovered it was true. In excitement, she squeezed his arm, willing herself not to smile. They'd obviously chosen to opt out of the process.

The trial proceeded smoothly. A statement of the charges, along with a long, emotional oratory by one of the members about the scourge of dueling and the cost of it in terms of young men's lives, and the need to halt it, for good. By the time the speech was finished, impatience was rife—the members wanted to be done with this spectacle. The case against Julian was presented straightforwardly, a cold-blooded murder, this, since Malvern himself was very drunk and the duel should have been avoided.

Then Julian's defense was presented. Malvern had grievously wounded Lord Albury's sister, publicly bragging about his sexual exploits with her. What man would not take up that challenge?

Finally, Adriana was given a chance to speak. She stepped up to the box, hiding her trembling hands in her skirts. For a long minute, intimidated, she could not find her tongue. Then, at a frown from Gabriel, she lifted her chin. "Gentlemen, I would like to offer an alternative to these proceedings."

A murmur went up. The judge raised his hand and gave Adriana a nod.

"Thank you." She took a breath. "My brother acted as any gentleman would have. He defended me, his little sister, by challenging the man who insulted my honor. However—" Her hands stilled their trembling and she let them relax at her sides. "—I did not conduct myself in a manner befitting my station and breeding.

"Many of you knew my father, and you know that he took the death of my mother in a most grievous fashion. We all went to Martinique to be with him, and comfort him, and thus, those years when I should have been learning to walk correctly and speak correctly, I spent running the beaches with my brothers, playing pirate."

A red-faced man she did not recognize stood up, "What has this to do with—"

The judge held up a hand. "Continue, Countess."

Adriana smiled faintly. "My error was in my belief that I was set apart from other women by my adventurous heart. If my mother had lived, she would have gently steered me in the right direction, but she did not. I learned to fight like a boy, and my heart was too lusty."

She had rehearsed this speech a dozen times before her mirror at home, and now bowed her head meekly. "I am ashamed of my willfulness in taking a lover, and I am even more ashamed that I did not insist upon dueling Malvern myself. If I wanted to play the man on one level, then I needed to be a man on all levels. As some of you have no doubt heard, I have chosen to defend myself in recent days, against the bold actions of man who wished to explore the truth of my scarlet reputation."

Suppressed smiles appeared here and there. Adriana waited.

"Are you finished?"

"No, my lord. I should like to offer myself as the object of transportation, to take Julian's punishment on my own shoulders. I ask to be transported to Ireland, and there live with my new husband, where I will be no offense to English society." She stepped back, then found Malvern's mother in the gallery. "And I do offer my most sincere apologies to Mrs. Pickering on the loss of her son."

Judgment was swift and relieved. The Lords agreed to transport Adriana to Ireland, where she was to remain for a period of two years, effective immediately. In two years she could again visit her family and ancestral home, but if she ever took up a sword or was discovered in a compromising situation, the banishment would be extended to the whole of her lifetime.

Julian was free.

They gathered in the drawing room some hours later. Adriana and Fiona were dressed as men. In this instance it was not nearly as unusual as in some cases. Women traveling the dangerous roads often donned men's garb to make the journey, and Adriana had insisted Fiona do the same.

She felt equal parts apprehension, excitement, and sorrow as her brothers stood to bid her farewell. She hugged Gabriel first, smelling the oil in his hair and the spicy water he liked to wear. His lean, long body was not nearly as thin as it had been only a few weeks before, and his arms were fierce as he embraced her. Tears gathered thickly in her throat, and she put her forehead against his shoulder. "I've only just got you back, and now I must let you go again," she whispered. "Write to me often!"

"Yes," he whispered, then let her go, and from his pocket took a fistful of wildflowers, only slightly crumbled. "I did not forget."

Tears spilled over as she accepted the offering, then clutching the flowers in her fist, she turned to Julian, feeling somehow shy with him. They'd barely spent a day's time together in all of this, and she felt his secrets and sorrows still buried in a tight little lump within him. "As soon as you are able, please come to Ireland. I have missed you."

And Julian, who had always been careful to reveal as little as possible, flung an arm around her and hugged her so tight she thought he would break her neck. "I will," he said. "I promise." Against her hair he whispered, "I'm so proud of you, Riana. And so glad you've found your love." He pulled back. "I am here now to see to our estates and our sisters. Go to your husband."

She nodded and stepped back, looking around her one last time.

"It isn't far," Gabriel said. "We'll come stomping around in such numbers and so often you'll be glad to be rid of us."

It was a long and arduous trip to the ferry at Holyhead, and took three days instead of the two the coachman had promised, thanks to the wheel-sucking mud. But at last they were aboard the ferry, on a sea that was calm in spite of the threatening clouds.

Adriana was stunned to discover how much she had missed the taste of sea air, and spent the long afternoon hours on deck, watching the waves spread away from the ferry in long, triangular swaths. Beneath her fingers the rail was crusted with salt, and by evening her own skin was similarly thick.

Mid-passage, they encountered a squall that sent the boat rocking and bucking, and most of the passengers scurrying for buckets, but although she allowed herself to be entreated to go belowdecks, Adriana still did not mind the rocking. It brought back a thrilling host of memories, and she thought that someday she would like to sail again. All these years, she had missed the sea, missed beaches and the roar of the winds and the lap of the waves and the unmatchable scent of salt and fish and water.

At Dublin they hired another coach, and it was yet another long drive across a countryside so green as to burn her eyes.

Her spirits till now had been high. All would be well. Her brothers were safe on English soil. Her sisters were looked after. The family seat could be coaxed to prosperity once again. And she had found her love.

And her first glimpse of Ireland seemed to only fuel that intensity of joy. Everywhere she saw Tynan—saw that wild beauty of his face, the untamed wonder of his heart and spirit. She thought, staring out of the window of the carriage, of his teasing words, that you could imagine the old kings riding over a hill at any turn. And as they passed mysterious glades, lonely under the gray and boiling sky, she thought of Fiona's description of the fairy folk here. *Beautiful, but dangerous, too.*

She could not stop drinking it in, feasting her eyes.

And then she began to see the cottages. And the folk who lived in them. Mean hovels and people with rags on their feet, their shoulders stooped with poverty. This was not the well-fed peasantry she knew. There were no neat plots of vegetables in side yards, no children running in the lanes, screeching.

Mile after mile. So many of them.

In alarm she looked at Fiona. "Why are they so desperately poor?"

Fiona looked out the window. "Catholic," she said, as if the answer were obvious.

Catholic.

What do you know of Ireland, Adriana? Tynan had asked her.

Nothing, she had to answer now. She had known nothing. The depth of her ignorance made tears spring to her eyes, made her heart ache for her husband, for only now did she understand what had caused that darkness in his eyes.

Fiona reached across the carriage and, in a most unseemly but welcome move, covered Adriana's hand with her own. Around the thickness in her throat Adriana asked, "And you, Fiona? Your family—are they out there?"

The maid only turned her face to the window. She nodded and drew from beneath her dress a crucifix that had lain hidden all this time. A crucifix she lifted now to her lips and let fall again, over her dress, in plain sight.

They did not arrive at Glencove till after the sun had set, mid-afternoon, on the sixth day after they left London. Both of them were stiff and cold and hungry, but the dark towers looming at the top of the hill did not appear particularly welcoming. "Here we are," the coachman said.

Adriana stared up at the crenellated tower and felt suddenly terrified at the reception she might face. After all, she did not know how Tynan would feel about her arrival. She thought of him in his bedroom at the town house, when she'd awakened to find him with his head in his hands in the middle of the night, could only remember the darkness that could cloud his eyes, and she was afraid.

Fiona stood beside her uncertainly. "Milady?"

She squared her shoulders. "Bring our bags," she ordered the coachman, and strode toward the heavy door, which swung open as she mounted the steps. It creaked loudly, as if giving warning, and Adriana couldn't help the nervous giggle that rose in her throat at the man who came out, tall and gaunt, white hair grown down to his shoulders in a thin mass.

In a most unfriendly tone, he uttered something in Gaelic. Alarmed, Adriana looked at Fiona. "What?"

"He wants you to state your business," she said, and grimaced. In an equally sharp tone, the girl rattled off a long rolling string of syllables in the same tongue. Adriana heard her name, but made out nothing else.

But it seemed effective. With a surprised grunt, the man moved backward, waving them in. "Where is Lord Glencove?" she asked.

"Wait here." He left them in a room that might have been cheerful had the fire been lit, the drapes open. Instead she shivered, apprehension crawling up her spine. She carefully did not look at Fiona.

The man returned. "Come on, then."

He led them through a cold passageway and up a set of stairs into what would have been a great hall in another century. It had been richly decorated with rugs, and tapestries hung on the walls, and a very warm, bright fire burned in a stag-sized hearth. Candles in an iron candelabra over the table cast long shadows up to the heavy beams of the ceiling, and cast them down upon the man who sat at the table, alone.

Adriana could not help herself—she laughed. "Why, Fiona, I believe we've stumbled into a Gothic novel. And who could that man be but the mysterious lord of the manor?" She strode over to the fire and warmed herself, covering her unease with a bright smile. "We're frozen to death, Tynan, and starving, too."

Only then did she see the gauntness of his lean cheeks, the dark circles below his beautiful eyes. His hair was loose on the shoulders of his shirt, open at the neck. "What are you doing here, Riana?" he said gruffly.

Pierced, she only looked at him, and realized she had anticipated a much different reaction. She'd expected to see him coming back down the hall himself, an expression of joy on his face. She had expected a wild embrace, a passionate kiss.

She swallowed and lifted her chin. "I am here to be with my husband. What else?"

He bowed his head. "Did your brother tell you the truth?"

"He did."

His eyes closed in an expression of defeat, and Adriana did not know whether to comfort him or slap him. She stayed where she was, frozen in uncertainty, nonplussed by her reception.

At last he raised his head. "Forgive me." He stood, gestured with one long-fingered, graceful hand to the table. "Please come sit. You, too, Fiona—we stand on less ceremony here. I'll call for some supper." He nodded at his man, hovering by the door like a praying mantis. "'Twill only be bread and cheese and apples tonight. We've buried seven men, and one was the son of my cook."

"Tynan, I am so sorry." Adriana reached for his hand, but as if he could not bear her touch, he pulled away.

Fiona stood. "Well, I know how to cook. You could stand with a meal yourself, my lord, by the look of you. Tell me where the kitchen is, and I'll make us all something simple and hot to warm our bones."

The expression on Tynan's face lightened as he looked at the country maid, and Adriana felt the most irrational sense of jealousy at Fiona's inherent usefulness. "I would be grateful," he said, then hesitated. "Tell James to bring it to my chamber later."

So he wouldn't even sit with her and have a meal, Adriana thought. In misery, she bowed her head.

When Fiona had gone, however, Tynan moved close and touched her shoulder. "I am humbled by your appearance here, Adriana, and I do appreciate your loyalty, but you may not stay."

A sorrow sailed through her. "Tynan!"

He shook his head, stubbornness on his mouth. "You do not know. . . ." He sighed. "I have decided not to buy a seat in the English parliament. My work is here. Your life will be easier there."

"Tynan, stop it!" She stood and put her hands on his face. "I want to be here, with you."

Gently, he took her hand away. "No," he said simply. "I'll see that you're made comfortable. Forgive me, but I must go now."

And as if they'd never kissed, never held each other through long nights of joy, he moved away, his back straight, his hair tumbling in a heavy fall down his back. Her husband.

Who did not, after all, want her.

21

A young woman with heavy black hair rolled into a simple knot on her head led Adriana up another set of stairs, and another, and to a bedroom set high in one of the towers. A fire burned in the grate, though it had not yet removed the chill of the room. Four arched windows, shuttered against the night and the cold, circled the room, four of them. The bed was piled high with down coverlets. A long-haired black-and-white cat had made itself comfortable in the center, and the girl was about to shoo it away when Adriana stopped her. "Let him stay."

"Do you need anything else, my lady?"

Adriana shook her head distractedly and waved her away. She drifted over to the bed then, suddenly feeling the exhaustion of the long journey, and curled up next to the cat. He stretched luxuriously and began to purr. His fur was sparkling clean and there were no burrs in the long tail. She smiled, scratching between his ears. "You're a spoiled one, aren't you?"

He meowed softly, cheerfully, and butted his head harder against her hand.

A vision of Tynan's face rose in her mind, and she ached to go to him. To lie down next to him and feel his skin, to smell his hair and just . . . be with him. Near him. Listening to him sleep.

She had come so far, she thought, not only in the miles from London and her home, but in her life. Lying now in an Irish castle. with a cat purring under her ministrations, she thought of her father and her mother, of Martinique and ocean voyages and Malvern and the long exile she'd put on herself after the duel, and it felt to her that all roads had led here. That somehow all of it had prepared her to be not just a wife, but a helpmate and soulmate to a man who would need her.

Outside, it began to rain, the sound a pattering softness, and Adriana lifted her head. She nudged the hollow spot in her chest to see what it was made of, and wondered, Was she afraid of this? Afraid of making this foreign place her home, of making the troubles of her husband's world her own?

Perhaps a little, she admitted to herself. Perhaps she was a little afraid of what might face all of them, not only Tynan and his people, but the children they would bear. Perhaps there would be sorrow.

But the world was changing—it was in the air, as her father had always said when she came to him as a girl, disturbed by some injustice or another. He'd often teased her that she had the heart of a revolutionary, and Adriana supposed it was true. Once, she'd imagined the adventures of overturning her woman's life for that of a man, a sea captain or a trader or a pirate.

Dear Papa, who'd always seen her so clearly. If he'd been able to grant her a commission in the navy, she had no doubt he would have.

Instead he'd asked this proud Irishman to be her husband.

He'd asked Tynan to be her husband.

Adriana closed her eyes in swift understanding. All this time, she had believed that her father anticipated the dire straits of his girls' financial situation, and knowing a rich Irish lord, had married her to him for the money.

Tonight, with her love hanging in the balance, she saw that he'd done it for her, to give her a chance to have a life worth the living, a life that would test her and challenge her and sometimes—yes, even put her at risk.

"Ah, Papa," she said aloud, rubbing the cat's belly, "you knew me so well." He alone had always seen through her faces, had understood that her passion and curiosity could be directed. And he'd found her a husband more beautiful than heaven, with a task too big for him alone, so she could be engaged, heart and soul, to something that would have meaning to her when she died.

In realization, she laughed, and let the tears fall. It had been a long, strange journey, but she could not think of anywhere on earth she would rather be than under the same roof as Tynan Spenser.

She awakened to such stillness that she could not think where she was. There was some sort of bird making a funny cry, one she didn't recognize, and there was something heavy against her neck. A cat.

And there was a voice, low and melodious, unmistakable. "Riana." His hand fell on her face, smoothing away a lock of hair.

She turned and opened her eyes, lifting a hand to clasp his hand to her face. "Tynan."

There was sorrow on his mouth. "There is something I want to show you. Get dressed and come down."

"What is it, Tynan? You needn't—"

"I do," he said, and stood. "Dress warmly. 'Tis cold and wet this morn."

He left her, and Adriana dressed quickly in a warm woolen skirt and blouse, with a shawl over her shoulders. Downstairs, she found him holding her cloak, which someone had dried by the fire. It smelled of wood smoke as he wrapped it around her shoulders.

"Are you hungry?"

She shook her head, intent on getting this over with.

"Come, then." He pushed open the heavy door and they stepped into a cold, overcast day. Rain had been falling, but had stopped, leaving behind that peculiar stillness punctuated only with birds. But below that quiet, Adriana thought she heard something else. She halted for a moment and listened. "Is that the sea?"

"Aye. Just over that rise." He pointed. "That's where we're going."

They walked in silence, leaving the path to climb a low green hill, barren of trees and studded with tumbles of rock. Overhead, seagulls circled and called, and

Adriana lifted her head to watch them, feeling a soft, blooming sense of something in her heart. In the air now she could smell the sea, that rich and evocative scent that so stirred her.

At the crest of the hill Tynan stopped. Adriana looked up at him as she came behind. Against the gray sky, he formed a silhouette of severe darkness, his hair blowing free from the queue in wisps, his dark cloak billowing on the wind. His face, still and severe in its beauty, dominated now in profile by that hawkish nose, seemed carved out of the granite that lay scattered in knots over the ground. She thought of his nickname, the Black Angel, and how it suited him, but in ways she would never have dreamed.

My blood came from that earth, he'd said to her.

She stood beside him silently, taking in the view. Behind was the sound of the sea, not quite visible—perhaps she would see it if she walked to the edge just there. Closer in, the hill dropped into an almost perfectly rounded bowl where winter-bare shrubs clustered in groups, as if to resist the sea squalls. A flat stone marked the middle of the clearing, and a scattering of rocks and hills rose on all sides.

"My brother died here," Tynan said without preamble. "They posted lookouts on all four hills, but that day they were short a man, and the murderers came through." His voice was dull. He lifted an arm and pointed. "They caught him there, on that slab, and cut his throat."

Adriana stared at him, a hand over her mouth. "Why?"

He swallowed and turned to her. "He was a priest.

It is illegal to hold mass." For a moment it seemed he might allow escape to the grief shimmering in his eyes—those eyes made of the land and the sky—but he pursed his lips tightly and shifted his face away. "So you see, it is not as simple as it appears, and I cannot allow you to stay." He sighed. "In truth, we are not even legally bound by my church."

It wounded her, quick and sharp, but in a rush she understood all of it. "You went to mass in London, didn't you?"

"Aye." Grimly, he set his mouth. "I will not ask that you take this life. I was selfish in imagining it, and more selfish still in lying to you."

And there, in that wild beauty of his face, she saw love, and her heart rocked. She raised a hand to his cheek. "I believed there was true feeling between us these past weeks, Tynan Spenser. If I am wrong, I'll go away and leave you." Tears welled in her eyes at the thought. "But in truth, I would follow you into hell itself if it meant I could lie with you at night." A tear slipped from her eye and slid down her cheek. "I do not mind taking new vows with you."

An expression of pain crossed his face and he ducked away, striding across the crest of the hill to stand with his back to her on the edge of that rocky outcropping. Adriana gave him a moment, watching the wind whip his hair and his cloak. Then she followed him.

Below stretched the wild sea, roiling gray in the wintry wind. It crashed to the rocks and roared out its song, and she paused, overcome. The wet wind touched her face, cold and exhilarating, and she closed her eyes in acceptance, lifting her chin into it, breathing it deep. "I have missed the sea," she said in wonder. "I had no idea how much. It's like coming home, to hear that song again."

Still he only glared at the waves, that hawkish nose so bold in profile.

She reached out a hand cautiously and put it against her husband's broad, strong back. "Let me help you, Tynan. Let me be a true wife, a helpmate."

"You don't know what you're asking." His voice was rough with despair. "There is so much struggle ahead, so many sorrows for my people until we are free. I cannot ask you to share such a burden when it isn't even your own."

"The world is changing," she said, hearing her father's voice. "The American colonies are free. There is revolt in the islands. Perhaps it will not happen peacefully, and perhaps not only you, but your children and grandchildren and great-grandchildren will have to fight. But freedom will never be won if you give up."

He turned to her at last. "It will be your children, too, if you stay."

She touched her belly. "It already is." She gave him a rueful smile. "I should have known, all that fainting nonsense."

"We've made a child?" he echoed, and almost as if his hands acted without his knowledge, he reached for her, putting that long-fingered hand across her lower belly. "Our own?"

She laughed. "Yes."

For a long moment he only looked at his hand on

her belly, then he raised his eyes to hers. "I fell in love with you the morning you came down the stairs to greet your brothers. There was such joy in you, and it made me feel the emptiness I'd been carrying since my brother was murdered." He paused. "Can you love me, then?"

She lifted her hands to his face and rose on her toes. "I can," she whispered, and kissed him. "I do."

With a soft sound, he swept her into his embrace, burying his face in her neck. "I love you, Adriana." A wind from the sea swept over them, and he murmured, "It will never be easy, but with you, I can face whatever comes."

She closed her eyes and sent a silent prayer upward. *Thank you, Papa.*

Then they joined hands and walked back to Glencove Castle, which had stood for six hundred years, and was strong enough to stand six hundred more.